DO YOU WANT TOTAL WAR?

Jerry – as one of my history teaching role models, you are no doubt well placed to give a proper verdict on the quality (or not) of this book... I can only hope I've done the topics I cover in here justice in your eyes. And, of course, that you enjoy the story! :)

All the best,

August 2015

ALSO BY THE AUTHOR

A Golfer's Education

DO YOU WANT TOTAL WAR?

A NOVEL ABOUT HISTORY

DARREN KILFARA

DUNBAR PRESS

To Heather, Lucy, Christopher
and the 60 million

First published in Great Britain in 2013 by Dunbar Press
Second edition published in 2014 by Dunbar Press

ISBN 978-0-9926687-0-9

Typeset by the author (using Adobe InDesign CC)
Text set in Adobe Garamond Pro and Hypatia Sans Pro

Cover design by Mark Mahaffey
Cover photography by Hugo Chang

Author's Notes and Acknowledgments

Totaler Krieg is a real boardgame, published by an American company called Decision Games. The version of the game referred to throughout this book is the second (*"Axis Empires"*) edition, which was published in 2011, and not the original version of *Totaler Krieg* published in 1999. (The formal title of both editions is *Totaler Krieg!*, but I have eliminated the exclamation mark for grammatical clarity.) Indeed, with the obvious exceptions of *Rasta-mon-opoly*, *Gallipol-opoly* and *Edna Krabappoly*, all of the boardgames and publishers referenced in the book are real, as are the Consimworld and BoardGameGeek websites, the CyberBoard computer application, and the Boardgame Players Association. While there is no official *Totaler Krieg* Play-By-E-Mail tournament at present, the BPA does in fact sanction many e-mail wargame tournaments every year, and any volunteer who might wish to organize an official *Totaler Krieg* tournament would be more than welcome to do so.

I have been playing *Totaler Krieg* for more than a decade. I helped playtest the 2011 edition of the game, I designed the CyberBoard gamebox for it (and used a modified version of it to create all of the maps and diagrams included in this book), I have written strategy articles about it, and I have been an active contributor to the *Totaler Krieg* discussion forum at Consimworld. I have also designed a variant module for *Totaler Krieg* and its Pacific-theater sister game, *Dai Senso*, called *Schiffskrieg* which is to be published as part of an official *Axis Empires* expansion kit. So to be completely transparent, because of *Schiffskrieg* I have a tiny financial stake in the success of *Totaler Krieg*. However, this book is a labor of love which has been years in the making, long before I conceived of *Schiffskrieg*. I chose to feature *Totaler Krieg* within these pages simply because it is one of my favorite games, because I am endlessly fascinated by the period of history it encompasses, and (most importantly) because I believe readers unfamiliar with the hobby of board wargaming will more readily grasp a grand strategic game about World War II than a game about a less popular period of history and/or something tactical or operational in scope. My hope is certainly that this book will be accessible to anyone interested in history and not just diehard members of the wargaming community – particularly once you move beyond the Prologue, which portrays the *Totaler Krieg* experience with a narrow focus, and at a level of detail, which is not representative of the rest of the book. But only the reader can decide if I have succeeded in that mission.

I would particularly like to thank Alex Aminoff for reviewing the entire manuscript prior to publication and providing much valuable and insightful feedback. My thanks also go to Louis Capdeboscq, David Hughes and Grant Flowers for their constructive input on various sections of the book; to veteran wargame artist Mark Mahaffey for his work, and his patience with me, in designing the cover; to *Totaler Krieg* game designer Thomas Prowell both for his general encouragement and his willingness to let me use his artwork to create the graphics you see in these pages; and to Pete Weinburgh and Dr. Louisa Moffitt, who taught my own Advanced Placement history classes in high school (many years ago!) and thereby clearly have much to answer for.

Most of all, I want to thank my family for tolerating my writing habits and believing that one day all of the words in this book might amount to more than a hill of beans in this crazy world.

Darren Kilfara
September 2013

"I ask you: Do you want total war? If necessary, do you want a war more total and radical than anything that we can even imagine today?"

—Joseph Goebbels, in a speech to the Berlin Sportpalast on 18 February 1943

PROLOGUE:
The War in Europe

1.

I'm looking at Dennis, across the thin stacks of cardboard that define our mutual hostility. He adjusts his eyeglasses, apposite wide rims of black plastic around oddly thin lenses, and plucks at his scraggly, mottled beard with thumb and middle finger, pausing periodically to inspect the tips or scrape a fingernail across one of his lower incisors. I hate watching Dennis pluck at his beard. I'm not old enough to grow a beard, so my expertise here is limited, but I can't help thinking that he will smear grease into everything he touches, or that Dad will eventually find tiny brown and grey hairs on or in something he cares about. Also, Dennis seems awfully casual about the hair on his chin when he has so little left on the rest of his head. Not that I would choose to look like Dennis, but if I had his beard and wanted to remove it, a shave would be more decisive.

It's two o'clock in the morning, and we're in Dad's "Second Study". Dad's main office is upstairs, but when he's working on multiple projects at once, the only way he can stay organized is to keep everything on separate floors. He hasn't had a second project for a while, though, so the room is pretty much mine now. It has a large, west-facing picture window across which I keep the thick velvet curtains permanently closed – otherwise, when the weather turns cold or breezy the room can get very drafty, and on late summer evenings like the one which yielded to night a few hours ago, the sun drains into your eyes across the tall maple and hickory trees in the adjacent woods. Bookcases inset within the adjoining walls heave with yellowing journals and faded tomes with cracked spines stacked two-deep; I've annexed two shelves for my own stuff, but the other contents have been left to decompose in peace. Above a pair of grey filing cabinets next to the door is a framed print of Pissarro's *The Boulevard Montmartre at Night*, bristling with blues and purples and an Impressionist energy the other walls conspicuously lack.

Centered on the picture window is a large, hand-carved oaken table of magnificent thickness and ballast. I'd thought antiques were by definition fragile until I first pressed my hand against its polished surface. It pins the Persian rug beneath it to the hardwood floor and is not easily jostled, which matters because although Dennis and I can choose to sit in upholstered leather chairs, I'm often pacing around it or bracing myself against it to get an aerial view. Dad used to keep a stapler, a pencil holder and pads of paper on it, but I've cleared them away to a dim corner of the floor.

On the table, illuminated by a row of harsh ceiling lights, is a large paper map of Europe stretching just beyond the Urals in Russia, just above the northernmost fjord in Scandinavia, across the Mediterranean to a coastal corridor of North Africa, and through the Middle East as far as Tehran and Basra. Superimposed upon the map is a grid of grey one-inch-wide hexagons at a scale where each "hex" spans 60 miles, as well as charts and boxes covering irrelevant sections of ocean or desert. A thin pane of plexiglass holds the map in place, canceling its creases and folds and presenting a smooth surface.

Upon the plexiglass, within the borders of individual hexes or boxes, lay the stacks of cardboard. Each piece of cardboard, half an inch square and one-eighth of an inch thick, is color-coded by country: grey for Germany, brown for the Soviet Union, tan for Britain, mustard yellow for Italy, green for the United States, and so on.

The pieces of cardboard are called "counters", a term coined by the first modern wargame designer because each piece represents a military unit's characteristics and abilities with numerical values. To give an example, there's currently a grey German counter on the East Map in hex e4012, which is three hexes south-southwest of Moscow and contains the Russian town of Orel. Printed on a white strip at the bottom are the numbers "5-4-4", which are the unit's respective ratings for attack, defense and movement. In the middle of the counter is an oval within a rectangle, signifying an armored unit; the designations "2P" and "XXXX" identify it as Second Panzer Army. Two dots in the upper-right corner mean the army has two "steps", each of which represents roughly 30,000 men and their materiel.

Second Panzer is at reduced strength. At full strength it's an 8-6-4 with three steps, but it suffered a step loss when I attacked Smolensk three turns ago, in July-August 1941, and I haven't yet gotten around to building it back up. Normally I don't remember that level of detail in my face-to-face games of *Totaler Krieg* with Dennis, but I've always had a soft spot for Second Panzer – Guderian's Second Panzer – especially during the 1941 Barbarossa campaign.

Colonel General Heinz Guderian has long been a hero of mine, at least to the extent that a lynchpin of Nazi Germany can or should be. I admire his tactical and operational skill, his leadership and motivational qualities, his innovativeness in the realm of armored theory, his flexibility (serving ably as battlefield leader, munitions coordinator and chief of the German General Staff), and above all his willingness to stand up to authority. Read the 1944 transcripts of Guderian in the *Führerbunker*, and you can't help but wonder what might have happened had more senior Nazis spoken to Hitler like him. If I'm playing the Axis and I manage to capture Moscow, Second Panzer often seems to get there first. If Hitler had listened to him in August 1941, Guderian may well have led the *Wehrmacht* into Moscow anyway, so if I can give the man his posthumous due, I will.

But nobody is getting to Moscow in my current game of *Totaler Krieg* with Dennis, at least not in 1941. Second Panzer led my attack on Tula – two hexes south of Moscow – in my half of the November-December 1941 turn, and the dice weren't with me. So now Guderian is stuck in the open steppe, waiting to get creamed by Zhukov's counteroffensive. For his Western Option Card, Dennis already unleashed his <u>Operation Crusader</u> offensive in the Med, attempting an amphibious invasion near Benghazi which I think primarily aimed to draw my Air units away from the Russian front. And now, having revealed his Soviet <u>Siberian Reserves Released</u> Option Card, he's poring over the map and making notes on a pad of paper between tugs at his beard.

As he studies the map, I realize something. "This game has almost perfectly replicated history, hasn't it?"

Dennis doesn't look up. "Yeah," he says absently, drumming with his tip of his pen on the paper. "A bit."

"More than a bit. Seriously, look at the front lines."

Dennis stops drumming and leans back in his chair. "You're right, Sean. It's pretty close."

"It's more than pretty close. The Germans and Finns are besieging Leningrad, but it's not cut off yet. I've got Kharkov, and I've sealed off the Crimea, but I haven't gotten into Rostov or Sevastopol yet. And Guderian just attacked Tula, in November-December 1941, but he couldn't capture it!"

"The Med is different."

"But it's within the margins of error. You've still got Crete, which should have happened if the British were competent. I've got Tobruk and have advanced to El Alamein, which would have happened if the Italians were competent. The coup in Yugoslavia didn't happen, and you didn't intervene in Norway, but everything else is just about right. We even got Italian aggression in Greece! How often does that happen?"

"You know what I think about Axis Aggression."

"Even when it happens to your opponent?"

"Yep."

"You should be playing *A World at War*, you know."

"Probably," sighs Dennis. "But I'm here playing with you." He leans forward and starts drumming his pen again.

Axis Aggression is one of the things I love about *Totaler Krieg*. When a "Minor Country Politics" Political Event occurs before Germany is at war with both Britain and the Soviet Union, the Allied player chooses one of five regional "Area Tables" and rolls a die: if the result is an Axis country, an adjacent neutral country joins the Allies. In our game, Axis Aggression occurred in August-September 1940 when Dennis rolled on the Western Area Table and luckily got Italy, which forced me to declare war on either Greece or Vichy France. When I chose the former, Dennis wisely deployed British forces to Crete but not the mainland; Athens eventually capitulated, but the invasion cost an Italian step and slowed preparations for my invasion of Russia.

A game about World War II in Europe with pretensions of historical accuracy needs to cast its players in plausible roles. Games like *A World at War*, *World in Flames*, *Europe Engulfed*, even *Axis & Allies* give the Axis player complete control over German and Italian decision-making – their armed forces, factories and diplomats do exactly what he tells them to, subject only to his opponent's interference and the luck of the dice. *Totaler Krieg* is different: in its designer's words, the Axis player "represents the tension between Hitler, the Army staff and the Axis allies." Mussolini's decision to invade Greece was idiotic. Some games let the Axis player use 20-20 hindsight to avoid such mistakes. Others give Italy special economic or political benefits for conquering a country on its own without German assistance, thereby encouraging the Axis player to make Mussolini's historical decision. But *Totaler Krieg* assumes that Hitler's allies occasionally get frisky and do stupid things, leaving the Axis player to clean up their messes as best he can. Control freaks may disagree, but I think the latter approach most accurately models history and creates the most interesting gameplay, which is one of many reasons I play *Totaler Krieg*.

❖ ❖ ❖

I often wonder what it felt like to be Heinz Guderian on Friday, 5 December 1941. I often wonder many things about history, but this intersection of date, place, person and context fascinates me more than most. The weekend to come would outline the course of human history for the next 50 years: on Saturday the 6th, the Soviet Union's first major counter-offensive of the war proved to the world that it was a global superpower; on Sunday the 7th, Japan's attack on Pearl Harbor motivated the United States to become one. Those two days foreshadowed the downfall of Hitler and Nazism, and the division of Europe into two armed camps. They predestined the decline of Imperial Japan, which led to the death of Asian colonialism in all its forms – the Philippines, Indonesia, India, Vietnam – and the dawn of the nuclear age at Hiroshima. Standing at the precipice on 5 December, with such vast, impersonal forces swirling around and preparing to throw the world over the edge, I wonder if any one person had even an inkling of what was about to happen on both fronts. Stalin? Maybe, *maybe* Stalin, if only thanks to his master spy in Tokyo, Richard Sorge. But Sorge was arrested by the Japanese in October, so no, probably not even Stalin.

Guderian certainly didn't, not that it was his job to know. On 5 December, his job was to decide when his orders couldn't be obeyed. Previously, he'd decided several times in 1940 and 1941 that his orders weren't to be obeyed, and his instincts were usually right. Hitherto, his insubordination aimed to secure victories he knew were within his reach – most famously in May 1940, where his daring armored thrust from the Ardennes to the Channel effectively won the war against France in two weeks. Now, it might be necessary to avoid a catastrophe. The brave and innumerable Russians, led by General Zhukov and abetted by the winter weather, could not be pierced. Attack was now impossible. Defense soon might be, if appropriate steps weren't taken immediately.

What was going through Guderian's mind? From *Panzer Leader*, Guderian's postwar memoir, we know the temperature near Tula on 4 December dropped to minus-31 degrees Fahrenheit. That day, Guderian interviewed several company commanders from his old Goslar Jaeger unit; they were anxious but believed further attacks could yet be successful. While returning in the dark to his headquarters, on Tolstoy's former estate at Yasnaya Polyana, his armored command tank drove into a crevice hidden by the snow – he was lucky to escape and quickly flag down a German signals truck, but this cannot have improved his mood. Attacks by several key units under his command were prepared on the 4th but not executed until the 5th, at which point they were repulsed after brief initial successes. Worse still for Guderian, it became clear on the 5th that Fourth Army, whose coordinated assistance was required for his Second Panzer Army to make significant headway, had gone over to the defensive.

So we know all of this, at least insofar as Guderian's memoirs are accurate. But what was he really thinking? He must have consulted his most trusted subordinates for advice: von Liebenstein, his chief of staff, and von Geyr, his senior corps commander. As the best battlefield general in the world's most skilled and professional army, he would have clinically weighed all the available evidence: bad weather and Soviet operational security reduced the intelligence at his disposal, but the threats to his flanks and the paralyzing effects of the cold were obvious. How heavily did recent history weigh upon him? He'd never conducted an unsuccessful offensive, never voluntarily surrendered ground he and his men had won, never faced the prospect of losing the strategic initiative his country had held for more than two full years of war and at least four years of peace before that. In addition, his immediate superior – von Bock – was out of touch with conditions at the front, and *der Führer* opposed retreat under any circumstances, not that Guderian was likely to consult either of these men for advice. Finally, he could hardly anticipate the full fury of a well-planned Soviet counteroffensive. Subconsciously or otherwise, the Soviets were still the *Untermenschen*; were they really capable of seriously hurting the mighty and as-yet undefeated German army?

Such are the decisions faced by the men of war. Many books and memoirs describe the experience and the horrors of the poor foot soldier; far fewer try to get inside of the commander's head and describe his day-to-day existence in the same way. I don't just mean examining the logic behind the decisions they make; I mean, what was it like to live the life of senior commander in World War II? They weren't all donkeys leading lions, living in lavish comfort miles behind the front and deserving full measures of derision. Many were conscientious leaders, highly skilled and more than a little brave, and if they got the best food and most comfortable billets, they probably benefitted from them when called upon to make the crucial, gut-wrenching decisions that commanders have to make. In this case, there's nothing to envy about Guderian – he chose retreat, shortly before the Soviets would have made his decision obvious, and three weeks later the *Wehrmacht* was in tatters and he was out of a job – except insofar as he was at least positioned to shape the course of events. Leaders get to lead. Someone has to. And look: I know I'm just a teenager at the end of my summer vacation, hyperactively pondering the past while a nerdy, middle-aged wargamer across the table from me plots my downfall. But if the full force of history ever threatens to engulf me, I want to be able to deflect its course and not merely flounder in its wake.

❖ ❖ ❖

November-December 1941 (Soviet turn). When Dennis is done thinking, he silently starts moving his counters. First, he places the 20 reinforcements steps granted to him by his Siberian Reserves Released Option Card on the map in Soviet cities. This Option Card also gives Dennis a "Blitz" marker: any Soviet units within its two-hex radius may attack twice this turn. After placing the marker and combining several one-step units into two-step armies, Dennis moves each Soviet unit up to its individual movement allowance, subject to the debilitating effects of snowy weather. Dennis has short, stubby fingers, so where necessary he uses a suction tweezer with a silicon tip to levitate his counters into position.

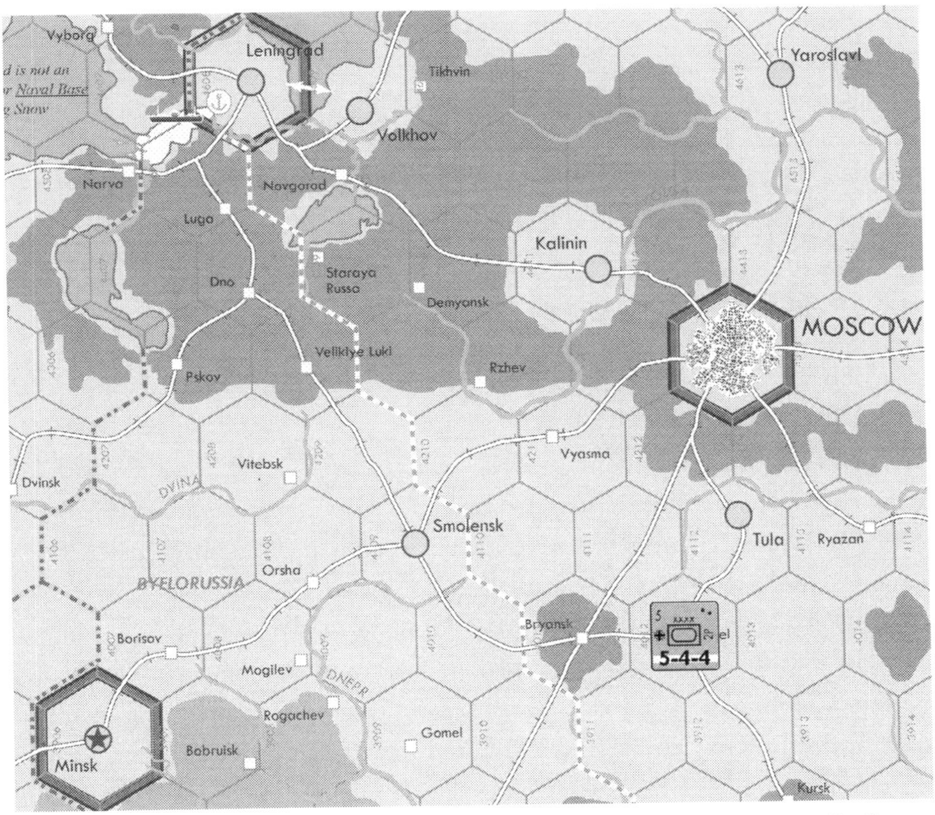

Fig. 1 – The Moscow Front (with Guderian's Second Panzer Army in Orel)

Dennis takes several minutes to move all of his units, but I immediately deduce that he is not attacking Second Panzer – he's pounding into my lines further north. When he's done, he declares the start of his Blitz Combat Segment and says, "First, the paras do their bit for the Motherland." He flips the Soviet airborne corps and places it on its "Airdrop" side in an empty hex behind my front line. "First Blitz attack is against Vyasma, with 21 factors and shifts for armor and the HQ. I assume you'll use your HQ?"

"Correct."

Dennis has 21 attacking factors to my nine defending factors – raw odds of 2:1 after rounding in the defender's favor – but his extra combat "shift" means he rolls on the 3:1 column of the Combat Results Table. Dennis chooses a translucent red die with white pips and drops it into a felt-lined wooden contraption called a dice tower. It bounces across several diagonal slats within the tower and emerges in the small, square basin at the bottom with four pips showing.

"The Defender Retreat is reduced to an Exchange by the snow," says Dennis, interpreting the "Dr1, 1/1" result he just rolled. "So we both lose two steps – a very bloody start."

Dennis eliminates a two-step armored cavalry army, while I kill my Yugoslavian cavalry step and replace the two-step German Twelfth Army with a generic, single-step German infantry unit. Twelfth Army goes to the "Delay Box" in the southwest corner of the map: at the end of the turn, the dice will determine when each unit in the Delay Box will again become available for use.

Next comes a more penetrating attack on Rzhev, two hexes due west of Moscow. Dennis rolls well and announces, "D-R two, oh-two after the snow." The "Dr2, 0/2" result means I lose two steps to Dennis's none and must also retreat two hexes. With Dennis's Airdrop blocking one retreat path, I must now choose whether to withdraw to the west or the southeast: the former exposes my forces between Vyasma and Orel to strong follow-up attacks during the Regular Combat Segment, but my gut tells me the latter might allow a devastating Soviet thrust through Smolensk. Is Dennis strong enough to encircle Army Group Center? If he is, this could be my Stalingrad, and I might lose the war right here.

Why did I have to attack Tula this turn? I should have anchored my winter defenses on Smolensk and Bryansk, instead of risking everything on Tula and getting dragged out of position like this. I keep falling into the same trap as Hitler, trying to keep my lines as far forward as possible even when it doesn't make sense to do so. Now I've only got one step in Smolensk, and if he can push Seventh Army back or exploit two hexes from Smolensk in Reserve Movement, and then the weather is bad again next turn…

"You still thinking?" asks Dennis.

Too many of my important decisions in *Totaler Krieg* seem to be made after midnight. West or southeast, west or southeast…screw it. I'm always, *always* too aggressive. If I go west, I can only lose a few steps; if I go southeast, I could spend the rest of the game digging myself out of the hole I've created. And then I'd have to blame Guderian for losing the war.

"I'll go west-southwest," I say. Third Panzer Army and Seventh Army withdraw to the northwest of Smolensk. Dennis exploits through Rzhev with six armies, three of which form the tip of his spearhead adjacent to Smolensk.

That concludes the Blitz Combat Segment. Dennis has planned his attack well and continues without pause: "To start Regular Combat, I'll soak off Army Group Center HQ at 1-to-3." This weak attack causes a Soviet army to flip and retreat to the northeast at no cost to me. However, by engaging my HQ unit and preventing it from supporting my other defenders, the attack accomplishes its goal.

"Next attack is against Smolensk at 3-to-1. What?"

"Nothing." I'm shaking my head because I now know I chose poorly. Dennis has nothing like enough force to threaten an encirclement – my attack of nerves will cost me several steps for no good reason. I'm such an idiot sometimes.

After Dennis clears Smolensk and occupies it with three Soviet steps, the rest of the turn passes quickly. Two final Soviet attacks near Vyasma cause additional casualties. During the Reserve Movement Phase, units adjacent to enemy forces cannot move, so there's not much for Dennis to do. In the Conditional Events Segment, Dennis gets two reinforcement steps via the Lend-Lease Table. Finally, in the Delay Segment, one of my Air units and all of my good armies return immediately, whereas the Soviet rolls are indifferent and the Western ones are horrendous. In particular, one British Fleet suffers severe damage and won't be back until 1943, which gives me breathing space in North Africa and perhaps even a chance to push beyond El Alamein to Cairo and the Nile.

❖ ❖ ❖

It is now two-thirty in the morning. "I hope you're ready to go to bed?" asks Dennis.

"Yeah. Can I make my Political roll first?"

"Sure."

The dice tower does its thing and spits out a '1'. I smirk at Dennis and slowly extend an arm to punch the air. My current Option Card, Mobilization Limits, models the effects of the *Wehrmacht's* first winter in Russia: normally, the weather is bad and the Axis suffers a "Command Failure", but this time my roll yields a "Mandated Offensive" result. Mandated Offensives can be bad later in the war, when Hitler orders attacks that have no chance of succeeding, but at present it's exactly what I need.

Dennis smiles, then yawns. "Where do you want me to sleep?"

"There's a room upstairs for you. Do you want to go now?"

"Yes, please."

"Go up the stairs at the front of the house, left at the top of the stairs, then follow the corridor all the way around to a door next to more stairs on your left. Go through that door – your bed is in there." Dennis arches his eyebrows, so I continue, "Really, you can't miss it. I'm gonna study the board for a few minutes."

"And in the morning?"

"There's a bathroom in there, but if you promise to behave you can use Dad's if you want – it's nicer. He won't be back until Sunday night. I'll wake you up if you're not up when I get up, but otherwise help yourself to breakfast."

"OK..."

"See ya."

Dennis shuffles out of the room. He's never stayed over before – we normally play on Thursday nights, but with Dad away for the weekend and the new school year not starting until Monday, this was an opportunity I couldn't pass up. I don't think Dad would want Dennis to use his bathroom, but I doubt he'll notice.

Meanwhile, what a break I caught in Russia! That changes everything – snow effects will still hamper movement, but at worst I can now organize my defenses properly, and I might even create an opening with my extra attack. I could ignore Russia and attack in Egypt, where the weather is lovely this time of year. I can try to reduce Smolensk ahead of a proper assault. I could engineer a voluntary retreat to disengage some of my forces, allowing them to reach deeper defensive positions or redeploy for a surprise attack. Or I can go after Tula again: I know I shouldn't, but it's only held by two steps and two factors, and if it might open the back door to Moscow, I should at least consider it.

The possibilities etched in my mind, I turn off the lights and march upstairs. What a game this is – so many twists each turn, so many interesting decisions, so many blunders to inevitably make and hopefully fix in the nick of time. Sometimes I really feel like I could rewind history and have Hitler let his panzers finish off the Brits at Dunkirk, or give Patton all the supplies and leeway he wanted in August 1944 and watch him reach Berlin before Christmas. And as I lie in bed, I can't stop counting the factors in my head – against Tula I could attack with 22 factors against four and one shift against two, so that's 3:1, and if I can soak off the HQ and hit the Moscow fort with 12 factors plus Air, that'd give me a shot... or was there another HQ within range of Moscow? I can't remember. Perhaps I can force a massive overstack in Vyasma – I'm sure I could do that from Tula, plus that would free up my own HQ. What if I freed everyone to turn southeast and attack toward Voronezh?

I'm exhausted, but it will be a while before I can get to sleep.

2.

I wake up late, sunshine peeking through my poorly closed curtains, with a lingering case of "gamer's headache", the feeling you get from doing nothing for hours on end but making intense strategic and mathematical calculations and eating pizza. You feel lightheaded, and your forehead and ears overheat; you can almost feel your brain tightening. I tend to get it most evenings with Dennis, but I had a bad case by the end of yesterday's all-day session, and waking up with it today doesn't bode well.

By the time I shower and stagger downstairs, it's already half past 10. Dennis appears to have eaten a bowl of cereal and is watching some sort of Japanese anime on the living room television. Sometimes I have to remind myself that Dennis is well over twice my age.

"Good morning." Hang on.... "Have you showered?"

Dennis's gaze doesn't leave the television. "I couldn't figure out how to work it."

"You've got to be kidding me. Five remote controls can't stop you from turning on this crap, but you can't get water out of a tap? Which one couldn't you figure out?"

"What do you mean?"

"Did you try the shower in your bedroom or the one in Dad's room?"

"I'm not even sure what room I slept in, so..."

"The real problem is that you didn't want it enough. OK, get up."

"What?"

"I need to eat, and while I do that, you need to shower. You *need* to shower. So get up."

At least I can adjourn to the gaming room while Dennis rediscovers the basics of personal hygiene. Why he wasn't studying the map when I came downstairs also escapes me, but that bothers me less.

I choose my immediate goal very quickly: I have to recapture Smolensk. Having confirmed that two Soviet HQs are indeed within range of Moscow and attacking Tula won't accomplish anything, there's only one smart choice. Beyond that, I need to decide when to play my Festung Europa Option Card, which brings the "No Retreat" marker into play and thereby directly affects how the game is won.

There are 39 "Objective Hexes" on the *Totaler Krieg* map, and at the start of each new season, you compare how many Allied Objectives are under Axis control with how many Axis Objectives are under Allied control. If the net total is 15 or more in the Axis player's favor, he wins the game automatically, but as this requires driving Russia beyond the Urals, invading Britain and/or overrunning the Middle East, it happens very rarely. Much more often, the No Retreat marker's arrival establishes a baseline Axis performance level that the Allies must exceed by V-E Day to win the game. In *Totaler Krieg's* historical storyboard, when the No Retreat marker arrives at the end of 1942 the Axis controls Oslo, Brussels, Paris, Athens, Minsk, Kiev, Sevastopol and Rostov, meaning the Allies must control at least 11 net Objectives at the end of the game to win. The trick for the Axis player is timing the marker's arrival to match his territorial high-water mark: too soon or too late, and the Axis victory level might not be high enough.

As my current game with Dennis retains a historical trajectory, I'll likely follow my <u>Case Blue</u> Summer offensive with <u>Festung Europa</u> in the Winter. My goal must be to capture the three Objectives I need to improve upon the historical Axis performance – but which three, and how?

❖ ❖ ❖

In real life, once the shock of that first Russian winter wore off, the *Wehrmacht* recovered its equilibrium surprisingly quickly. In May 1942, von Kleist and von Paulus routed Timoshenko at the second battle of Kharkov, and then von Manstein assaulted and captured Sevastopol to secure the Crimea. With those preliminaries concluded, Axis forces were now intriguingly poised to move in several different directions during the summer:

Donets and Caucasus. To me, the option Hitler did choose seems by far the worst of those available to him. I have no problem with pressing forward to Rostov and securely anchoring Germany's southern flank against the Sea of Azov; that could have been undertaken in conjunction with something bigger. But advancing beyond Rostov widened the front significantly, and when Germany's Sixth Army was sucked into Stalingrad, only Hungarians, Rumanians and Italians were left to guard its flanks. Hitler was probably lucky that Stalin's and Zhukov's goals for Operation Uranus, the eventual Soviet counteroffensive, were merely to surround and destroy Sixth Army; a firmer lunge toward Rostov could have trapped multiple German armies in the Caucasus and precipitated an unmanageable crisis in Berlin.

Hitler's motivation for the southern offensive was economic: more oil, wheat, manganese and nickel for Germany, less for the Soviets. But how many resources can you actually extract from conquered territory in a short space of time? Could Germany realistically expect to take and hold the Caucasus oil fields for long enough to make them prizes worth winning? Even denying them to the enemy seems a stretch – although the instant combustion of petroleum features in every action movie I've ever seen, I understand that oilfield fires can burn and burn and burn (and even be extinguished, which is beyond my comprehension). The paucity of prisoners netted during Germany's summer offensive certainly suggests that these economic objectives weren't as vital to Russia as the *Führer* reckoned.

(Note that Stalingrad is not an Objective Hex in *Totaler Krieg*. Why should it be one? It became important to Hitler and Stalin for the same reason that two brothers might fight over the same toy: one says "I'll have that," so the other throws a tantrum and says "No, you won't!" "Will too!" "Will not!" Interdicting the Volga would have been nice, and controlling the strategic corridor between the Don and Volga could have helped secure Sixth Army's northern flank, but can anyone seriously argue that victory at Stalingrad would have won the war for the Axis? And here's a thought: would the most grotesque battle in modern history have been fought in a city called "Tsaritsyn" or "Volgograd", the names of Stalingrad before 1925 and after 1961?)

Moscow. As for realistic alternatives, Russia's greatest political prize still loomed not far behind the front – Zhukov's winter offensive had created a buffer, but not one wide enough to completely secure his country's capital. The Soviets expected an offensive against Moscow in 1942 and defended it vigorously, so in that sense one might compare this option to Germany's disastrous Citadel offensive against the Kursk salient in 1943. But victory at Kursk was underpinned by a complete Soviet intelligence triumph, and it was created by an army forged within the crucible of Stalingrad; even then, the Soviets only prevailed after fierce fighting. Add up the variables and maybe someone like von Manstein breaks through to encircle Moscow; the Red Army loses cohesion; having fled to Kubishev, Stalin's authority wanes, exposing him to a palace coup; and 1943 in the East becomes a reprise of 1918, only without the subsequent German collapse in the West. Or maybe not, but that could have been a campaign for military historians to truly savor.

Leningrad. Russia's second city remained within German and Finnish artillery range well into 1944, and a determined northern operation likely would have led to its capture. Hitler was not inclined to accept the city's surrender in any event, and defending forces may have offered Stalingrad-like resistance, but once the siege perimeter could be tightened to block all Soviet reinforcements and supplies, the ultimate outcome would have been clear. It's one thing to conduct an impromptu siege at the end of a long supply line, another to consciously look for a street fight and plan accordingly. And Germany's rewards for such an undertaking could have been considerable: a secure northern flank, immense political and moral prestige around the world, and possible reinforcements from Finland if Mannerheim could be convinced to declare full co-belligerency against the Soviets.

Malta and Egypt. Not all of Germany's 1942 objectives lay within the Soviet Union. An airborne invasion of Malta and a vigorous offensive against and into Egypt could have been launched at a fraction of the cost of Case Blue in Russia. And once Rommel pushed beyond Alamein and reached the Nile Delta, Cairo was there for the taking, and the Suez Canal could be cut, and...actually, and then what? Where does Rommel go after Suez? Given the logistical difficulties of advancing beyond the Nile, is Egypt actually a strategic cul-de-sac? Any lunge for the oil of Arabia and Iraq, let alone Turkey and the Caucasus, would have been hugely risky – Napoleon-in-Egypt risky. What if the Arabs revolt against the likely excesses of German occupation? What if the Torch invasion of Morocco and Algeria sneaks through the back door while Rommel is driving into Iraq? The only outcome you could safely predict is the appearance of Nazis in Jerusalem, and that's not worth thinking about.

I do believe Hitler could have won the war in the Mediterranean – just not from the 1942 start line. But that's a discussion for another time.

Do nothing. Germany did have one other option: consolidate with limited attacks and mostly play defense. This notion isn't as unrealistic as it may sound, for Hitler and his generals strongly considered ceding the strategic initiative to Stalin in 1943 before the Kursk debacle. This planning process included one of my favorite Guderian dialogues, by the way:

> GUDERIAN: "Why do we need to attack Kursk this year, or indeed to attack in the East at all?"
>
> KEITEL: "We must attack for political reasons."
>
> GUDERIAN: "Do you think anyone even knows where Kursk is? It is a matter of profound indifference to the world whether we capture Kursk or not."
>
> HITLER: "I know – the thought of [this offensive] makes my stomach turn over."

In 1942, with German strength still mostly intact, an active strategic defense might have been truly formidable. Of course, in mid-1942 the Axis was widely perceived to be winning the war in both hemispheres: Russia was reeling, Britain was turtling, and America had thus far only offered U-boat victims in the Atlantic and ripe targets for Japanese conquest in the Pacific. Could Hitler have reconciled this logic with a Fabian strategy?

❖ ❖ ❖

While Moscow remains very seductive, I think I can accomplish more against Dennis by nibbling at the edges: Leningrad in the north, Sevastopol and Rostov in the south, maybe Cairo if the chance presents itself or I struggle taking one of the other three. But first, I must retake Smolensk.

When Dennis finally emerges after his shower, his dark brown hair is a damp, messy thicket, and his T-shirt – which says "SIMILIES ARE LIKE METAPHORS" in thick, white text on a blue background – is partially stuck to his torso. "The grunge look doesn't fit this theater of operations," I comment. "What would Mamie Eisenhower say? Or Kay Summersby, for that matter?"

"C'mon, let's get started."

The room is ours, unsullied by background music, television or natural light. Just a few drinks on coasters and last night's leftover pizza on a corner of the floor. This is our bunker. And this is what a game-year of *Totaler Krieg* looks like:

January-February 1942 (Axis turn). I use my Mandated Offensive to disengage my forces from Tula. During Operational Movement, Ninth Army slips unexpectedly into the vacant city of Voronezh, five hexes southeast of Moscow; meanwhile, Second Panzer Army wheels away from Tula, crosses 240 miles of snow at lightning speed and approaches Smolensk from the *southwest* – truly Guderian's finest hour – to help retake the city at 6:1 odds.

January-February 1942 (Western turn). All quiet. Egypt will likely remain stalemated until the fundamentals of the El Alamein position change – maybe American involvement, or overly hasty British redeployments to Crete or Malta, or possibly Italian defections.

January-February 1942 (Soviet turn). In the south, the Soviets are in more trouble than I'd first thought. Thanks to my incursion at Voronezh, Dennis has to disband an HQ unit and retreat two armies all the way to Saratov and Stalingrad. HQs are the most important units in *Totaler Krieg* – they increase your potency in combat and enable static defenses by converting retreats to step losses – and the Soviets would only disband one in an emergency. Nearer Moscow, Dennis narrows the scope of his counteroffensive so as not to overextend himself.

March-April 1942 (Axis turn). I reveal the Speer Appointed Minister Option Card and select my Case Blue offensive for the Summer, putting it face-down next to the board. Speer doesn't give me a Blitz marker, and I don't have obvious targets to attack anyway, so I take the ground I'm given beyond Voronezh and move my reinforcements forward.

March-April 1942 (Western turn). No American units will arrive in Europe until the Summer, so the Brits continue to mark time. The Western Option Card this season, Arcadia Conference, is a mundane prerequisite for the eventual Operation Torch offensive.

March-April 1942 (Soviet turn). Great Patriotic War brings five new Soviet tank armies into the game. Dennis further protects his most exposed Objectives; in fact, Moscow is so densely defended that I must be wary of the offensive threat posed by the Soviet armies guarding it.

April-May 1942 (Axis turn). Mud turns normally pass quickly, as enemy units adjacent to one another cannot move, but the Eastern Front is puzzling. Dennis's withdrawal to Tula, Saratov and Stalingrad has created a two-hex buffer zone between our lines; I think he is daring me to fill this vacuum, but to fill it properly, I'd risk not reaching my No Retreat target. However, if Dennis eventually fills it himself, he could threaten the rear of Army Group South.

I study the map again. I love a good *Blitzkrieg* as much as anyone, but where will a deep penetration take me? I can't seal up the Caucasus or sweep behind Moscow; the situation calls for something less glamorous. A straight line of 14 hexes connects Leningrad and Taganrog, in the south on the Sea of Azov; seven of these hexes feature good defensive terrain in the form of forests, rough ground, cities or rivers. Of my goals for Case Blue, only Rostov lies beyond this line – exactly one hex beyond – and if everything goes very well, I can gain a further line of 14 hexes connecting Rostov and the city of Volkhov, on Lake Ladoga in the north. On one of these lines I'll make my stand: this is where I want to be at the end of 1942. Every move I make in the East until then must be made with this goal in mind. I'll still threaten a wider offensive, but only as a strategic deception designed to help me reach this desired end state.

So, as far as Dennis knows, when I advance two armies adjacent to Saratov and Stalingrad, I'm taking his bait. In fact, I'm now baiting him. I think.

April-May 1942 (Western turn). The Allied build-up in Egypt continues.

April-May 1942 (Soviet turn). Dennis builds his two remaining Soviet HQs near Moscow and Rostov. His southern defense is quite elegant, but in the north, I might be able to exploit a gap south of Lake Ilmen.

❖ ❖ ❖

With the Summer about to begin, we exit the gaming room briefly to make a late lunch of ham-and-cheese sandwiches and, for nutrition, pickle spears. My muscles ache from disuse. Renewed exposure to sunlight is abrasive.

The kitchen is on the other side of the house from our game, and for the first time I hear lawnmower noises in our neighbor's yard. I squint through the kitchen window at a tall fellow, pacing back and forth between the trees in shorts and a T-shirt. I don't know his name; I think he's got a couple of kids who go to the elementary school up the road. I guess it's warm outside, but I grab a plain, grey sweatshirt from the kitchen table to defend against the air conditioning.

❖ ❖ ❖

May-June 1942 (Axis turn). All but one of my 17 Case Blue reinforcement steps are destined for Russia. I assault Rostov twice, but even with Air support my attacks aren't powerful enough to capture the city, and I know I must hurry so I can switch my focus to Sevastopol. However, in the north a sneaky panzer penetration helps me kill four steps and fully invest Leningrad, which will now definitely fall before the year is out. Elsewhere, I pull back from Saratov and Stalingrad, daring Dennis to come and get me.

May-June 1942 (Western turn). Unsurprisingly, Dennis reveals Arsenal of Democracy instead of US Victory Program, the historical choice to emphasize air and naval production over additional army expansion. More unexpected is Dennis's attempt to amphibiously attack the flank of my Alamein position in Egypt. He's rightly deduced that I'm no longer expecting to reach Alexandria and offers me a choice: I can repulse his invasion by fighting a massive naval and air battle, diverting forces from Russia and risking heavy losses, or I can let the Brits double their attack frontage and crack my lines uncomfortably soon. For now, I choose the former and hope I retain enough airpower to accomplish my goals next turn.

May-June 1942 (Soviet turn). Dennis accepts his fate at Leningrad, refuses to advance near Voronezh, and makes two spoiling attacks in front of Moscow before my reinforcements can reach the front.

May-June 1942 (Delay). Sometimes the Delay segment at the end of the turn is a game unto itself, albeit a game of *Yahtzee*. At the end of May-June, the Delay Box is a multinational purgatory holding no fewer than 25 Axis, Western and Soviet Air and Fleet support units, Convoy and Logistics markers, HQs, fortifications and armies. A separate die is rolled for each counter and modified by the current state of the game – e.g., late in the war, you'll usually subtract from the Allied rolls and add to the Axis rolls – and the lower the roll, the sooner that unit re-enters the game.

My Axis dice read '3-2-1-2-5-4-2-6-1'; the Western rolls are '3-6-1-5-3-5-1-6', while the Soviets get '1-2-4-1-5-1-3-6'. On the more important results – for the Air and Fleet units and my HQ – my luck is good, while Dennis gets a pair of '5's for his Western Fleets and a '6' for the Soviet Air unit. So I'm happy.

June-July 1942 (Axis turn). Leningrad falls without loss. However, I roll poorly in southern Russia, where after two attacks a single infantry step remains in Rostov and I've lost both my Airborne unit and a panzer step. I kill one of Dennis's two southernmost HQs, but Dennis can now reinforce Rostov if he wishes, and the Crimea still awaits my attention.

June-July 1942 (Western turn). An American armored corps sails across the Mediterranean to Alexandria. Historically, Montgomery drove Rommel across and out of Egypt and Libya with no American assistance, and US troops did not see combat in the European theater until Operation Torch in November 1942. I believe this was mostly for political reasons: when the US started fighting, it wanted to do so as an independent army and not as a token force under British leadership. But this needn't necessarily have been the case, and *Totaler Krieg* does not – and probably should not – mandate such behavior. So Dennis would be foolish not to send at least one US step to Egypt and establish a base from which American planes and ships can operate.

June-July 1942 (Soviet turn). The fall of Leningrad poses Dennis a real problem. My eight armies which had been besieging the city can now either march toward the two Lend-Lease ports of Murmansk and Archangel in the north or, more threateningly, move on Kalinin – two hexes northwest of Moscow – and sweep behind the Soviet capital.

So Dennis makes a perfectly rational decision, and does exactly what I want him to: he withdraws several hexes and builds a stronger, shorter line anchored on Kalinin and Tula. Better still, he abandons Rostov and withdraws fully behind the Don – I'll be able to capture one of the two remaining Objective Hexes I need without a fight. Now, I play quite a lot of poker with my friends at school, and I tend to do pretty well, but I have absolutely no poker face when I'm playing *Totaler Krieg* – all of my brainpower is transferred to the map. As Dennis finishes up his turn and rolls on the Lend-Lease Table, I'm grinning pretty broadly, so he looks at me and says, "What?"

"Nothing," I lie.

"You up to something?"

"I'm always up to something."

Dennis plucks at his beard. "I really needed Leningrad to hold out for another turn."

"Sure." I can't help myself. "But why abandon Rostov? You've just made my life a whole lot easier."

"If I fight for Rostov now, best case is that I hold on to it another turn, maybe two, and lose a lot of steps doing so."

"And?"

"Worst case, my whole southern army is vaporized like the planet Alderaan. You've got two Air units in the Delay Box – when you roll snake-eyes, as I'm sure you will, I'll have bigger problems than defending a single Objective. So I'll choose to live to fight another day."

I can see where he's coming from, but I think he's looking three moves ahead when one move would suffice. I'm not breaking through to Moscow or Baku, the red Objective Hex on the Caspian Sea. Beyond Rostov, the Caucasus is another strategic dead end; if Dennis had recognized that, I think he would have fought at Rostov.

July-August 1942 (Axis turn). After fighting a furious battle with the Red Air Force over the Crimea, I cobble together a patchwork assault force against Sevastopol. A 2:1 Blitz attack and a 3:2 Regular attack are barely passable, but I have to start the siege now, because I won't be able to make any Blitz attacks during the next two turns, and the city is well fortified. This is a rare battle where I'm glad to trade two panzer steps for two Soviet steps.

Apart from Sevastopol, I've now met all of my territorial goals for 1942, but Dennis probably doesn't know that, and I need him to think I've got bigger plans afoot to make sure I'm still where I want to be come December. Plus, every Soviet step I kill in 1942 is one less I need to worry about from 1943 to 1945. So I consciously thin my forces between Vyasma and Orel and scrape together two solid Blitz attacks, although Dennis cannily saves several steps in the north by not engaging his HQ and instead retreating along Lake Onega.

July-August 1942 (Western turn). Because my Air units were expended at Sevastopol, Dennis finally has support unit superiority in the Med and can amphibiously attack my flank in Egypt. As my Alamein position will soon be untenable, my goal now is to defend Africa to the last Italian and repatriate as many Germans as I can to Europe.

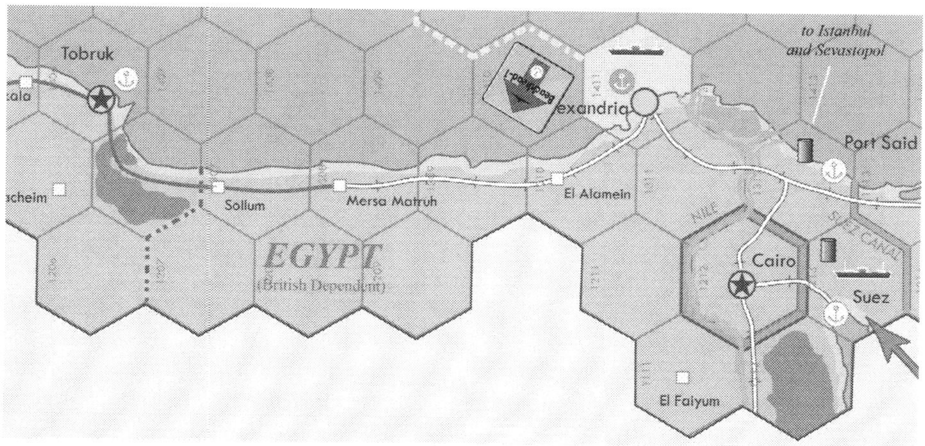

Fig. 2 – Western Beachhead counter placement near El Alamein

July-August 1942 (Soviet turn). I wonder what Dennis thinks I've planned for the Autumn. Because Germany cannot launch full-scale offensives in successive seasons, the only Blitz card I could have selected – Operation Felix – involves a series of dodgy Political rolls and foregoing four reinforcement steps. Thing is, Dennis knows I might be crazy enough to try a stunt like that, and if I had chosen it at the start of the Summer, I could cause real damage in August-September.

Dennis is certainly risk averse in the far north, retreating upon Archangel and sacrificing Murmansk. He also fortifies Tula. But in front of Moscow, he builds three new Shock armies which are strong in attack but weak in defense. Is he launching Operation Uranus next turn, one season ahead of schedule? Or is he trying to bluff me into retreating?

July-August 1942 (Delay). Two of my three Air units involved in the Rostov battle return to action immediately. I'm very blessed.

August-September 1942 (Axis turn). Total War Production is boring, but it gives me more reinforcements than any alternative, and that is what my current strategy demands. With Air support I have just enough strength to assault and capture Sevastopol, so I've finally reached my Festung Europa target. Finnish ski troops also glide into Murmansk.

August-September 1942 (Western turn). After Wartime Footing puts another stack of Western goodies in the Delay Box, Dennis interdicts the Central Mediterranean with a Carrier Fleet. I hadn't considered that; now my convoys to Africa are disrupted, so my units in Egypt are out of supply, which means my HQ in the desert can no longer support my Alamein position, and the Allies can drive me back toward Libya. Having fallen behind the Qattara Depression, I now must either defend two hexes at once instead of one, or abandon Egypt and Cyrenaica and withdraw to El Agheila.

I'm not sure I would have done anything differently – I was bound to get kicked out of Egypt eventually – but I hate getting caught out like this. There are so many variables to track in *Totaler Krieg*; miss just one of them, and you can be severely punished.

August-September 1942 (Soviet turn). Dennis reveals Operation Uranus and nods knowingly. "You saw that coming, didn't you?"

"More or less," I lie.

"I figured I'd need the steps, and that you'd give me a tempting target somewhere. But I'm not sure I see one. By your standards, you've been very conservative this game, haven't you?"

"I have, yes."

"And it's killing you, isn't it?" I laugh nervously.

Dennis looks down and starts scribbling on his notepad. I slump back in my armchair and glance beyond the Urals to a section of the bookcase sunken within the wall. I peruse several titles in one section:

- *The Origins of Freemasonry: Scotland's Century, 1590-1710*
- *Reluctant Cosmopolitans: The Portuguese Jews of Seventeenth Century Amsterdam*
- *Philosemitism and the Readmission of the Jews to England, 1603-1655*

Some real page-turners there. Even reading the spines drains me of purpose – it's like a morgue for books in here.

Every so often, Dennis waves a finger at the map, mumbles to himself and jots something down. He's often like this when planning a big offensive. A few months ago, Dennis was planning his Western move in a game which had reached July-August 1943, and I decided to follow his finger very closely as he pointed at different parts of the map. He kept motioning toward northern Italy, and I realized that he had a decent chance of sneaking into Bologna and causing Italy to surrender; he decided not to risk the invasion, and I immediately plugged the hole during my next turn, but that was my one and only foray into *Totaler Krieg* signals intelligence. The game is intense enough already – I need the mental downtime during Dennis's turns to get ready for my own – and I felt dirty doing it. Like, when my Aunt Jane forgets what she's doing during a family game of cards and lowers her hand so I can see it, I tell her to cover up again. She gets all upset, like I'm cheating instead of making sure I can't cheat, but then, she's not really a gamer.

Eventually, Dennis concocts a massive assault on Voronezh with airborne support which surrounds and destroys four Axis steps – a big loss, but expected in an offensive the size of Uranus. However, including Dennis's other attacks near Moscow, the Soviets lose four armored steps; it takes tanks to pave a road to Berlin, and expenses like this can add up as 1945 approaches.

August-September 1942 (Delay). With several large stacks again in the Delay Box, this time Dennis rolls better than I do. But with Winter approaching and Uranus basically finished, I think I can weather the consequences.

September-October 1942 (Axis turn). Our units in Europe are now locked together by mud, so there isn't much to do. Mud doesn't affect the desert, though, so after shifting my supply convoys from the Central Med to the Western Med, I boldly disband my HQ in Egypt – preparing it for reconstruction somewhere else – and withdraw to Tobruk, just far enough away so that Dennis won't be able to mount a strong attack next turn. I call this the "Brave Sir Robin" defense, after *Monty Python and the Holy Grail*:

Brave Sir Robin ran away.
Bravely ran away, away.
When danger reared it's ugly head,
He bravely turned his tail and fled.
Yes, brave Sir Robin turned about
And gallantly he chickened out.

Next turn I'll fall back again, just out of reach – I should be able to waste a few turns like this.

September-October 1942 (Western turn). The pursuit into Libya begins.

September-October 1942 (Soviet turn). Blitz attacks are prohibited during Mud turns, so Uranus peters out.

❖ ❖ ❖

I pause to phone for another pizza and fetch a bag of potato chips from the kitchen pantry. Daylight is fading now, and our neighbor's yard is quiet.

❖ ❖ ❖

November-December 1942 (Axis turn). Festung Europa arrives, bringing with it the No Retreat marker. For the first time, I deploy significant reinforcements to

Italy and the West, but after straightening my lines in Russia I still have at least five steps in each of the 10 hexes from Volkhov to Belgorod (northeast of Kharkov). Near Rostov, I bow my defenses forward along and above the Donets, but I can easily fall back to my linear position when required.

In the desert, Brave Sir Rommel withdraws toward Benghazi and El Agheila, knowing that Monty is too sluggish to pursue effectively.

November-December 1942 (Western turn). Right on schedule, Dennis launches Operation Torch and declares war on Vichy France. In the upturned *Totaler Krieg* box-top, which rests on a cushioned wooden chair at the end of our gaming table, is a storage tray of black plastic topped by a clear lid that neatly cuddles the tray's 20 narrow slots. This tray holds the pieces we're not using, and in one of its slots are the French counters we discarded when Paris fell in 1940. The counters marked with a small, white "V" represent Vichy's standing army – when I'm done sifting them from my French prisoners of war, I look at Dennis and mumble, "Um…what do I do with these again?"

"You put the striped units in the Delay Box and…hold on, I forget."

I reach for the rulebook. "How many times have we played this game?"

"Not enough to memorize the rules, obviously."

"It's been a long day."

I know I'm looking for Rule 13, "Factions & Countries", but it takes a moment before I find the sub-rule I need, on page 42 of the rulebook under "13.7.2 – Minor Country Setup Exceptions":

> **Vichy:** Select the following counters with a V in the upper left corner. These are placed as follows:
>
> - In or adjacent to City and/or Port hexes within Vichy (*not* Occupied France) *or* a Vichy Dependent, up to one unit per hex – three French 0-1-2 colonial infantry
> - Delay Box – one French 3-4-2 infantry, one French 1-2-3 infantry, one French 1-2-3 mech, one French 1-1-2 colonial infantry
> - Delay Box, *if Vichy has been activated as an Axis Minor and the counter has not already been entered or removed from the game* – one French Surface Fleet, French Convoy marker

Of course. The three Vichy steps go in Marseilles, Algiers and Tunis, so Dennis invades Oran with two armored corps. This triggers the "French Liberation" event (rule 16.4.1), dissolving the Vichy army and making France once again a Western ally, so I have several new cities to garrison.

November-December 1942 (Soviet turn). Dennis reveals Rumyantsev Reserves Formed, ensuring he will have all of the goodies he needs to launch a massive offensive next summer. Which of course is exactly what Hitler did with Operation Citadel in real life, and where did that get him?

❖ ❖ ❖

After Dennis makes two quick attacks, and as he's polishing off his Reserve Movement Phase, the doorbell rings. It's my turn to pay for the pizza, so I go to the front door. The delivery man – a freckly kid not much older than me and whose cheeks are festooned with acne – courteously announces the price of my order and hands me the usual cardboard box. The warm early evening infiltrates the foyer, and as the heat of the box bottom rushes into my fingertips, a gentle breeze whooshes through the trees at the side of the house before dancing across the back of my neck. I stare at the kid for several seconds. "You OK, sir?" he finally asks.

I blink twice and quickly shake my head several times. "Sorry," I stammer. "Here you go – please keep the change."

"Thanks very much. Well, you have a good evening."

"You too."

I step outside and watch the kid walk to his motorbike, put on his helmet, twist the ignition key to elicit two mellow growls from the engine, and slowly slip past Dennis's maroon Chevrolet and down the driveway. Attached to the rear of the bike is a large white cube in which to keep his cargo safe and warm; I start to imagine neat, circular black pips on each side, and immediately double-back inside and close the door.

"Dennis?" I call from the foyer. "Let's have the pizza out back."

"Really? You don't want to do the Delay rolls first?"

I let the suggestion sink in, then walk back to the study. "Just the big one, if that's OK."

"Sure." He hands me a white die with rounded edges. I drop it in the dice tower, and after wriggling through the slats it emerges as a '1'. The No Retreat marker is immediately placed at the "Axis Tide 3" victory level: to win the game, Dennis must reach "Allied Crusade 4" – i.e., control at least 32 of the game's 39 Objectives – by V-E Day in 1945.

❖ ❖ ❖

At the rear of my house is a paved patio with spartan wooden furniture shielded from sun and rain by a striped canvas awning. The yard beyond the patio is long enough for a game of touch football and wide enough for a game of catch, but not flat enough to do either comfortably; it slopes away from the house, imperceptibly at first but steeply at the far end to merge with the woods. When I was much smaller, I would lie on the grass by myself and look up at the impossibly tall trees, or shelter from rain beneath the sturdy awning on a hot summer's night and relish the mist formed by the wind and the splattering of moisture on concrete as it caressed my bare shins.

"This is a nice house you've got here," says Dennis, one leg raised and resting on a second chair, biting into a slice of pizza. "Have I told you that before?"

I look at Dennis, his face dimly lit by two wall lights at either end of the awning. I ask, "What is it you do for a living, uh, again?"

"I'm an electrical engineer." He takes another bite of pizza. "You?"

"Me? I go to high school."

"Kidding!" Dennis smiles. "I know – you go to high school, and you fight the Germans or the Allies every Thursday night."

"I do a few other things as well."

Dennis sips his drink and asks, "Do you do them as well as you play this game?"

I smirk. "That's highly debatable."

"Do you ever fancy playing something else? I mean, aside from *Totaler Krieg*. This isn't the only game you own, right? I'm sure I've seen others in this house before."

"Yes, I do own other games. But this is the one I like playing the most."

"Why is that?"

"How long have you got?"

"As long as you want. It's your house, it's your game, and you bought the pizza."

I pause for a moment. "Tell you what," I say. "Let me ask you a better question: is *Totaler Krieg* your favorite game?"

"Not really, no."

"I didn't think so – I've never really thought it was. So why do you spend so much time here, in my house, playing this game? How far away from here do you live?"

"About half an hour, by car."

"Exactly."

"Perhaps you haven't noticed, but wargamers aren't exactly a dime a dozen in this part of the world. And I'm not complaining: *TK* is a lot of fun."

"But it's not perfect."

"Of course not."

"And why is that? What has happened in this game today that wouldn't pass a historical sniff test?"

"Heh." Dennis smiles again. "There's more to it than that. Although for starters, how many amphibious invasions have I attempted in the past year-and-a-bit – three? There's no way the Allies had enough landing craft in 1943 for that, let alone 1942. And what about that silly little Beachhead I created in Egypt? I had, what, six steps marooned for months on my own little Gallipoli, never mind that there are no cliffs to hide behind on the Egyptian coastline."

"Design for Effect! It's a DFE game. Those 'invasions' don't just represent landing craft and an invasion attempt – they represent the air-naval war and everything that goes into it. Your Beachhead at El Alamein represented Montgomery building up his forces until he's sufficiently strong to make a decisive attack. It's not actually a landing on my flank."

"Yes, you keep telling me that. But I can't buy the abstractions as easily as you can. Believe me, I'd love to."

"You're more of a *World at War* guy."

"Given my present company, I wish it weren't so, but yes, I probably am."

A World at War also covers the whole of the Second World War, but includes the Pacific theater as well as Europe. Its rulebook is 196 pages long, not counting the 72-page "Status Sheet" booklet, a 24-page Research and Diplomacy booklet, and a 24-page Scenario booklet. That's not a game – that's a religion. And from what I've read and heard, I'm not convinced that the extra detail produces a more realistic game. At a certain point, "detail" becomes "noise".

But I'm not an expert on *A World at War*, and I can't judge it fully or fairly. So I say, "Look: I've found a game I like. I know how to play it, and how to play it pretty well. It does nearly everything I'd want a game on this topic to do – this is my desert island wargame. Why should I invest time and energy in a new system, studying a new rulebook and learning new Zone of Control rules and Weather rules and Diplomacy rules and suffering through the trial and error of failed strategies and tactics, when I could be enjoying this game and learning how to play it better?"

The breeze ruffles the tall trees across the yard. I think it might rain tonight.

3.

What *Totaler Krieg* and its peers can't do is make the Axis player believe into 1943 and 1944 that he can still win the war by forcing Britain or the Soviet Union to surrender. But nearly every grand strategic World War II wargame also lets the Axis player win the game simply by bettering Germany's historical performance – i.e., not surrender by May 1945. *Totaler Krieg* is more dynamic than many of its peers, as the Axis player's status in May 1945 is measured against his high-water mark circa 1942, but it still fits this pattern.

This is problematic, because Hitler wasn't merely trying to survive past May 1945. He was trying to win the war and perpetuate his thousand-year Reich, and if those are your goals, your decisions will reflect that. The impossible "stand fast" orders to Rommel at Alamein and to von Paulus at Stalingrad make sense in this context – Hitler wanted to win the war, not merely delay the inevitable. And Germany's Ardennes offensive in December 1944 should be properly understood as a final lunge at total victory. Hitler saw a chance, however miniscule, of striking through a weakly defended sector of the Western front and reaching Antwerp, dividing British and American forces from each other and perhaps driving Britain from the war; with the respite gained, he could amass enough strength in the East to stop the Red Army. Many historians have criticized Hitler's plan for its profligate use of reserves, and no intelligent Axis player in *Totaler Krieg* would instigate the Battle of the Bulge on the same terms and risk losing the war – and thereby the game – a month sooner. But if total victory is all that matters, even a million-to-one shot is better than no shot at all.

That said, forcing the Axis player to win the war to win the game doesn't work either. A realistic game with such victory conditions would be horribly imbalanced: by any reasonable calculation, Germany's chances of winning World War II were far less than 50 percent. Also, after a certain point Germany's fate was sealed, bar a series of Frederick the Great-sized miracles. What motivation would the Axis player have to continue any game beyond 1943, other than being courteous and letting the Allied player enjoy being on the strategic offensive? On balance, I think game designers have chosen the lesser of two evils; one can always rationalize that had Germany delayed the inevitable long enough, war weariness may have persuaded the Allies to settle for something less than unconditional surrender.

This brings me back to my game with Dennis, in which I'm now committed to a long, slow, pragmatic retreat. For the rest of Saturday evening and into Sunday morning, I push and parry in the East and withdraw from Libya in an orderly fashion. Several German steps escape across the Mediterranean to Italy; those that don't, along with their Italian allies, successfully prolong the African campaign until Summer 1943. Very historical, except I haven't sent any new forces to Africa since 1941, so Dennis's final bag of prisoners isn't extensive. Plus – and this aspect of the historical campaign is under-reported – with three Western armies now in Tunisia, Dennis is virtually forced to invade Sicily or Sardinia to progress further in 1943. A swift redeployment to threaten France, Norway or Greece is out of the question.

Meanwhile, I use my Festung Europa fortifications not to build the Atlantic Wall along the Channel coastline, but to construct a two-part "East Wall" on either side of the Pripet Marshes, from Riga to Minsk and from Kiev to the Black Sea. My Summer 1943 Option Card is not Operation Citadel, but rather a defense-minded card called Nation, Rise Up! which gives me more forts and improved war production. Beginning in May-June 1943, I slowly fall back from my Volkhov-Rostov line to the East Wall, which I'd begun fortifying in January-February at the rate of one hex per turn. This means sacrificing Rostov immediately, and Sevastopol and Leningrad (plus Finland) by the end of 1943, but the East Wall should hold firm well into the second half of 1944.

This is meat-and-potatoes wargaming, and in its own way rather like John Erickson's books on the Russo-German war: not at all sexy, but very filling and perfectly satisfying. I don't think Hitler could have countenanced the deliberate sacrifice of so much Soviet territory, to say nothing of adopting a Maginot mentality, but the military logic of such a withdrawal is inescapable. Some scholars suggest that Stalin extended peace feelers to Germany in 1943; perhaps an East Wall could have formed a basis for negotiations, had Hitler been so inclined.

Of course, to build and hold the East Wall, I must deplete my garrisons in the West. Dennis gets ashore in Sicily in June-July 1943, crosses to the mainland two turns later and collapses Italy via Operation Avalanche when he captures Naples in September-October. But I'm able to stabilize the front at the historical Gustav Line, south of Rome, and any serious effort on the Italian peninsula – three hexes wide at most and dense with mountains and rivers – will divert large forces away from Northern Europe. Still, when Dennis invades France in 1944, as he surely will, I won't be able to contain him on the beaches; another orderly withdrawal, to a fortified "West Wall" running from Antwerp to Switzerland, will be necessary.

❖ ❖ ❖

As Sunday afternoon fades into evening, Dennis and I are both running short of petrol. Dennis has twice expressed guilt about skipping church this morning and is rubbing his eyes a lot, while the painkillers I've taken are struggling to outflank my headache. We started this game around lunchtime on Friday.

It is now March-April 1944. The Russians are still blocked by the East Wall, although Dennis is trying to bypass it by oozing armies into the Pripet. The Yanks and Brits are now massing in England, but the Gustav Line in Italy remains unbreached. As the Western turn begins, Dennis reveals Operation Shingle and plops a British Fleet in the Adriatic Sea. I arch my eyebrows and peer across the board. "Huh?"

"Oh, sorry – it's not in the Naval Zone Box, I'm putting it in that hex there."

Nope, I'm still not following. "What?"

"It's a Fleet. You know how they can create Beachheads when you put them in sea hexes?"

"Yeah, I'm not an idiot. You're...you're invading Yugoslavia?"

"Do you want to contest the placement?"

"Do I?" I don't think I've touched a Yugoslavian counter since 1941. Three of Yugoslavia's four armies are in Zagreb, Belgrade and Salonika; the other is in southern Serbia, but it should probably be guarding Dubrovnik, Yugoslavia's sole port on the Adriatic.

"No, you don't," says Dennis. "But it's your choice, so do you?"

"Have it, then," I mumble. So Dennis places a Beachhead and points it at the Croatian coastline.

Just then, a door opens on the other side of the house, and I hear the thump of baggage on the tile floor by the kitchen. Uh-oh. Then comes a muffled shout: "Sean, it's like a bloody war zone in here!"

Welcome home, Dad. I look away from the gameboard to the floor of the study, at a whirlwind of pizza boxes, greasy plates and gaming paraphernalia, and say to Dennis, "Can you...I dunno, stack everything on top of each other for a minute?" I get up from my chair and wave a hand at the rubble. "I'll be right back."

"Take your time."

I maneuver out of the study and intercept my father in the living room. He stops and silently inspects me, arms folded, glasses perched on the front of his nose. It's a pose I know too well, although his hairline seems higher and more flecked with grey each time I notice it. "How was your trip?" I ask.

"The usual," says Dad. He softens his gaze and gives my hair a quick tousle. "You look terrible. Dennis is here, I guess?"

"Yeah – long weekend."

"How go the wars?"

"You know. Interesting game – played all the way to 1944 since Friday. You'd be impressed at how historical it's been."

"Mmm-hmm."

He crosses to the gaming room, through the half-open door, and shoots me a look of disgust. "You'll do something about that?" Neither of us are impressed at the quick repairs Dennis has attempted on the floor.

"Hi, Mister Lansbury," says Dennis.

"Hello, Dennis." The greeting drips from my father's lips with just the right amount of weariness and scorn for me to wince and Dennis not to notice.

He paces to the gaming table, presses his glasses to his eyes and scans the map. "Yugoslavia?" he asks.

"Dennis is the Allies," I answer meekly.

Dad turns, glances briefly at the bookcase on the wall, then points at the sloppy pile in the corner. "You'll do something about that, yes? Right now?"

"Of course – sorry."

"Is Dennis sticking around? Are you watching the baseball tonight?"

"We'll be finishing up soon, I think."

"Are you all set for tomorrow? Finished all of your summer reading?"

Bugger. First day of the new school year tomorrow. I shrug.

"Are you going to finish your summer reading? Have you done any of your summer reading?"

"Yes!" *On the Beach* was very readable. Slogging through Thomas Hardy, on the other hand, was like winter at Monte Cassino – I'm not going there again.

"I shall go upstairs for a few minutes and then get some food. Goodnight, Dennis."

Dad leaves the room. I slink into my gaming chair and slouch down low in the seat. If Dad had come home five minutes earlier, Yugoslavia wouldn't have happened yet.

"What do you want to do?" asks Dennis.

"Go ahead and finish up with the West. It's Mud next turn anyway, so this is a good stopping point." Dennis reaches over the board to continue his invasion, then I remember: "Oh, and I'll take our trash to the kitchen, thanks very much. Just carry on without me for a minute."

The tidying is my penance for leaving Dubrovnik unguarded, I guess. The irony is that I can justify the game's history: Prince Paul brings Yugoslavia into the war under duress, but Serbians dominate the war cabinet, and nationalist fissures begin to form. Civil unrest flares in the mountains, and as the Allies invade Italy, Croatian separatists contact the Allies. So when the invasion comes ashore, resistance is sparse, as was the case with Operation Torch in North Africa – only by now, the Allies know how to conduct an invasion, so they get ashore more quickly. (I wonder where Tito and his Partisans would fit into this storyline?) But Dad wouldn't see it that way: "An historical justification for the narrative, not a narrative explanation of the history," he'd bellow. Always "an historical" with him.

Dennis captures Dubrovnik, Split and Sarajevo, and the British Eighth Army crosses the Dinaric Alps during Reserve Movement, poised to surge into the plains toward Zagreb or Belgrade in the Summer. And with that, Dennis grabs his car keys, his wallet and his green, canvas duffel bag that has seen better days and heads for the front door. "You free on Thursday?" he asks.

"Of course."

PART ONE

1.

The thing that really bugs me about high school is that it's full of teenagers. Last spring, during a Friday afternoon English class Mrs. Fortune asked everyone what age they would be if they could be as old as they wanted, and my first six classmates to raise their hands picked numbers between 21 and 26. Gennifer Simms said she would be 23, "because I could stay out as late as I wanted, I'd have my own car and my own place and my mother wouldn't keep coming in and saying hi to my boyfriends." Mrs. Fortune must have seen my face, because she called on me even though my hand wasn't raised and asked for a dissenting view.

"I'd be nine months," I said. "My parents would look out for me, I'd play with toys all day, and I wouldn't have to worry about *anything*. I could spit out food I didn't like and get away with it. I could crawl around and break into forbidden cupboards and get up to all sorts of trouble, and everyone would laugh. No matter how ugly I was, people would say I was cute – they'd probably even think I was cute. Plus I'd have a woman's breast in my mouth all the time." This last line caused much sniggering. It's not often you can simultaneously play to your audience and laugh at its expense.

It's so true, though: babies don't have to worry about anything. Unless of course they come from broken homes or get sent to Auschwitz or wind up in Oradour-sur-Glane on the wrong day at the wrong time. But I try not to think about these things. It's much more fun to think of a child for whom the London Blitz or the Sack of Rome might have seemed hugely colorful and interesting, pleasant changes to the humdrum of kindergarten. Maybe small children in the right circumstances get to live the lives of historians' fantasy – experiencing the most dramatic events in history firsthand, unafraid of danger, oblivious to causes and possible consequences, easily retreating to a closeted Narnia of the mind should the danger come too close.

On the other hand, most of my classmates think history is something which fits on their schedules between Biology and French, and in reality between gossiping about transitory couplings or fashion crimes. This year I'm taking AP European History, which is fantastic, but it's being taught by Mr. Prendergast, which probably isn't. Mr. Prendergast also coaches the varsity baseball team, and I gather he likes to entertain his students with sensationalist stories. Both of these traits are good – and good history is sensational in the truest sense of the word – but I'm afraid that the combination might be toxic. You see, this is the first class I've ever wanted to take at school. I wanted to surround myself with smart students and have stimulating discussions about Oliver Cromwell and the French Revolution and Imperialism and Appeasement. I might even have learned something, though perhaps not about Appeasement. Now I'm facing a year on a fairground ride.

I go to Muhlendorf High School, which was founded in the 1870s by a wealthy German-American in a part of Middle America where the first-generation immigrants seemed indigenous. In 1917, before people came to understand that they were Americans first and German-Americans or Irish-Americans or any other form of hyphenated-Americans second, the school's name drew xenophobic criticism of the type that is so popular in the US at times of crisis. In both World Wars, at least three thousand miles, half a continent, an entire ocean and absolute naval supremacy separated us from our enemies, and yet many people – including those who should have known better, starting with FDR and Executive Order 9066 – behaved as though one never knew when the nasty Krauts or the dirty Japs were going to land on the shores of Lake Michigan and drive south until they reached the Rio Grande. (Come to think of it, this sounds like Soviet grand strategy in the movie *Red Dawn*.)

In the postwar education boom, Muhlendorf gained hundreds of new students and, in time, a clump of "modern" buildings to match. I've been to Europe before, and I've seen small cities in northern France like Le Havre that were quite ugly, but I can at least understand why: the Allies carpet-bombed them to smithereens during 1944, and *something* needed to be built after the war finally passed them by. Alas, the best you could say for Muhlendorf was that it expanded at just the wrong time, in the hands of just the wrong architect. How could anyone be inspired to attend this mishmash of windows, concrete, linoleum and right angles? We should be ashamed to offer an AP Art History course.

I'm told that Muhlendorf's academic standards compare favorably with anything in the state, even most of the private schools. I guess it basks in the warmth of the nearby College, and I'm one of many children of its faculty and staff who go here, but that wasn't always the case; Muhlendorf lagged behind many other schools in the district until about 15 years ago, when our PTA unsheathed its torches and pitchforks and marched on the local education board. As the squeaky wheel continues to get the grease, our catchment area is now incredibly fashionable among parents, even following the unfortunate incident my freshman year when two mothers came to blows upon discovering who had been cast as the female lead of the senior Spring Musical. It was in all the papers.

And that's the history of my school. Most students call it "M" or "the Mule"; I call it "Muhlendorf" because I can easily pronounce "Muhlendorf", and because the syllable "dorf" doesn't reduce me to fits of hysterical giggles.

❖ ❖ ❖

Lunch on the first day of school sees the return of the Big Game. This is the second year in which Muhlendorf is trialing a 60-minute lunch period. We can have lunch anywhere on campus. We can go to tutorials for some classes, or take time out to study; there are intramural sports competitions as well. But every school day since last October, five of us have gathered at the same round table in a sunlit alcove of the cafeteria to play poker. There's always the Gang of Four – that's me, Chris, Melvyn and Freddie – and we take turns inviting one other player to sit in, or two others if one of us is indisposed. There's a long list of students who want to take part, and we normally get a decent crowd of kibitzers.

The Big Game is No Limit Texas Hold 'Em, with a five-dollar buy-in, no rebuys and fixed 10-cent and 20-cent blinds. We play 10 hands per game, with each of us dealing two hands apiece, and the player with the most money left at the end gets to collect a bonus quarter from everyone else. It doesn't sound like much, I know, but it's pretty cutthroat. The four of us all know what we're doing, although seat five is usually dead money, which helps the rest of us stay in the black. I netted $56.40 last year, slightly down from a peak of around plus-$60.

There's a bigger crowd than normal watching us here on Opening Day, for we've invited the king of the Asses, Derek Stevenson, to be our fifth player. My Gang has divided the rest of the school into three categories: the Asses (the popular and/or stupid), the Masses (common folk) and the Glasses (the geeks), with a subset of pretty girls among the Masses called the Lasses. Derek is a senior and the starting quarterback of the varsity football team, and he's assured us all that he knows how to play poker and that he will emerge from the game 20 dollars richer. But Muhlendorf runs a wishbone offense – not very subtle – and Melvyn and I suspect Derek's quarterbacking traits might translate to the poker table.

Chris draws the button for the first hand and starts shuffling. Chris can riffle shuffle like a casino dealer – I love him for that – and his performance draws some admiring murmurs from the gallery. Then he shows us a new wrinkle: holding the deck steady with the thumb and middle finger of his left hand, he extracts and seems to juggle several groups of cards with his right hand in a blaze of movement until most of the deck is in his right palm, at which point he plops the few remaining cards in his left hand on top.

"Outstanding," I say. "Where'd you learn that?"

"That's called the Hindu shuffle," he says, beginning the ritual again. "I learned it in Bangkok over the summer when I was there with my mother. Apparently, everyone in Asia shuffles cards like this."

"I forgot all about that. Good trip?"

"I'll tell you more later. You wouldn't believe some of the stuff I saw over there." Chris is the man. He can shuffle poker chips between his fingers, too, but in the Big Game we just use nickels, dimes and quarters, which are easier to hide should the school Gestapo comes calling.

Chris slides two cards to each of us along the waxy tabletop. I draw the 8 of diamonds and the 3 of hearts and pass, then Derek, playing next, smugly announces, "All in." There's a gasp from a girl with blond hair across the table behind Melvyn, who looks at me and says, "That didn't take long." He folds as well.

Then it's Freddie's turn. Freddie is shy and quiet; he's got these startling green eyes and a wicked mop of curly brown hair that only God could have fashioned, and I keep telling him that the girls would drop dead for him if he'd just open up a little bit and let them in. But he keeps his cards, both literally and figuratively, close to his vest in life as in poker. As he calmly and without expression studies Derek's face, I'm expecting another pass.

But no, Freddie says, "I'll call." This produces much excitement and some applause from the cheering spectators, so I wave my hands and chide them with a "Guys, please. Calm it down."

Chris folds and says, "OK, Derek, what've you got?"

The football hero flicks his cards into the middle of the table, face up. "Two Queens," he says, arrogantly.

"Kings," answers Freddie, quietly. "Sorry." And there they are, the king of spades and the king of diamonds.

"What?" shrieks Derek. "C'mon! No way." He stands up and pushes his seat out from under him. "First hand? That's bullshit, man."

Chris kills the top card by turning it face down, and then he deals three cards for the flop: King of hearts, 8 of clubs, and 3 of diamonds. Derek is virtually drawing dead, and he can hardly contain himself – he grunts loudly and jackhammers his chair twice into the floor. The turn is a blank; just to salt his wound, the river card is a meaningless Queen.

"That is bullshit," hisses Derek. "Did you set me up? Are you guys setting me up?"

"Cards is cards," says Chris. "Sorry."

"Cards? What about that shuffle you did? The Asian thing. What was that? That wasn't a shuffle – did you set me up?"

"Are you accusing Chris of cheating?" asks Melvyn. The crowd is really stirring now.

"I can shuffle cards – I don't do magic tricks," says Chris.

"First hand!" bellows Derek.

"That's poker," says Chris. "Nobody put a gun to your head and made you go all-in."

"So that's it? I'm done? C'mon, let me buy back in."

"No, that's it," I say. "Big Game rules are no re-buys."

"This is so rigged. You guys suck."

Lowering my voice, I look right at the football hero and say, "Derek, we've been playing the Big Game for almost a year now. The rules are always the same. You knew the rules when you asked to play, and they've worked well for everyone else. Sorry."

"And nobody made you go all-in with Queens," says Chris.

"Shut up," says Derek. "Dammit." He pushes his chair in and makes to leave.

"By the way," I say, "you owe us another 25 cents. Winner gets to keep it. Big Game rules."

Raging, Derek reaches into his pocket and smacks a quarter firmly into the table, trapping it under his right hand. He seethes, "You're gonna have me back here, and I mean tomorrow, and I'm going to take you, you, you and you down."

"We'll be happy to put you back on the list," I say.

"For tomorrow?"

"We'll let you know."

Derek thunders away. Chris, Freddie and I get a few pats on the back and murmurs of appreciation, then the crowds begin to thin. One younger-looking boy who I don't recognize asks me, "Will Derek be back tomorrow?"

Chris answers, "We'll let you know," and smiles. The rest of us laugh.

Maybe the school lets us play poker in the cafeteria because the Big Game is so democratic. We don't discriminate: everyone can and does play with us. The rules are the rules. The Asses, the Masses, the Glasses and the Lasses are all equal, and the cards favor nobody. Where else can that happen on campus?

Actually, it's more likely that the school doesn't know what's going on.

I smile and look again at the table. "Funny thing is, if you guys would have let me play that hand, I'd have flopped two pair," I say.

"Yeah, right."

"No, seriously: I had eight-three offsuit. I would've gotten murdered by Freddie's trips, though."

"A note for next time," says Melvyn. "We should really have everyone ante up the extra quarter at the start of the game, to avoid this kind of unpleasantness."

"New year, new innovation – I like that," says Chris.

"The Big Game rules," I say, ambiguously.

"Doesn't it just," says Chris. "OK – button goes to Sean. Hand number two!"

❖ ❖ ❖

My first AP European History class begins at 1:45 in the afternoon. I'm sitting at a desk in the back of the class next to Chris, who is also taking the course with me. This trimester, we're borrowing a classroom from the math department, which means the teacher-created graffiti on the taupe-painted walls – square root symbols and algebraic formulae cut from colored cardstock, that sort of thing – feels both silly and out of place, instead of merely silly. But Stalin did say that a million deaths was a statistic, so maybe there's a larger point to bear in mind.

The "bell", an electronic drone spawned from two tests of the Emergency Broadcast System, sounds to start the class. Mr. Prendergast, a big, bearded man with an unusually round head, stands up and removes his leather jacket to reveal one of his trademark plaid shirts. "For many of you, this will be your first Advanced Placement course," he begins. "Welcome to the big-time: this is Major League Baseball. You do well here, you'll earn college credit, you'll improve your chances of getting into a good school, and you'll help your grade point average. All the girls will love you, and all the guys will want to be your buddy – or the other way round, and so on and so forth. You'll also learn something about the world: both how it used to be, and why it is the way it is now. It's not going to be easy, and the stakes are high, but so are the rewards. Is everybody with me?"

Surprisingly, nobody sniggers, and a few heads around the room nod in affirmation. There are 18 of us in the class.

"Let me start by painting a picture for you. It's the morning rush hour on the New York City subway system. The passengers are packed tightly together in their train cars on their way to work in Manhattan or wherever it is they're going. Somebody drops a glass vial on the floor of one of the trains: Is it from a scientist?

A terrorist? Nobody knows, but because it's so busy, nobody notices. And nobody knows it yet, but every person on the train is now infected with a deadly disease.

"They reach the next stop: some people get off the car, others get on. At the next stop, more people get off. Everyone who comes within breathing distance of someone who was on that subway train becomes infected with the disease. Every time an infected person sneezes and forgets to cover his mouth, or goes to the bathroom and forgets to wash his hands, the disease spreads further. Infected people get into work and spread the disease around, people get in their cars and take it home with them, they go to the airport and get on planes at JFK and LaGuardia and carry it to other cities, and within days it has spread around the world.

"Within three or four days, everyone infected with the disease begins to suffer fever, weakness in the muscles, nausea and vomiting. Big bumps start forming on their necks, under their armpits and in their, ah, nether regions. Within eight days of contracting the disease, three out of every four infected people are dead. The disease rages on for several months; before it dies down, one out of every two men, women and children in the United States are dead. No fewer than one billion people around the world are dead. Let that sink in for a moment.

"So, imagine that each of you are among the survivors. Half of the country is dead. What kind of world would you now be living in? What would be different?"

After a pause, Chris mumbles, "I probably wouldn't be taking this course!"

Mr. Prendergast smiles and says, "You were probably joking, but you might be right. I might be dead. Half of the teachers in this school might be dead. Half of your classmates might be dead. Muhlendorf would be a very different place. What else?"

More silence. Then Jenny Pedersen says, "It'd be pretty scary, wouldn't it?"

"More like total panic," says Hugh Johnson.

"Think of all the dead bodies – who's going to bury them?" asks Chad Sauerbrunner. "And where are you going to bury them? Or do they all get cremated?"

"And how would the country keep working?" offers Rebecca Fowler. "How many farmers are left? Who will ship the food to the supermarkets and keep them running for the people who need to buy it? What about doctors to look after the sick? Or bankers to run the economy? Or politicians to run the government? What if the president and half of the cabinet all got sick and died?"

"Indeed," says Mr. Prendergast. "What if the whole world fell apart at the seams, and nobody knew how to pick up the pieces and put them back together again?"

Ah, now I get it. I raise my hand and Mr. Prendergast calls on me.

"It's not a perfect analogy, though, is it?" I ask.

"What do you mean?" replies Mr. Prendergast.

"Well, the world nowadays is at least prepared for the idea of a global pandemic like this. Between advances in modern medicine, the existence of organizations like the CDC, and the ability to communicate quickly by phone and the internet, I would hope we'd be able to prevent a disease like this from spreading too quickly. In contrast, when the Black Death showed up in Europe, nobody had the slightest idea what it was or how to stop it from spreading."

"Exactly," said Mr. Prendergast. "Mister Lansbury stole my thunder – what I was about to say is that this scenario I've just outlined has actually happened already, more or less. I adjusted the scenario slightly to make it fit the 21st century, and shifted it from Europe to the US, but in the 14th century, the Bubonic Plague or 'Black Death' arrived in Europe, probably along trading routes from Africa and Asia, and within a few years something like 45 to 50 percent of Europe's population was wiped out. Dead. Finished. In some places along the Mediterranean, the death toll reached nearly 80 percent. And Mister Lansbury is right: people blamed everything and everyone for the plague, from earthquakes to astrological forces to the poisoning of wells by the Jews." Mr. Prendergast points gently at me and says, "I knew it was going to be dangerous, having you in here this year."

"Don't mention it," I say.

Mr. Prendergast then explains that the Black Death was like pressing "Reset" on a PlayStation game, causing Europe to start over again. I wonder why the dead died and the survivors lived. Was it just dumb luck? I guess city-dwellers suffered worse, because population density was greater and urban sanitation was non-existent. But within a given community, why does one poor schmuck get it and his neighbor not? Could an individual have done anything to improve his odds of survival? Was fleeing to the countryside, away from the crowds and the filth, the only sane option? And why is it always the Jews who get persecuted when something goes wrong? I suppose I know the answer to this last question, rationally if not emotionally. But everything about this scenario seems awfully capricious.

I could ask the same questions about World War II, of course. And I don't just mean about why does one house or one city get bombed and another not – suppose you're an able-bodied American male at the start of 1939. I know the Soviets and the Germans and the Poles and the Japanese and the Chinese suffered far more than the Americans did, but I was born in the United States, so let's start here. How unlucky would you have been to die because of the war? Particularly to have died in some godforsaken, muddy Italian trench or some equally godforsaken, malaria-ridden Pacific island, or some godforsaken Japanese prisoner-of-war camp. (All war deaths are equally bad, but some are more equal than others.)

Let's do the math: of the 130 million people living in the US in 1939, only one in 10 joined the armed forces. Of those in uniform, only 3 percent died during the war, and only 290,000 died in battle. So to be drafted and then posted to a combat unit, and for that unit to see serious front-line combat, is pretty unlucky to begin with. And even then, you'd have to be very unlucky to get shot or pierced by bomb or shell fragments – and more unlucky still to wind up dead and not merely wounded. Note that I've excluded the wounded from the above figures; it drives me batty when historians talk about "casualties" and fail to distinguish between the dead and the wounded, as though there's no difference between the two.

Hmmm. I seem to have started thinking like my Dad. I hate it when I do that.

(By the way, I didn't count the 1,700 American civilians that died during the war. Most of them were living abroad and were interned by the Japanese in the first few months of the Pacific war, although 68 civilians in Hawaii died on 7 December 1941, and another six – five schoolchildren and a preacher's wife – were killed during a church group picnic in Bly, Oregon on 5 May 1945 by a Japanese balloon bomb. It had been launched from Japan itself, floated on the jet stream across the Pacific, landed softly in a tree in Oregon, and was detonated by a 13-year-old girl who spotted it and tried to yank it loose. How unlucky is that? What a way to go.)

Speaking of my Dad, he'd love this: Mr. Prendergast is now passing out copies of the College Board's AP European History course outline, along with a separate syllabus of our own. This is disgusting. I guess I was naïve to assume that a course on European History would focus upon, you know, history. Topics for the course are grouped into three sections, each of which is given equivalent weight in the big exam at the end of the school year: "Intellectual and Cultural History", "Political and Diplomatic History", and "Social and Economic History". These topics include:

- *Major trends in literature and the arts*
- *Developments in social, economic and political thought, including ideologies characterized as "-isms" such as socialism, liberalism and nationalism*
- *Developments in literacy, education and communication*
- *The character of and changes in agricultural production and organization*
- *The influence of sanitation and health care practices on society: food supply, diet, famine, disease and their impact*

- *Gender roles and their influence on work, social structure, family structure and interest group formation*
- *Private and state roles in economic activity*

There's a single topic at the end of the "Political and Diplomatic" section called:

- *War and civil conflict: origins, developments, technology and their consequences*

One lousy, stinking topic. And here's the very first of the sample multiple-choice questions on the mock AP exam in the course outline:

1. *In early modern Europe, women were accused of practicing witchcraft more often than were men because of the belief that women:*
   a) lived longer
   b) had too much political power
   c) had more money
   d) were more prone to violence
   e) were more vulnerable to temptation

This was my Holy Grail of the American educational system? It's going to be a long year.

It's not just that I'm uninterested in much of this stuff and disinterested by most of the rest of it. It's that thousands of teenagers like me and my classmates will be taught that this is the history that matters. Never mind that the progress of a civilization is often enforced at the point of a sword, gun or bayonet, and on terms dictated by the dead white males about whom we're apparently not supposed to learn or care. History is now all about the progress itself, progress which takes the form of "trends", "developments", "influence", "changes" and "roles". History just happens. People merely experience it – nobody makes it.

2.

When Dad gets home, after the end of my first day of school, he asks he how it went. I respond with two words: "You win."

"What do you mean?"

I sigh. "They ought to call the course *AP European Culture, Enlightenment, Arts and Crafts, Minorities, Sanitation and a Little Bit of History.*"

"Hmph." He allows himself a tiny smile and leaves my bedroom.

Dad, of course, is a Marxist. Or rather, he's a Professor of History, although I gather the terms are now interchangeable. His specialist subject is the revolutions of 1848, particularly those in the Habsburg Empire. He's also what I call a colonic historian, by which I mean you need extended subtitles – the bits after the colons – to have any clue what his books are about. He's written five of them so far:

- *Radetzky's April: Suppressing the "Springtime of Peoples" in Northern Italy*
- *The Salons of Vienna: Free Thought, Free Speech and Revolution in Metternich's Austria*
- *The First Moves: Hungarian Separatism and the Road to Dual Monarchy, 1825-1849*
- *Lightening the Yoke: Feudalism in Austria Before and After 1848*
- *And I Have Forgotten It: The Schleswig-Holstein Question, 1848-1866*

The title of this last work, a rare digression from the Habsburgs to Danish nationalism and the two Schleswig wars, echoes Lord Palmerston's epigram: "Only three people understood the Schleswig-Holstein Question. The first was Albert, the Prince consort, and he is dead; the second is a German professor, and he is in an asylum; and the third was myself – and I have forgotten it." That quote might be the most interesting line in any of my Dad's books. If you ever see the name Alfred Lansbury on a book's cover, run away from it and the library in which you've found it as quickly as possible.

Dad is working on a new book now. Publish or perish, they say. But I'm reluctant to ask what it's about. For one, he's pretty secretive about these things. He recently started locking his upstairs study, his workshop, when he's not in it. I have no idea why, as this has never been a problem in the past; only the two of us live in the house, and previously I often tiptoed through the archipelago of sources, books and scribbled notes on the study floor – each cluster neatly positioned for easy access and remembrance – to ask him mundane questions and get blunt answers in return. He's never wanted me to linger, but I always assumed that's because he was busy. Even when he's been away and I have penetrated his lair, I haven't lurked for long. What would I be looking for? Tax records of Tyrolean farmers in the 1840s? Woo-hoo.

I do love my Dad – of course I love him – and it's because of him that I'm interested in history. But really, what kind of person reads what he writes? Do even other historians bother? I think his books are meant to be admired but not opened, like the works of James Joyce. Maybe he's finally writing something populist for the general public, or even a textbook: perhaps an overview of everything that happened in 1848 and how it changed the course of history. That still wouldn't explain the locked door, though. Plus, the story of 1848 has already been told before. If you're going to cover old ground in a new book, you must either tell the story better than anyone ever has, uncover new evidence and weave it into your narrative, or offer a convincing reinterpretation of the subject in question. Can Dad do any of these things? I don't know. Maybe he doesn't even know himself.

What drives Dad to do what he does? I haven't a clue, really, except I know it isn't money; ever since Mom died, we've been well looked after by her parents and my trust fund. Grandma and Grandpa understand Dad even less than I do, but their side of the family is made of money, and I think they're both fond of me. Point being, he doesn't have to dabble in esoterica forever. Maybe what he's doing is all he knows, and he wouldn't know how to write about a battle or a treaty even if he wanted to. Maybe the profession has brainwashed him into thinking that the "trends" and "developments" leading to the battles and treaties really are all that matters. Perhaps he just loves history and wants to make a contribution, but he's not quite brilliant enough to transcend the system, so this is the only contribution the system will let him make. Or maybe he has always believed that grain prices and demographic trends explain a revolution better than the men who make the decisions and lead the masses into conflict. Whatever it is, I'm afraid to ask.

❖ ❖ ❖

So he slaves away in his corner of the house, and I fiddle about in mine. On a school night, if the Gang of Four hasn't assembled, and I'm not with Melissa – my girlfriend, if you'd call her that – and Dennis hasn't come over, I'll do just enough homework to get by and then focus on what I like to do. I read history, by which I mean my kind of history. I watch television – mostly movies, documentaries and baseball games. I surf the web, most often within the discussion forums at Consimworld. And I play *Totaler Krieg* and other wargames via e-mail.

Tonight I'm reading the "History: World War II" folder at Consimworld, where the great North African logistics debate has broken out again. "Consim" is short for "conflict simulation", and Consimworld is the principal website where wargamers gather to discuss their hobby and form a community. Game companies and individual games all have their own forums; in the *Totaler Krieg* forum, we talk strategy and tactics, share game reports, ask questions about the rules and discuss or complain about various aspect of the game. But it's in the specialty folders that the inner nerd of many gamers truly blossoms – some of this stuff must be seen to be believed. There's one guy in the "History: World War II" folder to whom you can show a photograph of any WWII-era combat airplane, no matter how obscure – even a prototype of which only three were built – and he can not only name the exact make and model, he can usually tell you what the letters and numbers on the fuselage represent. There's another guy whose historical book collection surpasses the Library of Congress's – I've seen photos, and I'm not kidding. His complete, six-volume set of *Istoriia Velikoi Otechestvennoi Voiny Sovetskogo Souiuza 1941-1945* looks particularly impressive.

The North African logistics debate flares periodically and normally takes one of two forms. One debate asks whether the British under General O'Connor could have pressed on to Tripoli in early 1941, forestalling Rommel's arrival and shortening the Desert War by two full years. The traditional understanding of the Operation Compass offensive is that after the British had pushed the Italians back across Cyrenaica to El Agheila, Churchill shifted men and materiel from Libya to support and defend Greece, thereby denying O'Connor the resources he needed to finish the campaign. However, some posters argue – very convincingly, in my opinion – that the British offensive would have stalled on its own accord. Compass was a limited enterprise designed to capture a few forts, not march all the way to Tripoli. Not enough trucks were available to keep supplies flowing to the front. There were no enemy depots to be captured. Sea resupply wasn't an option – the *Luftwaffe* repelled several British convoys to Benghazi, and port capacity in the Sirte Gulf was non-existent anyway. The British tanks that had driven across Cyrenaica were worn out and needed refitting. Plus, German and Italian reinforcements were already trickling into Tripoli. By comparison, Montgomery's Eighth Army had far better logistical support in 1942-43 than O'Connor did, but Monty still paused for a month at El Agheila himself.

The other debate asks what Rommel should have hoped to accomplish once he arrived in Libya. The mainstream belief is that Rommel was a brilliant commander who twice pushed the British back across Cyrenaica, advanced into Egypt and nearly broke through to Cairo and the Suez Canal, all on a shoestring budget. If Hitler had only allocated him sufficient resources to build a full-strength Afrika Korps and/or invade Malta to secure the convoy routes from Italy, Egypt and beyond could and perhaps should have been his. The contrary view at Consimworld is that Rommel was a good operational commander who repeatedly exceeded his authority and caused his superiors to make poor strategic choices. His mission was to maintain a presence in Libya, keeping Italy motivated and Britain engaged, while Germany concentrated upon defeating the Soviet Union. Rommel could have accomplished this quite economically by remaining within Tripolitania and forcing Britain to operate along a lengthy supply line. Instead, he kept attacking and attacking, attracting more supplies and equipment than he should have needed. The trucks Rommel employed in 1941 could have increased the rail-to-front supply lift of the three German Army Groups in Russia by more than 25 percent, at a time and place where Germany most needed motor transport to successfully prosecute its most important campaign, so Rommel's gains arguably helped Germany lose the war. I'm not as convinced by this reinterpretation, for I don't think Rommel was sent to Africa with such a narrowly defined mission. On the other hand, Rommel's reputation in the West as the *Wehrmacht's* knight in shining armor bugs me, and I enjoy seeing it pegged back a notch or two.

The funny part is that because new people discover Consimworld and the "History: World War II" forum all the time, the same questions are often asked and re-asked. And because no consensus has formed on either side of these debates, and because the people who hang around Consimworld can't stop themselves, the same fights are fought over and over again:

- Uninformed questions are asked and a difference of opinion emerges.
- Member X contributes an exhaustively researched post including statistics on how many trucks were available, how many gallons of fuel were being transported across the Mediterranean (and how much of that was sunk along the way), and the airspeed velocity of an unladen African swallow.
- Member Y ignores most of X's post, calls one of X's facts into question by citing a dubious source, and for good measure mentions the airspeed velocity of an unladen European swallow.
- X calls Y an idiot.
- Member Z agrees with X that Y is an idiot, but cites his own sources to say that Y's point isn't wholly without merit.
- Y ignores Z and calls X a loser.
- Other members chime in to defend X, Z and occasionally Y.
- X then posts a detailed rebuttal of Z, including results of a time trial between laden and unladen African and European swallows organized by Rommel himself, and refutes one of Y's latest points to show that he's still an idiot.

This continues for several weeks.

Logistics bore me. History is forged at the sharp end of the sword, and in reading about a campaign's cut-and-thrust I want to know what the commanders were thinking, not their quartermasters. And most game designers agree with me: all strategic-level wargames have supply rules and penalties for being out of supply, but these rules supplement the games and don't attempt to dominate them. However, I also know an army marches on its stomach, and that it must be supplied well to fight well. And if a commander ignores his logistics requirements, he won't be able to make the right decisions. So if forced, I'd say that this is *Totaler Krieg's* greatest weakness as a simulation: logistics are too simplistic. The *Wehrmacht* can blitz into Iraq or beyond Moscow, and as long as there's a Supply Convoy linking Africa to Europe or an unimpeded line of railroads from Germany to the front, it remains fully effective.

There is at least one game that takes logistics ultra-seriously, or at least pretends to. *The Campaign for North Africa,* published in 1978, is the dark heart of wargaming. It covers the entire Desert War down to the scale of individual airplanes and supply trucks. The map is seven feet long. The designer suggests the complete game would take 1,500 hours to complete when played by two five-man teams, each side having a Logistics Commander and a Rear Area Commander in addition to air and ground leaders and an overall Supreme Commander. The game comes with charts for tracking the organization of each division and brigade, every truck convoy, every naval convoy, food and water usage, fuel and ammunition usage, prisoners, broken down and destroyed vehicles, supply dumps, airplane maintenance and a lot more; just setting up the game requires literally hours of paperwork. Infamously, the Italian units in the game use more water than the Germans or the Allies because they have to cook pasta. (According to the designer, this was meant to be a joke.)

The truly weird thing is that while the full game has almost certainly never been played to completion, many avid wargamers express a fervent desire to do so, if only you could get enough of them together for long enough and design the right Excel spreadsheets to assist them. Used copies regularly sell for more than $200 on eBay. It reminds me of Tolkien's Ring of Power: there's something irresistible about detail – even for its own sake – that draws gamers toward it, as though *The Campaign for North Africa* is as close to real warfare as you can get without joining the army. Sounds more like a vanity exercise to me, and nothing remotely resembling fun, but it is a free country.

❖ ❖ ❖

As usual, Dennis arrives shortly after 6:30 on Thursday evening to continue our game. He's wearing a black Motörhead T-shirt and stonewashed jeans with a faded splotch of what looks like ketchup on the left leg.

"Have you been following the North African logistics debate on Consimworld?" I ask him, as we make our way to the gaming room.

"No."

"Do you subscribe to the 'History: World War II' folder?"

"No."

"Why not?"

"Because I'm not that interested in history."

"Wha…huh? Come again?"

"No – I mean I'm not *that* interested in history. I'm a wargamer, not a historian."

"What's the difference?"

Dennis snorts. "Is that a trick question? I don't get paid to study and write about history. I'm not adding anything to the body of historical scholarship. This is all just for fun."

"But we're all historians, aren't we? I've learned things on Consimworld that I haven't anywhere else – not so much because wargamers are producing new data, but rather, they're reinterpreting existing data in new and convincing ways. Who's to say that the professionals in their ivory towers are doing a better job than we are?"

Dennis laughs.

"I'm serious," I continue. "Just because you can cull data from archival sources shouldn't make you judge and jury. It's like baseball – the quote-unquote 'journalists' perpetuate misconceptions about the importance of batting average and RBIs and a pitcher's wins and saves, while the interesting and valuable articles are written online, using research based on stats accessible to anyone with a computer. Meanwhile, I've been in AP European History for four days now, and we've spent three-quarters of our time talking about disease, life as a peasant and vernacular literature – which may itself be a disease, for all I care. We did the Hundred Years War in a hundred seconds."

"I was more of a math guy in school."

"Doesn't it bother you? Given that so few of us in America have any desire to learn anything, shouldn't the educational system be trying to encourage us instead of feeding us steaming piles of politically correct horse manure?

"Nope. Life's too short."

"That's it?"

"That's it. There are plenty of things I can be mad about with good reason, but none of them are this."

"Oh." I look at Dennis across the map, seated in his chair. His beard is super-scraggly today, like he hasn't touched it since Sunday. "Did you ever take AP European History?"

"Nope."

"Why not?"

"No idea. That was a long time ago."

Sigh. "It's your turn, you know. The Russians are up. And by the way, that shirt is horrible."

"I know."

"I know you know."

Only a minority of *Totaler Krieg* campaign games continue into 1944, so it's fun to have arrived here with both of us still hoping to win. The game includes scenarios which let you finish the war from the historical starting points in 1941, 1942, 1943 and 1944, but it's rare to start a campaign game in 1939 and see it through to 1945: usually, either the war becomes lopsided and there's no point in continuing, or you run out of time, energy or willpower to finish. Or you forget to lock up your cat and it leaps at the gameboard, kamikaze-style, between sessions. I don't see the point of cats to begin with – I'm not anti-cat as such, I just don't get why people are attracted to them. But if Consimworld is a fair indicator, the number of rogue cats that have ruined unfinished wargames is pretty staggering. Dennis and I normally require seven lengthy Thursday night sessions to complete a full game of *Totaler Krieg*; can you imagine making it through five or six of them, with the game poised like ours is now, only to have a feline ICBM break the fourth wall and knock 20 or 30 armies across the map into the Arctic? There are no pets in the Lansbury household, I can assure you.

Anyway, to Yugoslavia. In studying the map between sessions, I discovered several flaws in Dennis's landing at Dubrovnik. First, because the Allied penetration beyond Sarajevo is so narrow, the supply route to British Eighth Army is very exposed. Second, the only supply road from Dubrovnik to Zagreb goes through Belgrade; as long as I can defend the latter, the Allies cannot advance on the former. Third, Allied forces in the Med are now dispersed across two fronts instead of one, and Dennis must soon open a third Western front in France, further diluting his strength.

After pinning Dennis's units in Yugoslavia in the mud of April-May, I strike at Sarajevo in May-June, trying to isolate Eighth Army from Dubrovnik. I don't quite succeed, but by walling off Zagreb, shielding Albania and retaining an offensive threat in Italy, I neutralize the invasion long enough to minimize the danger. At the end of Summer 1944, the Allies have yet to reach my West Wall or fully batter down my East Wall, and the Mediterranean front is an Allied sinkhole.

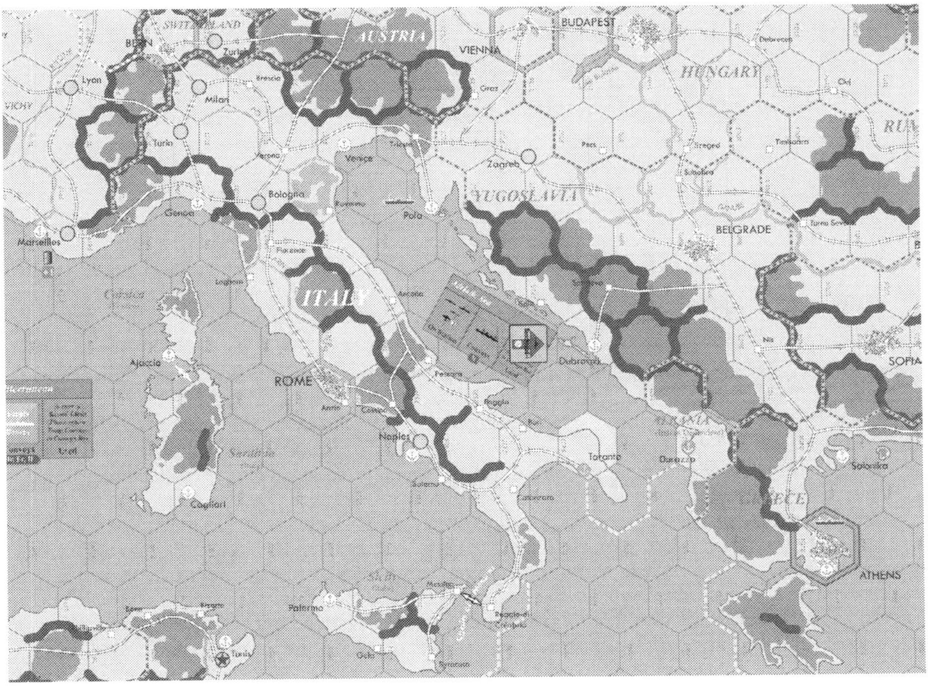

Fig. 3 – Western Beachhead counter placement near Dubrovnik

As we begin August-September 1944, I ask Dennis whether he would invade Dubrovnik again if given a second chance. “Good question – possibly not,” he replies. “In my defense, I was pretty shattered by Sunday evening – I’m not sure I was thinking clearly.”

“Had you ever invaded Yugoslavia across the Adriatic before?” I ask.

“No.”

“Me neither. Maybe there’s a reason for that.”

“It was probably worth a shot, just to see what would happen.”

“It’s a shame you can’t earn any Churchill Points for your invasion.”

“What do you mean?”

“The game should somehow reward the Allied player for doing stupid things that Churchill might have suggested.”

Dennis laughs. “I wonder if you could earn Churchill Points in *Gallipol-opoly*. Did you ever see that in *The Simpsons*?”

“No.”

"It was a throwaway line in the 'Brawl in the Family' episode. They were deciding which version of *Monopoly* to play, and Lisa pulled several games out of the closet: *Star Wars Monopoly*, *Rasta-mon-opoly*, *Gallipol-opoly*, *Edna Krabappoly*. No?"

"I've never seen *The Simpsons*."

"What? Really?" Dennis looks aghast.

"Actually, just having a set of three-player victory conditions would help. The West and the Soviets should be wrestling over the Balkans and pushing each other for Berlin, right? By invading Yugoslavia, you've probably guaranteed a happier postwar world for Yugoslavia, Albania and Greece, possibly Hungary and Czechoslovakia, and maybe even Rumania. But in game terms, you've just spread your Western forces too thinly, and on a part of the map where the Soviets will eventually arrive in force anyway."

"I can only hope. But go back a minute...you've never seen a single episode of *The Simpsons*? Seriously?"

"Never."

"Damn. You've gotta stay in more."

❖ ❖ ❖

Dennis and I agree about *Monopoly* itself. Hundreds of millions of people view *Monopoly* as the typical family boardgame, even though there must be literally thousands of more enjoyable and stimulating examples of the genre. Roll two dice, move your piece, pay money to the banker, try to get lucky. Repeat for hours and hours until everyone drifts out of the room or dies of boredom. Considering its longevity, influence and ubiquity, *Monopoly* might be the worst game ever.

Totaler Krieg, on the other hand, remains a captivating puzzle right to the finish. By the end of 1944, Dennis's Soviets have battered through the East Wall and into Poland, and the Yanks have captured Paris, but the Allies have yet to enter Warsaw, Rome, Zagreb, Belgium or Alsace-Lorraine. As predicted, by diluting his Western forces across three separate axes, Dennis has struggled to make inroads on any of them. Our session finishes just before one in the morning, just as our weeknight sessions always seem to: one more turn, always one more turn must be finished, even though we know we'll regret it in the morning.

As the end of the game nears, my thoughts turn to the end of the real war. I've watched the movie *Downfall* several times, and I'm fascinated by the psychology of its subjects. If the Bible is true, and the world as we know it will end and be judged after a time of extreme trial, that time of trial will probably look a lot like Berlin in April 1945: some tried to fight, some tried to flee, some looked for scapegoats, some couldn't bear to go on. The scene in the movie where Magda Goebbels forces her children to swallow cyanide will remain with me for a long time, even after I consider that those children had a much happier life and met a much less gruesome end than many of their peers across Europe during the war.

Some commentators believe films like *Downfall* do too much to rehabilitate the image of the German people by contrasting monsters like Hitler and Goebbels with the humanity and, be honest, raw sex appeal of characters like Alexandra Maria Lara's Traudl Junge in *Downfall* or Kate Winslet's Hanna Schmitz in *The Reader*. Without people like Junge and Schmitz and the active or passive actions they took which supported the Nazi regime, Hitler never could have wreaked so much havoc, and our emotions shouldn't be manipulated to the point where we root for these characters in a movie. I think that's true to a point: resistance within Nazi Germany was feeble, and national indoctrination nearly total. But *Downfall*, at least, is essentially a reenacted documentary of what actually took place in and around Hitler's bunker, and viewers should be trusted to know that a film shot from the Nazi perspective can only be fully be understood within its wider historical context.

There are many ways the war in Europe might have ended, of course. What if Hitler had fled Berlin to hide in Berchtesgaden? How long might it have taken to pry him loose, and how would the Soviets have interacted with the British and Americans in the interim? What if Hitler had allowed himself to be captured instead of committing suicide? What if the SS had successfully launched its "Werewolf" organization, and guerrilla warfare had carried on in Germany for years after 1945? On the other hand, what if key German generals had allowed the Allies to advance rapidly in the West after breaking out from Normandy? This is supposedly an idea under consideration within Rommel's circle as von Stauffenberg prepared to assassinate Hitler: if you feel certain by July 1944 that Germany will lose the war, why not make sure you don't lose it to the Soviet Union? Surely a united Germany under Western control would have been better for the German people than the historical Soviet domination and ransacking of Prussia, right?

This could have led to a justifiable rebirth of the "stab in the back" legend created in Germany after World War I, but it also might have created the Soviet-Western tension that Hitler dreamed of and even given him a path to survival. Imagine this scenario: it's July 1944, and Operation Cobra has finally levered the Americans out of Normandy and into the open country beyond. Hitler – or a new

Führer, after Hitler is assassinated – orders the *Wehrmacht* to completely pull out of France, Belgium, the Netherlands, Italy, Greece and Yugoslavia. A defensive line is formed in Germany, perhaps along the Rhine or maybe even as far back as the Elbe and the Alps. While the Western Allies advance into this vacuum, German reinforcements pour into Poland and stop the summer Soviet offensive well short of Warsaw. How does Stalin react? Not very well, I'm sure: paranoid at the best of times, this would look to him like a German rapprochement with the West, and who knows what might follow? A truce in the East? A complete breakdown in Soviet-Western relations, perhaps? Admittedly, this is all farfetched, but East-West tension was always present, and fighting between Communist and non-Communist forces broke out in Greece, Yugoslavia, China and elsewhere whenever it was safe to stop fighting the Axis. Is it completely irrational to imagine Germany emerging from this scenario in one piece, or even as an ally of one Allied faction in a war against the other?

All of this is irrelevant, of course, in the context of my game with Dennis. When he arrives the following Thursday to finish the war, he continues to pound at the edges of my empire with total air and naval supremacy. He captures a smattering of Objective Hexes: Metz and Bucharest in January-February; Brussels, Warsaw and Königsberg in March-April; and the Ruhr in April-May. But when the Soviet April-May turn ends around 11 o'clock, he's still far short of where he needs to be to win the game.

The game concludes as soon as the V-E Day marker is removed from the Turn Track. (Dennis often calls it the "VD marker" in a way that suggests no joke could possibly be funnier, no matter how many times he repeats it. He's wrong.) In a typical game where Germany invades Russia in 1941, the marker will be due to come off of the track prior to the start of May-June 1945. However, if the No Retreat marker is in play, when the game is due to end you roll a die, and if the result is equal to or less than the No Retreat level (Axis Tide 3, in our game), the game continues for at least one more turn. In other words, the game has no fixed end date: the higher the Axis high-water mark, the more likely it is that the Allies will get one or more bonus turns at the end of the game to gain extra territory and squeak out a win. This can feel arbitrary, but it creates drama and also mitigates the "end of the world" syndrome seen in other games with fixed endpoints, whereby players can undertake wild maneuvers and incur costly losses during the final turn without fear of punishment or reprisal.

So with April-May finished, Dennis hands me the die: I roll a '3', so the game narrowly continues. Fair enough...facing Operation Eclipse in the West and the

Soviets' Final Offensive, I tidy my lines as best I can and wait for a Summer turn of Allied blitzing. The Americans capture Frankfurt, the Brits liberate Athens, and the Soviets take Posen and advance to the Oder. But I'm still safe as we go to the V-E Day roll – I let Dennis make it this time, and he rolls a '1'. It's now nearly midnight.

In June-July, my lines are finally crumbling – I still have many armies with which to defend, but I can no longer shape them into a recognizable pattern. Munich and Vienna fall to the Americans, who rendezvous with the Russians for the first time in Hungary; the Soviets also take Budapest, Prague and Breslau. If Dennis can capture Berlin, he can also take credit for the pro-Western neutrality markers in Madrid, Stockholm and Ankara. But he hasn't yet, so I'm still winning when I make the next V-E Day roll: another '1'.

I pound the arms of my chair several times. It's now quarter to one in the morning. "You having fun yet?" Dennis asks.

"Not really, no," I say.

"You can have all of the luck you want throughout the game, but if I can have VD, I'll still win," he chuckles.

This is ridiculous. July-August has to be the final turn of the game, or I'll lose after all. The British finally capture Rome from the north – Dennis having long abandoned his quest to crack the Gustav Line – while the Americans take Hamburg and invade Norway at Trondheim, which I've abandoned. The Soviets occupy three hexes adjacent to Berlin and reduce my garrison in Berlin to two steps, but Dennis cannot yet capture my capital. The only Objectives I still control are Oslo, Narvik and Berlin, but by the margin of one Objective, I'm still winning. At 1:27 a.m., I make the final V-E Day roll, resolved to surrender immediately if the game doesn't end…and I roll a '5'.

I wearily thrust my arms in the air. "That was some finish, huh?" says Dennis. "I guess I should have invaded Norway sooner."

"You probably could have supported that fourth front sooner than you thought," I respond. "But, wow. Just wow."

"I need to go, obviously – do you want some help putting the game away?"

"No, thanks. I'm going to stare at the board a while, and then be a dutiful German and slit my wrists."

"OK – see you later."

Dennis sees himself out. I'll see him again next Thursday, of course, after reporting our finish to Consimworld and picking up the pieces to start over again. Tonight's conclusion has been draining, punishing and fascinating in equal measure, but that's the thing about *Totaler Krieg*: no sooner has the war finished, you get to start it all over again.

3.

We had an extraordinary guest at the Big Game today. We invited this freshman, a scrawny little kid named Lewis, to the table as our fifth player, and for nine straight hands he did nothing but check and fold – not a single bet. On the tenth and final hand, he made a 20-cent raise, and when Melvyn re-raised him, he folded. As the game broke, he said, "It was an honor playing with you."

"It was nice having you, too, I guess," I said.

As he left the table he went to two of his friends who had been watching on from the corner of our lunchroom alcove, and he high-fived them. He'd lost $1.25, and he high-fived them.

It's now after school, and the Gang of Four is recalling today's game and laughing on the steps behind the big gymnasium where Muhlendorf's basketball and volleyball teams play, and where I'm forced to lift weights twice a week during Physical Education. "He kept looking at you like you were Jesus," Chris says to me.

"Jesus?" I ask.

"Jesus Ferguson," clarifies Chris. "Minus the beard, of course."

"Same fashion sense, though," smirks Melvyn.

"I've never felt so insulted," I say. "Never mind what he looks like: as far as I can tell, Chris Ferguson hasn't made the final table of a televised poker tournament since before we were born. Why do they keep putting him on camera, anyway? I'm clearly more like Daniel Negreanu."

"But without the skill," says Freddie.

"And what's your bank balance like these days?" I retort.

"You're Daniel Negreanu," says Chris. "Melvyn is Howard Lederer, Freddie is Erick Lindgren, and I'm, uh..."

"Phil Hellmuth," I say. Melvyn and Freddie laugh.

"I'm not Phil Hellmuth," says Chris.

"Or Mike Matusow," I say.

"I'm not Mike Matusow either," says Chris, looking slightly uncomfortable. "Where did that come from?"

"Oh, come on," says Melvyn. "You don't do well with bad beats."

"I'm fine," says Chris.

"Really!" says Melvyn. "The other day, when Candace drew the Jack of diamonds on the river, and you stormed away from the table complaining it was 'amateur hour' and 'ladies night'? What was that?"

Chris's face goes slightly pink. "Don't get me wrong – you've got talent," I say. "One day you might be a contender again."

Chris punches me in the arm.

"The kid, Lewis, I bet you anything he was watching on opening day when Derek came to the table," says Melvyn. "One hand and out – didn't want to be that guy."

"Speaking of which, you guys going to the game tonight?" asks Freddie. Muhlendorf is playing Central Catholic at home.

Chris and Melvyn nod. "Not me," I say. "I'm going to Melissa's."

"Really?" asks Chris.

"Derek will be running the wishbone for three hours against the worst team in our division. The game will suck, it'll be cold, we'll score 70 points, and the Asses will be everywhere on Monday."

"He's got a point there," says Freddie.

"If I wanted to watch sports tonight, there are three good pennant races to follow on TV."

"So what will you be watching tonight?" asks Melvyn.

"None of your business," I say, grinning.

I don't know what's going on with Melissa. About six months ago, she became the third girl I'd ever kissed, and I've kissed her a lot since then – not just on the lips, either. She's very pretty, I think: shortish sandy blond hair, green eyes, smooth skin, wears this perfume that drives me crazy. We hang out on weekends, and we saw a lot of each other over the summer, but we don't go out of our way to find each other at school. And we never talk much, no matter where we are. We just do things with each other, and to each other.

We've rented a movie for tonight, and I hope I'm not quizzed about it afterwards, because I don't expect to see much of it. Which is nice, of course, but it's all part of an odd pattern: I converse with the Gang of Four and my other (mostly male) friends at school, not Melissa. I sense this pattern may explain why so many marriages end in divorce.

"I assume the two of you are going to Homecoming together?" asks Melvyn.

"Yeah, I guess," I say. "We haven't talked about it yet, but I'm sure we will. You going with Vicki?" Vicki is a tall, blond senior, and Melvyn just started dating her a few weeks ago – he's definitely punching above his weight.

"Yep. Who are you guys going to ask?"

"All will be revealed in good time," says Chris.

"Do you know already?" I ask.

"Possibly," he says.

"Coward."

"What?"

"Either you know who you're going to ask and you're afraid to tell us, or you're afraid to ask who you really want to ask," I say. "And of course, you'd be afraid to tell us that."

Freddie giggles. Chris turns on Freddie and asks, "So who are you going to Homecoming with?"

"I hear Angela Galloway wants you to ask her, Freddie," says Melvyn.

"Nah," shrugs Freddie. "I don't think I'm going."

"Not going?" the rest of us exclaim.

"The whole thing…I mean, Angela's nice and all, but I went to Homecoming last year and didn't like it. What's the point?"

"What's the…I mean, everyone goes to Homecoming!" says Chris.

"Not everyone," says Freddie.

"OK, everyone who isn't a loser goes to Homecoming," says Chris.

"Plenty of losers go to Homecoming, too," I say.

"You know what I meant."

"I don't like to dance," says Freddie. "I just don't. And the 'Hollywood' theme couldn't be more lame if I shot it in the leg."

After several seconds of silence, I ask, "But if you're going out with someone already, you kinda have to go, don't you?"

"Well, yeah," says Freddie. "Maybe. Actually…hang on, no, you don't have to do anything."

"With Melissa? No, I pretty much have to go," I say.

"Whatever," says Freddie. "She's your girlfriend."

"Is that what you're calling each other now?" asks Chris.

Embarrassed, I stammer, "Yeah, sure." Chris and Melvyn laugh.

"Maybe I'll ask Angela out, or maybe I won't," concludes Freddie. "Or maybe I'll ask someone else. But I don't *have* to go to Homecoming, and neither do you."

Chris, Melvyn and I blankly look at one another. Then I ask Freddie, "What if the theme were 'Las Vegas' instead of 'Hollywood' and we had a mock casino?"

"Oh, then I'd definitely be there," says Freddie, smiling.

❖ ❖ ❖

Friday night at Melissa's house goes well. Saturday at home, however, is another story. Overnight, in my quarterfinal match of the Boardgame Players Association (BPA) *Totaler Krieg* Play By E-Mail tournament, Hitler was assassinated, and now all hell is breaking loose.

E-mail gaming is very different to its face-to-face equivalent. I use an application called CyberBoard – there are others – and an online dice server to play *Totaler Krieg* via e-mail, pointing and clicking to move pieces around the virtual map. When I require a decision from my opponent regarding an HQ commitment, support unit contestation, retreat direction, loss allocation or anything else, I usually send an interim move file so he can watch what I've done and react accordingly. It takes a long time to finish a game this way; the BPA e-mail tournament time limit is four months, which is actually pretty aggressive for campaign games of *Totaler Krieg*. E-mail tournaments for many games can take literally years to finish.

Within CyberBoard, you can only view part of the *Totaler Krieg* map at any one time, but you can see the factor values for every counter in a stack simultaneously, which is very helpful when planning a move. And careful planning is far more central to the e-mail gaming experience than face-to-face play, as you can take as long as you want to plan a turn before making it. Sometimes I'll print a portion of the map and doodle potential moves on it while I'm eating a meal or half-watching something on television. I'll construct different versions of an offensive or a static defense in CyberBoard, resetting the position after each move and closely comparing the merits of each option. I enjoy this and find it stimulating, but I also have to do this lest I make a mistake; because most of my opponents are equally watchful, the quality of play in e-mail games tends to be much higher than in face-to-face games, and errors can be punished severely.

My quarterfinal opponent in the *Totaler Krieg* tournament is a man named Steven Ginsberg. I know he lives in Stockton, California; apart from that, I only know him by reputation from Consimworld as someone with liberal views about letting wargames deviate from history and/or reality. For example, for the Pacific-theater game *Empire of the Sun* he once proposed a rules variant based upon the novel *Weapons of Choice* by John Birmingham, in which a United Nations naval task force centered upon the aircraft carrier *USS Hillary Clinton* travels back in time from 2021 to 1942 and finds itself sailing toward the Battle of Midway. Even by normal Consimworld standards, this is rather fruity. That said, from our e-mail correspondence he's seems fairly normal, even if he hasn't demonstrated very good *Totaler Krieg* skills in our quarterfinal.

That said, he seems to have found an unusual way of recovering a losing position. Everything was looking good for my Allies: by the start of Summer 1944 I'd already retaken Rome, invaded Norway and reached the Vistula in Poland, and the No Retreat marker is only at Axis Tide 2. Then last night, Hitler was assassinated (via a "Military Takeover" result on the Materiel Shortages Option Card), which in *Totaler Krieg* means the Axis player suffers some penalties but can also engineer a one-turn truce with both Allied factions. Such a truce is annoying, but manageable; however, Steven's Summer 1944 Option Card was Peace Offer, a Hail Mary play which succeeded when in successive turns he rolled up "Political Option: Axis" events and extended his one-turn truce with the Soviets to a four-turn Armistice! Twenty-six times out of twenty-seven, I'd be sitting pretty; instead, the dice will keep the Soviets at peace until September-October, my Bagration Offensive is completely wasted, and most of the *Wehrmacht* can now turn to contain the already-delayed Operation Overlord.

So now I'm banging my head against the framed drawing of a Spitfire that hangs above the wooden desk in my bedroom, wondering why *Totaler Krieg* chooses to simulate Hitler's potential assassination this way. The full truce scenario we've experienced is hugely improbable, of course – less than a 4 percent chance, even after Steven's Peace Offer play. But historically, what would have happened if Hitler had been assassinated? There were apparently 17 planned attempts on Hitler's life during his reign as *Führer*, but I think three stand out as his closest escapes:

1) On 8 November 1939 a bomb planted by Georg Elser, a Swabian craftsman, exploded in the Munich Bürgerbräukeller shortly after Hitler had finished his annual speech on the anniversary of his failed "Beer Hall Putsch" in 1923. The bomb killed eight people and wounded 65, but owing to fog that prevented flights back to Berlin, Hitler had cut short his speech and left the hall early – 13 minutes before the explosion – to board a train.

2) On 13 March 1943 Hitler returned by airplane from his Russian headquarters in Vinnitsa to Germany via Army Group Center's headquarters in Smolensk. There, Colonel Henning von Tresckow and his aide, Lieutenant Fabian von Schlabrendorff, gave a box which they said contained two bottles of cognac to one of Hitler's aides, Colonel Heinz Brandt, for delivery to a colleague in Germany. The box actually held a bomb set to detonate 30 minutes after takeoff, but while nearly every part of the bomb's detonator worked as intended, the percussion cap

that was to trigger the explosion was too cold to react as it should have, because the bomb was in the plane's unheated cargo hold.

3) Most famously, Colonel Count Claus von Stauffenberg succeeded in exploding a bomb in the Wolf's Lair, Hitler's East Prussian headquarters, on 20 July 1944. The bomb killed four people, but Hitler emerged with only minor injuries because Colonel Brandt – him again – wanted to get a better view of a map on the room's conference table and kicked the briefcase containing the bomb against one of the table's thick oaken supports, which absorbed much of the explosion's impact. (Brandt himself had one of his legs blown off by the blast, and he died two days later.)

If any of these attempts had succeeded, how might history have changed? Elser's 1939 attempt is both the most tantalizing and most uncertain counterfactual: if Hitler dies then, who takes his place? Hess? Goering? Someone from the Prussian military establishment, after an extended power struggle? Does the war continue, or does Germany's new *Führer* convene an international conference to wind it down, perhaps on the basis of Germany's 1914 frontiers plus Austria, the Sudetenland and the Polish Corridor? Does persecution of the Jews persist? Presumably the Final Solution would not have been implemented, but could Nazism exist without some anti-Semitism? I'd guess that France, the *Wehrmacht* and Britain (in that order) would have jumped at the chance to institutionalize the *Sitzkrieg* and hammer out a settlement. Particularly if Russia had still gone to war with Finland in 1939, the contrast between a rapacious Russia and a Hitler-free Germany could have triggered a wave of revisionism. But here, the crystal ball becomes extremely murky.

On the other hand, I'm not sure Hitler's assassination in 1944 would have fundamentally altered the war. *Totaler Krieg's* theory of a temporary truce is at least plausible, as is the collapse (deliberate or otherwise) of Germany's Western defenses that I suggested previously, but von Stauffenberg's and his conspirators intended to save Germany's honor by conducting the war properly, not by ending it at once. That said, any attempt so late in the war to dismantle the SS or streamline the Nazi bureaucracy could have weakened Germany's capacity for resistance instead of strengthening it. Plus, the Final Solution had its own inertia by mid-1944, and many if not most of the Jews who died in the war's final year still would have died. All in all, while the overall death toll might have been somewhat lower, I think 1946 in this counterfactual reality would have looked similar to what occurred historically.

Rewind to March 1943, though, and the scenario changes again. At that point, British and American forces were still fighting in Tunisia, and Operation Citadel had yet to occur in the East. The Battle of the Atlantic was still raging, its outcome still uncertain. Germany may not have been winning the war, but it also wasn't clearly losing yet. So if Hitler dies then, what happens? If the plotters succeed in gaining power – more doubtful now, with the legitimacy of Hitler's regime still mostly intact – they might have managed to roll back the worst elements of Nazism and change history.

But here's where I'll stop this tangent, before I come anywhere near the excesses of Nazi fanboyism. An underbelly of interest in alternative history on the internet consists of adolescent, barely informed speculation along these lines: "If only Germany had done A, B and C, they would have won the war." I love making educated guesses at what might have happened had certain historical paths diverged from reality, but I don't concoct wild fantasies extending well beyond the point of realistic speculation, particularly when the fantasy exists for its own sake and not the historical reality underpinning it – and even more particularly when the fantasy glorifies obviously evil or immoral entities like Nazi Germany. The "If only…" construction is the giveaway: these comments never seem to begin, "Thank goodness Germany didn't do A, B and C". More often, you'll see a thread on the Axis History Forum website titled, "Assume you are Hitler. How would you have won the war?", with posts like:

"I would Invade France before Poland, the French were completely unprepared during 1939, then in the exact moment instead of invade Denmark and Norway i would Invade UK, then all the other small contrys, and in the end together with the Japanese, start an Invasion of USSR." *[sic]*

Doodz got pwned! 4 realz! ROTFLMAO! :-) I'd laugh if I weren't so disturbed that people actually think like this. I mostly stay well clear of the Axis History Forum; there's some thoughtful stuff there, but there's a stench about the place that makes me feel like I've walked into a room full of smokers, and that if I linger too long, everything about me will reek of nicotine and despair.

❖ ❖ ❖

On Monday, at the start of our AP European History class, Mr. Prendergast hands out a pop quiz about the Renaissance. There are 10 lines to complete across three columns labeled "A) Work", "B) Artist/Author", and "C) Importance"; either the work or its creator is given, and we have to fill in the blanks.

One of the works listed is *The Prince*, so in column B) I write "Niccolo Machiavelli", and in column C) I write, in very small letters, "A polemic about political power and how rulers of a state can gain, maintain and increase it. The book broke with previous works of political theory by addressing not how government ought to function, but rather how things actually are, and thereby represented a huge leap away from the Christian thinking of the time, particularly in analyzing whether leaders should want to be loved or feared. Ironically, the work was written during his own political exile, after the Medici family expelled him from the Florentine city government."

This answer leaks well into the space reserved for my analysis of Baldassare Castiglione's *The Courtier*, but that's fine. In columns A and C for that answer, and for every other blank space on the quiz, I write "(n/a)". Then I walk forward to Mr. Prendergast, who is leaning back in his chair with his feet on his desk, and casually flip my paper along the surface into the soles of his brown loafers. When I arrive back at my desk, and as the rest of the class attempts to complete the quiz, Mr. Prendergast is holding my paper and glancing quizzically in my direction.

At the end of the class, on my way out of the room Mr. Prendergast pulls me aside and asks me to find him after school.

So at the end of the day, I track him down in one of the History classrooms. Three ninth-graders have questions to ask him about the introductory-level World History class he also teaches, so I ease into a desk at the back of the room, put my backpack to one side and begin doodling on my Trigonometry homework. When they're gone, and the hall outside has finally begun to quieten, Mr. Prendergast slides between several desks and plops his ample frame into a plastic chair by a desk diagonally across from mine. I drop my pencil into the crook of my math textbook, snap it shut and look Mr. Prendergast in the eyes.

"Sean, why are you here?" he asks.

"You asked me to find you after school," I respond.

"That's not what I meant."

"No, it isn't."

Mr. Prendergast sighs. "Your quiz today," he says.

"Yes."

"Great answer on Machiavelli."

"Thanks."

"And your answers to the rest of the quiz? Positively Machiavellian."

"You think?"

"You tell me: what does '(n/a)' mean?"

"It means 'not applicable'. Isn't that what it normally means?"

"You don't think you're going to be tested on Michelangelo and Donatello on the AP exam next May?"

"And what if I am?"

"Could you answer it?"

My turn to sigh. "Donatello was a sculptor who revived the classical figure of the human body with self-awareness. Probably the greatest artist from Florence before Michelangelo."

"That's what I thought."

"I've actually seen the ceiling of the Sistine Chapel in person, you know."

"But you don't think it's relevant to European history?"

OK, let's do this. "It's 'history of', not history," I say. "History of art. History of agriculture. History of industry. History of minorities."

"Whoa, hang on."

"I'm serious. Look here – I bookmarked this for you." I push my Trigonometry book away and extricate *A History of Western Society* by McKay, Hill and Buckler from my backpack. "Pages 404 and 405, the section called 'Blacks in Renaissance Society'."

"Yes?"

"There were no blacks in Renaissance society in Europe! Blacks were slaves. That's it. They made no contribution to the advancement of history or society. They weren't beginning to rise up against their masters. There weren't even many of them around: see here? 'In all, blacks made up roughly 3 percent of the Portuguese population.' And that's in a country with a relatively large black population. Count 'em: one, two, three, four, five long paragraphs on blacks in Renaissance society, and there's nothing there!"

"So we should just ignore these people because of their skin color?"

"Yes! Not because they're black and because there's something wrong with that, but because they didn't have a place in the society of the time. The section on blacks in society immediately follows the section on women in society: again, there's nothing really to say, so why say anything at all? This book and this course are pigeonholing modern cultural values into a period where those values didn't exist. Why not just report that they were second-class citizens at the time and leave it at that, instead of digging up bogus material that cannot compare with the intensity or seriousness of everything else going on during this period of history?"

"And today's quiz on art and artists?"

"That's different, sort of, because the works being discussed do and did impact the development of society. But even then, it's 'history of'. Did societies and nations rise and fall because of art?"

"So what should we be covering, in the *History According to Sean* textbook?"

"I answered the question on *The Prince*, didn't I?"

"Yes, you did."

"So, let's study that! Let's talk about how wars and politics affected the Church and the papacy, instead of glossing over the Sack of Rome. There's one sentence about the Sack of Rome in our textbook. Insofar as we have to talk about art, why not talk about how the Sack of Rome affected the arts community in Italy, or how the Sack of Rome indirectly paved the way for Henry VIII's divorce of Catherine of Aragon and triggered the Reformation in England?"

"We'll come back to that later when we cover the rise of Protestantism, you know."

"Good, but it's relevant now as well. Or here's a question: are we going to study the Poland-Lithuanian Commonwealth at any point during this course?"

"We study Poland."

"But not Poland-Lithuania as such?"

"Not really, no."

"This was one of the most prosperous countries in Europe in the 16th and 17th centuries. How many of my classmates do you think know that Poland and Lithuania were the same country for more than four centuries, and that it was far larger than both of those modern countries put together for most of that period?"

"Not many."

"And why do you think that is? Because it lost. Because its political system proved too weak, and its military couldn't pick up the slack. It lost, it was divided between Prussia, Austria and Russia, and it ceased to exist."

"We cover the partition of Poland in the course."

"In how much detail?"

"Not too much."

"If, say, France had slowly ceased to exist and was then partitioned between England, Spain and Lombardy or the Papal States in the late 1700s, do you think that process might have earned more than a few random scribbles in my notes?"

"Probably."

"Well, if you're looking for a minority I care about, there's one – let's talk about the countries that failed and why they failed and the leaders that defeated them in battle and the battles where they were defeated. And let's talk about them instead of blacks before the fall of slavery, or women before the suffragettes except where royalty is involved and a queen or a princess did something that mattered."

Mr. Prendergast leans back in his chair, eyes me up and smiles. "You know," he says, "I know your Dad."

"Yeah?"

"Not well, of course, but he seems like a good professor and an interesting guy."

"Sure."

"But he's not half as interesting to me as you are."

"Why's that?"

"Because here you are, after school on a Monday, lecturing me about the Polish-Lithuanian Commonwealth. You care about history a lot, don't you?"

"Sure – that's what being the son of a History professor does to you. I blame my Dad."

"No. I'm sure that's part of it, but there's something else going on. You really, really like history."

"Yeah, I guess."

"And you don't like the way it's being taught in my class."

"Yeah – well, it's not really your class. I guess you're only teaching what you're told to teach."

"But that's part and parcel with the system: you can't separate one from the other. High-school math can be taught in absolutes, but fashions come and go in history, literature and even the sciences. And in each of these fields, we teach what we teach because the values of our society elevate some of those fashions above others, and a consensus of opinion forms."

"That consensus can be wrong."

"Of course it can. So what if I told you that in studying Renaissance history like we're studying it, we're actually teaching you, Sean Lansbury, more about modern society than Renaissance history? Not anyone else in the class: just you."

"I'd say you're probably right."

"So here's the deal I'm offering you: come pretend with me that everything we're studying matters. Play along with society – our society – to learn what it thinks we should know about the past. Do what you have to do to get through this class: make a deal with the devil, if that's what it takes. Churchill once said that if Hitler invaded Hell, he would make at least a favorable reference to the devil in the House of Commons. Do you think you can do that?"

I crack a small smile. "And what do I get in return?"

"You get a good grade in this course, a good grade on your exam, and someday you will be in a position to help rewrite our cultural values so that your children will be able to study history the way you want it to be taught."

"And how do you know that?"

"Because you've got a sharp mind, a sharp tongue and a sharp sense of self, and with those three things you can achieve anything. And don't let anyone tell you otherwise: just because you're humoring me and the system to do well in this course doesn't mean you should change anything about your passion for history."

"Really?"

"And don't worry about that quiz," he says, reaching into his pocket. "It was a bold gesture, and boldness will serve you better than any quiz will, both in life and AP European History."

Mr. Prendergast rips my quiz paper in half and then in half again, gets up from his chair, places the four ripped pieces of paper on my borrowed desk and looks at me with empathy. "You OK with that, Mister Lansbury?"

"Sure."

"Attaboy."

Mr. Prendergast exits the room. I remain seated at the desk, staring into space and feeling a slightly warm and fuzzy sensation I don't remember feeling before. It's quite pleasant, at least until Chris and Melvyn poke their heads through the doorframe and Chris asks, "What's up, loverboy?"

My head jerks up. "Nothing, I'm just…"

"Teacher's pet!" says Melvyn. They both laugh.

"Just the opposite," I say. "I got called on the carpet because I failed a quiz. Ten points out of a hundred."

"Nice!" says Chris. "But he…"

"Yeah, he ripped it up," I say.

"What a hero!" says Melvyn.

"Anyway, Freddie's waiting downstairs – he needs help making a decision about Angela Galloway," says Chris.

"What?" I ask, scrambling to put my books back in my bag.

"Yeah, and I need your help about how to suck up to History teachers," says Melvyn.

"Heh," I say, dashing out of the room with my friends. "Don't get my hopes up like that!"

4.

When I reported the final session of my game with Dennis on Consimworld, I expected to spark a discussion about whether the V-E Day rolls at the end of *Totaler Krieg* are fair. To my shock, I discovered that because we'd not reached V-E Day for so long, we'd forgotten the rules had changed since an earlier version of the game. There is no longer a V-E Day roll; instead, the game simply ends when the V-E Day marker is removed from the Turn Track. So much for that controversy!

When Dennis arrives for our next game, he's philosophical about our mistake. "These things happen when you're a wargamer," he says.

"I wonder what percentage of all wargames are actually played to completion with no rules being broken?" I ask. "It's gotta be pretty low."

"Such a shame, too. The old way was much better."

"Please tell me you're just saying that because you were the Allies."

"Not at all. *Totaler Krieg* is a game. It's nice to have a twist thrown in at the end now and again."

"A twist?"

"We don't get to a point in the game where VD matters very often." Dennis emits a reedy chuckle.

"Would you please stop saying that?"

Dennis ignores me. "When it does matter, and the roll goes the right way, it can make the game a lot more interesting – that's exactly what happened to us last week, right? I was dead, then I wasn't."

"But don't you think the better player should win the game? I completely controlled that game from 1942 to 1945, but four or five rolls at the end nearly messed everything up. Luck shouldn't decide a game like this."

"Luck? It's a game with dice – of course luck plays a role. The better player doesn't always win."

"But there's a difference between combat luck and what the V-E Day roll represents. The former is a meeting of strategy, tactics and skill; the latter involves none of that."

"What about that Naval Delay roll I got that took one of my Fleets out of action for a year? Where was the skill in that?"

"Fair point, but the difference is that you chose to commit that Fleet to an invasion and put it at risk. You made a decision that led to the possibility of bad luck."

"It's still luck, though."

I sigh. "Sure, there will always be luck in a game with dice. But luck shouldn't dominate *Totaler Krieg*. The better strategist and tactician should nearly always win. And when you play a game for weeks and weeks, should a few lucky rolls be allowed to undo all of the Axis player's hard work in building a dominant position, just because it's exciting?"

"There is another thing, though: VD also gives the Allied player motivation to carry on."

"Really, will you knock it off?"

"I mean, think about it: without VD, I could have safely resigned long before the game finished. I knew I needed a miracle going into the last few turns. And VD is a potential miracle waiting to happen."

"I would have gotten more sleep that night if you had resigned."

"Me, too. But you know, World War Two games are symmetrical. The Axis player has his fun at the start of the game, so it's only fair that the Allied player gets his fun at the end. And the old VD mechanism in *Totaler Krieg* encouraged that. Don't you think?"

"I'd still rather have my skills and abilities properly rewarded or punished."

Dennis smiles. "You're a very intense young man."

I grimace. "Shall we get started?"

"One other point: don't you think you'll remember that game far longer now because it ended the way it did? Apart from my misadventures in Yugoslavia, it wasn't the most interesting or unique game we've ever played, but the ending was nearly one for the history books."

"So to speak."

"Yeah."

"I'll remember it, all right." I'm not one to forget my own history.

Dennis is the Axis this time, and as if to demonstrate how dull he thought our previous contest was, he purposefully drives this game in a very different and ahistorical direction. After rolling over Poland, Denmark, Norway, the Low Countries and France by the end of June-July 1940, Dennis brings Franco into the war before Mussolini. As his panzers push into Iberia, a pair of Treaty cards ally Germany with Italy, Yugoslavia and Greece. In Spring 1941, Dennis invades Portugal and easily captures the Objective Hex in Lisbon, while Gibraltar also falls after a long siege. With only a skeleton German defense in Poland, in Summer 1941 I play Stalin Challenges Germany, but my Political rolls fail me and I cannot break the Nazi-Soviet Pact. Meanwhile, Turkey and Rumania also join the Axis via Dennis's final Treaty card ("New World Order"), and in Autumn 1941 Dennis invades Iran from Turkey in Operation Felix to capture Tehran, another Objective Hex. Outflanked by Turkey in the north and pressed by German and Italian armies in Egypt, my Brits retreat to the southeastern corner of the map, in front of Basra. Although my beleaguered garrison still holds Malta, the Mediterranean is otherwise now an Axis lake.

In *Totaler Krieg*, this is known as the "Long Limited War" strategy, and Dennis has executed it very well. From the Axis perspective, the strategy has several downsides, most obviously the distinct possibility that Stalin Challenges Germany will allow Russia to strike preemptively in the East. Germany must fight the Soviets no later than mid-1943 – that is hardwired into *Totaler Krieg* – but the Axis player benefits if he controls the timing of when hostilities start and "Total War" begins. Regardless, if Germany doesn't strike before 1942, the Red Army can grow very large; with the *Wehrmacht* likely dispersed across multiple fronts, even if one of these fronts is in the Caucasus Germany shouldn't be able to inflict a knockout blow against Russia. If the Allies can ride the storm and assume the strategic offensive, the "soft underbelly" of the Axis empire can become terribly flabby, and the road to Berlin may now pass through Madrid or Istanbul. And if Total War doesn't start until 1942, V-E Day will not arrive until 1946, giving the Allied player additional time to recover and win the game.

Having said all of this, the Long Limited War strategy can not only work in the game, it might have given Hitler his best chance of winning the war in real life. I envisage a three-step process: one, diplomatic pressure in Southern Europe; two, conciliation to Russia and respect for Stalin's desired spheres of influence; three, coordinated strikes against Britain's overseas empire and its allies. If the dominoes fall correctly, Britain is relegated from the league of elite nations, Stalin respects German strength and remains in his cage, and Germany possesses the Middle East and need never worry about synthetic oil research.

See? I can be a Nazi fanboy too!

In all honesty, I have conveniently ignored several details. One is that old chestnut, logistics: even with a friendly Turkey, any supply line from Germany to the Middle East would be very long and tenuous. A second is the fragile nature of this Axis coalition: Greece and Turkey are never the best bedfellows, while Spain, Italy and Vichy France each had competing interests in Africa and elsewhere. But this strategy assumes Germany can ally with all of them, even though Hitler only just managed to keep Hungary and Rumania – two satellite states far less independent than the likes of Spain or Turkey – at peace with each other in real life despite their shared hatred of Russia.

Most importantly, this scenario assumes that Hitler was totally rational and free of idiosyncrasy. Consider Spain's involvement in the war. In July 1940, Franco was keen to join the Axis but Hitler wanted nothing to do with him, and for the same reasons: the war seemed to be as good as over, and Spain wanted to reap its spoils without doing anything to deserve them. Three months later, Hitler and Franco famously met each other at Hendaye, a small French town near the Spanish border. By then, the equation had changed: the Battle of Britain had been lost and the war would obviously continue, so now Hitler wanted an alliance but Franco had lost interest. In essence, an alliance between Germany and Spain could only be forged if Franco believed Germany was bound to win the war but Hitler believed he would need Spanish help – not a likely combination.

But here's the thing: from 1935 to 1939, Hitler demonstrated a supreme mastery of *Realpolitik*. Through cunning, guile and posturing, he accomplished every one of his diplomatic objectives. So in 1940, even though Spain's territorial ambitions might have caused trouble with France and friction with Italy, why not offer Franco the French territory in Africa he craved, wait for Spain to join the war and become inextricably enmeshed in it, and then find excuses to delay and temporize? Instead, when Franco put the former German colony of Cameroon on his territorial wish list, Hitler refused to countenance it. Why on earth not? If Germany or Spain were ever in a position to annex Cameroon, the Axis surely would have won the war, and Germany could have dictated whatever terms it wished to absolutely anyone. Did Hitler develop a conscience because he was dealing with a fellow Fascist? Did he come to believe Spain wasn't a prize worth having at any price? I'm not aware of any evidence to either effect. So what happened? Why didn't Franco join the Axis?

My best guess is that Hitler wanted to win the war only insofar as he could win it on his terms. After the meeting at Hendaye, Hitler privately remarked that he would rather have three or four teeth pulled than sit through another conversation with Franco. Stalin, Churchill and Roosevelt each proved in their own ways that they were willing to do anything to win the war, and that they would bicker in earnest about peace terms only after the war was all but over. The same could not be said of Hitler. Also, Hitler told one of his generals in June 1940 that Germany's victories in the West "finally freed his hands for his important real task: the showdown with Bolshevism." I don't think Hitler ever could have embraced a Mediterranean strategy – he simply couldn't wait that long to pursue the Eastern *Lebensraum* he always coveted.

However, one final aspect of a Mediterranean strategy might have worked in Germany's favor: it could have encouraged Stalin to make the first move. In *Totaler Krieg*, this is a bad thing for Germany, but in real life I'm not so sure. In Russia's darkest hours at the end of 1941, Stalin invoked the Motherland and the spirit of 1812 in exhorting his countrymen to withstand the fascist invasion. This succeeded both at the front and in the factories, and the Soviet state not only continued to function effectively, but even encompassed a spirit of national unity which lasted well beyond the war itself. If Russia had attacked first, the reverse may well have happened: Germany would have been galvanized to repel the Communist invaders, Stalin's war of aggression may not have resonated with the average Russian, German atrocities in the East could have been painted as justifiable revenge, and after the first few Tannenberg-scale defeats Communist Russia might have imploded just as Tsarist Russia did before it. Just as Pearl Harbor awoke the sleeping American giant in a way that an attack on the Philippines alone might not have, a justifiable sense of national grievance and a permanent grudge against an aggressor should not be underestimated in predicting who might win a war.

❖ ❖ ❖

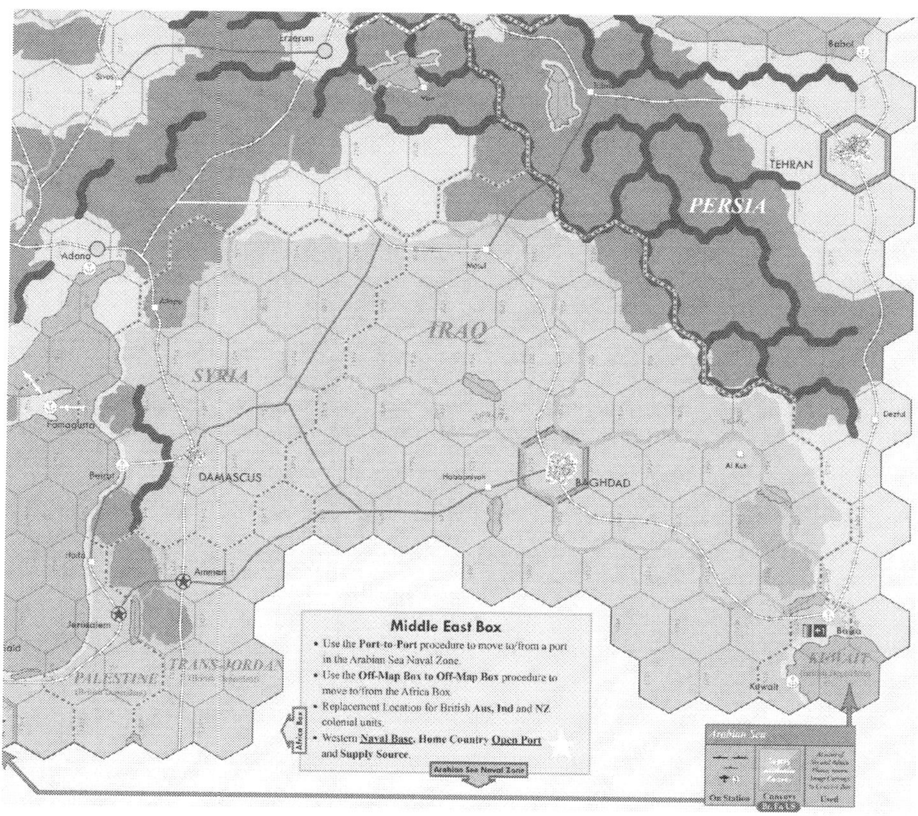

Fig. 4 – The Middle East

Late in the second session of Dennis's Long Limited War campaign, during my half of the July-August 1941 turn, Dad poked his head into the study. He rarely interrupts us during gaming sessions, but this time, after I said "hello" he silently sidled up to the gaming table and peered over my shoulder at the Middle East, where my very stretched British defenders stood guard at Jerusalem, near Aleppo in northern Syria and near Mosul in northern Iraq. "That's weird," he said eventually.

I'd been concentrating on my move, and planning a difficult *Totaler Krieg* defense is like adding a long series of two-digit numbers in your head: it's not impossible, but it's easy to lose your place, and if you lose it you'll probably have to start over again. But with Dad hovering, I was losing my focus and my nerve, and I let out an exasperated sigh. After a short pause, Dad said, "Knight to queen's rook four."

"Dad!" I turned around.

"What?" he said. "It's the obvious play."

"That's not funny," I said.

"It's a little funny," he said. "Particularly as you're getting the snot beaten out of you."

"Thanks a lot."

Dennis laughed and commented, "It's still early days." He was wearing a black T-shirt featuring a bright green army helmet over which "MAKE WAR, NOT LOVE" was superimposed in pink letters.

"Let me ask you something, Dennis," said Dad. "Why is it that a man of your age and with your wardrobe spends so much time with my son?"

"I just go where the action is," said Dennis.

Dad smirked. "May I sit?" he asked.

I made room on our spare chair by carefully lowering the game's box-top and our dormant counter trays to the floor. He sat down, leaned forward and put his left elbow on the table, cupped his chin in his palm and stared dolefully at me. I started to survey the map again, stopped, started again, then glared at Dad.

"What?" said Dad. "You go ahead – I'm just, you know, here."

"Why are you here?" I asked.

"I'm just here," he said. He crinkled his nose and pursed his lower lip, like a puppy spying me through a window while soaking in the rain.

"So, Mr. Lansbury – you're a History professor?" interjected Dennis.

"That I am," said Dad, pivoting his cheek on his hand to face my opponent.

"What's that like?"

"It's a carnival," said Dad. "Every day a parade."

Dennis paused, then asked, "Which do you like more: teaching or researching?"

"I don't know. What day is it?"

"Huh?" I said.

"Sometimes it's one and sometimes the other," said Dad. "Some students really, deeply, passionately want to learn. And some very much don't."

"How much do you know about World War Two?" asked Dennis.

"A fair amount, I suppose. Germany and Japan won, right?"

"Heh."

"The 'cycle of renewal', I've always called it," Dad said. "After a peace treaty is signed, the quote-unquote 'winner' usually remains complacent, while the 'loser' looks to fix what went wrong. Look at GDP growth, political stability, quality of life indices, education rates – all of that, decades on from 1945, and you tell me who won World War Two. It's not Britain and it's not Russia, I can assure you."

"So you weren't joking?" I asked.

"Not really," said Dad. "Always take the longer view."

"It helps if you don't have to fund a national defense," said Dennis.

"True," said Dad.

"Do you like World War Two?" asked Dennis.

"Like it?" countered Dad, with a confused look on his face.

"Are you interested by it?"

"It's not really my brew, if that's what you mean."

"Oh," said Dennis.

"Which makes it odd that he's here," I said. "Dad, you know we're really trying to keep to a schedule…"

"No, no, you're fine," Dad said. "Just go on like I'm not even here."

"I can't really do that…"

"So what does interest you?" continued Dennis.

"In history?" asked Dad.

"In history."

"I teach about the Revolutions of 1848."

"No kidding. Why that?"

Dad shrugged. "It's what I do. 'Ours is not to reason why,' and so on and so forth."

"But you must have started somewhere."

Dad leaned back in his chair. "I moved with my parents to America from Lincolnshire when I was 12," he said. "I've always liked it here, but things are different. The wide open spaces. The sunny outlook on life. The self-confidence of a detached and truly independent nation. And, of course, the nearly total ignorance of international history among the population at large. Present company excepted, of course."

"Indeed."

"So I was drawn back to European history – I wrote my senior thesis, found a little piece of academia to call my own, and here I am."

"So you made a career out of your senior thesis?" asked Dennis.

At that, Dad went quiet. He pivoted his face back toward me, again jutted out his puppy-dog lower lip, and stared vacantly beyond the map in front of him. I looked at Dennis, and Dennis looked at me, and then I asked, "Dad?"

"Yes?" he said.

"What are you doing?"

"Just carry on like I'm not here," said Dad. "Because I'm just, you know, here."

"Are you OK?" I asked.

"I'm fine. You know, I'm fine. I just want to see if my boy has what it takes to defend, you know, his queen, so to speak."

"You sure?" I asked.

"God save the queen," said Dad.

Then he was quiet again, and I looked at Dennis, and then I shrugged and looked back at the board, trying once again to catch my train of thought. I recalculated how far the Turkish cavalry vanguard could move into Iraq, the strength and positions of the Axis armies on the Syrian border, and how many factors Dennis could amass from Egypt to attack Jerusalem. And just as I'd nearly completed my analysis, Dad stood up and said, "Don't be up too late, OK? Goodnight, Sean," and he tousled my hair.

"Goodnight, Dad," I groaned.

"Goodnight, Mister Lansbury," said Dennis.

"Behave yourself," said Dad. And he walked out of the study and closed the door.

I shook my head. "Sorry about that," I said.

"Is he often like that?" asked Dennis.

"I don't really know."

"Oh."

I started to look at the Middle East again. Then I looked at Dennis. "When you said 'like that', about Dad, what did you mean?"

"He seemed a bit, you know, off."

"He's an intellectual," I said. "Normal behavior isn't normal for him."

"Oh. OK."

I stared again at Dennis's ridiculous shirt, then turned again to the board. Jerusalem, Aleppo, Mosul. Baghdad. Damascus. Basra. Jerusalem again. Aleppo and Mosul, again. The crossroads in hex e2119 (northeastern Syria). How to defend, fall back, protect, retreat, cover, fight, live to fight. It wasn't really happening.

Then Dennis said, "You would make a lousy general in real life."

"Really? Do tell."

"Generals have to put up with all sorts of personal stuff in war. Buddies of theirs get killed at the front. Their sons get killed at the front. They get 'Dear John' letters from their wives and girlfriends. They have to massage the egos of politicians who want to sack them. Whereas your Dad just looked at you kinda funny and now you can't make a decision, can you? That's all I'm saying."

I stared again at Dennis. "Too harsh?" he asked.

"Perhaps."

He's probably right, though. The next turn he invaded Persia – I never saw Operation Felix coming – and took Mosul, and I reentered crisis mode. I am comforted, though, to remember that of course *Totaler Krieg* is just a game. It has many qualities as a simulation, but it cannot recreate the visceral aspects of a battlefield: the sights, the smells, the sounds, the abject fear and utter terror. My decisions don't save or cost real lives, and thank goodness for that: as much as I love to put myself in the shoes of history's great commanders, I would never matriculate at West Point and try to become one myself.

5.

A few years ago, GMT Games published an intriguing multi-player boardgame set in 16th-century Europe called *Here I Stand*, in which up to six players can represent England, France, the Habsburg Empire, the Ottoman Empire, the Papacy and the Protestants. Players can form alliances with one another and earn victory points by completing various asymmetrical tasks – everything from winning wars and discovering the New World to translating the Bible into new languages (Protestant) or successfully burning debaters at the stake (Papacy). The British player also has a special card, The Six Wives of Henry VIII, and can play it to roll on the "Henry's Wives' Pregnancy Chart" in search of a healthy Edward VI. I wouldn't call it a flawless simulation, but it does immerse you in its history; I played it once via e-mail, and although the game eventually collapsed because one player had to withdraw and another's slothful play caused us all to lose interest, I'd definitely try it face-to-face if I could find five opponents within a 100-mile radius.

The game is named after Martin Luther's famous concluding statement at the Diet of Worms in 1521: "I cannot and will not recant anything, for it is neither safe nor right to go against conscience. *Here I stand. I can do no other.* God help me. Amen." Of course, the italicized text is apocryphal – it does not appear in contemporary accounts of Luther's speech, and the quote appears in my AP European History textbook without it. And yet, to me this is yet another black strike against the course I'm taking. To rephrase William Randolph Hearst, just because a myth isn't true doesn't mean you shouldn't print it. "Here I stand" is both famous and poetic; its fame in and of itself makes it historical, and its omission here without explanation feels wrong to me.

That aside, I really enjoy studying the Reformation. It's not like the other "history of" we've studied, because the history of the Church and the history of Europe are inseparable: international politics, diplomacy and war-making in this period cannot be understood without first understanding the Church. The key actors and their actions are larger than life: Luther nails 95 Theses to the church door in Wittenberg; Henry VIII embraces arch-villainy in a sweeping medieval soap opera ("divorced, beheaded, died, divorced, beheaded, survived" resonates independent of context); the Council of Trent and the Counter-Reformation it triggered play out like *The Empire Strikes Back*. This history sweeps grandly across Europe, with every petty duke and two-bit cleric lining up on either side of a vast ideological divide. Meanwhile, the Ottomans threatened to destroy all before them after the Battle of Mohács in 1526 and render the Reformation irrelevant. What if Suleiman the Magnificent had marched decisively on Vienna, captured the city as he surely could have, and subsequently found allies among the Protestant armies of northern Germany? Theodore K. Rabb speculated about this very scenario in the first *What If?* book of counterfactual essays, and he makes a compelling case that the Reformation easily could have turned out very differently.

The apotheosis of our Reformation studies will hopefully be the Thirty Years War, but that is still a few weeks away on our syllabus. At present, for his Reformation party piece Mr. Prendergast asked us to prepare for a great ecclesiastical debate in the spirit of the Diet of Worms. Half of us will make Luther's case for the prosecution, while the other half is defending the existing Church, and the winners will receive extra credit on the test we'll take at the end of our current study unit. Because I love a good counterfactual, to say nothing of an underdog, I'm in the Catholic camp.

Mr. Prendergast ostentatiously announces: "Ladies and gentleman, I am *Reichsmarschall* Ulrich von Pappenheim, convenor of this tribunal and lieutenant general in charge of men-at-arms within the Holy Roman Empire. Which is neither holy, Roman nor an empire, but that's not important right now. In the blue corner, we have the defending champion, Johann Eck, papal inquisitor and defender of the one true faith. In the red corner, we have the upstart from Saxony, Martin Luther, author of the *95 Theses*, *Resolutions Concerning the 95 Theses*, *On the Papacy at Rome*, *Address to the Christian Nobility*, *The Babylonian Captivity of the Church*, and *On the Freedom of a Christian*. Fight fair, please, and address all of your arguments to each other. First of all, Lutherans: what's the problem? Where's the fire?"

"To put it bluntly, the Church is going to hell," begins one of the Lutherans, and they take turns firing with both barrels. The sale of indulgences is a theological travesty designed purely to enrich the Church. Papal supremacy is all about temporal power and not saving souls. St. Paul's letters correctly show that salvation comes from grace alone and cannot be earned except through faith. Purgatory and transubstantiation are but two of many doctrines invented by the Church and not found in the Bible, the one authoritative and divinely inspired source of teaching about God. The Church was always meant to be the collective body of all Christians, and therefore the responsibility for achieving salvation must be shared among all and not sequestered within the clergy.

After six or seven minutes of this, *Reichsmarschall* Prendergast steps in and says, "That's enough for the moment. The prosecution rests. What say the Catholics in response?"

And then it hits me. I ask, "Can we request a short recess, your honor?" Several of my classmates giggle at this.

"What? Why?" replies the court.

"To coordinate our defense," I say. "This debate is lopsided: the Lutherans just need to repeatedly condemn the existing Church to score points, whereas we need to formulate a coherent defense. We could employ many different strategies, but some of them are mutually exclusive."

"Indeed they are," says Mr. Prendergast. "Mister Lansbury, do you know when Luther first posted his 95 Theses?"

"1517," I say.

"And when did the Counter-Reformation began?"

"Probably in 1545, when the Council of Trent kicked off."

"So it took the Catholic Church 28 years to even begin devising a unified and coherent defense of itself, right? I'm sorry, but we don't have that kind of time. Your objection is noted, but overruled." Both sides of the aisle titter gently. "However, as Mister Lansbury points out, the law firm of Eck, Eck, Eck, Eck and Eck can make some valid points for the defense – shall we hear some of them?"

Duly chastened, I yield the floor while my teammates trip over each other. Tim Rogers – a really nice guy who I know goes to Mass every Sunday – gamely argues that traditions like pilgrimages, the veneration of saints and relics and the adoration of the Virgin Mary have their place in the faith, and that the papacy descends from Peter, the rock upon whom Jesus built his Church. But he sounds lost and vacant, as though he no longer fully understands Catholicism. Jessica Biderman more firmly supports this argument, noting that the early Church traditions were vital in establishing Christian doctrine. The Nicene Creed, for example, was formulated at one of the early Church councils convened to define Christian beliefs and refute pervasive heresies.

"So are you saying that ever since Jesus died, you've basically been making it up as you go along?" asks Faith Evans. Faith is one of Muhlendorf's resident conservative evangelicals and the conspicuous wearer of a chastity ring that her demeanor renders entirely moot.

"What is your collection of Lutherans, Hussites, Calvinists, Anabaptists and many other 'ists' doing if not 'making it up as you go along'?" I retort. "But if by that slur you include 'deciding which books form the canonical version of the Bible', the book that you Protestants find so central to your argument, then yes, we agree."

"And we believe you made the wrong call on several of those books, but whatever," says Miss Evans.

"Please," says Mr. Prendergast. "Give the defense a chance to finish."

A new angle is introduced by Felix Randolph, a tall and fair-skinned kid from a religious family, who establishes that the Bible isn't just for Luther. "James, chapter 2, verse 20: 'Faith without works is dead,'" he says. "You pretend there's a huge difference between salvation through faith alone and salvation through faith and good works, but a real faith will produce good works automatically, and the two positions will come to look identical. It's a distinction without a difference. Here's another one – Romans, chapter 3, verse 23: 'All have sinned and fallen short of the glory of God.' Everyone falls short, including the Church's leaders, and to expect otherwise is unsound doctrine."

"Aren't you now defending Protestantism?" asks Belinda Macintosh, from Luther's camp.

"Not at all," says Felix. "Even Papal infallibility only applies when the Pope speaks on matters of doctrine – otherwise he's capable of sinning. Catholics have always believed that."

"For that matter," I interject, "did you guys know that the doctrine of papal infallibility won't be invented for another three-and-a-half centuries? It will be defined during the First Vatican Council, in 1870."

"Objection!" cries Mr. Prendergast. "Calls for future speculation – please try not to shatter the space-time continuum in forming your answers."

"Hang on…so even Catholics don't believe the Pope is infallible?" asks a bewildered Tim.

"On doctrinal matters, they do – the doctrine of infallibility just hasn't been formally stated yet," says Felix.

"Actually, I don't think that's true," says Jessica.

"This is what I was going to say," continues Chad Sauerbrunner. "The Church has made mistakes, and it needs to reform itself to some extent, but these reforms can take place within the existing Church."

"But given the checkered history of the Church, and particularly the papacy, do you really believe that can happen?" asks Belinda.

"Is the Pope Catholic?" responds Chad.

Several different arguments are now brewing simultaneously, and the class is getting out of control. In the middle of all this, my mate Chris, hitherto silent at the back of the class with his best too-cool-for-school face on, sarcastically wails, "There is no God!" Eventually Mr. Prendergast opens his desk drawer, pulls out a referee's whistle and gives it several tweets, which shuts everyone up.

"Another year, another banner day for the ACLU," he says. "Isn't it nice to see what religion can do to you? I know many of you will already be familiar with the passions religion can excite in us, but even though this debate has collapsed in similar fashion every year since I first started refereeing it, it's worth having it for that reason alone. The Reformation eventually became a life-or-death struggle precisely because each faction so passionately believed in the rightness of its cause. Those same religious passions can be seen throughout history: in the Crusades, in the persecutions of the Jews, most definitely in the Reformation, and even within the red state-blue state divide we now face in America. At least we no longer burn people at the stake, so that's something, I guess. As for the winner of the debate, as Mister Lansbury noted earlier, the debate was slanted in the Protestants' favor at the start, which is why everyone who contributed productively to the discussion will get extra credit on the test…Mister Lansbury, you have something else to say, do you?"

Indeed I do. "Actually, the best argument to be made in the debate on our side, on the Catholic side, has nothing to do with religion."

"Do tell."

"In secular terms, the Reformation was all about power and politics, nothing more. Before Luther, the Church and the Pope had the power, and every secular leader operated within their framework. But after Luther's revolt and the Church's rejection of him, his ideas spread and became popular: suddenly the papacy had viable competition. While some princes did become Protestant on religious grounds, and many of their subjects did as well, other leaders switched allegiance for secular reasons. Henry VIII in England is a perfect example: an entire denomination of Protestantism was formed over a minor religious issue – an individual divorce – that was all about secular power and politics. And so that's the point: if Luther could have looked into the future and seen how the Church's power would be diluted, and how many divergent Protestant groups and churches would form for all sorts of good and bad reasons, would he still have been inclined to shatter the Papal monopoly? Wouldn't it be better to work within the Church for more gradual reform, and not have your agenda hijacked by people who don't care about your issues or take them in other directions, way beyond what you intended?"

After a few moments of silence, Chris blurts out, "You are such a dork." I think he's smiling, sort of.

❖ ❖ ❖

A few days later, Melvyn's budding girlfriend Vicki joins the Big Game. This wasn't my idea.

I'm all in favor of inviting girls to our poker table. One or two of them have played well at the Big Game, and several others have gotten lucky. I'd love to have Melissa join us, but she's not that way inclined. If she were to come along, though, I'd treat her like any other player: respect her, show no hard feelings regardless of the outcome, and try like hell to take her money.

This is the problem with Vicki, and with Melvyn. Vicki is a big fish, and Melvyn has her on his hook but hasn't quite reeled her in yet. Last week, Melvyn asked the three of us if Vicki could jump the queue and play in the game. Sure, we said.

"Thanks," said Melvyn. "But I mean, not just play…I want her to do well. You know, so that, well, you know."

"Yeah, we get it," said Chris.

"No," I said.

"No? C'mon, why not?" asked Melvyn.

"That's not what the Big Game is about," I said.

"I know it's not, but this is different," said Melvyn. "This is important to me. Can you be a friend and lay off for once? I'll make up any money you lose."

"That's not poker," I said. "We play a serious game, and we play it to win. Always."

"But we've been playing it every day for a long time," said Melvyn. "How many games have we played – hundreds? Thousands? What's wrong with playing it slightly differently, just once?"

"You can't think of any other way to impress her?" I asked. "That's pretty sad."

"Of course I can, but she asked about this, and you can only play one hand of cards at a time."

"So to speak," said Freddie.

"So to speak," smiled Melvyn.

I grunted and looked away, and the rest of the Gang took this as reluctant connivance. I wish I'd told Melvyn that any relationship hatched like this is surely doomed to fail. This might work in a stupid sitcom, but really, if you think you can find true love by cheating at cards, good luck with that.

So I'm morose as Vicki joins our table, fashionably late by several minutes. I've got nothing against Vicki – she'd be intimidatingly blond and pretty even without the extra year she has on us, and she wears too much makeup for my tastes, but she's outgoing and friendly, and I'd be churlish to wish her ill just because Melvyn's brain is in his boxers.

"Hi guys – how ya' doin'?" asks Vicki. I'm across the table from her.

"Welcome to the Big Game," says Chris. "You're in Seat Four, just after Freddie and just before Melvyn in the dealing order." Melvyn had asked to sit next to her instead of accepting a random seat assignment – another breach of protocol.

"Thanks," says Vicki, pecking Melvyn on the cheek as she sits down. "So, can one of you guys teach me the rules before we start?"

I raise a hand to my forehead, attempting to shield my pain from the rest of the table. "Only kidding, Sean! Melvyn told me to say that," says Vicki, laughing.

I pinch my thumb and middle finger to the inner corners of my eyes and say, "Sorry, just rubbing my eyes – I didn't get much sleep last night." Which is true, actually; I spent far too long deciding whether to invade Norway as my *Totaler Krieg* e-mail tournament game against Steven Ginsberg nears its conclusion.

"So, do you know what you're doing?" asks Chris.

"Yeah, mostly. My Dad taught me and my brothers how to play when we were younger – we used to play for pennies. I haven't played in a while, though. Do you guys use jokers and wild cards?"

"No," I blurt.

Freddie has the dealer button and begins shuffling the cards. It's a cool, cloudy day outside our alcove window, with freshly fallen autumn leaves whipped by the wind into little cyclones pretending to climb the walls of the Facilities building, a few yards away from us. Several kids are half-watching our game from adjacent tables as they munch their food, while one regular kibitzer, a lanky sophomore named Michael, leans in his usual spot against the wall across from the window.

In our first hand, Vicki starts strongly and immediately raises to $1. Melvyn folds so quickly he almost pulls a hamstring – not a great actor, our Melvyn. Freddie folds, and then I peek at my cards: Jack of diamonds, 7 of spades. I fold, Chris folds as well, and Vicki lets out a small whoop of delight.

"Well played," says Melvyn.

"Thanks!" responds Vicki. "Do I show these cards to everyone?" she asks, even as she's flipping the Ace of diamonds face-up.

"No, no, no," says Chris. "Not like that – you only need to show 'em when you want to."

"Oh. Should I show the other one now?"

"Only if you want to," echoes Melvyn.

"What should I do?" asks Vicki. I glance across at Michael, who is listening to his iPod and typing on his iPhone.

"If you had a good hand, you could show us your cards so we might believe you when you next make a bet," answers Chris. "If you had a bad hand, you could show us your cards so we might not believe you next time. Or you could just keep us guessing. Which option sounds best to you?"

"I don't know. Tell you what – I'll show you." She flips over the 10 of spades.

"Yeah, those are good cards," says Chris.

"Impressive," says Melvyn.

"Cool!" coos Vicki.

I deal the second hand. Melvyn calls, then Freddie calls. I have the 8 of diamonds and 3 of clubs and am again compelled to fold. Chris calls. Vicki in the big blind, raises to $1. Melvyn folds, Freddie folds, and Chris folds.

Vicki laughs. "I'm not showing you my cards this time!" she exclaims.

"I bet they were pretty good," says Chris.

"Yeah, they were. But I'm not telling you how good!" says Vicki.

The third hand matches the second: Freddie calls, I draw more rags and fold impassively, Chris calls, and Vicki raises from the small blind, this time to $1.50. The rest of the table folds, and Vicki has now increased her starting stack of $5 to $6.50.

"Y'know," I say, "I was flipping channels the other day and wound up watching a few minutes of this nothing tennis tournament on ESPN. At one point, the commentators started laughing about an exhibition match coming up in a few weeks and predicted it would be a three-set barnburner."

"Who's playing?" asks Freddie.

"Doesn't matter," I say. "I learned there's an unwritten code between the two players in most exhibition matches. They play hard in the first set, and they play hard in the third set, but the second set is almost always won by the guy who lost the first set."

"Really?" asks Freddie.

"They want to give the crowd its money's worth," I say. "I guess it's pretty easy to lose a set of tennis in such a way that nobody can tell you're tanking."

"You don't say," says Chris. I glare over at Melvyn, who is whispering to Vicki and giggling with her, oblivious to the rest of the table.

For the fourth hand, Vicki deals the cards after letting Chris shuffle the deck for her, a common ritual for guests in the Big Game. I'm first to act, and this time my hand is passable: the Queen of hearts and the Jack of hearts. I gently raise to 50 cents and get two callers, Vicki and Melvyn. I suspect Melvyn is protecting Vicki more than playing his own hand; with Vicki, my only read on her so far is that she's still very blond and perky.

Vicki deals the flop: Ace of hearts, 10 of spades, 3 of hearts. Now I'm in business, with four hearts and a gutshot straight draw. I'm again up first and place an exploratory bet of 50 cents. Vicki quickly calls. Melvyn, realizing that this flop is too dangerous to play with a rubbish hand, pretends to ponder for a few seconds and then ducks out of the way. Normally he's much less obvious than this.

The turn is the 7 of hearts. Perfect. The only better hand Vicki could have is a higher flush, and she'd need the King of hearts for that. I twiddle several nickels and ponder my options: I can bet again and hope Vicki calls or re-raises, or I can check and try to trap her into making a big bet of her own. Given how quickly she called my bet after the flop, she must have at least a rag Ace, or maybe even Ace-10 or Ace-3 for two pair. Hmmm. I think betting out is more likely to win me money – maybe she hasn't even considered the flush? – but check-raising might work too. And because a check-raise or even a check-call looks less aggressive than leading with a strong bet, I could win the pot without looking like I'm out to ruin Melvyn's sex life. It's a rubbish reason, but in these circumstances it's as good a reason as any.

"I check."

Vicki looks at Melvyn. "So I can now…"

"Check to see another card, or bet and force Sean to call or raise you," answers Melvyn.

"OK, I check," says Vicki.

The river looks like a blank – 9 of clubs. The same betting logic applies, so I check again, this time more quickly. Vicki chews her bottom lip for a second and then says, "I call."

"Do you mean 'check'?" I ask. "Or do you want to bet?"

"Sorry," says Vicki. "I check."

I show my hand and say, "Flush to the Ace, Queen kicker. Do you have the King of hearts?"

Vicki blushes. "Do I have to show my hand?" she asks.

"Only if you've won," says Chris.

"I haven't won," says Vicki. "But here." She shows her cards anyway: a pair of sixes. "God, Mel, that was awful." Freddie and I glance at each other. "Mel"? We've never heard that before.

This is such a waste of time. Normally we chew up and spit out players like Vicki as fast as we can – dead money demands to be killed. I look again to Michael, who is still texting and headphoning. This game demands a showpiece execution.

Melvyn deals the fifth hand, and I'm in the big blind. Chris folds. Vicki bets $1. Melvyn and Freddie fold, and the action is to me: I have the Ace of clubs and the 9 of clubs. Any suited Ace is playable in a five-handed game, even out of position; against someone like Vicki, I'm definitely in. I stare intently at her for several seconds, then ask, "Are you a natural blond, Vicki?"

"Sure am," she says. Not a hint of fidgeting. Melvyn scowls.

"I call," I say.

Melvyn deals the flop, tossing the three cards onto the table together: Ace of spades, Queen of clubs, 4 of clubs. Brilliant. I have the top pair, and the nut four-flush in reserve.

"Is your mother blond?" I ask.

"No, she's brunette – my dad is blond," says Vicki.

"I check," I say. This isn't another feel-good check-call – this is real poker.

"I bet a dollar," says Vicki.

"Where are your ancestors from?" I ask.

"I'm half-Scottish and half-Austrian," says Vicki.

"That's nice." I look straight at Vicki again: "I re-raise." I take the eight quarters in my pile of coins and plonk them carefully down on the table, two at a time. "Two dollars."

Vicki bites her bottom lip again. I'm pretty sure it's a tell.

"I call," she says. She glances at Melvyn.

Melvyn silently kills a card and deals the turn – the 10 of hearts. What could I be losing to? King-Jack would be a straight, but she wouldn't have called for nearly half her stack with an inside straight draw. An Ace with a better kicker, or three of a kind? If so, then fair play to her – she'd fully deserve my money. But even then, I'd have outs on the flush draw. And nothing else beats me.

So that's it – I won't give her another chance to get lucky. "I'm all in," I say.

Vicki takes a deep breath and starts tapping a nickel on the table. I catch Melvyn's burning stare and gently shrug my shoulders. What could I do? I make eye contact with Michael, against the wall – he's put his phone away, and his headphones are out of his ears.

"Is your father Austrian?" I ask.

"No – my mother is," says Vicki. She sighs and says, "This is a tough one."

She taps her nickel on the table again, more loudly this time. Not in rhythm – there's no beat to it. Just a set of sharp cracks on the surface, amidst the chaotic backdrop of a high school cafeteria.

"OK, whatever – I call," she says.

I flinch in slight amazement. "You call?" I ask.

"Yep."

Chris and Freddie lean forward. We count our coins, and Vicki is actually all-in – I cover her by $1.10 – but either way this is a huge pot for the Big Game.

"I've got a pair," says Vicki. She turns over her cards: the King of diamonds, and the Queen of spades. Second pair. What a terrible call.

"Alas, I've got a higher pair, as well as a flush draw," I say.

"Yep," says Vicki. "That's what I thought. Oh well!" She puts her arm around Melvyn's shoulder – she seems pretty upbeat about it.

"King-Queen is one of those hands that usually looks better than it is," I say. "There's a lot of paint on those cards."

"Am I done for?" asks Vicki.

"Let's see," says Chris. "Any club gives Sean a flush, so you need a King, but not the King of clubs. You need a Queen, but not the Queen of clubs. And a Jack would also make you a straight, but again, it can't be the Jack of clubs."

"So you've got seven outs," I say. "Two Kings, two Queens, three Jacks."

"C'mon, King of spades!" says Vicki. She crosses her fingers and squints.

Melvyn deals the decisive river card: it's the Jack of diamonds. Dammit.

"Jack...it's a straight! I won! I've won!" Vicki claps her hands together excitedly, the bracelets on her wrists bobbing up and down, and gives Melvyn a hug. Melvyn looks very relieved.

I can only shake my head. What can you do? Anyone who has ever played poker knows the sinking feeling of a bad beat. I know the feeling very well.

"Harsh," says Freddie, quietly.

"That's poker," I say. Dammit.

"I'm sorry, Sean," says Vicki.

"Dammit," I say. "No, sorry, that's just the way things are going for me lately. This is just like that roll I had against Dennis the other night – I was attacking Tripoli..." Oops.

"What?" asks Chris, his head jerking up.

Think fast...

"I, well, I was playing craps online, and this guy named Dennis was the shooter – do you guys know how to play craps?"

"No, but we're not degenerates like you," says Melvyn.

"My grandfather taught me. Anyway, we had a side bet going where I was backing against the shooter, odds on, to make his six-point with double threes, which some players call 'Attacking Tripoli'. Tripoli, triples, double threes?"

"Oh," they say. "OK."

"Of course, then Dennis rolls double threes, and I get totally screwed. So that's my life story at the moment."

"You deserved better than that," says Vicki.

"Freddie's the dealer again, right?" I say. "I'm all-in."

"Without looking at your cards?" asks Vicki.

"Yep."

And sure enough, Freddie draws pocket Jacks, and I get nothing, and that's me done for the day. I've been eliminated from the Big Game before, but only rarely, and never quite like this.

My grandfather did teach me how to play craps, by the way. That much of my story was true. I'm just glad my ill fortune against Dennis last Thursday occurred during an amphibious invasion of Libya. My carefully conceived attack, which involved two corps backed by a Carrier Fleet and a Blitz marker, had a 5-in-6 chance of blowing open Dennis's stranglehold on the Mediterranean theater; it failed, but at least it failed against a city whose name I could instantly associate with something else.

❖ ❖ ❖

The next morning, Melvyn finds me near my school locker and offers to return the five dollars I'd lost yesterday. "Keep it," I say. "Vicki won it fair and square."

"I'm sorry – you're right, I was an ass."

"It worked out well for you, though. Didn't it?" I smile. "It's more than you deserve, of course."

"Vicki was ecstatic," says Melvyn. "That's the moral of the story, isn't it? I'd rather be lucky than good."

"Good for you."

"She wants to play again at some point now, you know."

I look sternly at Melvyn. He pats me on the shoulder and runs off to find Vicki.

And then I wonder…fair and square? When Melvyn dealt the river card in that fatal fifth hand, there were eight cards on the table – four community cards plus the two cards apiece dealt to me and Vicki. That leaves 44 cards unaccounted for, of which only seven would win Vicki the hand. That's 16 percent of the cards potentially in play.

I've always liked poker because I've thought of it more as a game than a gamble. I wouldn't buy lottery tickets or "play" the slots – that's pure gambling, with no skill involved. Craps and blackjack are hardly different: knowing the laws of probability helps, but you're still at the mercy of the dice or the cards. Poker is supposed to be a game in which you can win by reading your opponents well, even if you are never dealt the best cards.

But that's only true over time, and I now see why poker is actually closer to gambling than gaming, particularly if you define the 10 hands of one Big Game as the "game". Ten hands is nowhere near enough for skill to dominate luck. Skilled card sharks can make a living out of poker by giving themselves better-than-average odds of winning each hand, and by playing millions and millions of hands to virtually remove luck from the equation: each 60-40 hand in their favor is a crapshoot, but a million 60-40 hands is a jackpot. But how is that different from games like blackjack or roulette, where casinos earn their profits through the same logic? A single customer may win big during a weekend in Vegas; collectively, everyone visiting Vegas during any given weekend will lose more to the casinos than they win.

I'm beginning to think the poker community treats bad beats with too much respect. Everyone accepts that they're part of the game. Why? Aren't they more of a sign that the game itself is flawed? Put it this way: suppose you take the best 5,000 golfers in the world, the best 5,000 tennis players, and the best 5,000 poker players. How often will each game identify the most skilled player? In tennis, the four or five best men in the world between them will win most of the events that they play in, and nearly all of the grand slams. In golf, prior to 2010 Tiger Woods won around a third of the tournaments he entered as a pro, and he finished outside of the top 12 only around 5 percent of the time. In poker? How many players win more than one noteworthy tournament in any given year? In the past 10 or 15 years, how many players have finished in the top 100 of the main event at the World Series of Poker more than once, let alone the top 10? Nobody, with the possible exception of Dan Harrington in 2003 and 2004, has even come close to winning the WSOP twice in that period.

I'm not saying I prefer games with no luck – if I did, I'd play chess and not *Totaler Krieg*. And certainly, games that attempt to simulate history should incorporate randomness. Real generals can't feed perfect variables into a computer and know how their strategies will unfold on the battlefield; when I attack Tripoli at 2:1 odds and roll a '6', I'm able to imagine any number of reasons why my attack might have failed. Bless the English department at Muhlendorf for making me read this passage from Stephen Vincent Benet's *John Brown's Body*:

If you take a flat map
And move wooden blocks upon it strategically
The thing looks well, the blocks behave as they should.
The science of war is moving live men like blocks.
And getting the blocks into place at a fixed moment.
But it takes time to mold your men into blocks,
And flat maps turn into country, where creeks and gullies
Hamper your wooden squares. They stick in the brush,
They are tired and rest, they straggle after ripe blackberries.
And you cannot lift them up in your hands and move them.
– A string of blocks curling smoothly around the left
Of another string of blocks and crunching it up –
It is all so clear on the maps, so clear in the mind,
But the orders are slow, the men in the blocks are slow
To move, when they start they take too long on the way –

The General loses his stars and the block-men die,
In unstrategic defiance of martial law.

I know this poem isn't about wargaming – quite the opposite. But this is what randomness in war looks like. In *Totaler Krieg*, this randomness looks like luck because it arrives in a die-shaped vessel. However, beneath each pip lies a hundred small engagements fought by thousands of men marching across muddy roads and fording creeks and gullies, none of which appear on maps in which each hexagon represents 3,000 square miles. The dice speak of regimental orders misread or poorly implemented by my captains and majors, of gaps in the enemy's line my colonels and generals have failed to spot, of deserters and spies and codebreakers who fed my opponent vital intelligence.

The story of World War II features moments of pure luck, although not as many as one might think. For example, Britain's evacuation of more than 300,000 troops from Dunkirk in 1940 was hugely "lucky" in the sense of being an unexpected triumph in what may have seemed a hopeless situation. However, the Germans really only had themselves to blame: Hitler ordered his panzers to halt, not wanting to risk them in the Flanders mud while their flanks weren't secure, while Goering – not for the last time – promised more than the *Luftwaffe* could deliver. Luck didn't save the British: German decision-making did.

So where does pure luck enter the World War II narrative? Here's my list of the Top Ten Luck-Driven Moments in World War II:

10) The fate of the crew of the *USS Indianapolis*, 30 July 1945 and afterwards: Sunk by a Japanese submarine while sailing alone, each of the ship's three SOS signals were disregarded (one of them was received by a drunken watch commander, while another was thought to be a Japanese prank), causing hundreds of men to die needlessly of exposure. Would rank higher on this list if a decisive turning point of the war were involved.

9) Capturing the Rhine bridge at Remagen, 7 March 1945: How had a bridge over the Rhine survived every German order to blow them up? Not as vital to ending the war as first thought, particularly given how few US troops crossed the bridge before it collapsed, but still a monument to how men don't always behave like blocks and the best-intentioned orders aren't always executed.

8) Nagumo's task force remains undiscovered both before and after the Pearl Harbor attack, December 1941: More a combination of good Japanese planning and horrendous misreading of the available intelligence by the Americans than pure luck, of course, but in a raid so daring, when so many things can go wrong

but don't, luck is on your side. (Honorable mention: this could also be said of the German invasion of Norway.)

7) German leadership at the Second Battle of El Alamein, October 1942: Rommel was away on sick leave when the battle started, and his understudy, General Georg Stumme, died of a heart attack during the initial fighting. These absences didn't determine the battle's outcome, but with the possible exception of D-Day – with Rommel away in Germany for his wife's birthday and many of his subordinates on their way to Rennes for a wargame – I can't think of another time when battlefield leadership was so badly compromised by non-battle-related causes.

6) The weather on D-Day, 6 June 1944: What if Allied meteorologists had been wrong in guessing – and really, it was only an educated guess – that the weather on D-Day would be good enough to support the Normandy invasion? In a worst-case scenario, bad weather could have ruined everything; how would the war have evolved thereafter? (Plus, if the invasion had been postponed, the next suitable dates were marred by what proved to be the worst Channel storms for decades.)

5) Japan's destroyer at Midway, 4 June 1942: American dive-bombers desperately searching for the Japanese carriers near Midway stumbled upon the destroyer *Arashi*, headed for Nagumo's task force at flank speed after diverting to depth-charge a US submarine, and correctly changed course to follow it. Not long thereafter, *Akagi, Kaga* and *Soryu* were on fire, and the naval war in the Pacific had been radically altered.

4) The Mechelen Incident, 10 January 1940: One week before the planned German invasion of Belgium and Holland, an obsolescent Messerschmitt accidentally strayed outside of German airspace, suffered mechanical failure and crash-landed in a Belgian field. The two German aviators aboard failed to destroy the top-secret invasion plans in their possession before they could be confiscated by Belgian officials and analyzed by Allied intelligence experts; Hitler reluctantly postponed the attack indefinitely, at least partly because strategic surprise had been lost (although subsequent bad weather may have forced the postponement anyway), and ordered a review of the invasion plan itself, about which he had become increasingly uncertain. Eventually the *Wehrmacht* discarded its unimaginative reprise of Schlieffen's 1914 plan and adopted von Manstein's daring attack through the Ardennes, a revision which underpinned the spectacular victories of May and June 1940. For want of a good pilot, the battle was…won?

3) Assassination attempt, 20 July 1944: Von Stauffenberg's bomb gets pushed under a table leg, Hitler survives, the war descends into madness for eight-and-a-half additional months.

2) Assassination attempt, 13 March 1943: Von Schlabrendorff's bomb fails to trigger on the flight back from Vinnitsa, Hitler never realizes how close he came to destruction, the war carries on for two more years.

1) Assassination attempt, 8 November 1939: Hitler leaves the Bürgerbräukeller early because of the fog in Munich, Elser's bomb explodes 13 minutes too late, and the war isn't nipped in the bud as it might have been.

Elser's attempt ranks at the top because it carries the most counterfactual weight: in theory, the gap between life or death for tens of millions of people, and untold disruption to the lives of hundreds of millions of others, was 13 minutes or the clearing of fog at a single airport. "Luck" hardly seems the right word for it.

6.

La Coruña is a bustling port on the northwest coast of Galicia, near the great Spanish naval base at Ferrol. According to Wikipedia – and when I value specificity more than accuracy, as when researching a school report I don't really care about, where better to turn? – more than 400,000 people currently live in its metropolitan area, and if you were to tunnel straight down from La Coruña to its antipode on the other side of the earth, you'd emerge in Christchurch, New Zealand. "Corunna", as the British call it, hosted an important battle in 1809 in which Sir John Moore died while successfully evacuating his army from Iberia to England ahead of Marshal Soult's marauding French, but World War II mostly passed it by. Thirteen of its citizens died in Mauthausen concentration camp, having been handed over to the Nazis by Franco, and a German submarine – U-514 – was attacked by a British Liberator bomber very near the port on 8 July 1943 and sunk with all hands lost. But that's about it.

In my ongoing *Totaler Krieg* campaign against Dennis, however, La Coruña has become the nerve center of the Allied war effort in Western Europe. It's been a crazy game. Although the Mediterranean remains an Axis lake, Dennis never managed to expel me from the Middle East; by keeping and then growing a foothold on the Persian Gulf, I've tied up several German armies that Dennis would prefer to send to Russia. He launched Barbarossa in Summer 1942 and broke through in the Caucasus to capture my Objective Hex at Baku, on the Caspian Sea, but with so much firepower diverted southwards, the main German thrust from Poland initially stalled near Smolensk and Dnepropetrovsk. And in attempting to garrison every Atlantic port from Narvik to Casablanca, Dennis cut a few corners and I found a weak link, launching Operation Crusader to invade La Coruña and create a decent bridgehead. Now with American help, I hold a perimeter two hexes deep in front of La Coruña, from Oporto in northern Portugal to Oviedo on the Bay of Biscay. As we reach November-December 1943 – with V-E Day not scheduled until 1946, thanks to the late outbreak of Total War – Dennis reveals the Festung Europa card, content to place the No Retreat marker at Axis Tide 3.

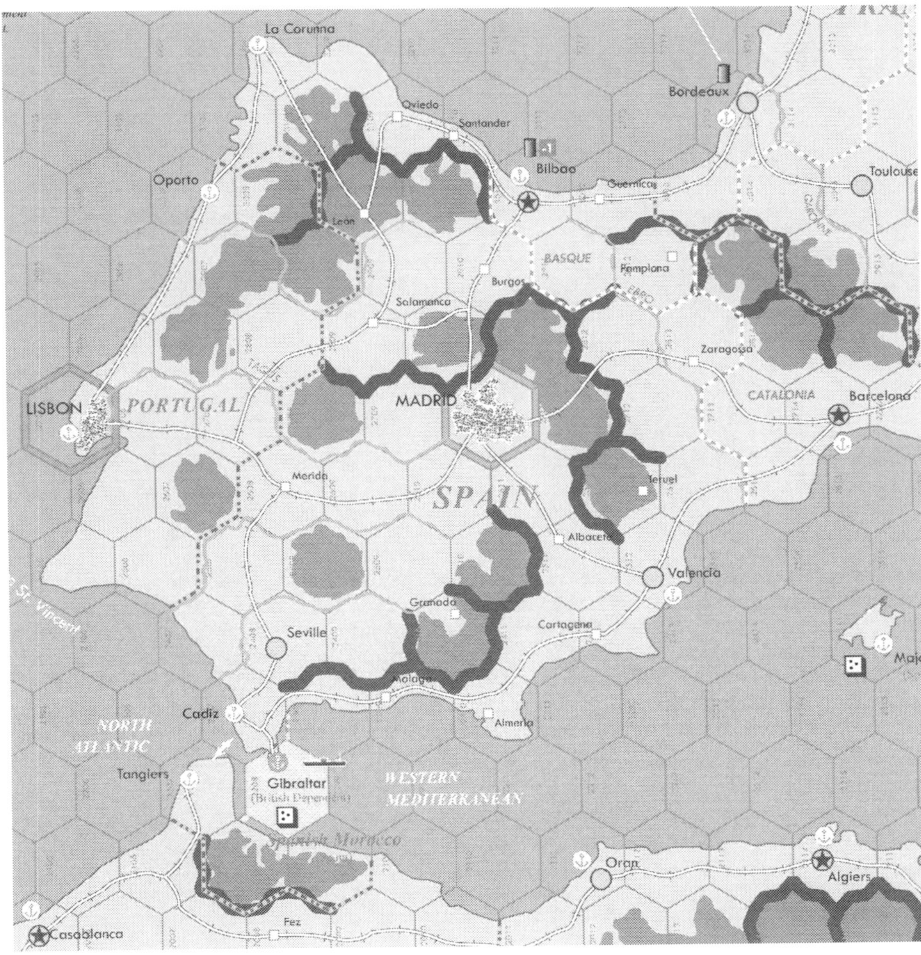

Fig. 5 – La Coruña ("La Corunna" on the Totaler Krieg *map) and Iberia*

This is my second game of *Totaler Krieg* in which the Allies have established a major foothold in Spain. Many within the *Totaler Krieg* community believe the Allies should almost always declare war on Spain, as a cheap and easy way of returning to the Continent. The terrain in Iberia matches Italy's for difficulty, but the available frontage is far wider, and the Pyrenees are less formidable than the Alps. While Madrid is much farther from Berlin than Rome is, any advance across France from south to north can be supported by outflanking amphibious invasions, so the distance from Bordeaux to Calais is far shorter in practice than it appears on the map. And while I can't imagine many circumstances in which the US would have declared war on a neutral country at all, let alone for purely strategic reasons, I wonder how much pro-Republican sentiment would have bubbled to the surface if such an attack had occurred. How many Spaniards would have greeted the Allies as liberators, with Napoleon circa 1807 being compared to Hitler in 1942? Quite a few, I reckon.

In my half of November-December 1943, I bypass Operation Torch to reveal Trident Conference. The point of kicking the Axis out of Africa is to then move on Italy, but I'm already back on the Continent, so why bother opening a new front? Instead, I'll save Torch's firepower for a season in which I can better use it. So I slowly continue building up my Spanish bridgehead: one British infantry step convoys to La Coruña during Operational Movement, and an American armor step follows suit during Reserve Movement.

"How many of my steps do you think will convoy to La Coruña over the course of the game?" I ask Dennis.

"A lot," he idly responds.

"How many hundreds of thousands of troops?"

"Yeah."

"The lives of everyone in sleepy La Coruña are going to be transformed forever, aren't they?" I sit up. "Think about it. My engineers will be hugely expanding the port facilities even as we speak, extracting every last ounce of capacity. Eisenhower and Patton, at the very least, will now be living there along with their headquarters staff. England won't be totally overrun by the Yanks and American culture – Spain will. I mean, the history of La Coruña, of Galicia, of Spain itself will become radically different no matter what happens."

Under his breath, Dennis mutters, "Who cares?"

"What?"

"Never mind." Dennis puts an elbow on the table, rests his chin in his palm and scrapes at his beard with his fingernails. He looks tired. "You're very sweet," he says.

"Why?"

"In a demented, demented way."

"How's that?"

Dennis sighs. "Well, for starters you make it seem as though all of this matters." His eyes light up slightly.

"Our game?"

"Yeah."

"Hmph."

"It doesn't." Dennis smirks.

"I know that."

"And I know you know that, which is why it's sweet. And demented."

I smile. "You said 'for starters'?"

Dennis jerks his chin into the air again. "You wanna take a short break? I could use a drink."

"Sure, OK."

I grab Dennis a can of Diet Coke from the fridge and pour myself a glass of tepid water, and we retire to the living room, sitting on sofas on opposite sides of the massive wooden coffee table in the center of the room. I've tried gaming on this table before, but I've concluded that playing wargames on a coffee table while sitting on a sofa will ultimately benefit a chiropractor more than me. Instead, Dennis slumps into the middle of his sofa and rests one of his sneakered feet on the table, risking my father's wrath should he emerge from his labors upstairs. It's dark, windy and chilly outside, and an early breath of winter penetrates the house because on principle, Dad refuses to employ our heating system before November. So it's sweaters for everyone.

Dennis takes a sip from his drink and sighs. "You were saying?" I ask.

"It's not a big deal or anything," he says. "But you do like to make mountains out of our little molehills."

"In what way?"

"Well, you know. 'Expanding the port facilities of La Coruña'?"

"I was just musing about what's going on in our game. Under the hood."

"I get that."

"To build up an army from scratch in northwestern Spain, an army that will be capable of crossing Spain, France and Belgium into Germany, you have to build a lot of infrastructure."

"But this is my point." Dennis shakes his head. "Who *thinks* like that?"

"You have to think like that if you want to get the job done."

"You have to think like that if you're Eisenhower and actually have to get the job done. You don't have to get the job done. You're a kid pushing pieces around a map of Europe."

"But that's why we play wargames, isn't it?"

"To pretend that we are Eisenhower? No, not really."

I rest my glass on the coffee table. "That's the whole essence of this hobby. *Totaler Krieg* puts you in the shoes of the great captains of World War II and lets you make the same types of decisions they had to make. Other games do the same with different wars and leaders at different levels of seniority. Without that, without the history that underpins the game, you're left with a fancy version of chess or backgammon. Why do you keep playing?"

Dennis smiles. "It's a question of degrees," he says. "I like blasting the Nazis back to the Stone Age as much as the next guy. They make good villains. And I like having a go with the Nazis too, because it's fun to play make-believe."

"That's something an eight-year-old would say," I say.

"Yeah? Well, maybe that's me. Maybe I'm Tom Hanks in the movie *Big*, and you're the little kid."

"So *Totaler Krieg* is just a fancy first-person shooter to you, but with a bigger rulebook?"

"And no need for good hand-eye coordination, thankfully. You have no idea how much I suck at video games."

"And that's it? That can't be it, because you obviously know a bit of history."

Dennis pauses thoughtfully. After sipping his drink, he says, "I think gaming has always driven my interest in history, instead of the other way round. I'll play a game or read a rulebook on a topic I've never studied, and then I'll watch a movie or read a book as a companion to the game. The more I learn, the more I enjoy the game. If *Totaler Krieg* were about werewolves or Martians, I probably wouldn't enjoy it as much. Although actually, *War of the Ring* is a wargame based on *The Lord of the Rings*, and I enjoyed it more after reading the books and watching the movies even though hobbits aren't real."

"So you're a multimedia guy, basically."

"Something like that."

"Do you collect the action figures as well? Why not go all the way and become a miniatures gamer?"

"Like I said – bad hand-eye coordination. I could never paint the damn things. But even if I could, that's beside the point: this is what I do. I play board wargames. And I like them, mainly because they're fun to play."

I nod my head. "On that, we are in agreement."

"Good – so, let's get back to you."

"Really?" I sigh.

"We were talking about Eisenhower, and I said it was a question of degrees. I enjoy *Totaler Krieg* as a piece of historical entertainment. However, sometimes you get so wrapped up in the pretend history we're creating, it feels like you're in a role-playing game. You don't get to live in Hitler's Bunker when you're the Germans, and you don't get to give real speeches to the 101st Airborne on the eve of D-Day when you're Eisenhower." Dennis waves a finger toward the gaming room. "And those people in La Coruña whose lives are being changed? They aren't real."

"Your powers of deduction astound me, Watson. What's your point? That I'm more into the finer details of history than you are?"

Dennis flinches. "We can drop this if you want to," he says. "I'm not trying to be a pain. I just think it's funny how much you care about the 'finer details' of fake history."

"Counterfactuals," I correct.

"Make-believe," says Dennis.

"No," I insist. "Make-believe is what little girls play when they're holding dolls or dressing up as princesses. Counterfactuals are a critical weapon in the arsenal of a good historian. To know what really happened and why, you need to fully understand both how probable the actual outcome was and also what else could have happened instead. The more you look at counterfactuals, the more you see that the course of history is littered with low-probability events. And the more you understand that, the more you come to appreciate the Butterfly Effect and the fragility of the strands of history that make us who we are."

Dennis chuckles to himself. "So sweet, and so demented."

"What? It's true."

"You're, like, the youngest existentialist I've ever heard of. Dude, you're a sophomore in high school."

"I'm a junior in high school."

"Do your friends at school know that you talk like this?"

"No! I mean, no, and it's probably best if we kept it that way."

Dennis laughs out loud. "Don't worry – your secret is safe with me."

"That's not funny," I moan.

"It wasn't meant to be. But it's funny that someone with so much of his life still to live is already so interested in what might have been."

I sigh. "Why am I always getting psychoanalyzed?"

"Because it's so easy?" Dennis smiles and stands up. "C'mon, let's get back to the game. You can take your existentialist angst out on me by leading the good people of La Coruña to better, more prosperous lives."

"Shut up." I stand up as well.

"I bet there's a thriving black market in La Coruña right now," says Dennis.

"I bet there is too," I wearily respond.

"Lots of prostitutes in La Coruña are lining up to sleep with the GIs on leave in the rear."

"Yep."

"And when I said 'in the rear', I meant…"

"Yeah, I figured it out, thanks."

❖ ❖ ❖

Freddie's right: Homecoming sucks.

The high concept of Homecoming makes sense – old people get to remember their youth, while young people get to pretend they're adults. Only it doesn't actually work like that. On a scale from "zero" to "sad", it's hard for me to tell which group scores higher: the codgers who ought to have forgotten about high school 40 years ago, or the teenagers who rent fancy dresses and fancy cars but become utterly childish as soon as they enter the dance hall. If Dennis needs more tutoring on the difference between "counterfactuals" and "make-believe", I could easily lecture him about it right now, within Naehring Gymnasium at Muhlendorf High School.

Don't get me wrong – the school put a lot of time and effort into decorating the gym, and the "Hollywood" theme works better than I'd expected. The red carpet, rope railing and spotlights at the entrance are a nice touch; the music system is good, atmospheric but not throbbing; and many of the props in the hall were carefully thought out and give a sense of occasion. There's a horribly kitsch rainbow of "popcorn" – four-foot boxes of red and white stripes connected by an arch of yellow and white balloons held in place by mesh netting – but that probably seemed a decent idea on paper. Less forgivable are some of the girls' dresses; irregular necklines don't look good on supermodels at the Oscars, so why 16-year-olds wearing fake tans and enough eye-shadow to restore a Picasso think they're a good idea is beyond me.

But all of this is window dressing. The real issue is that several hundred teenagers shouldn't be cloistered together for three hours with little to do but enjoy each other's company or try to sneak alcohol past airport-level security. Melvyn and Vicki are loving themselves, dancing and chatting and nuzzling into one another, and I'm sure the other 10 or 15 legitimate couples in the hall equally appreciate their time together. But for the rest of us? It's a big, loud, dark room with few distractions in it. Who thought this was a good idea?

And don't get me started about Melissa: she's been a ball of hyperactivity all evening. The six of us – Melissa and me, Melvyn and Vicki, and Chris and his no-longer-a-mystery date, Elaine Patterson – split the cost of a limousine that picked each of us up in turn, took us to a nice Italian restaurant for a quiet meal, and then dropped us off at Muhlendorf for the dance. Or that was the plan, anyway. I was last to be picked up; I was feeling good, having won my *Totaler Krieg* tournament quarterfinal against Steven Ginsberg several hours earlier. It was a tense final turn, and my move took a lot of planning, checking and re-checking to ensure I hadn't miscalculated the 5-in-6 chance I thought I had of capturing Vienna to win. You don't play a game for three-and-a-half months just to stupidly fritter away a well-earned victory! But I got everything right, the dice server was kind, and my relief and delight was substantial. I sent my thanks to Steven for his sportsmanship and then reminisced about my stout defense of Moscow, my coup de main at Naples in early 1943, and of course the crazy Hitler Assassinated/Peace Offer combination that nearly snatched defeat from my jaws of victory. You have to work very hard to win a wargame via e-mail, and you're thoroughly entitled to savor every victory.

Slightly too late for comfort, I then showered and began to change. The limo arrived as I was still putting on my rented tuxedo; Dad answered the door for me, and then embarrassed me in front of Melissa, Chris and Melvyn by insisting upon adjusting not only my bow tie but my cummerbund and boutonnière as well.

"I think you look just luurrvely," meowed Melissa, herself in a fetching, emerald green satin dress.

"I think he looks crooked," said Dad.

"Why do you care?" I asked him.

"Because that's what fathers are for," he said.

"Why are you wearing a cummerbund anyway?" asked Chris, himself sporting a matching yellow bow tie and suspenders.

"Why *am* I wearing a cummerbund?" I squirmed. "It's not a belt, it's not suspenders, and it's not attractive. It's the appendix of men's fashion."

"I think you look very nice!" exclaimed Melissa.

"Me too!" smiled Melvyn.

"Me three!" smirked Chris. Melvyn's and Chris's partners had remained in the limo.

So we headed to dinner, the brief novelty of six people talking together in the backseat of one car hardly justifying our expense. At the restaurant, the conversation was spoiled by Melissa's loud fascination with reality television. Maybe she was nervous, or maybe she'd had five cups of coffee that afternoon, but the meal reminded me why we rarely talk much. So while Melvyn and Chris made nice with their dates and everyone talked about MTV's latest crime against humanity, I silently munched my fettuccine and pondered how tough it was for my Western Allies to cross France in 1944 without any Soviet pressure in the East.

By the time we reached the dance itself, I was ready to go home. Melissa and I quickly got our picture taken together, and then she started pinballing around the room, repeatedly dragging me onto the dance floor and just as quickly bopping off without me to chat with different groups of friends. Her throat must be stronger than mine; at her current pace, I'd be hoarse already from trying to talk above the music. Currently, she's laughing and gesticulating wildly within a group of eight or nine girls at the edge of the dancing, so I've snuck outside for a moment to catch my breath. I call Freddie on my cell phone.

"Yo," says Freddie after we are connected. "You're missing a fantastic game. Eight-eight, bottom of the seventh, bases loaded, one out."

"Crap," I respond. Game Three of the World Series is on right now. "You're missing absolutely nothing, by the way."

"Melissa?"

"Yeah, she's a wild one."

"Go back in there and apologize for whatever you've done."

"Me? I've found some paint thinner I'm about to swallow. Can you send an ambulance for me?"

"I did warn you about this."

"Yes, you did."

"Hang on…" I can just hear the screaming coming through the television as Freddie falls silent. "Wow, that's something you don't see every day. Sacrifice fly to right, bang-bang play at the plate and the runner is safe, only now they've thrown to third base and it looks like he's out on appeal. I guess the runner left third early."

"Damn."

"So that's the inning over, only the manager is still out there, screaming at the umpires."

"I don't even want to know. Goodnight, Freddie."

"Later."

I breathe deeply and gaze across the dark campus, peacefully bathed in gentle spotlights. Then I get frisked for booze on my way back into the gym by a security guard, even though I was in plain view of him throughout the four minutes I spent outside. In the drinks room just inside the glass doors, I pour myself a cup of pink punch and sit in a hard plastic chair at the end of a long set of tables covered in frizzy white paper and silver tinsel. I wonder how long it will take for Melissa to find me.

Three boys – sophomores, I think – wobble toward the punch bowl at the other end of the room. They help themselves, liberally ladling pink liquid onto the tablecloth as well as their cups, giggling loudly and talking over each other with loud voices. Amid general laughter, one of them bellows, "I AM SO BUZZED RIGHT NOW!" I put my elbow on the table, brace my cheek against my hand and wonder what they all want to be when they grow up.

Rebecca Fowler, one of my AP European History classmates, gives the boys a wide berth and fills a cup from the bowl at my end of the table. We grunt hellos at one another. After a pause, as Rebecca sips her drink I nod toward the three boys and say, "You know, in 1968 a student in Paris painted a piece of graffiti on a wall that said, 'I AM A MARXIST OF THE GROUCHO FACTION'. Another student painted the message, 'I DON'T LIKE TO WRITE ON WALLS'."

Rebecca laughs. "You trying to say something?" she asks.

"Maybe." I crack a wan smile. "The aimlessness of modern youth, I guess."

"What do you mean?"

"I don't know…take a look at them." I point at the three boys, their backs now turned as they stumble toward the dance floor. "What kind of graffiti would they write?"

"In 1968, the students believed they could change the system," says Rebecca. "And humor was more than a way of making people laugh – it was a way of making them notice."

"It feels like 1968 was a century ago."

"But it must have been lovely to be there, and to be a part of it. Don't you think?"

"I'm not sure." I sigh through my nose. "Do you want my considered opinion?"

"Sure."

"Nearly every Prague Spring is followed by a more powerful counter-revolution. The original French Revolution led to the Directory, and then to Napoleon. The Russian Revolution gave way to Stalin. In 1968, De Gaulle remained firm, and the Czechs themselves were invaded by the Soviet Union and its Warsaw Pact allies. And in 1968 we elected Nixon, a true counter-revolutionary if ever there were one."

Rebecca laughs again. "That's a pretty cynical view of history. Sure, the Czechs suffered, but don't you think 1968 directly led to 1990 and 1991?"

I smirk. "How do you know so much about Czechoslovakia?"

"I went to Prague last summer with my parents. We toured Europe for a month."

"Really?"

"Or maybe I just like knowing something about the world I live in. Just like you, if I remember correctly."

"Ha!" I sit up in my chair. "So, Rebecca Fowler, if you were to take a spray can of paint to the front office at Muhlendorf, what would you write on the walls?"

"First of all, call me Becs." A sweet, innocent smile peeks through her lipstick.

"OK, Becs."

"But to answer the question, I wouldn't want to compete with the Class of '68, for humor or imagery. What about you?"

"Honestly? I probably would have been a Young Republican in 1968 – part of Nixon's law-and-order brigade. And if I'd been forced to paint something illicit on a wall, I would have drawn an arrow and written, 'THIS WAY TO NAEHRING GYMNASIUM'."

"Good one. OK, I'll play." Becs squints and purses her lips in thought, her left hand arched gracefully on her hip, the fingers of her right hand drumming on her thigh while she thinks. She's wearing a blue velvet dress that covers her shoulders but not her calves. She starts to speak, then exhales and pauses to reconsider her answer. Then she says, "I would probably write, 'IF IT WEREN'T FOR…'"

"There you are!" Melissa bursts into the drinks room, escorted by Elaine and another junior named Candi. "Stop hiding and come *dance* with me, Sean! Oh. Hi, Rebecca."

"Hello," says Becs.

"I'm coming, I'm coming – I just needed some air." To Becs, I say, "Hold that thought, OK?"

"I will."

Becs grins and reaches for her drink as I'm tugged again toward the dance floor. I playfully roll my eyes; Elaine glares at me like a truant officer.

Thankfully, Chris intercepts us just inside the hall. "There he is!" he beams. "What's going on?"

"I'm not sure. I've just seen a vision. Or had a vision. Or something."

"Whatever it is, I think that's the first smile I've seen on your face since we ordered dinner. Welcome back."

A Latin rhythm shakes through the sound system, and Melissa starts gyrating with more enthusiasm than decorum, hips and elbows flying in all directions. I can't suppress a guffaw, and my own feet start to twitch in sympathy. What a weird evening. I wonder who Becs came to the dance with?

PART TWO

1.

I meant what I said, by the way: I would have supported Nixon in 1968. Rules control the fun – that's true in games, and it's true in life. Graffiti, no matter how clever, is vandalism, and you can't condone vandalism in an orderly society. Indeed, hippies, yippies and anarchists couldn't exist in a country run by hippies, yippies or anarchists, and for them to piggyback on so many real protest movements in 1968 was reprehensible. Their only merit is that they at least stood for something, which is more than can be said for most of their latter-day counterparts at Muhlendorf.

On the Monday morning after the Homecoming dance, I seek out Becs before school, among the double-decker rows of weather-beaten, mustard-yellow lockers on the second floor of Building 2. The hall is bubbling with adolescent noise; Becs is wearing a saggy maroon sweater, a pleated black-and-white plaid skirt, white tights and black loafers, and her long, brown ponytail is held by a beaded white scrunchie. The inside panel of her locker is tidy and unadorned by superficiality.

"Did you have a nice time on Saturday?" she asks me.

"It got better as the evening went on." I grin. "You?"

"About the same, I guess. It was fun."

"I've got a quick question for you. I was wondering if you'd, y'know, be interested in forming an AP European History study group. With me. The two of us."

"With you?" Becs flashes a warm, toothy smile. "You don't really need to study for that class, do you? You seem to know all of the answers better than Mister Prendergast does."

"I've got some skills, yes." My face reddens. "But, uh, my knowledge doesn't always extend to the parts of history I don't like."

"There are parts of history you don't like?"

"You have no idea."

"Huh." Becs smiles again.

"So anyway, I thought you might be able to help me out. And maybe I can help you out as well. Or something. What do you think?"

"Sounds good."

"Great. Great. Um…who did you go to Homecoming with?"

"Hugh Johnson."

"Oh, right. Is he, I mean, are the two of you…?"

"No. Definitely not."

"Ah. Just curious."

"Of course."

"Oh yeah, I meant to ask, what were you going to say the other night before Melissa whisked me away? What was your graffiti going to be?"

"Oh. I forgot."

"Really? I think you started, 'IF IT WEREN'T FOR…', and then you were interrupted."

"No." Now Becs is blushing.

"What do you mean?" I ask.

"Sorry. I mean, I remember what I was going to say, but please don't make me say it. It's terrible."

"C'mon! It's OK."

"No, I would make a fool out of myself."

"No, you wouldn't. I promise."

"Anyway, I'm not going to tell you. And that's that."

"Got it. Maybe some other time."

Becs gently sags with relief. She closes her locker and says, "I've gotta do something before my first class, so…"

"No problem. Let me know when you want to start our study group, OK?"

"I will. Bye!"

"See ya."

Becs bounces away, ponytail flapping from side to side. I rest an elbow against her locker and breathe deeply…

"Boo!" A fist bangs into the locker above my right ear, and I lurch forward involuntarily. "What's up?" asks Chris.

"Bloody hell," I say. "It's Monday morning!"

"Yep," he says. "So you're starting up a study group with Becs?"

"Word travels fast."

"What about?"

"AP Euro."

"No kidding. I'm in."

"You're…oh, no you're not." I frown.

"What? Why not?"

"Because."

"Really, I need help with all of the names and dates and stuff."

"That's the bit I'm good at – names and dates. So we won't be looking at them, so we won't be able to help you. Goodbye." I start weaving toward my locker ahead of first-period Chemistry.

Chris persists, flitting along behind me. "Is something going on here?"

"No. Not really."

"Not really? What's with you and Melissa? Was Saturday night that bad for you?"

"No! It was fine. It wasn't great, but it was fine."

"So what's going on?"

I stop at the end of the hall, take a deep breath and look straight at Chris. "I had a quick chat with Becs the other night. She seems interested in history. She seems very interested in history, actually."

"Yeah?"

"So I sorta want to see if she's interested in history like I am."

"You're a history dork."

"Pretty much."

"And you think she might be a dork like you."

"Maybe."

"From one quick chat the other night."

"It was very quick."

"This was at the Homecoming dance?"

"It was."

Chris smirks. "You really are hopeless," he says.

"Yes. Yes I am."

"So what about Melissa?"

"The one has nothing to do with the other."

"You sure?"

"She's not taking AP European, is she?"

"Fair point." The bell rings our five-minute warning before first period. Chris looks at his watch and asks, "What class do I have now? Never mind – later!"

And he is gone. I shake my head and trudge toward the first class of a new week. I detest Chemistry, but some things must be endured.

❖ ❖ ❖

On my eighth birthday, my parents gave me a copy of *The American Heritage Picture History of World War II.* Although I've worn out the book's binding, to the point that pages snap away from the spine if I turn them carelessly, I still look at it from time to time. Its 610 pages of text hold up surprisingly well, but its 720 photographs were its star attraction to a young child who had never felt history come to life before. I had only ever lived in full color, and the black-and-white world of those pictures was impossibly exotic to me, even before I first noticed the Spitfire's elegant curves and the meticulous angles of an *Essex*-class aircraft carrier's flight deck. (I myself have moved on from such mechanical fetishization – I'm a "form follows function" guy when it comes to such things, and the Spitfire drawing hanging above my desk at home is a prepubescent relic – but many history geeks never do, and I can understand why.)

Among the book's many images detailing the horrors of war is a picture I still can't shake. Its central character is a gaunt figure, a man likely of Jewish origin with long, Slavic cheekbones. He stands at the precipice of an open mass grave, staring forlornly and uncomprehendingly at the camera, with dead bodies visibly stacked beneath him at the bottom of the photo. To his right is a German soldier, pointing a pistol at his head; behind him is a queue of other men and women in civilian clothes, each shepherded forward by other soldiers and waiting in turn to receive a bullet in the brain. It's a haunting picture that asks me many questions, both metaphysical and mundane: What goes through a man's mind, seconds before being murdered? Why would the victims simply queue for their fate like that and not offer resistance or try to escape? How could anyone impassively photograph a scene like this? When the photographer finished developing his film, how much would his sense of professional pride at the quality of his work be tainted by any understanding of what he had witnessed? How does a photographer come to be at that place at that time to take that picture? Was he the *Wehrmacht's* official Chronicler of Atrocities, had he signed up as a war correspondent and made a regrettable career diversion, or would he have gladly traded his Leica for a Luger and shot the victims himself? Is a pistol really the best weapon with which to conduct mass executions? What happens to the queue of victims while the executioner loads a new ammunition clip, or when he runs out of bullets altogether and has to wait for a new supply – does everyone just shuffle their feet in embarrassment, like supermarket patrons when the checkout lady calls several times over the loudspeaker for a price check? Or do different shooters take turns, like blackjack dealers in a casino?

Many horrible photographs were taken during World War II, so one might ask why I remember this particular image so well instead of, say, a photo of stacked skeletons at Auschwitz or any other depiction of carnage or brutality. Well, one of my fourth-grade friends – a kid named Stewart, the sort of friend you have before your tastes in friends become discriminating – discovered this image while flipping through the book at my house, and he thought it was hilarious. "Look at that guy!" he exclaimed, pointing and laughing. "His face, and the gun right next to his head!"

"He's about to get shot," I said.

"I know!" he said.

I forced out my own nervous half-chuckle. Stewart looked at the photo again, pointed at the condemned man one last time and shook his head, then continued thumbing toward the book's back cover.

It took me a long time to deconstruct that conversation. First, I thought Stewart was a complete idiot. Last year, I stumbled across the photo again and broke into a fast, chilling sweat: had I accidentally uncovered a psychopath? Was it my duty to inform the authorities? Now, though, I've come to view that exchange more sympathetically. Most fourth-graders couldn't begin to mentally process an image like that. Stewart was looking at an odd, Eastern European face contorted by stress and despair into something virtually alien; the gun pointing at it might as well have been held by Yosemite Sam. What response to this should you expect? Besides, laughter can be a defense mechanism; if you didn't laugh at some of these things, you'd surely cry. Stranger than Stewart's response, I now realize, is my parents' willingness to expose me to images like these at the age of eight. Perhaps my gaming hobby is an attempt to create order out of the chaos I've studied for more than half of my life to-date? That thought has crossed my mind, not that I intend to explore it too closely.

Like that book, my first wargame was unexpectedly foist upon me: for my 11th birthday, my Uncle Martin gave me a copy of the original version of *Axis & Allies*. Uncle Martin is my Dad's brother; he's a corporate lawyer living in London, and I've only met him once or twice. I can't remember receiving any other presents from him, so I'm not sure what prompted his life-changing act of altruism, but *Axis & Allies* immediately grabbed my attention, if not my intellect. *Axis & Allies* was first published by Milton Bradley, now part of the Hasbro empire, and can still be found on the shelves of major toy stores; as such, it is the rare wargame that non-wargamers might have heard of. It also comes with loads of cool toys: tiny scale models of tanks and battleships and anti-aircraft guns, and even tiny airplane models that fit on the decks of not-quite-as-tiny aircraft carriers. All of these models are placed and do battle on a map of the entire world, and as you roll the dice and the various armies sway back and forth across the map, it kinda looks like World War II.

But then I played the game, and I quickly realized that *Axis & Allies* is just for boys who like toys – any resemblance between it and World War II is purely coincidental. The map is a joke: instead of hexes, it is divided into connecting areas too huge to allow any semblance of tactics. For example, a single area called "Eastern Europe" encompasses a huge tract of land from Estonia to Bulgaria – in theory, the Soviets could attack out of "Karelia S.S.R." (i.e., Leningrad) into "Eastern Europe" and encircle Axis units trapped in "Ukraine S.S.R.". Meanwhile, due east of "Eastern Europe" one passes through "Ukraine S.S.R." and then "Caucasus" (which contains Stalingrad), before arriving in "Russia", The latter is east of the Caspian Sea but contains Moscow; I love counterfactual history, but counterfactual geography? As for the game itself, Japan is capable of overrunning all of China, India, Australia or even Alaska and Western Canada, while Germany can blitz through Kazakhstan or Persia and link up with the Japanese or drive south from "Anglo Egypt Sudan" through "Kenya Rhodesia" and into South Africa. There are no politics or diplomacy; the combat system is barely one step up from *Risk*; the production system is dependent upon immovable and indestructible factories; need I go on?

Many people like *Axis & Allies* purely as a game, independent of its historicity, but its main purpose for me was to instill a thirst that needed quenching. So I searched on the internet for alternatives and found Consimworld and its alter ego, BoardGameGeek.com. BoardGameGeek focuses largely on "Eurogames", loosely themed strategy games like *Settlers of Catan* and *Ticket to Ride* and *Carcassonne* that tend to play fairly quickly – sort of like *Monopoly*, but for people who enjoy thinking, and thereby several orders of magnitude more interesting. But BoardGameGeek does also feature wargames and hosts an exhaustive library of images, user reviews, discussions and downloads encompassing nearly every wargame that has ever existed. If I want to discuss a wargame in depth, or military history as filtered through the prism of the gaming hobby, I go to Consimworld, but if I want to see what a wargame looks like, or understand how it plays at a very basic level, I go to "the Geek". And kudos to the site for truth in advertising: everything you need to know about BoardGameGeek is in the title.

So, presented with an unimagined cornucopia of gaming possibilities, I began figuring out what I wanted to play, a challenging game in and of itself. If you want to simulate a war or a specific battle even remotely famous in the Western world, there's probably a game for it, and some topics – Waterloo, Gettysburg, D-Day/Normandy, the Battle of the Bulge, etc. – have been covered many, many times over. There are grand strategic, strategic, operational and tactical games: in some games one counter can represent one soldier and maps feature individual hills, houses, walls and even trees, while in others a counter can equal an army group and the map covers one or more continents. The rules for some games fit on one sheet of paper, while the rules for others like *A World at War* could kindle enough fires to keep all of Saskatchewan warm throughout the winter.

The hobby's rich diversity is both its greatest strength and its most frustrating weakness: wargamers always have many games to choose from, but any given game isn't likely to get played. In the 1970s, when board wargaming was arguably at its zenith, every game published by the two principal wargame companies – Avalon Hill and Simulations Publications, Inc. (SPI) – attracted a sizeable following. Their highest sellers sold hundreds of thousands of copies, and their in-house magazines (*The General* and *Strategy & Tactics*) offered strategy tips, game variants and even classified "Opponents Wanted" listings. If you wanted to play a wargame, chances were high that any wargamers living near you would know the game and would have studied it closely. Nowadays, many wargamers own hundreds or even thousands of rarely played games which mostly languish in semi-permanent storage on bookshelves or in attics.

Plus, gaming tastes are different. I like the huge scale and sweep of grand strategic games and seeing my actions change the course of world history, unlike tactical games in which the fate individual tanks or platoons of soldiers always feels self-contained. But I'm not just a grand strategic gamer: I'm a grand strategic gamer whose favorite conflict is World War II, who wants to solve tactical puzzles within a grand strategic focus, who isn't a control freak and enjoys having to respond to game-generated circumstances, and who is more fascinated by rules and subsystems relating to politics and diplomacy than technology and production. Rules complexity is also a thorny issue: too few rules and a game won't feel sufficiently realistic, but too many rules and I'll struggle to keep them in my head.

Now, by my unscientific count at least 25 grand strategic World War II games covering the war in Europe have been published and attracted a modicum of attention. I've researched most of these games, and *Totaler Krieg* comes by far the closest to meeting all of my criteria, which is why I focus most of my gaming energy on it. But there can't be more than a few hundred avid *Totaler Krieg* players in the world, and only a small minority of them actively post about the game on Consimworld. If I and my fellow gamers had fewer options available to us, would we perhaps be less persnickety and more willing to find common ground with potential opponents? Are the many gamers who continually purchase games they'll never play responsible for unnaturally supporting the hobby's over-extension?

At least e-mail and other online gaming options make it possible to find a perfect gaming partner, even if only via long-distance relationships. But finding face-to-face opponents with matching tastes is tougher than pushing your panzers to the Urals against a competent Soviet defense. I guess I'm lucky to have Dennis, who repeatedly plays *Totaler Krieg* to a decent standard with me even though he'd happily play any other game in his own massive collection if only I'd give him the satisfaction. I should remind myself of this more often – for all of his warts, Dennis lets me keep the physical board in "board wargaming".

❖ ❖ ❖

The final session of my latest game with Dennis kicks off in June-July 1945 – remember, because Dennis waited an extra year to invade Russia, the game won't end until mid-1946. Spain is now empty of enemies, and life in La Coruña is reverting to normalcy, but my Soviets are behind schedule, stalled at the gates of Kiev and Minsk. Dennis has withdrawn from the Middle East; the Turks have been pushed back to Istanbul, and I've successfully invaded Crete. But I'm surely still the underdog.

In the first half of June-July 1945, Dennis tidies his defenses either side of the Pripet Marshes – from Riga to Minsk and from Kiev to Nikolaev – before looking to the West. He still holds a solid line of five hexes from Bordeaux to the Franco-Spanish border on the Mediterranean, from which he'll need to conduct a fighting retreat until the weather turns in September-October. In real life, it's an unseasonably warm evening for early November, and Dennis is wearing a lime green T-shirt with the words "BONDAI BEACH SURF SHOP" in loud yellow and orange letters drawn beneath an abstract tiger and a messy image of a surfer riding a wave in black ink.

"It's an interesting balancing act you have there in France," I say to Dennis. "How much do you send to the south, and how much do you keep in the north?" While most of my Western Allied forces are in Spain, I have a strong HQ and two American armies in England, poised to cross the Channel if given the opportunity.

"I have to guard against the reverse Anvil," says Dennis.

"Exactly – the reverse Anvil. I like that. Or the reverse Anvil-Dragoon." Operation Anvil-Dragoon was the historical invasion of southern France in August 1944.

"Which part was Anvil and which part was Dragoon?" asks Dennis.

"Anvil was the operation's nickname during the planning stages, and then it was changed to Dragoon prior to its execution," I respond.

"So it's not like Market-Garden, where Market was the airborne element and Garden the ground forces."

"Right. It's more like how Sledgehammer became Overlord."

"Ah."

As Dennis studies the map, he pokes a fingernail between his upper front teeth, scrapes up to his gum, then reaches down and removes a German infantry corps from the map with that same finger.

"I've got a question for you," I say.

"Mmmm-hmmm." Dennis remains fixated upon France.

"Are you married?"

Now Dennis looks up. "What do you think?"

"I don't know – I'm just asking."

"No, I'm not married."

"Have you ever been married?"

"No, I've never been married."

"Oh. OK." Dennis pushes his glasses up his nose, looks down again, then reaches with his tweezers for a fortress counter in his Force Pool and carefully lowers it into Metz – another brick for his West Wall.

"Do you have a 'partner'?" I ask.

Dennis stares at me, over his glasses with the tops of his eyes. "No, I don't have a partner," he says.

"Have you ever had a partner?"

"Um…"

"I mean, have you ever had a civil partnership or anything like that?"

"No."

"Ever lived with another woman?"

"No."

"Ever lived with another man?"

"Yes."

"Wait – what? Seriously?"

"I went to college. We lived in these buildings called dormitories, yeah?"

"Ah. Heh-heh." My cheeks redden, and I shut up.

Dennis finishes his turn, and then I do mine – I drive up the Mediterranean coast to capture Montpellier in Blitz Combat and then Marseilles in Regular Combat. This broadens the French front considerably, but I haven't cracked

Bordeaux yet, I'm not appreciably closer to Berlin or the Ruhr, and another Summer turn is now gone.

After my Soviets finally lurch across the Dnepr and capture Kiev, Dennis rattles through his July-August turn. In western France, his defense is designed to bend but not break, while around Lyon and through the French Alps, he intends to stand firm in mountainous terrain along a four-hex line backed by three HQ units. The two halves aren't joined together; the hex containing the city of Vichy is vacant, but that is intentional, as none of my units are fast enough to reach Vichy during the Movement Phase. This is a familiar wargaming paradox: sometimes the most effective way of defending a hex is leaving it empty.

When my turn comes, I stare blankly at the map for several minutes, then I look up at Dennis, sitting back in his chair. "So, do you have a girlfriend?" I ask.

Dennis rolls his eyes. "Not at the moment, no."

"Are you looking out for one? Any prospects?"

"No comment."

"Hmmm. Have you ever had a girlfriend?"

"Yes, Sean, I have had a girlfriend," sighs Dennis.

"Aha! So, what was she like? How long ago was it?"

"Which one?"

"Seriously?"

"Is it that hard to believe?"

"No, I mean, of course not." (Yes, of course it is!)

Dennis smirks. "There was the first girl I kissed, in high school – she was called Denise."

"Was that awkward?"

"It was rather nice, actually. A little bit of tongue…"

"Not that!" (Ewww.)

"We were at *The Rocky Horror Picture Show*."

"I meant, being with someone called Denise. Dennis, Denise…"

"Oh." Dennis smiles. "I never thought about that before."

"Anyway, who else?"

"Well, I dated a few girls in college, and then most recently, I went out with this girl named Carolyn for a few years. Carolyn Johnson."

"How long ago was that?"

"It ended about four years ago."

"What happened?"

Dennis frowns. "She died in a skiing accident."

"Really?"

"She got run over by a Winnebago while trying to cross the freeway."

"What?"

"She flushed herself down a toilet." Dennis smirks again.

"So, she broke up with you?"

"Something like that."

"Not that you think about her that often."

"Nah, I'm over it. Really – we had some nice times together, and then we didn't, and now, here I am."

"OK."

"Although for a while, I was fascinated by the idea that she might flush herself down a toilet."

"I bet you were." I look at the map again and continue, "Let's get this over with. US Air unit in Genoa – will you contest it?"

"Nope – you got it." Dennis has been reserving his air support for Russia, where the *Luftwaffe* can still hope to gain parity with the Red Air Force.

"American Air in Milan – contest?"

"Milan?" Dennis thinks briefly. "No, you can have that one too."

"British Air there, northeast of Lyon – contest?"

Dennis bends forward and peers suspiciously at the map. "I'm not sure what you're up to, but no, no contest."

"I'm not sure what I'm up to either, but that's my Support Phase done. Tell me more about Carolyn, though. You said you had some good times together?"

Dennis raises his eyebrows, then sinks back in his chair. "We liked to talk to each other. She was smart – she had a really sharp mind. Very logical, very precise."

"Was she pretty?"

"Does it matter?"

"I don't know – you tell me. Did it matter?"

"She was pretty enough for me. I liked watching her think."

I begin shuffling my armies around southern France as I ask, "Did you ever play games together?"

"Heh." Dennis smiles and rests his head against the palm of his hand. "Why do you think we broke up?"

"She broke up with you over a game?"

"Not quite, but you're in the ballpark. We played a few entry-level Euros, like *Carcassonne* and *Lost Cities*, and she kinda enjoyed them, albeit not as much as I hoped she would. She wasn't very competitive."

"Neither are you."

"Compared to you, maybe. But compared to Carolyn? If she was competitive, it was at her job – she was a scientist, worked at a chem lab near where I lived. Playing games was beneath her."

"Did she know you were a wargamer?"

Dennis laughs. "You've obviously never been to my apartment."

"Ah."

"She used to cross her index fingers and hold them up to my gaming shelves, like they were vampires. Which was kinda funny the first time, but she did it again and again, and again, and again. Not cool."

"Did she not like history?"

"No, she was OK with that. It was just…every so often she'd tell me I needed to get on with my life, the implication being that, well, games were for children. Eventually I snapped and told her, look, this *is* my life."

"Huh."

"She did give me one chance to show her a wargame in action, and so I invited her to play one with me. Reluctantly, she said yes. Now, if you were in my shoes, what game would you pick to play with her?"

"I don't know. Probably an intro-level game like *Axis & Allies* – well, not *Axis & Allies*, because it's got the little soldiers and tanks and ships and airplanes in it. If she thinks games are for children, she won't be impressed by the whole 'boys with toys' thing."

Dennis smiles and covers his face with his hands. "You didn't!" I exclaim.

"Almost – I chose *Memoir '44*."

"Nice! I mean, ouch."

"Yeah, picking a game with model soldiers and tanks and artillery pieces and obstacles on the Normandy beaches was *not* my finest hour. And don't forget the dice with the little pictures on them – not pips from one to six, but silhouettes of soldiers and flags and stars and everything else. I'd barely explained the rules to her and started making my first move when she said, 'Look, this isn't working.'"

"That's not good."

"I sometimes wonder what might have happened if I'd showed her a game like *We the People* or *The Russian Campaign*, or one of those little titles by Victory Point Games with just the 20 counters on each side. Or a *Commands and Colors* game – same system as *Memoir '44*, but with stickered blocks instead of model figures. Or even *Totaler Krieg*, for that matter. Anything with cardboard pieces and a boring map. Even a long rulebook would have turned her off less than the figures."

"Of all the women in the world, you pick one who could have skipped straight past the gateway games to something serious, and you find a way to blow it."

"She might have hated the other games too. But now we'll never know, will we?"

"I guess not. By the way, how come you've never told me this stuff before?"

"Did you ever ask?"

"Good point."

"Why are you asking now? Are you in girl trouble of your own?"

"Oh, no you don't. Today we're talking about you. And anyway, look – it's time for Blitz Combat, or rather, it will be after I paradrop into Turin."

And there it is – a cockamamie plan, hatched in my subconscious during our conversation, but a plan all the same. I've walled off Italy from France with a cordon of air and airborne, and maneuvered a speedy British mechanized step adjacent to Vichy. Now, Dennis's HQ near Lake Geneva is out of supply, cut off because I exert a Zone of Control into the vacant Vichy hex, and I've discovered an alternate route to Berlin – not through France and the West Wall, but through northern Italy and the Alps.

"Damn," says Dennis.

At 9:1 odds, I destroy two Italian armies and clear the coastal road to Genoa. After exploiting into Genoa itself, during Regular Combat I attack the separate Italian corps in Turin and Bologna at 6:1 and 4:1, respectively, with a 55 percent chance of killing both steps. The dice favor me, clearing a path for Patton's Third Army – the fastest and strongest unit in *Totaler Krieg* – to dash through the wide-open Alps and all the way into Munich during Reserve Movement. The two German corps in southern Italy are hopelessly cut off. Milan, Turin, Bologna, Venice… they're all mine.

"You glorious bastard," says Dennis, after my Western turn is finished. "That's a great move. A really great move. I left you the chance, to be sure, but still. I'm not sure I can see a way back into the game from here. I'll keep fighting, but...damn."

"I guess I was inspired," I grin. "Sometimes you get just the one chance and you have to go for it, you know?"

2.

I'll remember my "Sideways Shift", as Dennis and I shall henceforth call it, from France to Munich via Italy for a long time. Lengthy games like *Totaler Krieg* rarely pivot on one unexpected offensive like that; Dennis was right in that it didn't end the game immediately, but in August-September 1945 Patton crowbarred his way into Vienna, and for the rest of the game Dennis was reduced to sticking fingers in the dyke. Eventually he ran out of fingers, and my hordes flooded through Germany to win a decisive victory.

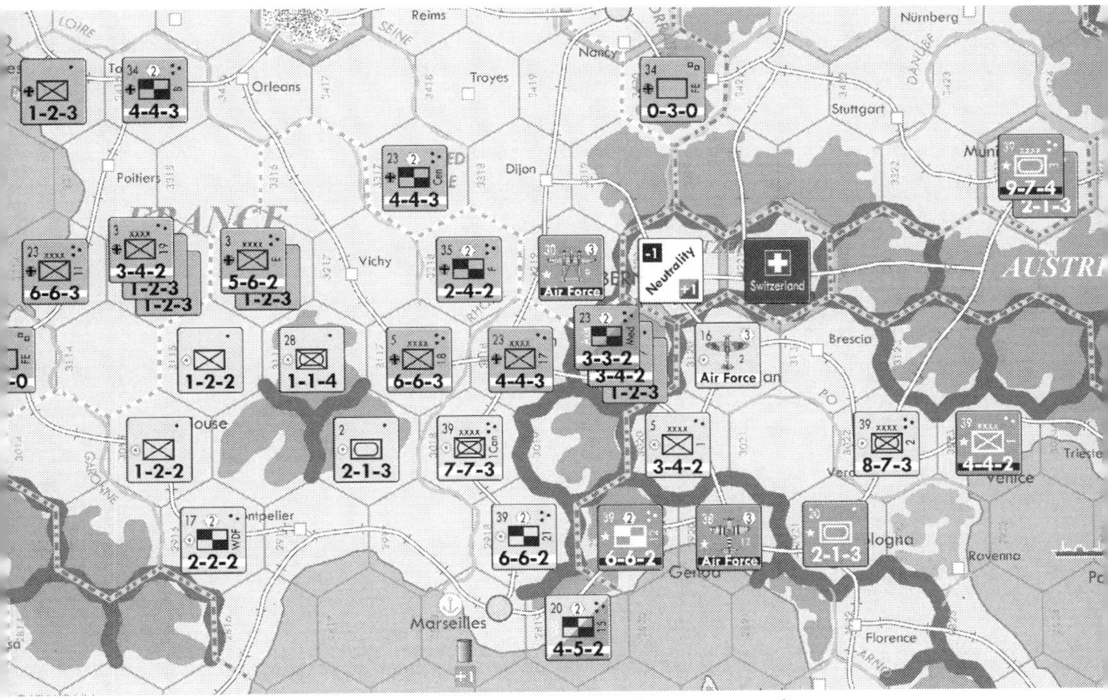

Fig. 6 – Position after the Western July-August 1945 turn

Upon reflection, I don't think I could have pulled off the Sideways Shift in an e-mail game. Before my move, Dennis could have withdrawn his HQ near Lake Geneva to Milan or shifted a corps from Turin or Bologna to Verona; either of these actions would have prevented or at least mitigated the effects of my breakthrough. My indirect approach to Dennis's defense solved the puzzle he'd presented me, and the odds held with the dice, but in an e-mail game Dennis would have studied the position more thoroughly and remedied these small defects. I would have kept pushing through France and not Italy, and I probably would have lost the game.

This is relevant because I've begun my BPA tournament semifinal, and I anticipate it will be a very tight game. My opponent, Gregory Spearman, is the defending champion, and he has a formidable reputation as a gruff, no-nonsense Brit who gives nothing away. When he posts on Consimworld, people listen, and

I'm almost certain he's played *Totaler Krieg* many more times than I have. In most e-mail games, there's usually a lot of banter – particularly to praise or complain about the dice – but so far I've hardly conversed with Gregory at all. He hasn't been rude or malicious or intemperate. He's just…blunt. Focused.

I'm not sure how to play an opponent like Gregory – usually, I'm the competitive one who really wants to win. You might be surprised by how many wargamers don't really care about winning: some are principally interested in history, or the social aspects of gaming; others have never outgrown the "boys with toys" stage; still others enjoy deconstructing the mechanics of a game more than playing it well. I don't really understand these perspectives – wargames are, you know, *games* – but as I've said before, the hobby is a big tent, and there's room for everyone.

I've drawn the Axis against Gregory, which I think is advantageous insofar as I can dictate the flow of the game and keep it as simple as possible. More experienced players can often turn unusual situations to their advantage, but if I stick to France in 1940, Russia in 1941-42 and holding on for dear life in 1943-45, all I have to do is work hard and outperform Gregory at the tactical margins, and/or get better and more timely luck. Easier said than done, but it's a plan, and I'm not about to shirk the challenge.

❖ ❖ ❖

Three days before my first-trimester AP European History final exam, Becs comes to my house for our first study session. She arrives just after sunset; as I open the front door, she's waving goodbye to her mother. "Mom needs the car tonight," she apologizes. She's wearing blue jeans and a demure white cardigan beneath her brown, suede jacket.

I lead Becs to the soft seats of the living room, where we quickly swamp the coffee table with backpacks, textbooks and study notes. "How do you want this to work?" she asks.

"I'm open to suggestions," I respond. "What areas do you want to focus on?"

"All of them," she says. "But then, you're the one who could teach our class, so perhaps you should choose. I don't want this to be boring for you."

"Unfortunately, it's the boring bits I need to work on. I'm hoping to make them less boring by studying them with someone else."

"What do you find boring?"

"Short answer: I'm not interested in history that doesn't move history forward."

"Which means what, exactly?"

"Well, consider our most recent subject, Absolutism and Constitutionalism. Think of all of the decisions that Richelieu and Louis XIV made to shape the destiny of France, and thereby Europe. Louis XIV revoked the Edict of Nantes, expelling the Protestant Huguenots from France: this shaped the future of his regime and the wider Christian Church, and the thousands of Huguenots who emigrated took their skills and their hatred of France to Holland, England, Prussia and wherever else. That's a big deal, right?"

"Yeah."

"The next section in our textbook is about French Classicism in the arts. Nicolas Poussin was a painter. Molière and Racine were playwrights. Now, I'm not a philistine: I tend to enjoy English class, and I learn from the works I read there. But did Poussin, Molière or Racine really impact the course of Europe? I'm sure their works influenced the art and literary world, but how much do the arts contribute to the rise and fall of nations?"

"It's a fair point."

"Sure, they contributed to the progress of European thought in some way. But can you compare even Shakespeare with the contributions of Hobbes or Locke, or Machiavelli before them? Machiavelli directly influenced the people who made the decisions who did make an impact."

"That's OK – you've sold me." Becs smiles. "You can stop now."

"Sorry." I blush. "I get worked up about this sort of thing."

"You've made that argument before, haven't you?"

"Yeah."

"To Mr. Prendergast himself?"

"Perhaps."

"You're always willing to speak your mind, aren't you? You don't seem afraid of what other people may think of you."

"Not in History class, anyway," I say. "But I'm trying to be more open-minded. I need to be, if I want to pass our exams. You can't get by on political, diplomatic and military history in this class."

"And that's where I come in?"

"I hope this will be a mutually beneficial relationship, but yeah, that's the idea. Anyway, what are you hoping to get out of our class?"

"I don't know – I'm just here to learn, really. I like how history connects everything in the world together. For example, did you know that you and I are both direct descendants of Charlemagne?"

"How could you possibly know that?" I ask.

"Everyone in the Western world is – it's a simple question of genealogical math," answers Becs. "So many generations have passed since Charlemagne was alive..."

"...that we all must be related to everyone who lived that long ago. I get it."

"Exactly. We're all connected through people and events of the past, or through great symphonies we've heard or great books we've read and shared with one another. And I guess the more I learn about history, the more those connections feel real to me."

"That sounds...almost noble."

Becs blushes. "It's not meant to be," she says.

"OK, then – let's talk about some of those great books. What do you know about *Don Quixote*?"

So we get started, beginning with our most recent material and working backwards. I know more about the "history of" stuff than I like to let on, of course, but when Becs quizzes me on baroque architecture and Colbert's economic policies in 17th-century France, the review we undertake is helpful. She likes to listen to classical music, so she possesses the same innate understanding of composers and their works that I do about wars and their instigators. And when I throw names and Roman numerals like Philip II and Charles V at Becs, she's quite handy at describing where they came from, what they did and why they were important. It's actually rather fun.

Still, when Becs asks me to say something insightful about the Spanish artist Diego Velázquez, I can't help myself. "He popularized the use of gunpowder in Europe, right?"

"What?" Becs looks confused.

I smirk. "I know, that's not right. But given that gunpowder was introduced to Europe around Velázquez's time and sort of, you know, revolutionized the nature of warfare in Europe, don't you think it might be appropriate to know who was responsible for that?"

Becs relaxes. "And he's off," she says, grinning.

"Even a single mention in our textbook of, like, one technological advance in warfare before World War I would be nice. I'm not asking for too much, am I?"

Becs starts flipping through our textbook in search of something. "What is it?" I ask.

"Hold on...there. Ha!"

"What?"

"Page 467, right after the Treaty of Cateau-Cambrésis – a treaty which, by the way, ended the conflict between which two countries?"

"Cateau-Cambrésis? France and, um, er...the Holy Roman Empire?"

"Bzzzzz – we were looking for France and Spain, not the Holy Roman Empire." Becs laughs.

"I should have just said 'the Habsburgs' and covered myself."

"Anyway, I quote from the book: 'The use of gunpowder altered both the nature of war and popular attitudes toward it. Guns and cannon killed and wounded from a distance, indiscriminately. Writers scorned gunpowder as a coward's weapon that allowed a common soldier to kill a gentleman.' And then, skipping a bit: 'Gunpowder weakened the notion, common during the Hundred Years' War, that warfare was an ennobling experience. Governments had to utilize propaganda, pulpits and the printing press to arouse public opinion to support war.' Happy now?"

"I happily stand corrected," I say. "Still, I bet there's no mention of the *trace italienne*, the fortifications developed to help protect cities and other strategic locations from cannon fire."

"Wow, you're right. This course is a travesty. Let's just pack up, and I'll have my mother pick me up early."

"I'm just saying that maybe we should learn something about Vauban, France's greatest military engineer, instead of looking at more paintings by obscure artists who should stay in AP Art History where they belong."

"Vauban, you said? What did he do?"

"He revolutionized the art of building fortifications, which helped Louis XIV win his wars, which helped perpetuate the existence of absolutist monarchism."

"Maybe the reason we study artists rather than military engineers is that artists contribute to building up civilization, whereas warmongers just find faster ways of tearing it down."

"Michelangelo himself designed one of the first *trace italienne* forts, at Florence."

"And he shall have to answer for that some day."

"You know who Robert Oppenheimer is, right?"

"Yes."

"Well, Vauban contributed at least as much to the science of warfare over a far longer period of time than Oppenheimer did. So if we're studying history – and I mean all of history – why shouldn't we know who he was?"

"I wish I'd never heard of Oppenheimer, so..."

"Why not?"

"He led the project that created the atomic bomb."

"Arguably the most amazing scientific accomplishment mankind has yet achieved."

"Great, so we've figured out a way to not only annihilate ourselves as a race, but also blanket the world with radiation so that nothing will grow on it ever again. No thanks."

"But you have to view everything in the proper context."

"Hang on." Becs looks genuinely alarmed for the first time. "Are you about to justify Hiroshima and Nagasaki to me? Because you can't. It's not possible."

"You don't think we should have used atomic weapons against Japan at the end of World War II?"

"Absolutely not, and I don't believe there are any circumstances under which their usage could ever be justified."

"Will you give me the chance to make that argument?"

"You think their usage was justified?"

"Absolutely. One hundred percent."

"I may never speak to you again, but OK. Make your case."

"I'm not even nervous – it's absolutely watertight. I can go into as much detail as you want, but I'd make four basic points. The first is that dropping the A-bombs was absolutely necessary in forcing Japan to surrender. The Japanese behaved throughout the war in a manner totally alien to the West, from the kamikaze attacks and banzai charges to the universal preference to die for the Emperor rather than be taken prisoner. As the war came closer to Japan, these attitudes became more intense, not less: Japan was willing to risk national suicide to make America back down from its unconditional surrender demands and win a negotiated settlement. Even the Soviet Union's entry into the war didn't change this calculus – it took two atomic bombs to make Japan's leaders understand that the Allies no longer needed to invade Japan to win the war. The Japanese prime minister at the time, Suzuki, said as much immediately after peace was declared, and I'm convinced by other evidence that his testimony is accurate. Plus, Japan's leaders were able to save face with their people and the military by being able to claim they were defeated by supernatural forces."

"We nuked Japan so its leaders could save face?"

"Not as such, but you have to understand how important saving face is within Japanese culture – it's much, much more important than it is in the West. Anyway, the second point is that America's leaders had also concluded that invading Japan would cause losses on a scale unacceptable to the American public."

"So the Bomb saved American lives," says Becs. "I've heard that one before."

"The most realistic planning estimates made by the Joint Chiefs for just the opening invasion of Kyushu, based upon America's casualty rates on Okinawa, determined that in the first 90 days alone, around 150,000 American soldiers and sailors would be killed and another 350,000 would become wounded or missing in action. And that estimate was made before further reconnaissance and intelligence reports revealed the Japanese had deployed their strongest remaining army and air units to Kyushu, right where the Americans were planning to invade. On 9 August, the day of the Nagasaki bomb, America's top naval commander in the Pacific – Admiral Nimitz – weighed up the evidence and informed his boss that he could no longer support an invasion. MacArthur was an idiot, as usual, and refused to believe the intelligence reports, but there's no way Truman would have endorsed the invasion after a second review."

"How do you remember all of this?"

"I just do. As for my third point, the A-bombs almost certainly saved the lives of many, many more Japanese than Americans. The estimates I quoted didn't include Japanese casualties: there were roughly 500,000 Japanese committed to defend Kyushu, plus another 3.5 million civilians on the island. Again, given the Japanese casualty rates on Okinawa, you'd have to think that at least a million Japanese would have died, whereas the most aggressive estimates of those killed in Hiroshima and Nagasaki combined are around 300,000. But never mind the proposed invasion: at the time of the two A-bombs, America's conventional strategic bombing campaign against Japan was about to stop targeting cities and instead hit transportation-related targets like railway centers and the system of bridges and ferries that connected the four Home Islands with one another. The US had closely studied the effects of its bombing campaign against Germany and had come to understand how sensitive Japan's system of food distribution was to these transportation links: by destroying this infrastructure, mass famine would have ensued, resulting in millions upon millions of civilian deaths and probably massive civil unrest even if Japan had chosen to surrender at this point, which is far from certain. So, unless the US and the Soviet Union simultaneously abandoned their pursuit of unconditional surrender – which was never, ever going to happen – the next-best scenario for the Japanese people *by far* involved the use of atomic weapons."

Becs nods her head, slowly and passively. "You said there was a fourth point?" she asks.

"Yes, there is. By the way, my first three points were cribbed from a historian named Richard Frank – I'd highly recommend his book, *Downfall*, if you want to read more about all of this. But the fourth point is basically my own: in short, weapons are created to be used. At Hiroshima and Nagasaki, atomic weapons were used under arguably the best possible circumstances – using them helped end a vast and interminable war almost immediately, saving many lives in the process. After peace had been declared, their usage could be fully investigated, and their horrible and unexpected side-effects revealed. Before the next war could break out, a consensus had emerged: many countries wanted atomic weapons, but nobody wanted to use them. By way of comparison, a similar international consensus formed after World War I around the use of poison gas, which after the 1930s was only ever used on a wide scale during the Iran-Iraq War of the 1980s. But because poison gas was first used in 1915, near the beginning of the war, its usage became repeated and widespread, and more than 1 million soldiers became gas casualties before the war ended in 1918. Imagine if the US had acquired its atomic capability in 1943: how much additional carnage might have occurred before the war ended?"

"I don't know," says Becs.

"I don't know either, although I'd certainly wager that more than two bombs would have been dropped. But the more important counterfactual is this: what if the US doesn't use A-bombs in 1945, or doesn't perfect the technology until after the war is over? When the Cold War breaks out and America's atomic monopoly ends, now you have two superpowers armed with nukes and possibly willing to use them. Who makes the first move, and where? Korea? Cuba? Berlin? Maybe everyone keeps the genie in the bottle, but with no stigma attached to the usage of nuclear weapons, and their destructiveness continuing to increase, it's increasingly likely that any attempt at localized usage would escalate into widespread holocaust or even global apocalypse. But all of this was thankfully avoided, hopefully forever, when Truman pulled the trigger on Hiroshima and Nagasaki. The US now bears the stigma of being the only country to actively employ atomic weapons, but it's a stigma America is capable of bearing, and it's probably part of the price you pay for being the world's dominant superpower."

I finish, and Becs remains quiet. When I can no longer stand the silence, I blurt out, "Like I said, that last argument was my own, and it's not as solidly backed by evidence as the ones I've provided from Frank. That's Richard Frank, of course, not someone named 'Frank'. And I didn't mean 'frank', as in truthful – well, I mean, I am trying to be truthful, and frank, but that's not what I'm trying to say…"

Becs sniggers gently. "That's OK," she says. "You did well."

"Really?"

"You made a lot of very good points."

"Oh, OK – thanks."

"What was the book called?"

"Frank's book – Richard Frank's book – is called *Downfall.* You can borrow my copy, if you'd like."

"You've got your own copy?"

"The book made a powerful impression on me." I smile. "And anyway, that's who I am. I'm the one who reads history for fun."

"I like that," says Becs.

"Now, shall we get back to business?"

"Good idea."

"Great. So, where were we?"

❖ ❖ ❖

We study on for a while, but my mind isn't in it. I can't quite believe I've just preached about American nuclear strategy in 1945 to the girl in my class with the ponytail and the long legs, and not some double-chinned wargamer with an attitude and body odor.

At bedtime, I lie awake in the dark for hours, fidgeting and replaying our conversation in my head. As soon as Becs left, I retrieved my copy of *Downfall* to fact-check the arguments I'd made – I did OK, but I wish I'd changed several things. Firstly, I overplayed the point about more Japanese than American lives being saved, which is true but irrelevant: armies have always developed and used the weapons at their disposal to save the lives of their own men and inflict greater casualties on the enemy. Truman dropped the bomb to end the war; saving Japanese lives was a secondary effect, not a goal. If anything, I should have mentioned the thousands of American prisoners of war in Japan, all of whom almost certainly would have perished during a long blockade or after an amphibious invasion of the Home Islands.

Secondly, the casualty estimates I gave for Operation Olympic – 150,000 American dead and 350,000 wounded or missing in the first 90 days – were both too high and too low. In an essay Frank wrote for the second *What If?* book called "No Bomb: No End", he presented a table with four different casualty projections and reported this conclusion: "The overall range of American losses *just to seize one-third of Kyushu* [Frank's italics] would probably rest between 140,000 to 527,000, including between 32,700 and 147,500 deaths." The figures I gave were at or above the top end of this scale, so in that sense they were too high. But on the other hand, Frank was undoubtedly constrained by a burden of proof: the historical record only includes casualty estimates prepared by the US military for the first 90 days of Olympic, and like most good historians he refrains from undue speculation. Furthermore, even though the higher-end figures seem way, way more credible than low-end figures derived by analyzing protracted campaigns in Europe, he is obliged to report the lower figures as well to cover himself.

This, I think, is where professional historians can outthink themselves. All of Frank's research points to one conclusion: America's decision to use atomic weapons against Japan was correct. However, an intelligent but uninformed observer may see the estimate of between 32,700 and 147,500 deaths, compare it to reasonable estimates of more than 200,000 deaths from all causes between the Hiroshima and Nagasaki bombings, and conclude that Truman was somehow inhuman in sacrificing more Japanese lives than American lives to end the war. Frank himself cites a November 1994 poll reporting that only 55 percent of Americans agreed with Truman's decision to use atomic weapons, with 39 percent opposed. I suspect even many of those who agree with the decision would admit to having reservations about it, both through abhorrence at how the victims were killed and guilt that many Japanese civilians were killed to save fewer American soldiers. This first feeling is understandable but ultimately misplaced: *every* civilian and indeed military death inflicted in war is abhorrent, and many other methods of civilian death in World War II were far more ghastly than instantaneous atomic vaporization. But the second feeling is simply wrong on every level, and I blame historians for not drawing obvious inferences in their conclusions for fear of overreaching. They settle for what they can prove, instead of what they could reasonably conclude as experts from the evidence and with the tools that are available to them.

So you get sentences like this from Frank's essay: "If the Japanese had committed at least a half-million men to southern Kyushu for the customary fight to the death, it is hard to imagine that fewer than a minimum of 200,000 to 250,000 of the emperor's loyal soldiers and sailors would have fallen by the end of the campaign." And then: "If only one in ten of [the civilian population on Kyushu, roughly 3.8 million people according to Japan's 1944 census] died, a much lower rate of loss than on Okinawa, another 380,000 would have perished, bringing total Japanese fatalities to the 580,000 to 630,000 range." Show the courage of your convictions, man! Give us your best guess! Or at least give us a worst-case figure at the other end of the scale with which to compare your conservative estimate. Use the actual Okinawa loss rates but revise them upward, on the reasonable basis that casualties are likely to increase as the Home Islands are invaded and desecrated. And don't just stop on Kyushu: do the same for Honshu, and even Shikoku and Hokkaido if you can, and add American estimates to the Japanese ones. Frank eventually concludes that "the Pacific War would have dragged on for probably two to five more years – perhaps longer – and the overall cost would have easily exceeded five million deaths in Japan alone by conservative estimates [along with another five to ten million deaths elsewhere in Asia]." I think he can do better than that. Come up with a completely logical and well-argued figure showing how many millions or tens of millions of Japanese might have died in the Home Islands, and then demonstrate how an extended campaign to conquer all of Japan likely would have killed more than a million Americans – i.e., *four times the total American military death toll in the rest of World War II,* and one-and-a-half times as many as died on both sides of the Civil War from 1861 to 1865. Maybe then we might begin to win the battle for the truth.

Of course, several potential counter-arguments never entered my conversation with Becs. One asks whether the Nagasaki bomb may have been superfluous: couldn't Truman have waited to fully evaluate the effects of the Hiroshima bomb, not to mention the Soviet declaration of war on Japan, before destroying a second city? Frank is adamant that both bombs were needed to force a surrender: the available evidence suggests that Japanese officials remained bullish after Hiroshima and were ignorant about and/or indifferent to the scale of Soviet attacks in Manchuria, whereas the Nagasaki bomb on 9 August caused several important ministers to shift in favor of peace. But although the key decisions to surrender were made on 10 August, the same decisions might have been made several days later, without any need for a second attack. So while Frank is right in proving that the second A-bomb was a major and immediate factor in forcing Japan's surrender, he never speculates about reasonable scenarios in the absence of a second attack and whether the shift toward peace might have happened anyway.

The second counter-argument is much more problematic: what if the Soviets had invaded Japan? Stalin apparently hoped to invade Hokkaido by the end of August 1945, after key staging positions on Sakhalin Island were occupied and cleared. The main military and moral justification for using atomic weapons was that they would save lives – American lives first and foremost. But if you're Truman, and Stalin proves he's willing to sacrifice Soviet lives to conquer Hokkaido (and presumably Honshu thereafter if you let him), this justification is significantly compromised. Now you're dropping the A-bomb partly for political reasons, to hold Stalin to his promises at Yalta and ensure that America gets to Tokyo first and can take full credit for Japan's defeat. Does that justify the release of atomic weaponry? Certainly nobody, Truman or otherwise, could have reasonably factored Soviet participation into estimates of Japanese and Allied death totals with and without atomic devastation.

(As an aside, could Truman and the United States have been best served simply by waiting for the Soviets to invade Hokkaido and then Honshu? Let the Soviets win the race to Tokyo, losing millions more of their own men in the process and exacerbating their already severe manpower shortages at the end of the war. The Soviets thereby gain the right to occupy part or all of Japan after the war, but at a frightful human cost that will weaken it if and when the Cold War warms up; meanwhile, the average American is thoroughly roused to resist the duplicitous Communists even earlier than he was historically. Only a Talleyrand or a Kissinger might have actively embraced such an amoral strategy, so this never would have happened, but it's an interesting thought.)

As I ponder these imponderables, one question keeps coming back to me: how much of this should I share with Becs? I don't want her to think I've been withholding exculpatory evidence, and I know I was showing off during our debate, recklessly bombarding her with numbers and figures and ideas. Should I apologize for letting my ego interfere with her education? And then there was that stupid mix-up about Frank's surname...that was simply hopeless. I just hope she doesn't think tonight was a waste of her time. For me, I'm afraid I now need a study session to catch up on my study session. Which parts of European history were we supposed to be reviewing tonight?

3.

The day before my AP European History final exam, Craig Foster joins the Gang of Four for a special post-lunch, spectator-free edition of the Big Game. Craig is a good lad – a Biology geek, in truth, but he hides it well. And not behind glasses, either.

Somehow we all have a free hour this afternoon starting at 1:15, so we meet at our usual table in the cafeteria, having agreed to double the game to 20 hands and a 10-dollar buy-in. As Craig and Freddie post the blinds for the first hand, it's odd to so clearly hear the thudding clunks of change on the table echo around our alcove, the gentle buzz of lunchtime having dissipated. The only other noise is the sporadic, distant cracking of wooden chairs being pushed into metallic table legs by an elderly black woman in Janitorial Services.

After Chris steals the first hand with an early raise, Craig takes the button from Melvyn and starts dealing. Chris, wasting neither time nor words, looks to his left at Melvyn and asks, "How's Vicki?"

"Vicki is…divine," purrs Melvyn. "She's heavenly."

"You're smitten, aren't you?" asks Craig.

"Yes, yes I am. In fact, last night we were on the phone, and…"

"And how's Melissa?" interrupts Chris, turning away from Melvyn to face me. Craig and Freddie laugh.

"Hey!" says Melvyn.

"No, you're done," says Chris, dismissing Melvyn with a shake of the head. "Young love in full bloom is too sad for words. Sean, how's Melissa?"

"How would I know?" I grunt, peering at a hand of 7-4 offsuit.

"She's your girlfriend, isn't she?" asks Chris. Melvyn announces a small raise to the pot.

"Have you been avoiding her calls?" interjects Craig. I'd forgotten Craig is a good friend of Melissa's.

"Have I?" I ask. I honestly don't know, but Freddie tuts and Chris emits a low whistle. I quietly muck my cards from the small blind.

"She told me this morning she left you a voicemail two nights ago, but you haven't responded and she hasn't seen you since."

"Two nights ago? Oh, yeah – Becs was over at my house for a study session. AP Euro. I probably didn't hear the phone ring, and as these guys will tell you, I'm terrible at remembering to check for messages."

"Becs?" asks Melvyn.

"Rebecca Fowler," I clarify.

"I know – but 'Becs'?"

"That's what she asked me to call her."

Melvyn raises his eyebrows, but with the flop now on the table he raises Freddie, who in turn patiently ponders and then calls. Our focus returns to the cards.

As the game carries on, we talk about exam schedules, and how we think we've done so far, and who has spent the most time studying, and which teachers ask the best, worst and toughest questions. Before long, I realize I've mucked 11 hands in a row before the flop and have yet to see a hole card better than the 10 of spades.

On the 12th hand I draw the Jack of hearts and the 9 of hearts. I haven't seen better cards in at least two weeks, so I gently raise from the small blind and get action from Chris and Melvyn. The flop is great for me: Jack of clubs, 5 of hearts, 2 of hearts. With top pair and a four-flush I check, hoping to draw a bet, but both

Chris and Melvyn check as well. The turn is the 7 of clubs, so with two clubs on the board, this time I bet a dollar. Chris calls quickly; Melvyn thinks, then mucks.

The river is the 9 of clubs. I've got the top two pair, so even though straights and flushes are possible, I lead out with a stronger bet of $1.50. Chris quickly says, "I'll raise – three-fifty." He counts out a tower of 14 quarters and lets them topple into the middle of the table.

"You think too quickly." As Chris purses his lips and raises his eyebrows, I frown and continue: "This isn't good. OK, here's what I know: my pre-flop bet didn't chase you away, so you must have at least a King and probably an Ace in there. You couldn't have 6-8 for a straight, I don't buy that – you wouldn't still be here. And as much as I want to believe you're bluffing, you're not bluffing. You're not that clever. You got a piece of that ugly flop, probably second pair, and then you hung around looking for two pair or a running flush. And now you get the prize, because my bet on the turn wasn't big enough." I muck my cards again, but this time face up. "You win with the 5 of clubs and either the Ace or the King of clubs – probably the Ace. Am I right?"

Chris smirks, then slowly nods his head. He lays each card on the table in turn, face up: first the 5 of clubs, then the Ace of clubs. "That's really good," says Chris in admiration. He gives me a quiet round of slow golf applause which is quickly copied by Craig, Melvyn and Freddie. I roll my eyes and grimace.

"That's a world-class fold," says Freddie.

"It's still a fold," I say. "You don't get partial credit for playing well when the cards are against you."

"Yeah, you do," corrects Chris. "You get to keep two dollars that should have been mine."

"Or you could have gone all-in and lost the lot," says Melvyn.

"Keep playing like that, and the cards will come around," says Freddie.

"Yeah, but when?" I ask. "If you flip a coin a hundred times and it comes up tails every time, what are the odds it comes up tails the hundred-and-first time?"

"Fifty-fifty," says Melvyn.

"Exactly," I say.

"Really?" asks Craig. "Doesn't luck always even out in the end?"

"It doesn't have to," I mutter.

I did play that hand really well, not that it matters. Poker is a game where good play can become bad luck on a single turn of the card all too often. You play the game for money, not the admiration of your peers. And yeah, I'm in a rut, but when the cards eventually start falling my way, what will I have done to deserve it?

While mucking my next few hands on auto-pilot, I wonder what life would be like if *Totaler Krieg* regularly featured on television instead of poker. I mean, I've seen backgammon tournaments on television, and the great Fischer-Spassky and Kasparov-Karpov chess matches were broadcast live with expert commentary from other grandmasters. Heck, in the late 1990s several *Magic: The Gathering* world championships were televised on ESPN2. Maybe the History Channel would be interested in *Totaler Krieg* – it likes World War II, right? The *World Poker Tour* shows are each two hours long, so let's aim for that; maybe you edit a full game down to an extensive overview and a few key highlights plus the odd historical reenactment, with Mike Sexton joined by Laurence Rees and Robert Cowley instead of Vince Van Patten. You could really educate people about history this way, and if you put a really big prize pot up for grabs, you could see some world-class, Hellmuth-level hissy-fits by gamers who get unlucky dice at key moments. That could be riveting television, couldn't it?

As this daydream passes, Melvyn is yapping about Vicki again, this time at Craig. I interrupt Melvyn to ask, "What is it with you and Vicki?"

"What do you mean?" responds Melvyn.

"You both seem very happy together. Some people might even get the impression that you're in love. Why? What makes it work?"

"We just love being together and talking to each other, I guess," says Melvyn, sheepishly.

"But why?"

"I don't know why – it just works."

"There must be some reason, right?" I notice Chris edging forward in his seat.

"I'm not sure you can analyze it. Is this going somewhere?"

"Hear me out, OK? It's a serious question. It's obvious to me that you've never felt this way about another girl before; I'm just keen to understand why. Is the attraction purely physical, or are there other factors?"

"Of course there are other factors," snaps Melvyn. The poker has ground to a standstill – the action is with me, but everyone seems happy to wait.

"It'd be OK if there weren't," I insist. "Vicki is very attractive. But what are those other factors? What do you have in common with her? Do you share any interests? Movies you both like? Do you both hate the New York Yankees? Anything at all?"

Melvyn pauses, breathes deeply and then says, "I know it's exam week, but I thought I had this hour off."

"So it is purely physical," concludes Chris. Freddie sniggers.

"I promise, I'm not yanking your chain," I say to Melvyn. "Your relationship seems to be working really well – pretend I'm asking you for advice."

"I don't want to think too much about it. We're having a great time together wherever we go, and it's wonderful. And I'm not going to start thinking about her like a series of poker bets that need to be decoded or something."

"I can respect that," I said. "Even if you're not really helping."

"Hang on," says Chris. "Is something else going on here?"

I sigh. "Craig, let me ask you question: you know Melissa very well, right?"

"Yeah," says Craig.

"What do you think she and I have in common?"

"I knew it!" says Chris. Freddie glares at Chris and scrunches up a piece of paper to throw at him.

"I don't know," says Craig. "I don't know how to answer that question. What do you think you have in common with Melissa?"

"That's the thing," I say. "I don't know myself. We're doers rather than talkers – we go to the movies, or we play miniature golf together, or we watch TV together and do, you know, other things. But I'm not sure we've ever had a serious conversation about anything. Is that enough to sustain a relationship?"

Chris, Melvyn, Freddie and Craig glance furtively at one another. Finally, Freddie says, "That's your call, isn't it?"

"Absolutely," I say. "I just wish I had a better frame of reference for what a relationship could feel like."

"Is this about Rebecca Fowler?" asks Chris.

"No. It's not even about Melissa, really. I'm just trying, and failing, to better understand an abstract concept. Anyway, here's something less abstract for you: I fold, yet again."

I flick my two hole cards with my fingertips to the middle of the table.

❖ ❖ ❖

I arrive five minutes early to Room 302 in the English department, the venue for my end-of-term AP European History exam. I suspect that at some point this year I might do something history-related in a History classroom, but that hasn't happened yet.

When I arrive, Becs is one of three students already seated. She waves hello; I meander over and sit diagonally across from and in front of her. I'm not sure I could concentrate on my answers if given the option of staring at the back of her head.

"You nervous?" she asks me.

"I'll tell you after I see the questions," I respond. "You?"

"Yeah. It's an exam – you're supposed to get nervous." Her hair is held in a black-and-white band, and I don't think she's wearing make-up – she's got her game face on. I like it.

"Thanks again for the study session the other night," I say. "It was helpful."

"Yeah – let's do it again."

"Brilliant. By the way, I'm sorry about the whole Hiroshima-Nagasaki thing."

"Don't be."

"No, it was a distraction, and I was arrogant about it."

"Sean, I'm in this class because I like history. Please don't apologize for caring about it, OK?"

"Got it."

"But now you're distracting me." She smiles and holds up her notes. "I'm still getting the Calvinists and the Anabaptists confused."

"You can't cram for this exam at the last minute – you've either got it or you don't. And I know you'll do great."

"Thanks, but shhhh…" She smiles again and tilts her head into her notebook.

As more students file into the classroom, Chris grabs the desk to my left. "Twenty bucks if you let me copy your multiple-choice answers," he mutters.

"Twenty bucks if you let me copy yours," I respond.

"You ready for this?"

"Like I just said to Becs, I'll tell you after I see the questions."

"Good luck with that," says Chris.

"Thanks."

"And good luck with the chatting-with-Becs thing."

"Shut up."

Our final exam is a miniature version of the AP exam itself. Today we have 90 minutes to complete 25 multiple-choice questions, one Document-Based Question (DBQ) encompassing a selection of primary sources to be used in crafting our answers, and one of two Free-Response Questions (FRQs). It's a tall order: proportionately, we'll have less time to finish each question today than we will during the full exam in May. That said, Mr. Prendergast has told us that if we're running out of time, a detailed outline of our proposed essay for the FRQ will suffice.

At the top of the hour, our exam proctor – a short and squat lady with curly black hair who I think is a Fine Arts teacher, possibly a choral instructor – waddles around the room with our exam papers, placing them face down on our desks. I resist the urge to peek as she recites a tired spiel about No. 2 pencils and bathroom break procedures. Then come the magic words: "Your time…starts…now."

I flip past the multiple-choice section to see what I'm really up against. First to the DBQ, which reads as follows:

"The Thirty Years' War pillaged through Europe from 1618-1648. During that time, many countries suffered detrimental losses. Discuss how the Thirty Years' War led to an age of absolutism in France."

Oh, yes. The nine primary sources include three quotes from Louis XIV, an excerpt from the Treaty of Westphalia, and a table of French military spending figures in the 1620s, 1630s and 1640s. More of that, please.

On to peek at the FRQs, then – here are my two choices:

1. *Analyze examples from literature and art that demonstrate the influence of humanism, classical Greece and Rome and religion on the Renaissance.*
2. *How did the conflict between Catholicism and Protestantism lead to the growth of power for nation-states and other political figures in Europe?*

Yeah, I'll take option two. I've got 89 minutes and 20 seconds remaining, and I've all but aced the exam already.

Even the multiple-choice questions befriend me. The Renaissance section shuns obscure artists:

1. *Which of the following passages appeared in "The Prince"?*
   - *a) "It is much better to be feared than to be loved."*
   - *b) "Civilization reached its lowest point during the Roman Republic."*
   - *c) "In diplomacy, honesty is the best policy."*
   - *d) "Loyalty to a small city is a foolish diversion of human devotion."*
   - *e) "Only through prayer can a man achieve his full measure of virtue."*

4. *The Medicis and Sforzas played a significant part in the Renaissance as*
   - *a) painters of everyday themes*
   - *b) writers who made important contributions to Renaissance literature*
   - *c) military leaders whose conquests spread the Renaissance to northern Europe*
   - *d) scientists who furthered scientific knowledge*
   - *e) rulers of Italian cities and patrons of culture*

7. *The term "da Vinci of today" would best describe a person who seems to be*
   - *a) a cruel tyrant*
   - *b) a conformist*
   - *c) a genius in many fields*
   - *d) only seeking pleasure*
   - *e) behind the times*

The Reformation questions are more political than spiritual:

9. *The dissolution of the English monasteries*
   - *a) resulted in a more equitable distribution of land*
   - *b) was the result of rebellious activities by the monks*
   - *c) resulted in Henry's excommunication by the Anglican Church*
   - *d) resulted from Henry VIII's desire to confiscate their wealth*
   - *e) deeply disturbed the English upper class*

13. *By the Edict of Nantes, France granted religious toleration to the*
    - *a) Huguenots*
    - *b) Muslims*
    - *c) Hindus*
    - *d) Catholics*
    - *e) Jews*

15. *The Reformation in Germany resulted in*
    - *a) Italian control of Austria*
    - *b) the abolition of Catholicism*
    - *c) political fragmentation*
    - *d) a unified German state*
    - *e) secular freedom for the peasantry*

And while some of the questions on Absolutism and Constitutionalism are tricky, they're surely trickier for my classmates than they are for me:

17. *During the 16th century, the main reason for the increase in power of the English monarchy was the*
    - *a) ability of the Tudor monarchs*
    - *b) marriage of Queen Mary to Philip II of Spain*

c) Glorious Revolution
d) ability of the Stuart rulers
e) increased position of the nobility

22. *The most significant Romanov ruler of the eighteenth century was*
    a) Alexander III
    b) Gustavus Adolphus
    c) Nicholas II
    d) Ivan the Terrible
    e) Peter the Great

24. *Which of the following exerted the most influence on Italy in the eighteenth century?*
    a) Spanish
    b) Austrians
    c) Dutch
    d) Turks
    e) English

I could have passed this exam back in August, no question. Now, in mid-November, I blitz through the multiple-choice questions in five minutes and finish the DBQ within half an hour, embroidering my response with salient extras about Sully's financial reforms and Richelieu's domestic and foreign policy successes. With 38 minutes still on the clock, I've sketched a detailed outline for my response to the second FRQ, including a multi-jurisdictional history of Catholic dominance prior to 1517 as well as the emergence of both Protestant Christianity and secular power politics in the 16th century. That outline is sufficient for my exam, but with so much time left and so little to do, I knuckle down to practice my penmanship and write the essay from start to finish. I even finish with a counterfactual flourish, wondering where the Catholic Church would have been in 1617 – 100 years after the 95 Theses – if Protestantism had failed to emerge and comparing its weaknesses to those of the Byzantine Empire as the Seljuk Turks became ascendant. My toughest opponents today have been over-confidence and cramp in my writing hand.

At the conclusion of 90 minutes, the proctor asks everyone to stop writing – "C'mon, drop them now!" she bellows, and in one corner of the room Hugh Johnson's pencil clatters noisily to the floor. "Faces forward, please," she demands as she silently marches around the room, collecting our essay booklets and pencil-dotted multiple-choice papers. When she returns to the desk at the front of the room, she sits and blurts, "You are free to go. Dismissed."

The class collectively exhales, then bubbles into nervous chatter. Chris rolls his eyes toward our proctor and whispers, "All the charm of a lesbian nun."

"Did you use that line on your exam?" I giggle. "I don't think lesbian nuns were at the heart of the Reformation."

"How'd you do?" asks Chris.

"Honestly? I think I was born to take that exam."

"I bet you were. That could have been worse. Anyway, I should leave you to, you know."

Chris winks and abruptly swivels toward the exit. I turn around and see Becs gathering her belongings from under and around her desk. Funny, in the heat of battle I'd forgotten about her.

"So?" I ask.

"That was OK," says Becs. "Hard, but fair. You?"

"I got lucky. I think I did pretty well."

"Great. Better for our study session?"

"Of course."

"Me too. When do you want to meet up again?"

"What are you doing for Thanksgiving?" I ask.

"I'll be around," she says. "Nothing too exciting."

"Would you like to get together on the Friday and maybe catch up on everything we've learned so far?"

"Um, yeah. Why not? Do you want to come over to my house this time?"

"Sure, if that's OK."

"Call me tonight and we can set it up." She smiles, wanders toward the door, waves a hand at me and passes out of sight. You won't find Becs' smile in a Renaissance painting – it's far too warm. Far too human.

I'm floating down a corridor toward my locker, still savoring that smile, when I almost literally bump into Mr. Prendergast as he emerges from a Biology classroom. He's wearing khaki cords and a striped, knitted sweater beneath his open leather jacket.

"Mister Lansbury," he growls.

"Sorry about that," I say.

"No need to apologize. How was your exam?"

"That's for you to decide, but yeah, really, really good."

"Top man."

"The questions were perfect – it's almost like you wrote that exam just for me."

Mr. Prendergast raises his eyebrows. "Have you got a minute?"

"Sure…what's up?"

"Come in here."

We enter the Biology room together, and I perch myself atop one of the two-seater lab tables at the front near the chalkboard. Mr. Prendergast leans against the teacher's desk, folds his arms and smirks. "Take a look around," he says.

I glance at posters of butterflies and the obligatory vivisection of the human body, and at cupboards probably full of severed frogs' heads and legs.

"Do you like Biology?" he asks.

"It wasn't my favorite subject, put it that way."

"Nor mine. Do you plan to ever study it again? Maybe at college?"

"Not if I can help it."

"OK. So why do you think you were forced to learn Biology?"

I think for a moment, then answer, "Muhlendorf tries to teach us everything, and expose us to all subjects so we can decide what we like."

"That's a large part of it. But then, once you decide you don't like a subject, why can't you just say 'No thanks' and give it up?"

Hmmm. "I'm not sure," I respond.

"Here's my answer: I believe everyone should learn to think in as many different ways as possible. From Math you learn logical skills; from English you learn verbal and emotional skills; from others you learn different types of analytical skills. You don't take Chemistry to learn how to diagram a nitrous oxide molecule. If that naturally interests you, great, but your real goal is to sharpen your brain in different ways, so that someday you might be able to make a split-second decision in a board meeting, or plan your family budget, or generally process information more quickly and efficiently."

"That makes sense. But if you don't mind me asking, what does any of this have to do with anything?"

"Ah. Yes." Mr. Prendergast unfolds his arms. "In the past, I've always been guided by this principle when teaching my classes. I want to prepare everyone for the AP exam, but I also want everyone to learn how to learn, and to think in different ways."

"Right."

"But then I have this nephew, yeah? My sister lives in Louisiana, and her son plays the clarinet. And I mean, he really plays the clarinet. Justin is a freshman at

Juilliard now, and he wants to play the clarinet for a living. Which is such a ballsy decision, I can't tell you. How many jobs are there in the world for professional clarinetists?"

"Not many?"

"Not many. Anyway, last year the music director at Justin's high school did something really interesting: he programmed as many clarinet solos as he could into his repertoire. He himself arranged Aaron Copland's Clarinet Concerto for wind ensemble. He heavily featured the clarinet in the school's jazz band. And for the marching band, he scripted a show around Gershwin's *Rhapsody in Blue* which began with a clarinet solo. He was hard on Justin throughout the year, but he knew that Justin was by far the most gifted musician in his school, and everything he did was designed to ensure that Justin's talent was properly developed."

"Ah."

"So there's that."

Mr. Prendergast stands up. He looks at me closely, his eyes wide open and his forehead creased with wrinkles, and opens his mouth as if to speak. Then he exhales, closes his mouth and smiles, and starts walking out of the room. "See you next week," he says, and disappears into the hallway.

4.

Dennis frowns. "There will be hell to pay in Chelyabinsk," he says.

I agree. "This game is running away from you pretty quickly now."

"I don't know what happened. I shouldn't be summering in the Urals, though."

"You could always surrender."

"Nope. I'll never give you the satisfaction, and you know it. I'll keep fighting until your panzers or the NKVD come and cart me off to the glue factory."

It's a cold evening outside, and our first dusting of snow is tickling the ground and the window ledge behind the thick curtains of my study. The landscape outside would have augured ill for the German army in 1941, but Dennis and I are near the end of Summer 1942 in our latest game of *Totaler Krieg*, and from my omniscient perch above our counterfactual world of warfare, warm air wafts from the ceiling vents to caress my face and fingertips. My *Wehrmacht*, far from facing defeat, stands ready to drink from the cup of ultimate glory: Chelyabinsk is the new seat of Dennis's Soviet government, Stalin having been chased from Moscow and then Kubishev, and I'm on the verge of "Automatic Total Victory". In layman's terms, Germany is about to win not just the game, but also the war.

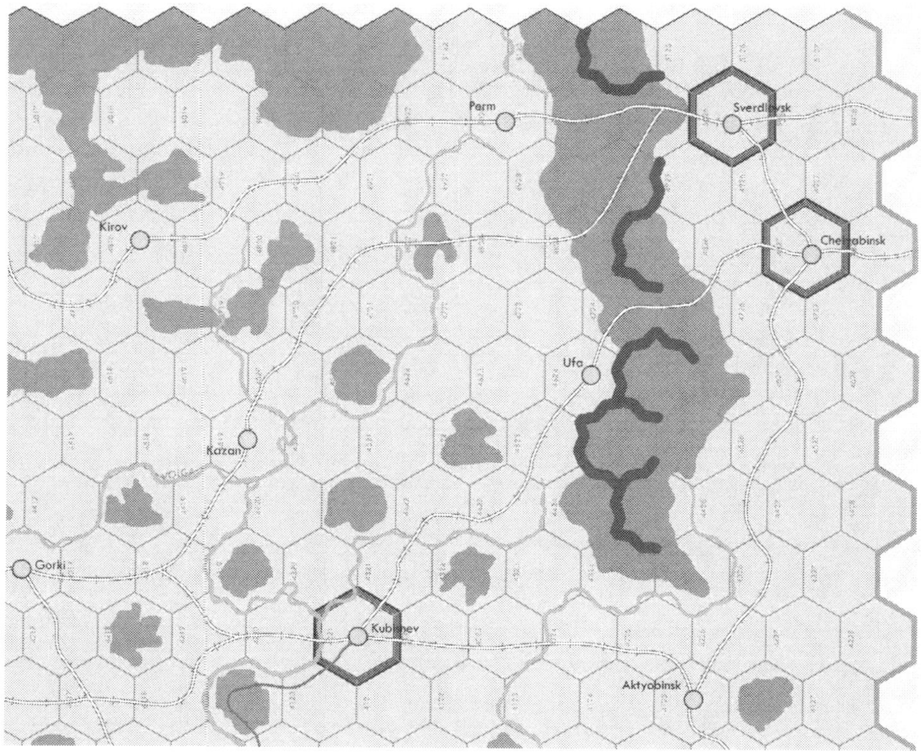

Fig. 7 – The Urals and the northeastern map edge

"Have we ever seen an Axis ATV in any of our games?" I ask.

Dennis looks fidgety. "I can't remember one," he says. He's wearing a hooded sweatshirt with a tie-dyed swirl of yellow, red, blue and green spiraling out from his stomach. It looks like the self-portrait of a sea horse on acid.

"This game, right here, is how Germany could have won the war," I say.

"Germany couldn't have won the war," says Dennis.

"You sure about that?"

"Yes. Now, shush for a minute and let me try to stop you winning this one."

Dennis is wrong, of course. Germany absolutely could have won the war. It might have won by pursuing a different strategy – perhaps in the Mediterranean, as previously discussed. Less plausibly, it might have won with the help of an alternative government – e.g., imagine if Elser's assassination attempt in 1939 had succeeded, only to bring about a right-wing coup of army officers who retained the totemic inspiration of Hitler while discarding the inefficiencies of Nazi government. (That *could* have happened, right?) But most plausibly of all, Germany might have won the war simply by performing slightly better while its opponents performed slightly worse – just enough to knock Britain or the Soviet Union out of the war before the industrial might of the Allies could manifest itself on the battlefield.

My current game with Dennis fits this latter scenario. I conquered Poland, Denmark and Norway on schedule before turning against France, to which Dennis had committed most of the British army. I didn't capture Paris until July-August 1940, but in doing so I killed four British steps – akin to the Dunkirk evacuation never having occurred. With the remnants of the BEF back in England, Egypt was weakly defended, and by Summer 1941 I forced a passage into Alexandria and Cairo. This duly impressed many European heads of state: between Autumn 1940 and Spring 1941, I got lucky on five of my six 50-50 Treaty rolls and gained Hungary, Rumania, Yugoslavia, Greece and Turkey as Axis allies. Dennis, now needing to guard the Caucasus as well as western Russia, tried to bend the Soviet army backwards without letting it break, but my hard-charging panzers turned a small mistake near Kharkov into a major blunder as I encircled and destroyed seven Soviet armies in July-August 1941. In August-September, Rostov fell and Guderian entered Moscow, and as Dennis backpedaled toward the Volga, the stranded bastions of Sevastopol and Leningrad capitulated early in 1942. Unhindered by any serious Soviet counter-offensive in Winter 1941-42, my Case Blue offensive of Summer 1942 has driven successfully on Kubishev and besieged both Archangel in the north and Baku on the Caspian Sea. I'm not strong enough to march much further toward the Urals, but I shouldn't need to.

Over at Consimworld, members frequently debate how optimal Germany's performance was in World War II, and how this should be reflected in games about the conflict. As mentioned previously, in virtually every wargame on this topic (including *Totaler Krieg*), the Axis player wins the game by bettering Germany's historical performance. In a game where both players have an equal chance of winning, presumably the Axis player should therefore do better than Hitler historically did about 50 percent of the time. But is that a fair proposition? Should the historical outcome of any situation always be treated as the 50th percentile result, with variation in either direction being equally likely? Arguably, the historical German performance was nearer the 90th percentile than the 50th: in particular, the rapid fall of Norway and France, Rommel's recovery in North Africa and the stunning early successes of Barbarossa were very low-probability events only made possible by incredible German luck and horrendous Allied mistakes. History fixates upon key German mistakes but ignores far more serious Allied errors: the Dunkirk evacuation is viewed as a key turning point, while the three weeks of barely imaginable German successes that preceded it (and necessitated it) are taken for granted. Diverting the panzers from Moscow toward Kiev in August 1941 is a mortal error that might have cost Germany the war, but if Stalin had taken any precautions whatsoever before the German invasion, or if the Red Army hadn't impersonated the Royal Yugoslav Army for two solid months after it started, Hitler wouldn't have been so well positioned to win the war in the first place.

So how do you design a wargame about World War II? If you give the Allied player perfect hindsight – let him abandon the Dyle Plan and cover the Ardennes in 1940, or conduct his Soviet defense in 1941 exactly as he wishes – you probably won't be left with a game that resembles the war. Because if the French campaign bogs down in stalemate, as it might well have done, Germany probably can't invade Russia in 1941. And even if the *Wehrmacht* performs perfectly in France, Russia might still be able to stop the Barbarossa invasion near Kiev and Minsk. This works as a simulation, and it could still yield a balanced game if the Axis player is only required to prolong the war beyond 1943 to win. But would such a game feel like World War II? Would gamers want to play a "simulation" that regularly features trench warfare in Flanders in 1940, Italy and the US staying on the sidelines, and Stalin attacking through Germany's back door in 1942? Nobody has designed that game yet, so it's hard to tell, but I have my doubts.

Instead, like other games *Totaler Krieg* artificially weakens France so that it almost always surrenders in the summer of 1940, and it forces the Soviets to commit nine armies on border defense duty in Poland as cannon fodder. This ensures the median game will reach the end of 1941 in a historical position, and the Allies will normally have to work hard to win the war by 1945. On the other hand, this means the Axis player doesn't need to greatly outperform history to capture Moscow, or Leningrad, or Suez – and if he significantly beats the baseline, his panzers might well reach the Urals or the Persian Gulf. That doesn't feel right either, and because game design decisions like these seem to force the Allies into repeating their historical mistakes in ways that the Germans and Italians are not, some gamers accuse these games of Axis fanboyism. The charge isn't fair – I'm sure the designers' goal in all of these games is to recreate World War II, not fantasize about the triumph of Nazism – but its basis is understandable.

That said, everything in my current game with Dennis passes the historical sniff test. The only questionable element of my impending triumph is the logistics of operating more than a thousand miles beyond the 1941 frontier as early as August 1942; everything else is a natural byproduct of my French campaign. Call it a test case of what might have happened if the BEF had capitulated at Dunkirk: the snowballing consequences thereafter all ring true to me. Maybe Dunkirk really was the key turning point everyone says it was?

I put that question to Dennis.

"If Dunkirk hadn't happened, Hitler would have found some other way to screw things up," he responds.

We're in July-August 1942, and Dennis has exactly two turns to avert a decisive defeat. He'll probably lose the game regardless, but with Baku doomed to fall in August-September, Dennis must recapture an Objective Hex by the end of Autumn or the war will end in a comprehensive German victory. Kubishev looks the most likely target.

"I love exploring parts of the map we rarely get to use," I say. "I mean, actually defending the Volga north of Stalingrad, or the forests around Kirov. If you make it back into Kubishev, you'll probably be the first leader to fight his way across the Volga from the east since Genghis Khan."

"Are you not counting the Russian Civil War?"

"Oh. Good question – you might be right. Anyway, do you remember that game we played when you had Norway and Finland and I had Sweden?"

"Yep."

"That was a weird one, figuring out how to use the geography correctly."

On the *Totaler Krieg* map, Norway is full of rough terrain and mountain hexsides, while Sweden is full of forest hexes and parallel rivers. Trying to defend Sweden from the north, against attacks starting at Lulea and ending in Stockholm, was enough to permanently instill in me a deep understanding of Baltic topography. I can't imagine many wargamers ever failed a high-school Geography class.

As Dennis ponders his last-minute bid for salvation, I'm struck by how calm he looks. Bored, even. "Nothing fazes you, does it?" I ask.

"What do you mean?"

"The front line in Russia is basically in Asia, and you don't seem very bothered."

"It's just a game."

"I know, but you're losing it pretty badly."

"How many times do I have to tell you? The play's the thing. Better to have played and lost than never to have played at all. Right, let's go – I'll attack Uralsk, using my HQ and everyone else adjacent to it. 3-to-1 if you use your HQ – what do you want to do?"

"I want to win, of course. I'll defend with my HQ." Dennis rolls a '6', and his miniscule chances of winning recede still further.

You know, for all of my discussions and daydreaming about the different paths World War II might have taken, I've never thought about what Europe might have looked like after a German victory. Counterfactuals fascinate me, but dystopian visions frighten me: I might as well ponder the future of humanity after global thermonuclear war. I know some people enjoy that sort of thing, but we all set our own boundaries and have lines we refuse to cross. I guess mine are near the point at which intellect gives way to imagination: the ramifications of a Nazi triumph are just too nightmarish to contemplate. And yet, I have no problem simulating the war itself right up to the final peace treaty. Strange. Maybe Dennis will psychoanalyze this part of me during our postgame recap.

❖ ❖ ❖

Becs lives in a cozy, three-bedroom house with a bright red front door flanked by white, timber cladding. Her older brother John is a sophomore at UC-Santa Barbara, her father is a tax attorney, and I recognize her mother as an active supporter of various school functions at Muhlendorf. Today being the Friday after Thanksgiving, and John being home for a few days, the three of them have gone to the mall and then the movies together, leaving Becs alone with me in her living room for our next AP Euro get-together.

When our Winter term begins on Monday, we'll begin studying the Scientific Revolution and the Enlightenment. "This is going to be a weird topic for me," I remark, settling into a leather sofa as Becs reclines on an adjacent armchair. "Enlightenment philosophy is barely history and deadly dull, but without it, I wouldn't be able to critique it."

Becs is wearing jeans and a scruffy grey sweatshirt. "I used to think the brain was the most fascinating part of the human body," she says. "Then I thought, well, look what's telling me that."

"Nice one."

"I didn't come up with that myself, but thanks. So, what do you want to do today?"

"I thought, you know, we could look at our notes for the course so far, maybe focus on the areas where we didn't do so well on the exam."

"OK."

"Would you rather do something else?"

"No, that sounds fine. I've just never studied anything shortly after a final exam or during a school holiday. Have you?"

"Huh. Good question. I'm not sure I have either. Is this a bad idea? Should I just go home?"

"No, it's fine." Becs smiles. "What did you struggle with on the exam?"

Good question. "There was the FRQ about art and literature," I say.

"You didn't actually answer that one, did you?"

"No, I chose the other one."

"Anything else?"

"There were one or two multiple-choice questions I wasn't sure about."

"And that's it?"

"Kinda. Yeah."

"Do you remember the questions you weren't sure about."

"No, not really."

Becs laughs. "So to sum up, you're here to study for an exam you aced already, during a break when we're not in school anyway, and because we don't have our exam papers or a list of the correct answers with us, there's not actually much for us to study."

All the blood in my body races into my cheeks. "Yep," I mumble. "This was a great idea."

"No, I'm sorry. That came out the wrong way. What a horrid thing to say – I apologize."

"That's OK – you're right."

"Don't worry about it."

I slouch into the sofa and clear my throat. "What do you think of the course so far?" I ask.

"It's been good. I enjoy it more than my other classes, even if it isn't always easy."

"Do you like Mister Prendergast?"

"Yeah. Yes. He's a bit out there sometimes, but mostly in a good way. I've had a lot of teachers I've liked a lot less. You?"

"I'm not sure yet. I'm still trying to figure out what he wants to accomplish with us."

"What do you mean?"

"Hmmm. Imagine two different teachers in two AP Euro classes. In the first class, everyone gets at least a 4 on the AP exam, and eight or ten students develop a passing interest in history which stays with them as adults. In the second class, there are some 3s and even 2s on the exam, and at the end of the year only four or five students remain interested in history – but in two of them, that interest becomes really deep, and one of those two eventually earns a PhD and discovers something important about our past. Based upon those results, which teacher has been more successful?"

"I'm not sure."

"I'm not sure either."

"Which kind of teacher do you want Mister Prendergast to be?"

"I don't know. I mean, for a subject like Physics or Chemistry, it's a no-brainer: it's better to make a few deep connections with your students than lots of shallow ones. Unless we encourage our smartest students to progress in the sciences, all of humanity will eventually suffer – we need scientists to cure cancer and fix global warming and desalinate water and save the rest of us from ourselves. But with History, I'm not so sure. I can't really grasp what big breakthroughs might be made or where they might lead. Plus, I think everyone should have an interest in our past and know where we've come from, at least to some degree. Everyone can and should be an armchair historian; do you even get armchair physicists or mathematicians?"

"You get people who like Sudoku."

"Sure, but Sudoku isn't exactly Advanced Calculus, is it? Take the highest level of knowledge a student could be taught in high school – AP classes across the board. Don't you think the knowledge taught in History classes is more likely to be useful to the average person than the knowledge taught in Math and Science classes?"

"No."

"No?"

Becs shakes her head. "I think you're biased. Don't you think exposure to the sciences might inspire students to become engineers and doctors and pharmacists, even if the specific knowledge taught in their classes doesn't become directly relevant to them? I also think you should broadly understand how the human body works, or how the earth revolves around the sun, or how equal and opposite forces react with one another. Isn't that knowledge at least as useful as knowing what the Edict of Nantes was or what Richelieu did?"

"I think you've just compared apples to oranges, but I take your point."

"You concede I might be right? That perhaps History isn't the only subject we should study at Muhlendorf?"

"Sure, as long as you concede that History is the best and coolest thing to study ever. *Ever.*"

Becs laughs. "OK, it's a deal."

"Excellent. This could be the beginning of a beautiful friendship."

Becs' eyes light up. "*Casablanca*!" she says.

"I know the line from Bugs Bunny, to be honest."

"But you know *Casablanca*?"

"Not really. Actually, not at all. I've never seen it."

"You've never seen *Casablanca*?" Becs shimmers with sudden energy. "You, a student of World War Two, have never seen *Casablanca*? You'll love it."

"Yeah?"

"Let's watch it." Becs stands up. "Right now."

"Now?" I ask. "This minute?"

"Absolutely." At the front of the living room, Becs opens the doors of a wooden hutch to reveal a widescreen television and a small selection of DVDs, including *Casablanca*.

"How many times have you seen *Casablanca*?" I ask.

"You can't see *Casablanca* too many times. And remember, you came over here to study history, so, you know, this counts."

"I think I've already stated my position on the history of art as real history," I smile. "And that includes the history of film."

"Just watch the movie, OK?" Becs closes the blinds and curtains at the windows to darken the room. "It's not like we were really going to study today anyway."

That's an unfair suggestion, but I restrain myself. Becs scrambles onto the sofa next to me and presses "Play" on the remote, and for the next 102 minutes, we sit together in silence.

Casablanca is an odd movie. It begins with five minutes of incredibly clunky exposition – including the worst voiceover I've ever heard, a jerky monotone during the scene-setting right after the credits. Then it settles into what I first think is a formulaic plot full of clichéd dialogue and characters, but then I realize *Casablanca* may have invented both the formula and the clichés, which is pretty impressive. Its historical accuracy and tone are only two degrees north of propaganda, but an hour into the film, when Victor Laszlo starts leading *La Marseillaise* and the other French patrons in Rick's café join in, I get a few goosebumps.

And as that scene ends, something unexpected happens. Becs nuzzles up to me, leaning her head on my left shoulder and entwining her right hand in my left hand. I stiffen: I'm not prepared for this. What's going on? Is this a movie cuddle that will end when the credits roll? If not, how should I respond? What about Melissa? Sometimes I wish I could deactivate my brain; Becs' presence on my shoulder might be rather wonderful if I could.

I focus on the movie even more intently, trying to postpone the inevitable reckoning. As the denouement approaches, at several moments Becs grips my hand more firmly and tensely, and she begins to sniffle as Ilsa and Victor walk into the mist toward the airplane on the final runway. Rick becomes human, a gun is fired, the usual suspects are rounded up, and a beautiful friendship begins…it's a great ending, but one thing doesn't add up.

"Where are they going?" I mumble, still staring ahead as the screen goes blank.

"What do you mean?" asks Becs, still sniffling.

"Rick and Louis," I say. "They're walking into the middle of an airfield on a foggy night."

"I don't know. It's a metaphor."

"Maybe there's an ATM for the Banque Nationale de Morocco at the far end of the runway, where Louis can withdraw his ten thousand francs."

"Don't be silly," says Becs, gently breaking our clinch to turn off the television. "Did you like it?"

"Yeah, I did." I turn to look at Becs, her eyes glistening softly with tears. "It's a great movie."

"I'm so pleased."

"It's not great history, though."

"Uh-oh." Becs smiles.

"Vichy Morocco wasn't really like that. The Germans weren't allowed to run the show there so blatantly – and I'm not sure any German officers or soldiers were ever stationed there."

"Really?"

"Also, those letters of transit were weird – didn't Captain Renault say that they were signed by General de Gaulle?"

"Yeah."

"General de Gaulle led the Free French and directly opposed the Vichy government. Why would letters signed by him have any standing in Casablanca? Why would he sign such letters in the first place?"

"Look…"

"And the idea that there was a single 'last train out of Paris' is a gross simplification…"

"Stop it."

"…like anyone knew exactly when the Germans would reach that particular station, or that the train would definitely make it to Marseilles without being bombed or captured first…"

"Shhhh…"

Becs puts an index finger up to my lips and presses them very gently. She smiles, leans close to me and softly says, "Don't you dare ruin this film for me!"

She withdraws her finger, stops smiling, tilts her head to the side and brings her lips to mine, closing her eyes. We kiss twice: timidly at first, then in earnest as I fully reciprocate, cupping her face in my hands.

"Did you like that?" asks Becs, keeping her face close to mine.

"Yes, very much," I reply, my voice cracking into a whisper. I clear my throat, then summon the courage to ask, "You know, the Christmas Dance at school is coming up soon. Would you, maybe, like to go with me?"

Becs smiles. "Maybe we could watch another movie instead?" she suggests.

"Good answer." I grin.

Becs places a tender hand on my cheek, and our lips draw together again.

PART THREE

1.

Here's my personal and highly subjective list of the Top Ten Movies about World War II:

10) *Saving Private Ryan* – Only the first 30 minutes, obviously. Everything after Omaha Beach is Hollywood drivel, although it gets bonus points for inspiring a porn film called *Saving Ryan's Privates.*

9) *Midway* – An unforgivable typo in one of the captions suggests that the final Japanese carrier, *Hiryu*, sinks on 6 June instead of 4 June (and that nothing at all happened on 5 June), and the B-movie plot involving the fictional Captain Garth and his son is terrible. But it's good fun and mostly depicts the battle faithfully, even though large chunks of battle footage were cannibalized from #6, below.

8) *The Bridge Over the River Kwai* – The plot is only vaguely historical, but the movie is very well done and gives a real taste of life in a Japanese prison camp.

7) *Das Boot* – The eponymous submarine is completely fictional, but the movie is very well done and gives a real taste of life in a German U-boat.

6) *Tora! Tora! Tora!* – A docudrama ahead of its time, superb history on a huge budget spoiled only by some surprisingly bad acting. Were Japanese admirals and aviators only able to communicate by shouting? No wonder the title has three exclamation marks, not that most of the American cast is much better.

5) *Valkyrie* – Tom Cruise as Claus von Stauffenberg? Seriously? And yet, bizarrely, it works and the history is really good, giving an accurate sense of what might have been and why counterfactual history is so enticing.

4) *The Longest Day* – The definitive D-Day movie. I only wish the melodrama involving Richard Burton could be cut, and the Omaha Beach scene from *Saving Private Ryan* spliced in at the appropriate moment.

3) *The Great Escape* – A sentimental pick, as I saw this for the first time with my father on Christmas Day when I was very young. (Watching *The Great Escape* on the BBC at Christmas is an annual British tradition.) The farfetched American presence of Steve McQueen and James Garner notwithstanding, the story is both riveting and accurately told.

2) *Downfall* – As referenced previously, it's wonderful history and storytelling from start to finish, and Alexandra Maria Lara...wow. A feast for my adolescent

eyes. Plus, parodies of Hitler's rant in the bunker went viral on YouTube. For a well-told and truthful World War II film in a foreign language, how cool is that?

1) *A Bridge Too Far* – No doubt a controversial selection, but it tells a uniquely moving story brilliantly and accurately through the starriest of all-star casts: Redford, Connery, Caine, Caan, Hopkins, Bogarde, O'Neal, Fox, Gould and some amazing bit-part players. (Laurence Olivier as a Dutch doctor! Denholm Elliott, aka Marcus Brodie from the *Indiana Jones* franchise, as an RAF meteorologist! John Ratzenberger, aka Cliff Clavin from "Cheers", as a random US lieutenant! Wolfgang Preiss, aka "that German general in every other war movie", finally receiving his field marshal's baton as von Rundstedt! And of course Gene Hackman with the best comedy Polish accent ever!) Plus, I first watched it on a VHS tape of a network television broadcast – yes, *A Bridge Too Far* once aired in prime time on NBC – in which Elliott Gould gets drenched at Son Bridge and says "Sh…oot", and then back at HQ his use of the word "schmucks" is drowned out by vehicular noises. They needed to censor the word "schmucks" for network television? Really? Anyway, I know the movie is baggy and unfairly soiled the reputation of General Browning – I guess Monty himself was still sacrosanct in 1977 – and I'm sure it can be blamed for the multiplicity of Market-Garden wargames even though it's a really poor topic for counterfactual history. (Seriously, even if XXX Corps struggles into Arnhem and crosses the Rhine, what happens then? Not much, I'd wager.) But I read Cornelius Ryan's book and then saw the movie at an impressionable age, and were the latter to pop up while I'm flicking between channels at home I would absolutely watch it to the end. Maybe I'll screen it for Becs as the second act of a doubleheader.

Note: I won't consider *Casablanca* for my Top Ten because it's not about World War II. Ditto *The Guns of Navarone* and other action capers in which any similarities to World War II are purely coincidental. Oddly, though, one movie which gave me great insight into Nazi Germany was Oliver Stone's *JFK*. After watching the film, I was outraged and certain that Lee Harvey Oswald could not possibly be the lone gunman who assassinated President Kennedy. Then I dug deeper into the facts and was equally outraged to discover how much of the film was utter fantasy. But that led to my epiphany: expose anyone to such a gross tonnage of lies and innuendo, and he's bound to believe that *some* of it must be true. Stone himself has said *JFK* attempts to create a "counter-myth" to the "myth" of the Lone Gunman theory: buy into any of the counter-myth, and your belief in Oswald's guilt must be shaken. Substitute Goebbels for Stone, and you can begin to understand how so many ordinary Germans could be seduced by Nazism and anti-semitism. Even if you thought most Nazi propaganda was loony, it couldn't all be lies, could it?

Given Hollywood's proficiency at portraying the Nazis as slimy weasels – *Casablanca* definitely included – I'm struck by how few films in my Top Ten vilify the "bad guys". *Saving Private Ryan* clearly does this, and for classically Hollywood-ish reasons; *The Bridge Over the River Kwai* and *Valkyrie* do as well, but Japanese cruelty and Nazi thuggery are at the core of their narrative arcs, so in them the vilification seems justified. Otherwise, it can't be coincidental that my favorite films are so even-handed: you may not like what the Japanese or Germans stood for, but you can sympathize with the actions and decisions of the individuals portrayed. Even *Downfall* is remarkably fair toward its subjects: Hitler does rant and rave, but he also calms down and shows lucidity and humanity, just like most of his acolytes. And while the viewer is expected to root for the Allies in each of these movies (apart from *Downfall* and *Das Boot*, where they are barely present), he is not incited to unfairly hate the Germans or Japanese. Even Kommandant von Luger is sympathetic by the end of *The Great Escape*.

That said, I was first drawn toward World War II largely because its "good guys" and "bad guys" are unmistakable, particularly relative to most other wars and periods of history. The dirty Nazis invaded most of Europe and gassed or shot Jews, gypsies, homosexuals and anyone that looked at 'em funny for sport, while the sneaky Japs bombed Pearl Harbor without warning, tortured POWs and repeatedly launched suicide attacks by land, air and sea. Meanwhile, the noble Brits and ingenious Yanks stood for truth, justice and the Anglo-American way – after persevering through Dunkirk and Bataan, we whipped 'em at Midway, El Alamein, Normandy and the Great Marianas Turkey Shoot, and thanks to us, tyranny was comprehensively avenged. This is the popular view of World War II in the English-speaking West, and in this story I'm sure there's a religion waiting to be founded.

Of course, it's not that simple. One can at least argue that Nazi Germany was an unfortunate historical accident of circumstance, a national hypnosis that could have afflicted any of the great powers after World War I. The nation-state and its *Führer* were evil, and all of their citizens deserved to bear collective guilt for Germany's behavior, but only a minority overtly perpetrated conscious acts of evil. Imperial Japan possessed an alien culture – one of great nobility as well as primitive barbarism – that the West found difficult to comprehend; atrocities deserve condemnation, but the collective spirit which animated the kamikaze attacks is worthy of admiration in the right context. Anyway, Japan didn't intend for the Pearl Harbor attack to be as sneaky as it turned out, so can you really blame it for that? As for Italy, Mussolini was a despot and a buffoon, but no worse than many tinpot dictators today; his guilt as an Axis leader is mostly by association – fairer comparisons would be with Franco or Gaddafi, not Hitler – and once he was removed from power, Italy quickly defected.

Among the "good guys", the elephant in the room is the Soviet Union. From August 1939 to June 1941, the Soviet Union was a de facto German client, and Stalin's reign before and after Barbarossa was in many ways worse than Hitler's. (Who is worse, the dictator whose twisted morality compels him to exterminate massive but specific groups of people, or the dictator with no morality who would kill anyone and everyone to enhance his personal power?) And were the Western powers immune from immorality? Of course not: Britain would have become an aggressor in Norway in early 1940 but for its own incompetence; France was stained for decades by its willingness to collaborate with Germany; and the Allied strategic bombing campaigns from Hamburg to Nagasaki via Dresden and Tokyo caused intense postwar guilt among the victors. And then there's the *SS John Harvey*: an American merchant ship carrying 100 tons of mustard gas bombs, it was attacked and sunk by the *Luftwaffe* in port at Bari, Italy on 2 December 1943, killing nearly 1,000 people. That was the largest tally of gas-related deaths in the European war – thank goodness Hitler retained a lifelong aversion to gas warfare after being blinded by gas in World War I! (The mustard gas at Bari was being stocked for potential retaliatory use only, but Churchill told his advisers in July 1944 that he wanted to "drench" Germany with poison gas and took much persuading to change his views.)

I mention all of this partly because I'm a wargamer who plays the Axis in roughly half of my games of *Totaler Krieg*. Do I feel at all squeamish when playing the Germans? Yes, I do. But if you're going to simulate a battle or a war, both players can't be the "good guys" simultaneously – someone has to represent Hitler and the Germans, just as someone has to represent Stalin and the Soviets. And as I've tried to show, the "good guys" are never as good and the "bad guys" never as bad as popular culture would have you believe. In any case, I always try to maintain my intellectual distance. I'm not "being" Hitler, and if I lapse into role-playing at times, I never pretend I'm a Nazi, never glorify atrocities or lightheartedly reference acts of evil, and never downplay the real human suffering we're poorly representing on the gaming table. I always try to honor and respect history for what it is, and what it means to people who might want to forget it.

Of course, a dispassionate observer might agree with the movie *WarGames* and decide the only winning move is not to play *Totaler Krieg* at all. I can respect that position; indeed, sometimes I wonder if the Axis player should be able to win at *Totaler Krieg* by remaining at peace. (Surely the safest way of surviving beyond 1945 with Germany's borders intact involves not going to war in the first place, right? Not that there's much of a game in that.) But ultimately, I have to disagree. Just as good war movies and books are entertaining, educational and thought-provoking in turn, wargaming increases my understanding of history and helps me enjoy it and connect with it much more intimately. And a good wargame has the added benefit of sharpening my logical mind far more than a thousand math classes at Muhlendorf ever could. Apart from the 60 million deaths that made *Totaler Krieg* possible, what's not to like?

❖ ❖ ❖

"Something happened," I say. "I was at Rebecca Fowler's house on Friday night for a study session."

"You were studying during the Thanksgiving break?" asks Melissa.

"Yeah, I know."

"You're really strange sometimes."

"And that's the point: we didn't really study much. Instead, we watched a movie together."

"OK…"

"And one thing led to another, and we sorta wound up kissing each other. A bit."

Melissa's face goes blank. I feel bad for her – I wouldn't want this to be my first experience of school after Thanksgiving, early on a Monday in an empty hallway of lockers and linoleum.

"I'm really sorry, Melissa. It just kinda happened."

"OK, well, we're done," she says. Her face is still dead, but her eyes are alive and angry.

"I didn't want you to not know."

"Do you like her?"

"We're friends."

"Do you like her?"

"Things just got out of hand."

"Are they going to get out of hand again?" Melissa grits her teeth, then says, "Never mind. I don't even care."

"No, I know you do, and…"

"Go to hell."

I still think Melissa is very pretty – as I watch her stomp toward the restrooms at the end of the corridor, her hips swaying and her recently clipped hair bobbing firmly up and down, I realize I might soon think she's downright beautiful. But she's not for me anymore. My eyes have been opened.

❖ ❖ ❖

That's not the conversation I'd feared the most today, although after three hands of the Big Game I think I might be safe, because none of Chris, Melvyn, Freddie, Peter Kasprowicz – our fifth player, and the starting power forward on Muhlendorf's varsity basketball team – or anyone else in our gallery has mentioned Melissa or Becs at all. But then on the fourth hand, Chris casually folds his hand from first position, then turns over his cards to reveal a pair of Kings.

"Wha…what was that?" I ask, incredulous.

"Just proving that you're not the only one who knows how to throw away a good thing," he responds. As he breaks into a grin, Melvyn stretches across the table to high-five him while Freddie cackles.

"Nice one," I say.

"Just for the look on your face, that was definitely worth it," says Chris.

"So what's up?" asks Melvyn.

"These things happen," I say.

"They don't normally happen to you," says Chris.

"Has this been going on for a while?" intrudes Peter.

"Not at all," I say. "Things just got out of hand the other night, and so I did the right thing and came clean with Melissa this morning. And word gets around quickly in this place. So that's that."

"What do you mean, 'Got out of hand'?" asks Melvyn. "What were you doing there in the first place?"

"Were you on a date?" asks Peter.

"Not that it's any of your business, but it was supposed to be a study session…"

"Over Thanksgiving?" guffaws Freddie.

"You really are the dorkiest dork who ever dorked," says Chris. "There's no way Rebecca realizes what she's getting herself into."

"And what about Melissa?" asks Melvyn.

"Well, unlike some people at this table, I did actually pause occasionally to analyze my relationship."

"Meow!" says Chris, punching Melvyn in the arm.

"Look, we've talked about this before. I like Melissa a lot, but we don't have much in common. I like Becs a lot, and we do. I didn't mean to leave Melissa for Becs as such, and I'm not sure what's going to happen with Becs anyway. But here I am. Go ahead, have a go at me – let's get this over with."

Chris looks at Melvyn. Melvyn looks at Peter. Freddie shrugs his shoulders. "Yeah, that sounds fair enough," mumbles Chris, and the others mutter in agreement.

"Really?" I ask.

"Yeah," says Chris. "For now, at least. Anyway, I'm pretty sure I just folded a pair of Kings, so the action is now to Melvyn."

❖ ❖ ❖

Becs is facing her locker, fiddling with her cell phone during the last few minutes of our lunch hour. She's wearing…actually, does it matter what she's wearing? She looks fantastic.

I approach her from behind, tap her twice on the shoulder and gently ask, "What's up?"

"I can't get the text function on my phone to…oh. Hello!" She beams warmly at me.

"I've got a present for you."

"Yeah?"

"Here you go."

She unwraps a tiny parcel in waxy purple paper, revealing a rectangular fridge magnet bearing the image of a *Casablanca* movie poster. "Awww…" she says, and blushes. Her mouth melts into a warm, bashful smile.

"Your locker seemed bare to me – I thought I'd help out."

"Where did you get it?"

"From a shop."

"Which shop?"

"One I normally wouldn't be caught dead in."

"You went out of your way to get this? Just for me?"

"Yep."

She doesn't speak for a moment – she just smiles, then looks down at the ground. She coughs quietly, then murmurs, "That's really sweet."

"The other night…that was really great," I say.

"Yeah."

"Let's do it again sometime. Soon."

"Yeah."

"We should schedule another study session."

"Or something."

"Or something, yeah."

Becs pauses. "I heard you broke up with Melissa," she says.

"That's not quite how I'd put it, but yeah, word travels fast. I don't think she'll want to talk to me for a while."

"I'm sorry."

"No, that's a good thing. Put it this way: I've never shared a study session with her."

"OK."

"By the way, when we do meet for our next study session, I want to make sure we don't forget to, y'know, study."

"Yeah?"

"I like history, and now I know I want to do really well in this class, so I don't want to always get sidetracked by, you know."

"Me?"

"Yes. Well, I mean…no…I didn't mean it that way."

"I know! I was kidding."

"Really? Well, OK. Good."

"We should study, well, whatever it is we're about to learn in a few hours' time. You don't have to justify yourself to me."

"I didn't want you to think I'd been using our study session as an excuse to see you. Because I hadn't."

"If I tell you that I believe you, that I know you like history, that I know you like me *and* that I like you too, will that be enough to stop you from wigging out like this?"

"Heh." My turn to blush. "Yes, yes it will."

"Excellent."

"So I'll see you soon, then?" I ask.

"In AP Euro, if not before."

"And after that?"

"We'll figure something out."

Becs places the fridge magnet neatly on the inside of her locker door, halfway up and halfway across. "It's perfect," she says, and she kisses me on the cheek.

❖ ❖ ❖

Sometimes I stare at the map and nothing happens. My BPA tournament semi-final against Gregory Spearman has reached the crucial May-June 1941 turn, and I'm ready to invade Russia...but I've got nothing. I'm looking at replacement locations in East Prussia, airbases in Hungary and Rumania, stacks of German armies in western Poland and thinner lines of Soviet armies in what used to be eastern Poland, but no plans are forming in my head. My mind is stuck at Becs' locker, images of her smile lapping at my cortex like gentle ocean waves eroding a sand castle.

So I'm relieved to hear the door jangle downstairs, followed by the thump of Dad's heavy briefcase on the floor of the kitchen. I push in my desk chair and bound downward to find Dad is scooping ice cubes from the freezer into a glass. When he turns around, he looks worn down: red tinges around his nose, wider wrinkles on his forehead, hair fraying around the temples.

"Are you OK?" I ask. "Bad day at the office?"

"No," he says, removing his glasses and rubbing his eyes with his fingertips. "I'm fine. I'm fine, really."

"Everything all right?"

"I'm fine. I had a...no, I'm fine." His eyes look red and irritated, maybe from the rubbing. "Very busy. I need to get going."

"You just got back."

"I mean, upstairs. Going upstairs."

"Do need some medicine or something? You don't look great."

"Really, I'm fine."

"Well, guess what happened to me today?"

"You went to school." Dad turns his back to me and fills his glass halfway with water from the sink.

"Yeah, and I seem to now have a new girlfriend."

"Really?" Balancing the water in his left hand, Dad bends over to pick up his briefcase with his right hand and walks around the kitchen table toward the front staircase.

"Can I help you carry that?"

"No, I'm fine."

I follow him through the hallway. "So, Melissa and I are now through, and Becs – do you remember her coming over a few weeks ago to study with me?"

"Not really."

"I think we're together now."

"That's great."

"The thing is, she really likes history."

Dad is climbing the stairs now. "When you're through with her, can I have her?"

"Dad!"

"I mean, as a research assistant or something. Were you thinking something else?"

"I don't know what I'm thinking. But I've got a really good feeling about this – about Becs."

"That's great." We're at the top of the stairs now. "Maybe you'll start playing that game of yours with her instead of Dennis."

"That's a bit premature…"

"Yes, well, so were you."

"What?"

"I'm just kidding. Here." He hands me the glass, withdraws his keys from his pocket and unlocks the door to his upstairs study. "Tell me about her sometime, OK?"

"I will – whenever you're free. Are you sure you're OK, Dad?"

"I'm sorry, Sean – I'm fine, but I'm not fine, you know? So much to do, so much in my head. I'll maybe catch you for dinner later?"

"Sure." I hand him the water glass. "Good luck in there."

"Thanks." He shuts the door, and as I trudge away I hear it lock behind me.

2.

Totaler Krieg comes with a scenario booklet as well as a rules booklet. Dennis and I normally start in Autumn 1939 with the invasion of Poland, but you can also begin the game at eight other points from Spring 1937 to Summer 1943, and several smaller scenarios facilitate faster play or help you learn different sections of the rulebook. Additionally, an expansion to the standard game includes a "Random Campaign Game" generator and a few wildly counterfactual scenarios, one of which Dennis and I have decided to tackle in our next game: "World War One Revisited" assumes Germany, Italy and Austria-Hungary have won the First World War, leaving a vengeful France to trigger the Second.

Dennis, ever the fantasist, is very excited about this scenario, but I'm also attracted to it for two reasons. First, because I trust the *Totaler Krieg* game engine to produce plausible results from a historical starting point, I also trust it to generate a believable narrative from this wacky premise. The game we're about to play might well represent what World War II could have looked like had the world taken several different paths between 1914 and 1938. More than that, though, in one sense a scenario like this is more historical than recreating history. In the normal 1939 campaign game, our expectations are colored by what actually happened: we know Poland should fall quickly, and there is usually a 1940 campaign in France and the Low Countries, etc., and we can measure our progress against the historical timeline. But in this scenario, I have no idea what's about to happen – I know how to use the forces at my disposal, and I know my ultimate goals, but I'm not sure how to achieve them. Instead, I can only follow my gut and hope for the best – just like Hitler, Stalin, Churchill and Roosevelt had to.

To prepare for the game, I scanned relevant sections of the *Totaler Krieg* map and digitally doctored them to exaggerate the new national borders of Austria-Hungary (now including Yugoslavia and Rumania), the Ottoman Empire (encompassing everything from Greece to Iraq and Egypt), and the now-independent buffer states of Siberia and the Armenian Republic. I then printed these overlays and positioned them precisely atop the map, holding them in place with tiny pieces of adhesive putty before carefully lowering my plexiglass cover. An aesthetic marvel it is not, but it does the job and won't keep us guessing which countries do and don't exist as we play the game.

When he arrives for our session and sees the map for the first time, Dennis is impressed. "How long did that take you?" he asks.

"Long enough," I reply. "I haven't attempted an arts-and-crafts project like this since elementary school."

"Not bad for a guy who doesn't paint minis."

"Yeah, I'm into DFE, not DIY. Anyway, we agreed you will be playing the Germans, right?"

"Yep," says Dennis. "Let's talk through all of the changes in the scenario."

"First of all, we begin in Summer 1939 instead of the Autumn, which means you can start with a full campaigning season if you wish. You've got the Nazi-Soviet Pact in place, or the "Imperial-Soviet Pact" as we ought to call it. You can also impose a truce upon the Western Allies at the start of the game if you wish, which according to the scenario 'represents Imperial Germany's influence in the League of Nations and her ability to hinder the West'. Sounds fishy to me."

"I'm sure it's there for a reason."

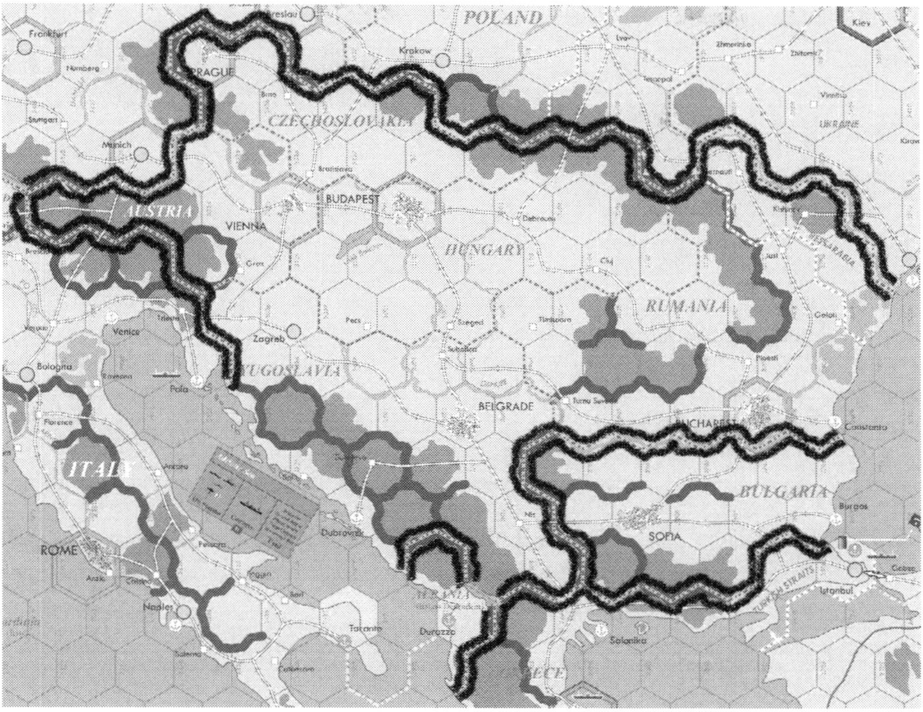

Fig. 8 – Greater Austria-Hungary and the Ottoman Empire in Europe, as redrawn on the Totaler Krieg *map*

"You think this scenario was heavily playtested?"

"I'd be happy if it was played once before publication and found not to be a runaway victory for either side."

"We'll find out soon enough." I scan the scenario rules again. "Alsace-Lorraine and all of Poland are part of Germany, the Maginot forts don't exist, and 'Anglo-French Non-Cooperation' means British and French units can't stack together until after France collapses."

"Where's the bad news?"

"I'm not sure. The French army is larger than normal, and you do have to capture every French city to force a Case Yellow collapse – and there's no Vichy option, so France will always fight on from North Africa. Plus, France is an 'Aggressor' country and doesn't begin under Appeasement, so you'll definitely have to deal with it first. And then there's Spain, which starts as an active Soviet ally on the grounds that 'Imperial Germany didn't support Franco.' I'm not sure I buy that either, but it does mean that when you eventually attack the Soviet Union, you'll have to neutralize Iberia as well."

"And we both know how much fun the Allies can have in Spain," comments Dennis.

"We certainly do," I say. "So, what do you have in mind – how are you going to play this? Or are you not going to tell me?"

"Patience, Jedi – all will be revealed in good time."

"In good time" proves to mean "almost immediately". I had guessed Dennis might open conservatively with German Mobilization and maybe Limited War Production, growing his army before attacking through Belgium in Spring 1940. Instead, Dennis immediately tries to Treaty the Low Countries, with a 1-in-3 chance of success, but a Coup d'Etat forces him to invade. Although he quickly captures Brussels, Rotterdam remains mine through the Summer and France is as yet unbreached; better still, German entry into Belgium triggers immediate expansion of the French and British war economies. Dennis does successfully Treaty both Denmark-Norway and Finland by the end of the summer, but even with Anglo-French Non-Cooperation in effect, as the war progresses into its second year it feels like "World War One Revisited" in more ways than one. At the end of May-June 1940, Dennis has only just captured Paris and Lyon, and Calais remains firmly held by a strong British pocket with HQ support from London.

With our evening drawing to a close, Dennis is preparing one final turn of attacks when I blurt out, "So, I kinda have a new girlfriend."

"I didn't know you had an old girlfriend," says Dennis, still looking at the board and nibbling the lid of his ballpoint pen.

"I did, sort of."

"And what happened?"

"I traded up."

"Outstanding." Dennis drops his pen to the table. "What's her name, the new one?"

"Rebecca."

"Is she nice?"

"Yes. It's early days, but I have a good feeling. I think she could be the one."

"Why is that?"

"She's very pretty and really intellectual, and she's got a deep interest in history as well."

"Yeah? You should invite her to play *Totaler Krieg* with us."

"Heh. My Dad made the same joke the other day."

"I'm serious. She could be the West, and you could be the Soviets and coach her on the rules."

"Ha! Not a chance in hell."

"Or we could play *Maria.* That's a proper three-player game, on the War of Austrian Succession – it uses normal playing cards for combat, so she'd probably get right into it. Plus, she could be a woman – Maria Theresa."

"She won't be joining us at the gaming table."

"Why not?"

"Do you think she has any idea I play games like this?"

"She doesn't?"

"Hell no."

"Maybe you should tell her that you do."

"Maybe you're wrong, and maybe I'm sorry I ever brought this up."

"Why wouldn't you tell her?"

I stare incredulously at Dennis. "Because I don't want her to think I'm a freak."

"But you are a freak."

"No, I'm not."

"I hate to break it to you, but yeah, you are. You enjoy playing wargames. That's not a bad thing – it's unusual, but it is who you are."

"But I don't just play wargames. I have a life away from this table, you know."

Dennis crosses his arms. "You said this girl, Rebecca…she might be 'the one'?"

"Yeah."

"If that's true, at some point you'll need to let her know who you really are. And not just part of who you are – all of who you are."

"Says the guy whose most serious girlfriend left him because he's a wargamer."

"And we weren't destined to be together. We broke up because Carolyn couldn't understand or accept who I am."

I look down at the map in front of me, then back up at Dennis. "That's very mature of you," I say.

"And because she's a bitch."

I snort. "Yeah, not so much."

"Really, though, this could work out great for you. What if you tell Rebecca about wargames and she wants to play then – or better yet, that she loves them? I mean, you could be living the ultimate wargaming fantasy."

"Settle down, OK? She's been my girlfriend for about a minute-and-a-half."

"That threesome for *Maria* could happen one day."

"Hypothetically? Sure, I guess – anything's possible. But not any time soon."

"OK. But give it some thought, yeah?"

"I will."

❖ ❖ ❖

That's the last I see of Dennis before Christmas – one Thursday he has to stay late at work, then the next Thursday we get a foot of snow and it isn't safe to travel. And soon he'll be home for the holidays – he's off to see his parents in Kentucky. So our current game is hibernating.

I'm seeing a lot of Becs, though. We've had three more study sessions, only one of which degenerated into kissing. One night we had a fascinating discussion about the Middle East's historical progress, my central thesis being that the Islamic world is about 150 years behind the West but catching up rapidly thanks to modern technology. Another night I convinced her that the West's fascination with D-Day reflects its ignorance of Russia's role in World War II; she had no idea how heavy the Soviet share of the Allied burden really was.

Today Mr. Prendergast is lecturing our class about the Agricultural Revolution, which is just as exciting as it sounds. He opened by comparing 18th-century cottage industries to modern globalization, sweatshops and the movie *Slumdog Millionaire*; it might have helped if any of us had seen *Slumdog Millionaire* or if, you know, this class were called "AP Economics". I know the Agricultural Revolution is vital to the grand sweep of history, but economics is to history as logistics is to battles, a subject best left to people like my father while the rest of us talk about the interesting bits. I'm trying my best to pay attention, but it's a struggle, and I can tell I'm not alone.

When Mr. Prendergast asks us to tell him about Jethro Tull and says "either one will do", he is met with stony silence and blank faces. "Nothing? Really?" he asks. "Forty years together and sixty million albums sold, and nobody has a clue? I'm clearly getting too old for this."

"It says in the book that he was one of the first advocates of using horses in plowing instead of oxen," says Hugh Johnson.

Mr. Prendergast sighs. "Ten years ago we could have wasted a good five minutes on the merits of *Songs from the Wood* versus *Crest of a Knave*, or the guitar skills of Martin Barre, before moving on to innovations in English agriculture. But yes, Mister Johnson is right…"

My textbook says that "Jethro Tull (1674-1741), part crank and part genius, was another important English innovator." That's him sorted, then. I scan the page in reverse: Charles Townsend (1674-1738) was another English pioneer regarding crop rotation. The Dutch engineer Cornelius Vermuyden directed several large drainage projects in Yorkshire and Cambridgeshire in England, reclaiming 40,000 acres of arable land in the Cambridge fens. The Dutch became experts in water drainage to ameliorate population density and facilitate the growth of towns and cities like Amsterdam. Yawn…then this astonishing paragraph jumps out at me:

> This agricultural revolution, which took longer than historians used to believe, was a great milestone in human development. The famous French scholar Marc Bloch, who gave his life in the resistance to the Nazis in World War Two, summed it up well: "The history of the conquest of the fallow by new crops, a fresh triumph of man over the earth that is just as moving as the great land clearing of the Middle Ages, [is] one of the noblest stories that can be told."

Becs is sitting at the desk to my left, legs crossed, doodling in pencil on her notebook. I fold my own notepad over and, in the top-left corner of the back page, write:

READ → 1ST PARA, P. 601

I carefully and quietly tear the page from the pad and, with Mr. Prendergast's gaze diverted elsewhere, pass it across to Becs. She glances quizzically at me, then does as instructed. Then she crooks her head at me and squints uncomprehendingly. On the paper she responds:

HUH?

She slips the note back to me. Below her response, I write:

NAZIS? REALLY???

Becs receives the paper and smiles. Mr. Prendergast is prattling on about English landowners and the enclosure movement. Becs responds again:

MORE INTERESTING THAN ZZZZZ…

I barely stifle a laugh and receive a tap on my right shoulder from Chris, who motions to the paper Becs and I have been passing back and forth. I shrug my shoulders and slip it across the aisle to him. I watch him open his textbook to page 601, read the passage, reread my and Becs' comments, and shake his head. Then he scribbles:

YOU GUYS PLAYING DORK DORK GOOSE?

I smirk, draw an arrow pointing to Chris's sentence and write:

CARE TO ANSWER THAT ONE?

I pass the paper again to Becs. Upon reading Chris's comment, she chuckles a little too loudly, then starts drafting a lengthy reply. In doing so, she doesn't notice that Mr. Prendergast, without breaking the rhythm of his lecture, is now meandering in our direction. I suggestively clear my throat, but to no avail. "So that's how England had become thoroughly 'proletarianized', to use a good Marxist word, by the late eighteenth century, completely dependent upon cash wages earned in...*Miss* Fowler, would you like to share with the rest of us what could *possibly* be more amusing than the livelihood of subsistence farmers in England at the end of the enclosure movement?"

Becs blushes, amidst sniggering from the gallery, then silently hands Mr. Prendergast our piece of paper. He scans it, then shakes his head and glances at me before addressing Becs. "I've collected some notes in my day, but never one quite as on point as this. Miss Fowler, what does it say in the first paragraph of page six hundred and one in our textbook?"

"It's a quote from Marc Bloch," I interrupt. "He died while resisting the Nazis in World War II, it says."

"And what's so remarkable about that?" Mr. Prendergast asks me.

"In possibly the blandest section of the most stony-faced history book I've ever read, and that's saying something, they cite the French Resistance in World War Two," I reply. "It's like the authors don't even believe themselves that this is interesting and are forced to resort to gratuitous Nazi references to keep us all awake. Like this is the History Channel, only in book form."

"Mister Lansbury..."

"I know, I'm sorry – but I'm really trying to care. And I know modern history is founded on the Agricultural Revolution and then the Industrial Revolution. But it'd be hard to make the history of farming sound interesting even if there weren't, like, three feet of snow outside right now."

"I was more right than I ever could have guessed," mutters Chris under his breath.

Mr. Prendergast smiles gently and shakes his head, then crumples our note in his hand. He turns to the class and asks, "Out of curiosity, are any of your parents farmers? Anyone's father, or mother, make a living out of the agriculture business?" Three people raise their hands. "Mister Sauerbrunner, do you have any response to Mister Lansbury's assertion?"

Chad Sauerbrunner coughs, then says plainly, "I wouldn't call this stuff interesting, but I've got more in common with farmers in England than I do with the Nazis."

"Yes, I'm a schmuck, and I do apologize," I whimper.

"No, this is good," says Mr. Prendergast. "Mister Lansbury's horizons have been neatly broadened: perhaps he'll think twice before assuming anyone else in here has ever watched the History Channel. Meanwhile, everyone gets a nice mnemonic for the AP exam: think enclosure movement and think…think what, Miss Fowler?"

"Nazis?" asks Becs.

"Think Nazis," beams Mr. Prendergast. "Excellent work, Mister Lansbury. Meanwhile, speaking of the AP exam, let me share a DBQ with everyone from a previous exam called, 'Why did the chicken cross the road?' And no, I'm not making that up – AP exams don't come wittier than AP European History, let me tell you."

As Mr. Prendergast tosses our note in the trash and fetches a set of handouts from his desk, Becs gives me a quick tap on the arm, then tilts her notebook toward me. She has written:

THANKS FOR TAKING THAT BULLET ☺ XXX

I shrug my shoulders, then grin and wink at her. She flicks her hair upward and turns bashfully away. I'm so in love right now. Mind you, counting her aborted graffiti-writing attempt at Homecoming, that's twice she's been saved by timely interruptions. But I suspect I can find a way to make her pay me back.

3.

Over at Consimworld, an argument is raging about whether Denmark is to blame for World War II. I'm almost as in love with this thread as I am with Becs.

These are the undisputed facts: on 9 April 1940, Germany invaded both Norway and Denmark, and the tiny Danish army offered almost no resistance before formally capitulating two hours after Germany's declaration of war. Because it was so cooperative, and because it possessed impeccable Aryan credentials, Denmark was alone among Germany's conquests in being allowed to retain its government and a large measure of sovereignty, at least until mid-1943. Openly democratic elections were permitted, and King Christian X remained in the country throughout the war; also, most of its Jews were ultimately saved from extermination thanks to governmental and then popular resistance.

On the other hand, Denmark's rapid surrender allowed Germany to quickly seize airbases in northern Jutland which were vital to the much more complex and strategically important operation in Norway, and it is around this point – within a broader discussion of neutrality in World War II – that the Consimworld drumbeat begins with this question:

Why didn't the Danes resist?

To which this quite reasonable response is posted:

> They judged, correctly in my view, that it would be utterly pointless. Resistance would not have delayed the occupation by a single day, would have cost no doubt many Danish military and civilian lives, and risked Copenhagen getting what Warsaw and later Rotterdam got. For no benefit to the Allied cause whatsoever except maybe a few dozen dead German soldiers, which the others would no doubt seek revenge for.

And then the fun begins:

> The Danish army and government, rather than perform an army's and a government's most basic tasks, chose to surrender instead....The Danes failed to stand up for their own independence. As in the case of Sweden and Switzerland, they collaborated in support of Nazi Germany. Of the three, at least the Swedes and Swiss took their people's taxes fairly – they preserved their national independence. The Danish government chose to facilitate German success while hoping her enemies would restore a freedom they would not defend....A week's resistance might have saved Norway and emboldened the Dutch and Belgians. Might have given pause to the Swedes to defend their own sovereignty. Might indeed have thrown the whole course of the war off the horrible track we know, saving millions of lives. We'll never know, because it wasn't tried.

Which inevitably produces this:

> What an utterly ridiculous statement.

And the even more inevitable counter:

> And now you claim to know "utterly" how an action could or could not alter history. Priceless.

And then:

> Next, let's discuss how those Luxemburgers rolled over! They could've stopped the Germans, they could've!

But even jokes can elicit fascinating factoids:

> Luxembourg had made provisions to prevent Germany from crossing the border (reinforced concrete blocks) but the wily Wehrmacht engineers had prepared wooden bridges to roll right over them when the time came. Overcoming concrete obstacle with funny contraptions wasn't invented by the D-Day Allies!

The same contributor then posts a series of intelligent responses to the whole debate:

They could have fought – that's what armed forces are for – and I believe they should have, too. If countries only fight when attacked by one no bigger than themselves, then none of Hitler's targets should have fought back until he attacked the USSR or the USA! So I believe the Danes should have fought, though not to the point of passing global moral judgement on the whole nation, as opposed to blaming their government's decision at the time. Bear in mind that the Danish government had less time to make up its collective mind about the issue than we've spent discussing it here, and it's not as if the country had any recent military experience (and besides, when was the last time Denmark hadn't lost a war anyway?).

That said, suppose a junkie decides to come at you with a knife to mug you. You can give him your money or decide that you'll resist, but according to [you], the quality of your choice won't be affected by your being a little old lady or your being the world free fight champion, heavyweight category. (It's a dark alley.) ☺

Sweden and Switzerland weren't attacked. The Swiss and Swedes did exactly what the US and every other neutral did: they tried to rearm so as to be in a position to defend themselves, and once reasonably secure that they couldn't be invaded they started talking back to Germany. For the Swedes, this was in mid-1943. For the Swiss, it never was (it took Allied diplomatic pressure to make trade with Germany stop in mid-1944). In both cases, economic collaboration was a necessity in any case. The USA had alternative, non-German-controlled sources of food or raw materials; the Swiss and Swedes hadn't. Check where Swedish coal and food were coming from.

I'm not trying to argue that the neutrals' behavior was noble. My point is that absolutely *every* country behaved roughly the same, and the first step invariably was to try not to be sucked into the war: appeasement for the British, the French and the Poles, neutrality for everyone else. And in that regard, it was not US policy to become a belligerent.

Britain and France were the only countries to take a serious military risk that they could have avoided. Everyone else on the Allied side either was attacked and therefore never got to make the decision, was "kindly persuaded" to attack or else (Turkey by the US/UK, Romania and Bulgaria by the Soviets), or was in no particular danger when it joined the war (like Mexico). Note that I am emphatically *not* arguing for any kind of British and French moral superiority, here. On the other hand, I do think that recent statements about nations earning their freedom and standing up to the aggressor (to include the US) contrasting with more cowardly ones are good political rants but very poor history.

Of course, the discussion doesn't end here – debates like this on Consimworld burn on as long as at least two people remain passionate enough to perpetuate them. Usually intelligence dissipates as passion precipitates, but even as the

Denmark discussion turns rancorous, we're still blessed with nuggets of retrospective wisdom:

> Hitler was not perceived as an evil whack job until after the war started in 1939. Until then, many nations viewed German aggrandizement within the boundaries and context of 500 years of European balance-of-power struggles. No one knew Hitler would not play by the rules until it was too late.

And comparisons between Denmark in 1940 and Warsaw in 1943-1944:

> The Ghetto thought resistance worthwhile. The Home Army thought it worthwhile. They both failed to win but was their sacrifice without value?
>
> The Ghetto had nothing to lose. The Home Army tried to time it right, but got smashed by the Germans while the Soviets dawdled (thanking them for the favor?). Poland suffered a horrible occupation. The locals had nothing to lose by fighting back. They had nothing to gain by collaborating. This was a nation neither Germany nor Russia believed should exist. To this day, Poles are very worried that those attitudes have not changed, especially since Germany and Russia are enjoying a cozy relationship.

And interesting perspectives on moral equivalency:

> Germany's attack was a direct consequence of starving the army during the 30s (Denmark came within one parliamentary vote of abolishing its army twice during that time), failure to mobilize or take any other step to secure the borders after September 1939 and ordering the army to stand down and be invaded.
>
> I agree, it wasn't the *army's* fault, but the whole disgrace was an abdication of the basic duties of any government. If Denmark was unready and had no allies, it was as much or more the Government's fault as anything else. Had they even made provision to destroy or block their major internal communications link – a mission well within their capabilities – the German plan to use Jutland as stepping stone to Norway (or Sweden) would have splintered. That alone would increase the chances of surviving the war uninvaded.
>
> Refusing to prepare any effective action and then acquiescing because no effective action was possible gains no credit.

And reminders of Denmark's own history before the war:

> The Danes already had their war against Germany/Prussia in 1856, which nobody remembers, and got their heads handed to them. That was really Denmark's last attempt to act as a military power in Europe. They tried for alliances then, too, and got nothing.

> What would an alliance with, say, Britain have gotten them? Britain couldn't have defended the country, and so the alliance just means a 100 percent chance of getting smashed instead of the chance of staying out of the war.
>
> Neutrality spared the Danes the horror of WWI. Why would they be quick to change strategies? The argument seems to rest, consciously or unconsciously, on the belief that the Nazis were uniquely horrible and terrible monsters, so all right-thinking people should have started shooting at them as soon as possible. Except that's not how the world worked, then, before, or since.

And humorous corrections about the aforementioned "war against Germany/ Prussia in 1856":

> You make the point yourself. It was in 1864, and yes, it is a year better to forget. ☺

And detailed analysis of what the Danes might have done:

> Look at Switzerland. They mined every railroad and highway overcrossing, armed and organized resistance in every hamlet, ensured the population's national sport was rifle marksmanship, prepared every important industry for demolition.
>
> The Danes could have, in addition, prepared their major islands for protracted defense (against a nation without a serious opposed landing capability), and mobilized and deployed significant military forces, in comparison to their size. The Belgians mobilized 22 Divisions from a population a bit over double the size. The Danes had two regular army Divisions, WWII mobilization levels would have given them approximately 6-8 conscript Divisions.
>
> Historically the Germans used one motorized brigade group and a follow-on infantry division. Against a mobilized army with a corps on the border and the rest on the islands, the Germans would need a minimum of a small army and *Luftwaffe* support to match.
>
> Diplomatically, a Scandinavian alliance adds another 10 Divisions (four Norwegian, six Swedes) and a small navy, probably enough to contest the waters around Denmark. That aggregation of troops, plus depriving Germany of Swedish steel and manufactured goods, is a powerful contribution to any anti-Nazi coalition.
>
> Even a fallback defense, buying time as the Poles attempted to do, would potentially be worthwhile.
>
> Why should they do so? Well, the examples of Austria and Czechoslovakia provide at least a six-month warning of what appeasement means to a neighbor of Germany. The fate of the Jews, Gypsies and "defectives" as of January 1940 was already enough to foretell the fate of those Nazi "untermenschen".

Instead, the Danes chose to bet their national existence on a) German goodwill and b) other people's blood.

There are four increasing levels of participation in international politics:

1) Defending one's people when attacked.

2) Refusing to aid an aggressor nation.

3) Giving all aid short of war to opponents of the aggressor.

4) Intervening in opposition to an aggressor.

Several of the participants in this discussion have registered opposition, mild or extreme, to nations who intervene, though in this case the mob opinion seems to be that was what was required. However, Denmark failed in even its basic duty to defend itself.

Denmark might well not have been the only one who failed in its moral duty. Most nations did, to one extent or another. Why, for example, did Canada let its volunteers fight on without replacements in 1943 and 1944 rather than send over conscripts? Why did it insist on building its own RCN anti-submarine force rather than accept cheaper US- or British-built vessels? (Hint – the shipbuilding industry was catapulted into modernity thereby.) And that was a nation which, for ethical duty and reasons of state chose to involve itself alongside Britain.

So not *only* the Danes deserve criticism. Nevertheless they cannot avoid it, since they took no steps to avoid the catastrophe that, had the Germans won, would have overtaken Denmark.

And a thorough rebuttal of said analysis:

OK, what if Denmark had a 10-division army, totally mechanized. We're talking two motorized infantry regiments and one tank regiment (150 AFVs, Pz. III or better), with an artillery regiment (48 tubes, half 105mm, half 155mm) plus one engineer battalion per division.

There is not enough space on the Danish peninsula to line up all 10 divisions, so think mobile defense in depth, relying on river and peninsula/island chokepoints to do the job. Germans would have to detach double that number of divisions, bleeding their way up the peninsula.

But wait...Denmark is also an archipelago! You will also need a Danish navy. Nothing impressive, mind you, just a dozen E-boat squadrons, about 24-48 coastal subs. You have lots of bays, inlets and islands to go knocking about it. Just dash out, fire, and dash back. That should put a dent in that German BB/CA/DD task force.

> But you also need air superiority. The Danish air force should be pegged at 1,000 aircraft, evenly split between fighters (ME-109 equivalent) for air superiority and strike aircraft (HE-111 equivalent) to maul German ground and naval assets. Germany would have to deploy two Luftflotten to neutralize Luftflotte Denmark.
>
> And let's not forget, Denmark has Neils Bohr, so include a tactical nuke capability to be used *in extremis*.
>
> All this is nonsense, of course. Denmark got invaded in about 24 hours, not leaving a lot of time for regular army mobilization to stop less than a division's worth of German troops. The two divisions they did have would have been overwhelmed in a second attack if the first one didn't work.
>
> After all, that is what happened to Greece and Finland. They defeated the first round of bad guy attacks, only to be defeated in round two by far larger enemies.
>
> I suppose the British could have intervened. Jutland would then be synonymous with Dunkirk.
>
> So let us dispense with all this Denmark bashing. The nation had three options: roll over and play dead, die like one speed bump, or die like two speed bumps. Any way you cut it, Germany is either annoyed, inconvenienced, or pissed off.
>
> And it is a waste of a low factor, zero-attack piece in a future strategic WWII game.

This is real history. It isn't dictated by academic loners within inscrutable tracts – it blossoms in discussions between smart people, with nothing at stake except the truth, and it branches in directions as unexpected as they are fascinating. History is meant to be lived, and relived. I wish Dad could see that.

And the best part? All of the above posts and literally hundreds of intervening comments like them (and insults unworthy of them) were made within 24 hours of each other, and I'm sure plenty more are still to come. God, I love the internet.

❖ ❖ ❖

My mother died eight years ago, two days before Christmas. I don't like to talk about it.

I don't enjoy the holiday season. This year feels worse than most, as most of my friends – including Becs – are either trapped with their families or traveling on vacation. Even Gregory Spearman is away, so my BPA *Totaler Krieg* semifinal is on hold. I have some reading to catch up on, and Consimworld remains a handy crutch, but otherwise it's just Dad, me and melancholy.

On Christmas Eve, I tried filling the void by writing an article on German diplomatic strategy in *Totaler Krieg* during 1940 and 1941 and relating it to my ongoing e-mail tournament game. *Totaler Krieg's* diplomatic model follows the domino theory, in that Germany can only attempt to ally with neutrals already bordering an Axis country, and a diplomacy-heavy German strategy can use three consecutive Treaty cards for a six-turn diplomatic offensive along one of these axes:

- Hungary-Rumania-Bulgaria-Turkey (then Greece)
- Hungary-Rumania-Yugoslavia-Greece (then Turkey)
- Hungary-Yugoslavia-Greece-Turkey (then Rumania)
- Yugoslavia-Greece-Turkey-Hungary (then Rumania)

Hungary and Rumania are Germany's two primary military allies against the Soviet Union. Greece contains an Objective Hex, and ownership of Crete forces Britain to defend the eastern Mediterranean. Turkey opens up both the Caucasus and the Middle East, but later in the war the Allies can use it as an overland passage into the Balkans. Yugoslavia and Bulgaria are gateways to Greece and Turkey, but little else.

I enjoyed writing the piece; one day I might develop it further and submit it for publication in a wargaming magazine. Of course, Dad thinks I'm wasting my time. He came up to my bedroom as I was writing it and asked me what I was doing. So I told him.

"Have you ever considered writing an article about Germany's *actual* diplomatic strategy during 1940 and 1941?" he asked. He dislikes the holiday season as well – we haven't been talking much.

"No," I said.

"You should. Make yourself useful."

"I'm sorry, Dad, but I don't have that kind of time."

"You seem to have plenty of time."

"Not to be a scholar like you."

"Don't be a smart-ass. On Christmas Eve as well."

"As if that matters," I muttered as Dad exited. He locks the door to his study when he's working; why should he be able to barge into my room?

Long gone are the Christmas mornings when I would dash downstairs before dawn to see what Santa had left under the tree. There's barely a tree now; this year's misshapen triangle of needles is leaning into a corner of the living room, trying to avoid drawing attention to itself. If it could tunnel under the carpet and out of the house, *Great Escape*-style, I'm sure it would. There are no stockings, and no turkey dinner in the offing; we have received cards from friends and family, but the handwritten ones read like condolences. Our one concession to tradition is the Bing Crosby Christmas album on the old record player – his scratchy warbling infuses our morbidity with wistfulness.

We exchange gifts quickly. I give Dad an Amazon voucher, a nice bottle of malt whiskey I got my Uncle Martin to send me, and a packet of chalks for his teaching blackboard; I meant the latter as a friendly joke, not that he seems to get it. (I have no idea what he really would have wanted.) Dad gives me a sweater, a baseball signed by Stan Musial, the DVD boxed set of *The Pacific* and several books – none written by him, thank goodness. The last present I unwrap is Adam Tooze's *The Wages of Destruction*, a detailed study of the Nazi war economy.

"Did you get this for me because you think I'll like it, or because you think I ought to read it?" I ask.

"Both. Neither."

"I'm just curious." I try to force a grin, and fail.

"It's a good book, Sean, and an important one."

Bing starts singing *Silver Bells*. Dad, still wearing his flannel pajamas, slumps down on the sofa and rubs his eyes. "Believe it or not, Sean, I want you to be happy," he whispers.

"I know."

"I've always wanted that. I've always loved that you love what I've loved."

"More or less."

"Yes."

Dad tilts his head downward and stares at the table for ages. Bing croons, *It's Christmas tiiiime in the city.* Eventually, Dad slowly closes his eyes. "Are you OK?" I ask.

"Why is it so goddamn hard?" he whispers.

"What do you mean?"

Dad clenches his fist. "Why," he growls more loudly, "is it So. God. Damn. Hard." He punches the sofa with each syllable. "Why?"

I'm confused, and getting frightened. "What do you want me to say?"

"I don't know. I just...I don't know." He's softening now, and choking back sobs. "I just wish it wasn't so, so...hard."

"I'm sorry, Dad," I say, unsure of what I should be sorry for, tears welling up in my own eyes.

"Me too, Sean," Dad says. "Me, too." He takes a deep breath and clears his throat. "Right. Give me that bottle of whiskey."

"Yeah?"

Dad stands up. "That was very thoughtful of you," he says, and pats me on the head.

"Thanks." I sniffle.

"What will you do now?"

"I guess I've got some DVDs to watch."

"Jolly good. I know this isn't the best Christmas ever, but I bet it beats front-line duty on Guadalcanal."

"Yeah, probably."

"Merry Christmas, Sean."

"Merry Christmas, Dad."

And that's my Christmas with Dad. I don't see him again until Boxing Day.

❖ ❖ ❖

While rewatching *The Pacific* over the next several hours – I've seen it all before, of course – I ponder Dad's last assertion. Guadalcanal would have sucked, Bougainville would have sucked, Peleliu would have really sucked, and Iwo Jima (to quote *Good Morning Vietnam*) would have sucked the sweat off a dead man's balls, but rarely would they have been lonely. They call it *esprit de corps* for a reason. The European predecessor to *The Pacific* was called *Band of Brothers* for a reason.

So I phone Becs.

"Can I come over?" I ask. "I miss you. And I need you."

"Really?"

"Yeah. I can explain."

"OK," she says. "We've just started playing *Monopoly*, though."

Yet another reason to hate that game. "I'll give you 45 minutes to creatively bankrupt yourself."

"Yeah?"

"Trust me – it's more fun than trying to win."

When I arrive at her house, Becs has indeed extricated herself from the game her mother, father, brother, grandmother and grandfather are still playing. "You were right – that was more fun," she says.

"Could anyone even tell you were trying to lose?"

"I don't think so." Becs laughs. "Although when I sold my three railroads at a discount and called myself 'The Trust Buster', John looked at me kinda funny."

We go upstairs to Becs' bedroom – she lounges on the bed, and I sit on the carpet across from her, leaning against a bare wall. Pink wallpaper aside, the décor is spartan, just like her locker at school: a white-painted dresser; a white iMac on a glossy white desk; a round, black-and-white clock on the wall; a full-length mirror on the closet door; one small poster, a cityscape of Prague at sunrise; and several framed photographs of her family.

I tell her about my morning, and Becs is horrified. "I can't imagine a Christmas like that," she says.

"I'm used to it, unfortunately. Ever since Mom died."

"Do you remember what Christmas was like with your mother?"

"I try not to think about it."

"Really? I'd probably think about nothing else today." Becs blushes and puts a hand to her mouth. "If you don't mind me saying so."

"No, it's OK. It's just, it was so long ago, and I never really talk about her, ever."

"Would you like to talk about her?"

I shrug my shoulders. I'm not sure.

"What do you remember about her?"

"Like what?"

"Anything. What did she look like?"

"Brown hair. Dark skin, I think. We don't have any pictures of her around the house, really – my memories aren't distinct."

"No pictures?"

"Nope. You'll see, next time you're over. I don't think there are any pictures of me or Dad either. It's nothing personal."

"How did she…how did she die?"

"She fell down the stairs at my house. Broke her neck."

"Oh."

"It was instant, apparently. They said she wouldn't have suffered any pain."

"Were you there, in the house with her?"

"No. Dad was. It was during the day – I'd gone out sledding with some friends and a few of their moms, and I didn't know anything until I got home. One minute she was part of my life, and the next she was a huge bloodstain at the foot of the stairs."

"That's horrible."

"Funny thing is, I don't miss her – I'm never thinking about what it would be like for her to be around. I guess I've mentally processed and accepted that she's gone, and that part of me is now dead. Like there's a crime scene in my brain cordoned off with black-and-yellow tape saying 'DO NOT CROSS', so I just know not to go there. Christmas is different, but less because she's gone and more because Dad and I struggle to get along."

"Did you love her?"

"Yeah, of course I did. She was my mother, and she loved me; she didn't abuse me or do anything to separate herself from me, so I loved her. But then, you don't choose your parents. I loved her because sons are supposed to love their mothers, just like I love my Dad because most sons love their fathers. But I love you because of who you are – not by circumstance, but by choice."

Becs sits up. "Did you just say you love me?"

"Oops. Did I say that out loud?" I blush. "I mean, not 'oops' that I love you, because I do, but that's not how I meant to say it. Or when. I meant to say it, but…gosh, this is awkward."

"It's OK. Come here."

She beckons me onto her bed, so I push myself off the floor and slump down next to her. "I'm sorry, I'm rubbish at this," I say. "I'm not sure I've ever talked about my mother."

"It's absolutely fine," says Becs, putting an arm around my shoulder. We swivel to awkwardly hug each other. "I'm honored that you would open up to me about this."

"Yeah? I'm just pleased I can talk to you, about this or anything else. So thanks for that."

"Thanks for calling and asking to come over."

"Honestly, I'd even have been happy to join your game of *Monopoly*."

"If you'd like, we can go downstairs and ask to buy back in…"

"I was just going say how happy I am it didn't come to that."

Becs smiles. "That's OK. I can think of better things to do." She pushes me gently down onto the bed. "By the way, I love you too."

"Really?"

"Absolutely." She lies on top of me, wraps her arms around me and whispers, "Merry Christmas, Sean." Then we kiss, and kiss again, and again.

4.

The first Big Game of the new year has only four players. This happened last year, when the Gang of Four failed to find a fifth before the holidays; this year, we agree we're carrying on a tradition, but I think we all know we simply forgot again.

Having repeatedly discussed each other's holiday misadventures and Christmas gifts already, our lunchtime session is pure poker. Ice and fog on the windows filter the sun from our alcove, and I'm cold despite the vest beneath my sweater. Nobody is watching us muddle along, and just as well, for my first five hands are as follows:

- 6 of diamonds, 3 of clubs
- 9 of clubs, 2 of hearts
- 8 of diamonds, 4 of spades
- Jack of hearts, 4 of diamonds
- 4 of clubs, 2 of hearts

Even in a four-handed game, there's no play in these cards. In our sixth hand, after Chris folds I discover I've been dealt the 7 of spades and – for the third hand in five – the 2 of hearts. "Can we play something else?" I ask.

Chris laughs, looks at Freddie and says, "Here comes a two-dollar raise."

"If I raised, would you believe me?" I ask.

"Probably not," admits Chris.

"I'm going to put my cards over here, in a little stack of their own, and let you guess what they are after the hand is over," I say.

"That's a fold, then," says Melvyn.

"F, O, L, D. Folderama. El Foldo. This is an ex-hand."

"I think he's bluffing," deadpans Freddie.

"I mean it," I say. "Have you guys ever thought about playing something else?"

"You want to try Pot-Limit Hold 'Em?" asks Chris. "Or maybe Five-Card Stud? Omaha High-Low? Shanghai? Minnesota Triples?"

"Please tell me you made that last one up," says Melvyn. Chris shrugs.

"Poker isn't the only game there is," I say.

"Burn the heretic!" exclaims Chris, a little too loudly.

"You guys finish your hand," I remember. "Freddie, do you want to have a go?"

"Sure – I fold," says Freddie, surrendering his small blind and the pot to Melvyn's big blind.

"Right. Chris, tell Melvyn and Freddie what I just folded."

"7-2 offsuit?"

"7-2 offsuit. Turn 'em over if you don't believe me."

"That's bad luck," says Melvyn.

"My previous five hands were worse," I say.

"That's poker," says Freddie.

"But when you get bad cards in poker, the game gets boring in a hurry. I've been freezing my butt off for 20 minutes and have actually played cards for about 20 seconds, including the shuffling and dealing. Do you know how many hours of my life I've spent watching other people look at their cards?"

"But that's the beauty of poker," says Chris. "It requires patience and discipline as well as skill and knowledge."

"And a high boredom threshold," I counter.

"It's like fishing," continues Chris. "Some days the fish don't bite, some days you catch a few little ones, and then occasionally you catch a big one, and when you reel it in perfectly you know you've done something spectacular."

"Honestly, Chris, what the hell do you know about fishing?" I ask. Melvyn chuckles.

"Maybe it's like baseball," offers Freddie. "A lot of games are blowouts, but once in a while someone hits a walk-off homer to beat the Yankees, and it feels extra special because you've endured all the crappy games to get there."

"To be fair, you're also allowed to bluff in poker occasionally," offers Melvyn. "You seem pretty resigned to your fate at the moment."

"You're just in a rut," says Chris. "You had bad cards before Christmas, and you've had bad cards today, but they'll come around."

"You're all missing my point," I say. "There are other games in which I can have bad cards without being stuck on the sidelines."

"Like what?" asks Freddie.

"I dunno," I say. "Maybe a trick-taking game, like Spades or Hearts. There are four of us, which is perfect, and everyone plays every card. Or Bridge."

"Bridge?" asks Freddie.

"My grandmother plays Bridge," says Melvyn. "I'm not playing Bridge."

"Or Pinochle," I offer.

"Pinochle?" asks Freddie.

"Do you even know how to play Pinochle?" asks Chris.

"Kind of," I say. "It doesn't even have to be a card game – it could be a boardgame."

"Like *Monopoly*?" asks Freddie.

"I'm *not* playing *Monopoly* in the school cafeteria," says Chris, crossly.

"Always bloody *Monopoly*," I shudder. "There are so many better boardgames than *Monopoly*."

"Yeah, I'm not playing a boardgame either," says Melvyn.

"You wouldn't try something else?" I ask. "Not even once?"

"We've got a good thing already," says Chris. "The Big Game is poker. Everyone knows how to play it. Other people watch us. Other people want to play with us."

"The game itself doesn't matter to you, does it?" I ask. "It's all about getting the cool kids to play with us, or helping Melvyn get into Vicki's pants."

"You've said it yourself: poker brings people together," says Chris. "And we've had plenty of the not-so-cool kids play with us. Including Vicki."

"Nice," says Melvyn.

"Anyway, this is all moot," concludes Chris. "You'll get better cards tomorrow, or the next day, and then you'll be right in the game. So just chill out, OK?"

I slump back in my seat. "Pass me the cards," I say to Chris.

"Why?"

"Because it's my turn to shuffle."

Chris smiles. Freddie teases Melvyn about Vicki again. I stare blankly at the table, shuffle the cards a few times, and deal myself the 10 of spades and the 6 of diamonds. Maybe the game will get better tomorrow.

❖ ❖ ❖

The dining room in Becs' house is bright and cheerful, its white wooden table lit by cube-shaped glass lights dangling from the ceiling. Becs' father is watching television in the living room, so Becs and I are sitting at the table while her mother tidies around us and washes dishes in the adjacent kitchen.

Tonight's study topic is the French Revolution, the historian's ultimate Rorschach test. Everyone seems to have their own theories, and "pure" interpretations are impossible to come by: Was the Bastille stormed because of high grain prices? Enlightenment ideas and the Third Estate? The breakdown of social order? Monarchical despotism? How do you explain the progression from limited monarchy to the Republic, the Reign of Terror and the Directory? Can you ignore the leadership of Danton, Robespierre and other individuals and focus purely on amorphous causes? The "Great Man" theory of history may not be central to the French Revolution, but I firmly believe any theorist who ignores it should not be taken seriously. Great Men are often driven to do Great Things by complicated and often contradictory pressures.

"How are the French and American Revolutions connected to each other?" I ask Becs, ostensibly as an AP study question. She's sitting across from me, leaning forward, her fists propping up her chin as her bare elbows rest on the table.

"I would say the French Revolution was influenced by the ideals behind the American Revolution, but their causes were different, and they unfolded in very different ways," she says. "The American Revolution also created a new country, while the French Revolution transformed an existing country."

My question seemed more interesting before Becs answered it. "You're very good at simplifying complex answers," I say.

"Thanks, I think."

"Seriously – that'll be a real skill in completing the AP exam."

"As long as I don't skimp on the detail," she says. "You also have to hint at vast reserves of knowledge beneath your simple answers."

"You can do that."

"Sometimes."

"Which interests you more: the American Revolution or the French Revolution?"

"Can I pick the Glorious Revolution?"

Heh. "No."

"Then I'd pick the American Revolution, because I'm American. Duh. You?"

"Definitely the American Revolution, unless I can count the Napoleonic Wars as part of the French Revolution."

"You can't."

"Then you have my answer."

"Why?"

"Because when you talk about the American Revolution, you talk about Washington and Jefferson, John Adams and Sam Adams, Nathaniel Greene and Benedict Arnold. When you talk about the French Revolution, you talk about the bourgeoisie and the peasantry, and letting them eat cake. Or you talk about mobs, terrorists and the guillotine."

"You like it when your dead white males die a little less quickly than that," laughs Becs.

"Two of my ten favorite moments in history also come from the American Revolution, so there's that. I wonder if I could list my ten favorite revolutions in history..."

"Hang on – you have a list of your ten favorite moments in history?"

"Yes, I do."

Becs exhales. "You're about to tell me them, aren't you?"

"If you want," I say. Pause. "In chronological order – number one: 1519. Hernan Cortes is at Villa Rica, on the Caribbean coast of modern-day Mexico. He packs one of his 11 remaining ships with gold and sends it to Spain as a gift to his king – and then he burns the other 10 ships to prevent his men from deserting him. With no alternative but to band together, they march with Cortes on Tenochtitlán and conquer the Aztec Empire. More than anything else, that single-minded act of willpower is why most of the countries south of here speak Spanish.

"Number two: 1777. British Captain Daniel Ferguson spots a rebel American officer in the woods near Brandywine Creek in southern Pennsylvania and calls upon him to surrender. The American quickly mounts his horse and starts riding away. Ferguson has him in the sights of his rifle, but chivalry compels him not to shoot an unarmed man in the back. Unbeknownst to Ferguson, the man he fails to shoot is George Washington. The American Revolution lives on."

"So when you're talking about favorite moments in history, you actually meant just that – specific moments in time?" queries Becs.

"Pretty much. I couldn't pick something like the fall of the Berlin Wall or the battle of Gettysburg, because those weren't 'moments' – they each took days to play out. There are other rules."

"Of course."

"Number three: 1783. George Washington again – he's trying to stop the Newburgh Conspiracy, speaking to a hall full of mutinous officers who want an advance on the pensions promised to them by the revolutionary government. The speech isn't going well when he withdraws a letter from his pocket and puts on a pair of glasses. He says, 'You will permit me to put on my spectacles, for I have not only grown grey but almost blind in your service.' The men are overcome with emotion, realizing everything Washington has done in leading the revolution; the threats are withdrawn, and the American government grows independently, without being dominated by the military."

"I've heard of the Newburgh Conspiracy," says Becs. "I'd never heard that story before, though."

"Number four: 1804. Napoleon Bonaparte is crowned Emperor of the French by Pope Pius VII on the 2nd of December, in Notre Dame Cathedral in Paris. I just love the idea of Napoleon, who rose from humble origins to the pinnacle of European power entirely by merit, being crowned and groveled to by that ultimate symbol of status and privilege, the Pope. I would like to have studied everyone's faces throughout the coronation.

"Beethoven had just finished writing his Third Symphony and dedicated it to Napoleon when he heard about the coronation," comments Becs. "He flew into a rage and promptly changed the symphony's title from *Bonaparte* to the *Eroica*."

"I did not know that. Interesting."

"Thanks."

"Continuing with number five: 1896. William Jennings Bryan delivers the 'Cross of Gold' speech at the Democratic National Convention in Chicago, uniting the party behind the Populist plank of repudiating the gold standard in favor of silver. Bryan said, 'You shall not press down upon the brow of labor this crown of thorns, you shall not crucify mankind on a cross of gold!' This triggers a spontaneous demonstration lasting nearly an hour, as weeping and shouting delegates carry Bryan aloft on their shoulders and ultimately demand his nomination for the presidency. Bonus fact: Bryan's main rival for the nomination was a Missouri congressman named Richard Bland whose nickname was 'Silver Dick'."

"Silver Dick!" snorts Becs.

"Number six: 1916. Four days into the battle of Verdun, the key fort anchoring the French defenses around the city is effectively captured by a single German soldier. A sergeant named Kunze, armed only with a rifle, enters Fort Douaumont by himself and wanders around until he finds the artillerymen commanding the fort's guns, tricks them into surrendering and locks them up. Then he loses his way trying to get out and gets distracted by a table of food, but while he's gorging himself 10 of his comrades enter the fort behind him and secure it. So in a war full of senseless carnage, the only casualty on either side at Fort Douaumont was a German soldier who scraped one of his knees.

"Number seven: 1942. Commander Wade McClusky, leading a mission of dive bombers from the USS *Enterprise*, is searching for a reported enemy task force when he spots a lone Japanese destroyer, the *Arashi*, heading somewhere at flank speed. McClusky correctly deduces that *Arashi* is heading toward the Japanese task force and turns his squadron in that direction; several minutes later, three Japanese carriers are aflame, the Battle of Midway is all but won and the Japanese advance across the Pacific is stopped."

"Isn't the *Enterprise* Captain Kirk's ship in *Star Trek*?" asks Becs.

"It was a real aircraft carrier first," I respond. "Anyway, number eight: 1944. On the 5th of June, RAF meteorologist J. M. Stagg delivers possibly the world's most famous weather forecast and persuades General Eisenhower, in front of all of his key commanders, that the weather on the 6th of June will be sufficiently good to launch the invasion of France. The weather is indeed tolerable on the 6th, and D-Day is successful."

"What are the two of you studying?" asks an older lady with brown-bobbed hair and bright red lipstick.

"Oh, hi, Mrs. Fowler," I say. "I forgot you were over there."

"Did you just mention D-Day?" asks Mrs. Fowler. "I thought you were studying the French Revolution."

"Sean likes to talk about history," says Becs. "He also likes to digress."

"What's your favorite moment in history?" I ask Mrs. Fowler.

"Probably the moment this girl's father proposed to me," she says, patting Becs on the head.

"That's not…I mean, that's very sweet," I say.

"Sorry, I've got some laundry to fetch – I'll be right back." Mrs. Fowler disappears into the hallway.

"Maybe you can summarize your last two moments for me?" asks Becs.

"Should I wait for your Mom to get back? I don't want to be rude."

"When she said she'd be 'right back', that could mean any time in the next six months."

"OK, well, number nine is when Truman fired Douglas MacArthur in 1951 as the American commander in Korea, pretty much for being Douglas MacArthur. Like McClellan in the Civil War, MacArthur was popular back home, but he was also an idiot, and I'm very happy he finally got the fate he'd deserved for years. And number ten is the meeting in 1962 between Robert Kennedy and Anatoly Dobrynin that effectively ended the Cuban Missile Crisis and guaranteed the future of the human race. I don't see any way to exclude this moment from the Top Ten, because without it, we're probably not here to have this conversation."

"That's fair. And that's a good list. But Sean, if I can put this delicately…you know how I love listening to you talk about history?"

"Yeah?"

"We can talk about other things too, right?"

Oh. "Of course. You name it."

"I'll settle for more 'Silver Dick' jokes, for a start."

I laugh. "Thanks for humoring me," I say."

"You've been waiting a long time to share that list with someone, haven't you?"

"I couldn't possibly say."

5.

Dennis finally returns for round two of World War One-and-a-Half on a bitterly cold night in mid-January. If he's wearing a stupid T-shirt, it's hiding under his sweater and sweatshirt – he almost looks normal. He is complaining about frostbite in his extremities, which isn't helping him manipulate counters with his pair of tweezers. The effects of winter weather on the Germans are supposed to be simulated in *Totaler Krieg* by the Mobilization Limits Option Card, not the command paralysis shown in Dennis's stubby fingers.

In the last two turns of Summer 1940, Dennis reduces my forces on the Continent to a French pocket around Bordeaux and the small British outpost at Calais. With the writing on the wall, the Brits evacuate to Kent – Dunkirk-style – while my best three French steps depart for North Africa. In the Autumn, Dennis plays Case Yellow and allies with Austria-Hungary after mopping up Bordeaux to collapse the French. The Ottoman Empire signs a Treaty and joins the Axis in the Winter, while Spring sees Limited War Production boost Germany's depleted army ahead of Barbarossa.

Summer 1941 is wild and woolly. The Turks declare war on the Caucasus Republic to get at Baku. Austrian armies surge into the Ukraine as the Red Army masses between Smolensk and Leningrad (or Trotskygrad, or whatever it's called in this reality). The Republican Spanish fall back upon Madrid as an Anglo-French battlegroup wanders north from Gibraltar. Meanwhile, Britain establishes a foothold in under-garrisoned Norway at Bergen. The position is tremendously intriguing…but for some reason, it isn't.

"What's wrong?" asks Dennis, putting the Kaiser's Fifteenth Army in Barcelona and leaning back in his chair. "You keep looking at your watch and yawning. What time is it?"

"About quarter past ten," I respond.

"That's not normally your bedtime, is it?"

"No."

"So what's up? You're the one who normally keeps me here until two in the morning."

"It's cold in here. Maybe I'm using all of my energy to fight hypothermia."

"That's never bothered you before."

I list to one side and poke several knuckles into my right cheek. "I think I might be playing too much *Totaler Krieg*," I say.

"Is that even possible?" asks Dennis.

"The e-mail tournament I'm playing in – my semifinal match. Gregory Spearman. It's doing my head in."

"Yeah?"

"We're into 1942. I've surrounded Leningrad and cut off the Crimea, so No Retreat 3 looks doable. But he's so clever with the Russians, making constant low-odds attacks to keep me on my toes and infiltrating spare armies behind my front lines. Maybe I should have dragged him into a Long Limited War, or even an East First opening for which he might have been less prepared. Because if you're not winning with strategy, you have to win with tactics, and his tactics are razor sharp. The past two months of gaming have been like living in constant fear of a sniper attack."

"And that's bugging you now? Tonight?"

"I'm just saying, I might be short of mental energy right now. I wish I could have been the Allies."

"You are the Allies."

"I meant against Gregory."

"OK."

I pause. "I don't know. This scenario…look at the map. I know wargaming is about creating alternate history, but most wargames start from a historical position. This started in fantasyland and is getting sillier and sillier as we go along."

"Didn't you say something last time about this scenario feeling more historical than real history, because we'll be experiencing this war for the first time?"

"I might have."

"And?"

"I might be changing my mind."

"How decisive of you."

"Plus, look at what's happening in Iberia," I say. "You'll never be able to divert enough force from Russia to kick me out of Spain, so this will be like our other game with the 'Sideways Shift'. When the Allies get into Spain early, games always go the same way. Eventually I'll creep into France again, and that'll be it – game over. Mark it down."

"Let me get this straight. A few minutes ago, you were saying this game is too unlike anything you've ever played before. Now, you're saying this game is so much like the one we played a few months ago, you know exactly what is going to happen."

"Um, yeah."

Dennis is smiling. "I've smelled some cow dung in my day, but get a whiff of you, eh?"

"When you put it like that…"

"Who are you trying to convince?" asks Dennis. "If you want to stop for the night, or just quit this game altogether, I'm happy to leave right now. This is supposed to be fun. If you didn't think this scenario was a good idea, we shouldn't have started it – but then, I'm not the one who custom-made a map to play it. And regarding your e-mail game with Gregory, it sounds like you could use a release from it. Some good, clean, harmless fun in a silly scenario like this one."

"I already have a release," I mutter, almost under my breath.

"Huh?"

"I don't need a release from my other game, because I've already got one. And no offense, but she's much better looking than you are."

Dennis snorts. "None taken!"

I gaze at the Frankenstein map of fantasy Europe I've stitched together. If a perfect wargaming opponent exists for me, I haven't found him yet: Dennis and Steven Ginsberg are too geeky, Gregory is too intense and competitive, and others are too anal-retentive, or not anal-retentive enough, or not into the right games, or into too many games. With Becs, I'm not worrying about any of that. The contrast between debating real history with Becs and fantasizing about pretend history with Dennis could hardly be clearer.

After what feels like several minutes of silence, Dennis stands up. "Shall I go home?" he asks.

"Yeah," I mutter, masking my mouth with one hand. "Probably best for now. I'm sorry, I'm just…"

"Don't worry about it," shushes Dennis. "It's late for mere mortals – get some sleep."

"Thanks."

"And build a fireplace or something while I'm gone, will you? It's like Ice Station Zebra in here."

I shrug. Before he leaves, I promise Dennis that I will keep the game set up for now. But I think we both know we're unlikely to finish it.

❖ ❖ ❖

The other day, Mr. Prendergast said something ridiculously inaccurate about Napoleon in class, and I bit my tongue. I'm proud of myself. Perhaps I'm finally learning how to control my inner geek.

Then again, Becs is over tonight, and we're watching *A Bridge Too Far*. She asked me to pick one of my favorite movies, so I picked this. I regretted the choice almost instantly, and I must have asked her five or six times if she was really OK with watching a war movie.

"*Casablanca* is a war movie," she said.

"Sure, in the sense that the *Twilight* films are horror movies," I responded.

But she's not a sensitive soul, so we agreed upon a Friday night screening in my living room. She doesn't know anything about Operation Market-Garden, and I have to remind myself that *A Bridge Too Far* was designed for mass consumption and grossed more than $50 million at the US box office (against a production budget of $27 million). Within the *Consimworld* domain, the movie is pure geek chic – an essential text for gamers and game designers alike. You can quote obscure lines of dialogue in any *Consimworld* forum and receive knowing nods and winks in return. You can play games about the battle at any scale, complexity level and price point: for example, Multi-Man Publishing has issued both *Target: Arnhem*, a free giveaway covering the whole campaign at a high level to help introduce new gamers to the hobby, and *The Devil's Cauldron*, a company-level simulation of just the battles around Arnhem and Nijmegen with four maps and 1,600 counters which you need a full wallet to buy and a forklift to move. In this universe, the idea that anyone could spoil the plot of *A Bridge Too Far* is too outlandish to fathom, but with Becs I must watch my words carefully.

In fact, watching the movie with Becs proves surprisingly miserable. I suppose when you introduce two close friends from different social circles and around whom you behave differently, you fret constantly about how they are interacting and struggle to "be yourself" in two different ways. When watching *A Bridge Too Far* on my own, I reflexively mutter lines of dialogue in unison with the movie – I can even parrot whole sentences in German and Dutch. With Becs, I'm torn between showing off this knowledge and repressing it: I'm not sure if she would find my lip-synching cute, silly, impressive or revolting. (The movie itself must think I'm an utter tart.) Additionally, because I prefer the edited-for-television version of the film I watched growing up, I'm inclined to apologize for several clunky scenes only present in the DVD version we're watching, like the set piece in which James Caan and his nearly-dead captain escape in a jeep from a squad of the *Wehrmacht's* worst marksmen. Amidst this mental turmoil, I also want to look like I'm enjoying myself and am neither pathetically conflicted nor desperate to gauge Becs' reaction to every scene. So it's a struggle.

Understandably, Becs' eyes glaze over during some of the battle scenes. She asks what is going on when Elliot Gould and company build the new Bailey bridge at Son. She also asks me if "Scheisse!" means what she thinks it means during Captain Grabner's vehicular charge across Arnhem Bridge. (It does.) But she is attentive, at least faintly interested, occasionally amused and sad at the right places. Or so it has seemed when I ask her the big question at the end: "What did you think?"

"I liked it," she says. "It's not a masterpiece, but as a movie I never would have watched without your recommendation, I'm glad I saw it."

"That's as much as I could have hoped for."

"There were a lot of explosions, though."

"Yeah, it was a war movie. I don't think you were its target audience."

"How historical was it? In 50 words or less, if you can." Becs smiles.

"Short answer: very. Slightly longer answer: some of the star turns were exaggerated, and General Browning was an unfair caricature of Field Marshal Montgomery. But pretty much everything else was spot on – many of the more detailed scenes were minutely accurate."

"How long did the war go on for, after the battle was done?"

"The battle was fought in mid-September 1944, and V-E Day was May 8, 1945, so another eight months."

"Could the battle really have ended the war by Christmas?"

"Almost certainly not. Market-Garden only could have succeeded if the Germans had remained in full retreat, in which case the airborne carpet barely would have been necessary. Capturing Arnhem could have saved the British airborne division, but it wouldn't have won the war, and for that matter, it mightn't have won the battle. The Allies would still only own a narrow corridor of land in Holland, and a weak bridgehead over the Rhine. I guess the movie doesn't really make that clear."

"How many times have you watched *A Bridge Too Far*?"

"Can I plead the Fifth?"

"Heh. Do you remember how old you were when you first watched it?"

"That's a good question. I don't know, maybe eight?"

"How many times have you watched it with a girl?"

"I think some women may have passed through the room while I was watching it – does that count?"

"To quote Michael Caine, 'Yes, that counts.'"

"Nice – you were paying attention!"

Suddenly there's a sharp crack at the back of the room – a thick bottle banging into a wooden table – followed by a slosh of liquid. Becs and I crane our heads to see my father, leaning against the table behind the sofa we're sitting on. "Hello, children," he says. I can barely discern his face in the dull light.

"How long have you been there?" I ask.

"Not long," he says. "Can't resist a potshot at ol' Monty, though, can you?"

"Hello, Mister Lansbury," says Becs, politely.

"Always the historian, that kid," says Dad. "The written and the spoken word."

"You've raised a very smart boy," answers Becs.

"I can't believe – I really can't believe – I can *not* believe that my son, my Sean, just watched *A Bridge Too Far* with his girlfriend."

"*Dad!*" But no, it's too late.

"I enjoyed it," says Becs.

"You like history?" Dad asks.

"Yes, I do," says Becs. "We're in AP European History together."

Dad waves a dismissive hand. "Do you like Sean's version of history?"

Becs laughs. "He's very opinionated," she says.

"Has he told you his Top Ten Favorite Moments of History list, whatever it's called? He shared that with me once."

"Yes, he has."

"History's Greatest Hits." Dad sighs deeply. "You know the Newburgh Conspiracy speech? 'I have grown blind in your service,' et cetera."

"Yes, I remember."

"The key moment wasn't spontaneous," says Dad. "Washington was a politician. Playing to the gallery, when reason alone didn't work. That ought to count for something."

My right hand is now on my forehead. "Dad, honestly, what are you on about?"

"I'm just saying, if you're going to have a definitive list of the Ten Greatest Moments in History, it ought to be grounded in truth and not legend. Also, there ought to be less of Sean's war pornography on it."

"What do you mean?" asks Becs.

"What he means is that I like military history," I respond. Now I'm angry. I push off from the sofa and work my way around the coffee table to confront Dad directly. "One, half of my list isn't war-related at all. Two, wars are an obvious source of dramatic moments in history – that's a simple fact. Three, it's *my list*, and I'll put whatever I want on it. And four, *I'm spending time with my girlfriend!* Would you just go away? Please?"

Dad stares blankly at me in the half-light for several seconds. Then he removes the cap from the bottle on the table, lifts it to his lips – it's whiskey, I think – and takes a swig. Silently, and without emotion, he puts the cap back on, turns around and slowly walks away.

I slink back across the room toward Becs. "Maybe you were a little harsh?" she enquires, gently.

I sigh. "You don't know my father. He's not a normal human being."

"Yeah?"

"As someone in that category myself, I know what I'm talking about."

Becs smiles. "Come here," she beckons.

I crawl to the sofa and crumple into her arms like a talking doll whose string has just run out. As she cuddles me close to her chest, she cannot guess my true anxiety: Dad easily might have revealed my wargaming secret just now. And that, to again reference *A Bridge Too Far*, is not in Monty's plan at all.

PART FOUR

1.

I blame 1848 for everything. The rise of nationalism fragmented the Austro-Hungarian Empire, united Italy and Germany, and sparked two world wars. My father's career studying the former indirectly sparked my interest in the latter. And now I'm over at Becs' house, sharing thoughts and mnemonics about 1848 for AP European History. Studying this topic in our class is extremely disorienting. Mr. Prendergast, bless him, asked if I'd like to invite Dad to give a guest lecture; I said I'd rather write 30 pages about suffragettes in the Ottoman Empire.

Before this evening, I didn't know the history of 1848 very well, likely for Freudian reasons. But it's good to be here, and quite healthy: I'm like a small boy discovering that broccoli actually tastes OK when smothered with cheese and followed with the promise of a favorite dessert. As revolutions go, the narrative structure of the French Revolution was more dramatic, but the Springtime of the Peoples possessed intricate layers of multinational tension which exploded sequentially across Europe like a grab bag of fireworks. Here's how I summarize it to Becs: "Unlike 1789, the 1848 revolutions seemed futile on the surface: new states and governments in France, Sicily and Hungary were overturned, and the status quo was restored within several years. Their only lasting achievement in the short term was the abolition of serfdom in Austria-Hungary by 1850, but they unleashed forces of nationalism and republicanism which prevailed in the longer term."

"Write that on an essay, and you'll be good to go." Becs smiles across the table at me.

"I could have cited the fall of Metternich as another lasting achievement, but that might get me in trouble with the Dead White Males Police," I continue. "It's funny, the closest thing the revolutions of 1848 had to an overall leader was probably Karl Marx."

"The original Communist. And a Dead White Male, I would point out."

"All white males eventually die," I counter. "The question is one of individualism and leadership, skills which the historical profession has deemed..."

"Yes, I get it," interrupts Becs, impatiently but not impolitely.

"Sorry. What's your take on 1848?" I ask. "Does this period interest you?"

Becs bites her bottom lip. "That question no longer interests me," she says.

"What do you mean?"

"I no longer want to take sides. I just like history. I like knowing where we've all come from, and why we are the way we are. I don't want to rank it and classify it – I just want to learn it."

"You must have a favorite period of history, though. Or a country that interests you more than others."

"The more I think that way, the less history interests me."

"Oh."

"This is where you should learn to take a hint, by the way."

"Yeah. Good safety tip."

Becs pushes her chair out from under the table and stands up. "Would you like something to drink?" she asks.

"Um, sure. A soda would be nice. Whatever you have."

She slowly walks across from the dining table to the kitchen area and collects two glasses from a cupboard and two bottles from the fridge. With her back to me, she calls out, "Hey, have you been following the Republican debates at all? Who do you think is going to win the nomination?"

"No idea," I respond.

"Who do you want to win it?"

"I refer you to my previous answer."

"Is that because you're a Democrat?"

"I'm more of a Federalist. Or maybe a Whig."

Becs brings the drinks to the table. "Will you be old enough to vote in the general election?" she asks, sitting back down.

"I think so."

"Will you?"

"Vote? I don't know. Probably not."

"Why not?"

"I'm not really interested."

Becs frowns, then sips from her glass. "Do you even know who is running for the Republican nomination?"

I pause, then ask, "Wendell Wilkie?"

"You know, I really have no idea whether you're serious."

"I read an old book on American presidential elections once. There have been some fascinating contests. McKinley-Bryan in 1896 was a real clash of styles – that's how I know about the 'Cross of Gold' speech. Same with John Quincy Adams versus Andrew Jackson in 1828, and Nixon versus Kennedy in 1960. The three-way contest between Taft, Wilson and Teddy Roosevelt in 1912. The four-way battle between Lincoln, Douglas, Breckenridge and Bell in 1860. Rutherford B. Hayes only won the disputed election of 1876 over Samuel Tilden after a supposedly bipartisan commission voted eight to seven in Hayes' favor on every important issue, months after the general public had voted."

"No mention of the Bush-Gore election of 2000?"

"I think the book was published in 1983."

"I was referring to you. You were actually alive for Bush versus Gore. What do you think – should Gore have won?"

"I think those wounds are still too fresh to be properly analyzed."

Becs smiles faintly. "You haven't answered my original question."

"What was the question?"

"Whether you were serious, about Wendell Wilkie. And not knowing who is running for president."

"What do you think?"

Becs sighs. "I think you never talk about the present like you do the past."

"The present scares me."

"What about the future?"

"Terrifying."

Becs titters. Then she stops, and realizes I'm not joking. "Are you serious?"

I breathe deeply. "Yeah. Mostly. The past is finite. Generally speaking, we can figure it out. The present is loud and obnoxious. There's no perspective. No nuance. Politics is a battlefield, and truth is its first casualty. The present is so messed up, it's messing up how we teach the past."

"And so you disengage from it?"

"The past is safer. It's more real, in many ways."

"And what about the future?"

"That's the other thing. If the past teaches us anything, it's that the future will be scary."

"So you're a pessimist."

"I'm a realist."

"You're 16 years old, and the future scares you? That's pretty depressing."

"This is how I think, OK? Do you remember the first day of AP Euro, when Mr. Prendergast compared the Black Death to a modern disease outbreak?"

"Yeah."

"What's to stop something like that from really happening? Billions of people dying in a mass pandemic?"

"I don't know." Becs thinks for a moment. "Luck, I guess."

"It's a low-probability event, but history is full of low-probability events. There's been quite a lot of it, you know. Recorded Greek history and what we now call 'classical antiquity' started almost exactly one million days ago."

"Yes."

"And as technology improves, the pace at which we make and record history accelerates. The Spanish Flu killed between 50 and 100 million people in two-and-a-half years from 1918 to 1920; how much more quickly would a disease like that kill many more people in an era of fast cars and global air travel? Could modern medicine even keep up with it?"

"I don't know."

"It doesn't have to be a disease. It could be a terrorist attack – if the wrong people get their hands on a loose nuclear weapon, they could make 9/11 look like a traffic accident. Or it could be a war between Israel and Iran, or Pakistan and India, or North Korea and everyone. Or a global famine. Or a huge natural disaster. Or a second Great Depression. Or it could even just be the normal degeneration of the United States into a second- or third-rate nation – which is scary precisely because it's so likely to happen."

"What do you mean?"

"People in this country seem to think the US has a divine right to remain the best and most powerful country in the world forever. But isn't that pretty much what people in every dominant empire have thought throughout history, right up until and even beyond when it's no longer true? From Alexander the Great and Ancient Rome to Victorian Britain and Soviet Russia, every superpower eventually loses its power and influence. And the US is at a dangerous period where fewer and fewer smart and capable people are entering politics and government. If we're lucky, our slide will be gradual like Britain's and not destructive like Rome's and the Soviet Union's. But ever since our War of Independence, the US has been very lucky throughout its history in a way that, say, Europe really hasn't been."

"You think so?"

"Absolutely. Think about this: Colonel Ferguson easily could have shot and killed George Washington, as I described to you in my Top Ten list, and that's only one of at least 11 or 12 turning points where the American Revolution might have collapsed but didn't. But in Europe, the assassination of Archduke Ferdinand and the whole chain of events leading to World War One were incredibly improbable, while Adolf Hitler somehow survived both World War One and numerous assassination attempts between 1939 and 1944. Meanwhile, what if Robert E. Lee had listened to many of his advisors at the end of the Civil War and encouraged his army to melt into the hills? We could have had a guerilla war across the South, and the Confederacy may have become to the United States what Serbia was to Austria-Hungary. Or even look at the Japanese attack on Pearl Harbor: through a series of amazing mistakes and bad luck, America suffered a huge defeat, but it only served to unite the country and galvanize it to become the most powerful nation on earth. If Japan's attack had failed, would America have become a superpower?"

Becs ponders the question for a moment. Then she smiles and stifles a laugh. "How did I let you segue from a talk about the present into another lecture about the past?" she asks.

"It's a gift, I guess." I sip from my own glass. "Anyway, I'm just trying to talk about the future by referencing the past. We can't even begin to imagine what the world will look like 20 years from now. Think back just a few decades: in 1985, who would have guessed that 20 years later we would be enmeshed in Iraq and Afghanistan, trying to avenge the destruction of the World Trade Center? We were still fighting the Cold War, and it wasn't clear we were winning! Or go back to 1930, at the start of a vicious depression, and try to imagine the world in 1950. Or try envisioning 1930 from 1910. And so on, and so on. Do you follow me?"

"Yes."

"So, come back to the present and try to predict the future. Do you think this country will be a better place 20 years from now? Might it be worse? What if it's much, much worse? The government could break down completely – not a huge stretch, given how much the Democrats and Republicans hate each other. There could be a popular military coup, possibly after a nuclear terrorist attack. We could be goaded into launching a nuclear attack of our own and become an international pariah. Or dozens of other things could happen which I've never thought of – which nobody could possibly think of. *That* is what history teaches us."

Becs looks blank for a few seconds, then creases her mouth into a faint smile and lifts her glass to her lips. Her movements seem so graceful, even in the simple act of taking a drink, that my own awkwardness stands in sharp relief. "You think I'm paranoid, don't you?" I ask.

"Not really," she replies.

"It's not so much that I expect these things will happen as I am aware that they could."

"I was actually just wondering how you and Melissa ever got together."

I relax. "Yeah. Weird, isn't it?"

"A little."

"Obviously I never would have talked about stuff like this with her."

"Obviously."

"You're smart enough to get what I'm saying. And I guess I feel safe enough with you to say it."

"Thanks."

"Not that I would want you to think like I do."

"Oh, God no."

I laugh. "You know, when I get on a roll like that, you can ask me to stop at any time and I'll stop."

"What makes you think I haven't tried?"

"Really?"

"I can be ruder next time, if you'd like."

"Oh."

I must look quite crestfallen, because Becs' response is thoroughly warm. "You're incredibly smart, and listening to you is very thought-provoking, not to mention entertaining. I just can't absorb everything in such large doses, that's all."

Becs gets up from her chair, walks to where I'm sitting and kisses me on the forehead. "I'll be right back, OK?"

"Will you marry me?" I ask. I'm not sure if I'm joking.

Becs chuckles. "Don't go anywhere," she says. And she disappears through the door to the hallway.

❖ ❖ ❖

Freddie lives in an expansive house of grey stucco walls and black slate roofing which in February is of course blanketed in snow. Behind the house, a sloping path meanders for several hundred yards through a forest of tall pines before stopping short and curving away from a small stream. To a boy who can jump, the stream poses no obstacle, and in any case it is now frozen solid; beyond the stream, the land is more jagged as it rises, slowly at first but then more steeply. But as long as the snow isn't too thick, you can climb the hill easily enough, grabbing at the thinner and shorter tree trunks for purchase and bracing against the thicker and longer ones for balance.

At the crest of the hill is a golf course. The gates to the club that owns it are guarded year-round, but this side entrance is unpatrolled during the winter, and it is via this route that my Gang of Four regularly makes our sneak attacks. We emerge at the fifth hole, a downhill par three which – according to a wooden sign dangling by two chains from a metal pole – measures 241 yards from the tee farthest from the hole. The sixth hole, a par four which bends to the right around a cluster of trees, also starts with a downhill shot from a mounded teeing area. The fifth green and sixth tee are separated by two sand bunkers, three ornamental oak trees, and the artificially steep curb of a concrete path on which members must drive their golf carts. The Gang of Four, however, comes to the fifth tee armed not with clubs or carts but with sleds: good, strong wooden sleds with metal runners on wide bases. We have learned over the past several winters that on a properly cold day, when the snow is icy but not too thick, expert steering – around the bunkers, between the trees and avoiding the curb and teeing mound – can yield a thrilling ride of nearly a third of a mile, from the fifth tee to within a snowball's throw of the sixth green.

Sadly, one of our pilots on this bright Saturday morning is missing: Melvyn has opted to escort Vicki to the mall. So it's just me, Chris and Freddie. I'm annoyed – we only do this two or three times a year, and I'm here even though I'm just as besotted with Becs as Melvyn is with Vicki. I'm also the least skilled sledder among us: while Chris and Freddie more often than not avoid the obstacles and cruise the full distance, in steering to miss the trees I frequently catch the corner of the sixth tee and either tip over or ascend onto the mound and lose my speed. From there I must either glide slowly down from the sixth tee, which is dull, or climb back to the fifth tee and try again on my own, which is antisocial. It's still great fun, but Melvyn's absence is irksome. The Big Games notwithstanding, we hardly see him.

Today, on my first run I veer too far left and spin around one of the bunkers onto the fifth green. The snow is a touch powdery, but the sunshine and the stillness of the cold air are memorable, and when I judge my second descent to perfection and zoom to the end of the run, I forget about Melvyn and savor a high-five and a chuckle with Freddie, who is two for two. Conversely, the normally assured Chris is having a bad day, steering once into the forest behind the fifth green – an amateur mistake – and then overcompensating into the sixth tee on his second run. As we scale the big hill for our third attempts, each new climb always more draining than the last, Chris is boasting between gulps of air about the speed and distance he will certainly achieve this time around.

Usually we stagger our starts to maximize our chances of successfully navigating the full course. Sometimes, though, we begin simultaneously and race each other head-to-head for speed and distance. And with Chris in this mood, we have little choice: he wants to redeem his earlier failures. So after briefly recuperating on the bench behind the tee, we line up together at the crest of the hill with Freddie on the left, me in the middle and Chris on the right. As we push off, Chris and I make the fastest starts, while Freddie steers wide to the left before looping behind us. Chris and I are locked close together and gathering speed, when suddenly Chris veers sharply to the right: distracted, I squiggle to the left, lose my balance and wobble directly toward the oak trees. With seconds to spare before a thumping collision, I spin out and roll down the snow, instinctively covering my face and leaving my sled to chart its own course, like a racehorse that has unseated its jockey. My momentum dispersed, I collide tamely with the first of the oak trees; I'm not hurt, but the snow has ruffled my face, and as I gather my wits I know my muscles will be sore in the morning.

I lie in the snow, perpendicular to both the tree and the line of the sixth fairway. I've never thought this pastime to be dangerous, but then, I'm young and rather more stupid in many ways than I like to let on. As I ponder my lack of protective padding, a snowball suddenly grazes the back of my head and lands at the base of the tree. Startled, I sit up immediately. Chris is standing 20 feet away.

"What are you doing?" I call.

"Trying to hit something I'm aiming at, for once," he responds. He bends over, collects another chunk of snow in his dark blue gloves, and fashions it into another ball.

"I could have been seriously hurt!"

"Are you hurt?"

"Well, no, not really…"

"Then here, have this." Chris cocks his arm and throw the second snowball at me, this time hitting me in the stomach.

"Owww!" I call, more in shock than injury.

"That's better," says Chris.

"What's going on? Why are you doing this?"

"That's for being such a geek."

"Really? Where's Freddie?"

"Down there." Chris points down the sixth fairway – craning my neck around the oak tree, I can just about see Freddie in the distance, waving his arms and pumping his fists in delight.

"I guess we have a winner," I say, clambering to my feet and dusting myself off. "What happened to you?"

"Mind your own business," says Chris.

"It would have been my own business if I'd have smacked into this tree," I retort. "Why did you veer off to the right like that?"

"I'm sure it's your fault."

"Thanks. So, I'm a geek again? What did I do this time?"

"Do you really have to ask?"

"AP Euro?"

"Duh."

"Mr. Prendergast was being stupid, and I called him on it."

"OK, both halves of what you just said are nine kinds of wrong."

"But he was!"

"Why can't you shut up during class and write a love letter to Becs or something?"

"You mean like the last time I got caught writing notes to Becs?"

"Oh, God." Chris leans down and gathers another wad of snow in his gloves. "How could I forget?"

"You're going to throw that at me, aren't you?" I ask.

"Depends what you say next," answers Chris.

"Let me ask you this: what's your favorite class in school?"

"Study hall." Chris pats the snow in his hands into a ball.

"Apart from that."

"I dunno. English, maybe. Depends on the teacher."

"OK, say it's English. Have you ever read a book or a poem you really liked? Something you were actually excited to talk about in class? Something that made learning fun?"

"No."

"You're an idiot."

Chris raises his throwing arm and I flinch, raising a hand to guard my face. Instead he kicks some snow onto my boots and laughs. "Yes, I have a brain," he says. "I have read books I was happy to discuss in class."

"Give me one example."

"I liked *Hamlet*."

"Who was your teacher when you studied *Hamlet*?"

"Mrs. Gilfillan."

"Did Mrs. Gilfillan ever say anything about *Hamlet* you strongly disagreed with? An interpretation of the play? A fact you thought was flat-out wrong?"

"I have no idea! That was, like, more than a year ago. How much do you think I pay attention in class?"

"More than you're letting on – your grades are better than that. You're not really cheating on your exams, are you?"

"Even if I did disagree with her, Mrs. Gilfillan is paid to teach English, and I would never correct her in front of the class. One, I don't know that much. Two, I don't care that much. And three, it's rude."

"Hmmm. You might be right about the rudeness."

Chris quickly cocks his arm and slings his snowball into my chest. He's only five feet away, and the contact stings even through the layers covering my torso.

"Why did you do that?"

"For being rude and a dork at the same time."

"I wasn't wrong, though."

"About what?"

"About Mr. Prendergast."

"Here we go again…"

"Nationalism doesn't spontaneously combust. Would Italy have unified without Cavour and Garibaldi, or Germany without Bismarck? And yet Mr. Prendergast is teaching as though the 'Great Man' theory doesn't exist."

"Shut up."

"What?"

"No really, just shut up. Do you ever listen to yourself?"

"Becs has asked me that as well…"

"Stop it – I don't even want to know. The thought of your geeky little History love-ins gives me more shivers than the snow does. I'm so glad I'm not in your study group."

"Me too."

"Why do you care so much about this crap?"

"Because it's not crap. Look at this another way: do you consider yourself to be patriotic?"

"Sure."

"How? Would you travel to the Olympics or the Ryder Cup or a US soccer game just to wave a flag and support our teams?"

"To a point, given enough money and time."

"What about joining the armed forces and defending America's interests around the world?"

"No way. Like the chances of one of these in hell." Chris scoops up another handful of snow and quickly squeezes it into a ball.

"Right – only a few people are patriotic enough to risk their lives for their country. So what would it take to change your mind? Or to put it another way, what convinced so many Italians and Germans to become so patriotic in the 1860s?"

"What are you guys talking about?"

That other voice belongs to Freddie, who has finally ascended from the sixth fairway and rejoined us by the fifth green. Chris immediately whirls and flings his snowball, catching Freddie in the neck.

"Dude!" calls Freddie. "Down my back as well – not cool!" Ice is trickling down Freddie's skin and inside his clothes, and he starts wriggling as if afflicted with bedbugs.

"That's for being too good at sledding," says Chris.

"It's not my fault you suck," responds Freddie, reaching to the ground to grab his own ammunition. Chris immediately ducks behind the tree into which I almost crashed a few minutes ago.

"We were talking about nationalism and the 'Great Man' theory of history," I say to a dodging Freddie. "What do you know about 'Great Men'?"

"You have to be pretty great to ride so well so many times in a row," says Freddie.

"That's not what I…"

"Shut up," says Chris to me. "I mean it." He jukes from behind the tree and wings another snowball toward Freddie, which misses. Freddie jumps into a defensive crouch.

"I can throw snowballs too, you know," I respond.

"Which historical figure do you throw like the most?" snarls Chris, forming another ball in his hands. "I'm guessing Susan B. Anthony."

"OK, stop for a second," I yell. "Stop it!"

Freddie relaxes. Chris peeks around his tree and asks, "What?"

"Let's make it interesting," I say to Chris. "You and me, top of the hill, one more race. Simultaneous start, furthest distance without stopping wins. If you win, I promise to shut up about AP Euro for the rest of the term, both inside and outside of the classroom."

"Awesome," says Chris. "And if you win?"

"If I win…." I haven't thought this through – but then it hits me. "If I win, we get to play something other than poker at the Big Game."

"What, for the rest of the term?" asks Chris.

"No, just once is fine," I say. "I'll figure something out."

"A card game, just not poker," echoes Chris.

"Sure," I concede. "A card game. You OK with that, Freddie?"

"Cool," says Freddie.

"Melvyn lost his vote by not being here today," I say.

"You cut off your penis and give it to your girlfriend, what do you expect?" says Chris. I smile, then Chris blurts out, "First one to the top of the hill gets inside position," and then he's sprinting with his sled.

2.

"I went through the motions of racing Chris to the summit, but I was really trying to conserve my energy," I say. "He was so jacked up it was untrue."

"So what happened?" asks Dennis.

"He flipped over halfway down the hill, and I won easily. He was not a happy snow bunny."

"So what are you going to play?"

"I have some ideas."

Dennis has come over for our first *Totaler Krieg* session since our "World War One Revisited" game fizzled out. I'm not that excited about playing again; my tournament game against Gregory Spearman is still bubbling along, and I hadn't been desperate for Dennis's company. But I guess he's been desperate for mine: he was happy to start from scratch, and he's even wearing a collared shirt with no outlandish colors, patterns or logos on it.

Once again, into the breach…our opening moves zoom by gracefully, like a game of speed chess in Washington Square Park. We barely need move the pieces to conquer Poland: Air between Krakow and Warsaw, Blitz attacks against Danzig and the weak units southeast of Posen, exploitation and mopping up as necessary. The Soviets then move into Eastern Poland, Germany redeploys from East to West, and the Allies convoy reinforcements to France, all with forensic efficiency. Unlike Hitler, Stalin, Chamberlain and Gamelin, we know exactly what to do and what to expect in the first year of the war; that our results so often match theirs is a trick of wargame design, nothing more.

Today I'm the Axis, and after losing a panzer step in Poland, the German airborne unit is slow to arrive and I can't invade Norway on schedule. Instead, I choose Limited War Production for Spring 1940, and when I reveal Case Yellow in the Summer I select Operation Weserübung for the Autumn – a Blitz card to get ashore in Britain if circumstances warrant, or to snag Norway if not. Regardless, I'll get to Axis Tide 1 in time for my Treaty rolls in the Winter.

Dennis's defense of France is unorthodox. France starts the game with only one HQ unit, and it cannot cover every hex from the Channel to Switzerland. If the HQ goes south to Troyes, the Axis player will normally wheel Schlieffen-style through Calais, but if the HQ goes north to Reims, the Maginot forts are unsupported and the *Wehrmacht* can lunge through Strasbourg. Dennis puts his HQ in the north, but he also puts his best armies in the Maginot Line, whereas his forces in Flanders are relatively weak. He's trying to have it both ways, but as I study the board – at greater length than normal prior to Case Yellow – I spot a promising opening.

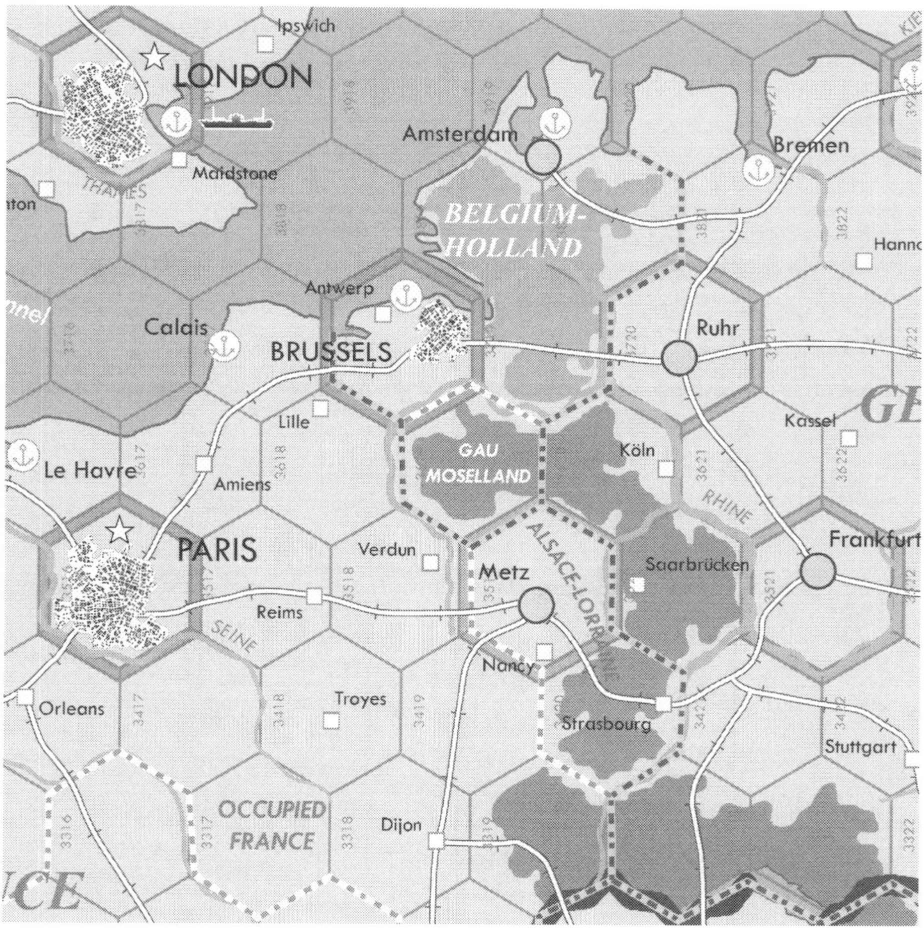

Fig. 9 – The Case Yellow battlefield

I have two HQs at the start of Case Yellow, and I swing them both to the north. Amsterdam falls comfortably, and although I fail to exploit into France after routing the Belgian army (a 50-50 chance), I can now strongly attack both Calais and Lille in Regular Combat. At worst, I will occupy one of the two hexes; at best, I could exploit all the way to Paris and checkmate France in a single turn.

"I'll attack Lille first with my stack in southern Belgium and the HQ in Cologne," I say. "That's 18 factors with HQ and Air shifts; without your HQ, it's 6-to-1, or with it I'm down to 3-to-1. What will you do?"

"I've got a River shift as well," says Dennis. "Right?"

"Oh." So he does – I'm attacking across the Meuse. "Hmmm. Hang on a minute." Well, that sucks. I forgot about the River shift. And despite my best efforts, I cannot reconfigure my attacks against Lille and Calais to guarantee at least one roll at 6:1 odds as I'd hoped. "I won't change anything," I mutter.

"I won't use my HQ – roll it up at 4-to-1," says Dennis.

On a '1' or '2' against Lille, I will force a two-hex retreat into Paris and advance into Amiens, cutting off Calais in a remarkably historical scythe to the Channel. On a '3', '4' or '5' I will force a one-hex retreat and be slightly better off than normal after the first turn of Case Yellow. But instead, I roll a '6' – an Exchange, with no retreat at all. Oy veh.

"Brutal," says Dennis.

"Horrible," I say.

In my 3:1 against Calais, I kill a single step without loss, but a bad situation is made much worse at the end of the turn. Overall, Dennis's Delay dice are poor, but on his most important roll – for the second French HQ – he gets a '1'.

"How to stop a *Blitzkrieg* cold in two easy die rolls," I laugh.

"A perfect storm," says Dennis. "I couldn't have planned that any better."

"You know the line, 'We'll always have Paris', from *Casablanca*? I think you can now say that literally."

"I'm sure you'll get there eventually."

"Not soon enough to give me any chance of winning the game."

"You still have your airborne unit, as well as uncontested Air supremacy. It isn't over yet."

In theory, Dennis is right: I don't have to capture Paris by the end of the Summer to collapse the French. But in practice, my fallback option involves taking three French cities in the south – Metz, Lyon and probably Marseilles or Toulouse – whereas the focal point *(Schwerpunkt)* of my offensive is in the north. The Maginot Line remains unbreached, and unless I capture Strasbourg and Metz, I won't even be able to attack as far south as Lyon. And if I fail to collapse France by the end of the Summer, it will fight on until all of Continental France is conquered, and even beyond in North Africa thereafter.

Desperate, in June-July I launch attritional infantry attacks against Strasbourg and Metz even as I again hit Calais and Lille, this time with *Luftwaffe* support.

I break through at Calais, inflicting heavy losses and pushing the French back – my spearheads reach Amiens and Reims as well, giving me two hexes adjacent to Paris and a puncher's chance of capturing the capital next turn. However, not only are my Maginot attacks unacceptably costly, in my haste to pursue the French to Paris I forget that the current Western Option Card – Dyle Plan – is itself a Blitz card. So now Dennis can punk my *Schwerpunkt*: after my only HQ in range repulses a Blitz attack on Amiens, Dennis forces a two-hex retreat with his second attack and recaptures both Reims and Lille. Then in Regular Combat, a diversionary push toward Brussels distracts my HQ and allows a 3:2 attack on Amiens, and when Dennis rolls a '2' to force another retreat, 10 of my steps are stuck in Calais. As you can only stack up to six steps per hex, I have to eliminate the German Fourth Army and another infantry corps, and I am monumentally screwed.

"I'm sorry, man," says Dennis. "If it weren't for bad luck…"

He lets the thought drift away – I'm shaking my head and smiling. "Should I resign now, or wait until the end of the Summer?" I ask.

"No, I'm happy to stop now. There's no way back from here."

"Congratulations. Well played."

"You mean, 'well rolled'."

"Seriously, I do want to consider your French defense more closely," I say. "You may have discovered something."

"I discovered that rolling sixes at 4-to-1 odds are hazardous to your health," responds Dennis. "That was like a 'swindle' in chess – nothing more."

"I'm not sure about that. I know he who defends everything defends nothing, but you've asked some tricky questions in both the north and the south. Any hex with 13 defense factors and two shifts is a tough nut. And if you can prevent a 6-to-1 attack in Flanders during Regular Combat, you've got a 1-in-6 chance of keeping the Germans out of France on the first turn of Case Yellow."

"That assumes the Belgians don't retreat three hexes during Blitz Combat."

"Well, yeah. That's a 50-50 shot, so I guess it's 1-in-12 overall."

"Plus you have to get the second HQ right away to make it really count."

"I'm not saying it's a likely sequence of events. But it happened in our game, so I know it's possible. And if your defense gives the Allies even a 5 percent chance of winning the game in 1940 without materially affecting them if it doesn't work, that's enough to take a perfectly balanced game and make it 52-48 or 53-47 in the Allies' favor. That's not inconsiderable."

"But what if it does materially affect the Allies if it doesn't work?"

"That's what I want to study. Do you mind if I keep the game set up like this for a few days?"

Dennis glances at his plasticky digital watch and asks, "I guess we're done for tonight?"

"What time is it?"

"About quarter to nine."

"Really?"

"Time flies when you're not having fun."

"Oh. Well, um, I guess we could set up to start over, although that might take some time."

"No, it's fine. It's not every day you can play a full game of *Totaler Krieg* and still get a good night's sleep after you're done."

"True."

"You should show the final position to your girlfriend, by the way. This is fantasy history anyone can embrace!"

"Yeah…it is."

"I'll see myself out. Have a good night."

❖ ❖ ❖

Dennis leaves, but I remain entranced in my chair, my heart fluttering and then pounding. Maybe he's right. Maybe this is my opening with Becs. I am Guderian, this is May 1940, I've just crossed the Meuse, and I see no Allied armies between me and the Channel.

Consider three low-probability events:

1) The 1940 German *Blitzkrieg* in France between 10 May, when the great offensive in the West was launched, and 20 May, when Guderian's panzers reached the Channel at Abbeville.

2) A successful defense of France in 1940, with Dennis's performance in our game suggestive of what might have been.

3) Becs becoming a wargamer, and the two of us never leaving our house except to buy food and books and to drop off our home-schooled children at Harvard for the start of their freshman years.

What happened in France in 1940? With hindsight it does seem as though Germany, to quote Hitler, "need only kick in the door and the whole rotten structure will come crashing down". The Third Republic's institutions were decaying, its leaders clueless, its morale plummeting lower every day. France dreaded the prospect of re-fighting World War I and cowered behind the Maginot Line, happy for the *Sitzkrieg* to last as long as Germany allowed it to. When Germany struck, it struck hard and fast with a plan and a vigor Gamelin and his dilapidated colleagues couldn't match. The campaign itself could have evolved differently, but the end result was preordained: France would fall during 1940. This is certainly the view endorsed by wargame designers – the French campaign is little more than speedbump, a scenario generator for the real war to follow.

That said, in the above quote Hitler was actually talking about Russia, not France. Nobody in Germany dared presume a speedy French collapse. And if Germany had attacked in December 1939 or January 1940 as originally intended, France might have survived indefinitely. France was already outproducing Germany by May 1940, and while the *Sitzkrieg* undeniably harmed French morale, Julian Jackson in *The Fall of France* convincingly argues that British morale was just as low. The difference was that Britain had time and space to recover from the French campaign, just as France itself survived in 1914 and thereafter could dig in figuratively as well as literally. The French army learned quickly and was already fighting demonstrably better in June 1940 than it was in May, and either Reynaud or Pétain – the former had only become Prime Minister in March, while the latter was a beloved figurehead not yet tainted by the stench of Vichy – could have become for France the war leader Churchill became for England. But by the start of June, France was already out of time.

Even then, the real German attack in May 1940 was a very near run thing. The *Wehrmacht* achieved total strategic surprise for its drive through the Ardennes – to quote Jackson, "If only the French High Command had realized what was happening, the huge concentration of German armor moving through the tangled mess of the Ardennes would have offered an easy target to Allied bombers." Instead, the panzers reached the Meuse virtually undetected. Even then, the steep-banked river was not easy to cross, and tiny French detachments were able to cause significant casualties among the German assault parties. The German bridgeheads were small on the evening of 13 May, and a determined counterattack may have bought France the time it needed to find its balance. Instead, the counterattack was delayed, and several others fizzled out in the days that followed, so Guderian's panzers kept streaming west. The *Wehrmacht* still could have squandered victory: Guderian's boss, von Kleist, tried to slow him down and on 17 May even ordered him to halt to let the infantry catch up and protect his flanks. But Guderian kept pushing forward, creatively disobeying his orders and even threatening to resign.

We know how the Dunkirk evacuation was made possible by Hitler's famous "halt order" of 24 May and the four precious days it bought for the BEF; what if a similar order had been obeyed a week earlier, with the sickle-cut to the Channel incomplete, and Weygand's plan to strike into Guderian's northern flank had been given room to breathe?

In my May-June 1940 attack against Dennis, I made one small mistake (misjudging the odds by one terrain shift or two attack factors) and got one unlucky die roll (the '6' at 4:1 vs. Lille). That's all it took to transform certain victory into another Flanders bloodbath. My eventual margin of defeat was massive, compounded by another poor decision and more bad luck, but I'm comforted to know that in a campaign between evenly skilled players, a French victory – or at least the denial of German victory for long enough to turn World War II into World War I – is at least possible in *Totaler Krieg*. And while I know a wargame like *Totaler Krieg* cannot prove the plausibility of a French victory in 1940, it can make us reconsider history and ask new questions about it.

Think about the greatest upsets in sports history. If the USA-USSR hockey game in the 1980 Winter Olympics had been played 100 times, the Soviets may well have won at least 95 of them. They had won a best-of-three series against a team of NHL all-stars in 1979, they crushed the US Olympic team 10-3 in an exhibition the week before the Olympics, and they won their group games by scores like 16-0, 17-4 and 8-1 while the US was scraping come-from-behind victories and even a late tie with Sweden. The Soviet players were virtual professionals; the US team was full of college kids. Objectively, the Soviet team was clearly better, even if the US won the game and then the gold medal. The Miracle on Ice was a supreme triumph of the underdog; nobody thinks the US timed its player development cycle perfectly and therefore possessed more great talent in 1980 than anyone else in the world.

Why don't we think this way about wars as well? Rewind to the end of the Polish campaign and let the next 12 months unfold again: if Germany had invaded France 100 times, who would win the series, and by how large a margin? How often would Germany attack in the winter, without first adopting von Manstein's plan to attack through the Ardennes? How many times would the Allies leave the Ardennes virtually unguarded and allow Germany to gain decisive strategic surprise? Decisions upon decisions, strategies upon strategies...how often would Germany do better than it did historically, and how often would it do worse? I imagine Joshua, the computer from the movie *WarGames*, fighting and refighting the campaign hundreds or even thousands of times at hyper-speed, with Matthew

Broderick and Dabney Coleman staring at a panoply of colliding pixels in wonderment – only to conclude that different decisions and strategies *do* matter, because sometimes Germany wins the campaign, sometimes France does and sometimes they battle to a draw.

And if enough of these hypothetical campaigns could be seen to end in German draws or defeats, perhaps we would stop asserting that systemic causes preordained a German victory. Hitler wasn't fated to cancel his winter offensive and embrace von Manstein's plan as his own. Gamelin wasn't predestined to gamble his strongest armies on a headlong rush into Belgium, and forget his own army's map exercises from 1938 – which posited Germany moving armored forces through and beyond the Ardennes in 60 hours. When France's Parliamentary Army Committee suggested in March 1940 that the defenses of General Charles Huntziger's Seventh Army at the Meuse near Sedan possessed "grave insufficiencies", Huntziger need not have strongly rebutted its report. (Equally, Hitler might not have approved the "halt order" and thereby made Dunkirk possible; the pendulum of fate swings in both directions.)

Inadequate information and intelligence notwithstanding, why do leaders make mistakes? If Huntziger had gotten a better night's sleep before that committee inspected his front, would he have been more amenable to accepting constructive criticism? Gamelin had a reputation for astounding intelligence, and an ability to see both sides of every argument; surely he, more than any other leader in the campaign, might have made different decisions given the chance to make them again? For example, Gamelin initially wanted to advance into Belgium only up to the Escaut line, much further west than the Dyle; might he have resisted British pressure to enact the Dyle Plan, and also kept a healthier reserve to better contain any German penetrations?

Or forget about leaders and focus on the front line. What if an additional 1 percent of all French bullets and shells had successfully pierced enemy skin or armor, and 1 percent of Germany's hits had become misses? Or 2 percent? Or more? How random is individual marksmanship within a given day, battle, campaign or war? It isn't all down to training; sometimes even the best snipers miss. And until someone adds up all of the variables and can accurately conclude that Germany's offensive performed at the 93rd percentile or the 64th percentile or the 31st percentile relative to the hypothetical mean of those 100 French campaigns being fought over and over again, I won't know how much the real French campaign of May and June 1940 owed its result to systemic causes like training, tactics and morale and how much might even have been a triumph of the underdog. Which event was less probable: Germany's historical triumph, or French resistance along the lines of what Dennis achieved? Could Dennis's accomplishment have been much closer to the historical mean than I'd ever suspected?

Now...if I were to show Rebecca Fowler my *Totaler Krieg* map at the moment of Germany's capitulation to France 100 times, how often would she be ensorcelled and how often repulsed? How many of those scenarios are clear-cut wins for me? I suspect the odds are low, but the stakes are high: this could be the beginning of much more than a beautiful relationship. Should I rethink my plans and metaphorically plunge through the Ardennes? If we keep drawing closer to one another, she's bound to discover my hobby eventually; should I actively draw her into that world, or let her discover it herself? What factors influence the female mind? Is Becs' reaction preordained, or can I apply any positive shifts to improve my attack odds?

I don't know the answers to these questions, but one thought keeps entering my head: decisive action is required to win the battle. Guderian and von Manstein gambled and won for Germany. Dennis gambled and won for France. If I pick the right moment and time my offensive perfectly, can I gamble and win Becs over to my hobby? Can I afford not to try?

3.

It is a Tuesday evening, the twenty-first of February. The temperature crept above freezing this morning, so the snow began to melt, but now it's cold again, and untreated roads are getting slick. At school today, I lost another 50 cents in the Big Game, but I aced an English pop quiz on Virginia Woolf's *A Room of One's Own*, proof that my only bias against feminism is its over-emphasis in history classes. On this date in 1613, the Romanov dynasty in Russia began, whereas in 1848 the *Communist Manifesto* was published by Marx and Engels. I'm guessing Mr. Prendergast didn't know these things, but his lecture today about Pan-Slavism and the Russian Revolution of 1905 was no less timely for that.

Our next exam on Thursday covers our current topic of Nationalism and Imperialism, so Becs has come over for another study session. We're at the oval-shaped table in my large and well-lit kitchen: the lacquer faded from its wooden surface years ago, and felt-covered cushions are required to temper the discomfort of lattice wicker chairs, but in present company it always feels like a good place to learn. Sprawled on the table are books, notepads crammed with dog-eared handouts yearning to escape, ballpoint pens in several colors with tooth-marked lids, and the fluorescent markers we use to deify the men and their deeds we feel we must know, at least until the AP exam is finished. The best single gauge of immortality must surely be the number of times your name has been highlighted in scholastic textbooks.

For Thursday, we've been told to expect the usual multiple-choice section plus any one of these four essay-based questions:

1. *Contrast the impact of nationalism in Germany and the Austrian Empire from 1848 to 1914.*
2. *To what extent and in what ways did nationalist tensions in the Balkans between 1870 and 1914 contribute to the outbreak of the First World War?*
3. *Identify and analyze the political and cultural issues in the debate over Pan-Slavism.*
4. *Analyze the pressures on Great Britain's Liberal government during the Sudan crisis (1884-1885) and explain why the government acted as it did.*

The latter two are Document-Based Questions, so we would have assistance from primary sources in answering them. I'll gladly answer any of the four, of course – this is my kind of history.

Becs and I assess our options in reverse order. Our textbook doesn't reference the Sudan crisis of 1884-1885 – much less prominent than the Fashoda Incident of 1898, Britain's last great conflict with France – but we assume the DBQ will cover general themes related to imperialism. Pan-Slavism is fresh in our minds from this morning, and nationalism in the Balkans relates to Pan-Slavism and Russia's role in crumbling the Ottoman Empire, so we speed through those questions as well. To be honest, I think Becs fancies progressing to something more intimate than our studies.

Then we look at nationalism in Germany and Austria. "*Zollverein* must be the most German word I've ever heard," I muse.

Becs is skimming through our textbook. "It says here that Bismarck was the most important figure in Germany between Luther and Hitler," she reads.

"I'm surprised the authors didn't pick Bach or Beethoven."

"Hey – don't mock Beethoven, OK? I won't allow it." Becs smiles. "Anyway, 'Sedan'...I guess that's where the car name comes from?"

"From the city, not the battle as such."

"Dad drives a family sedan." Becs clears her throat and sips from the soft drink on the table in front of her. Then she comments, "Louis Napoleon was an idiot, wasn't he?"

"Pretty much. If France and Austria gang up on Prussia in 1866, maybe Bismarck can't forge a united Germany. And then Louis Napoleon personally led the French army straight into the encirclement at Sedan. He did some good things too, but it's hard to ignore the disastrous outcomes of his diplomatic strategy."

"Here's a military question for you: Why did Germany conquer France so easily in 1870 and 1940, but fail to do so in 1914?"

I stare incredulously at Becs. "You want to kiss me right now, don't you?" she says, coquettishly.

"Oh, you have no idea." Her thin, lightly painted lips are very kissable indeed, but a deeper opening also beckons. To be safe, I first offer an escape hatch: "Do you actually want me to answer that question?"

"Try me."

Becs' elbows are resting on the table, chin cradled in her interlocking fingers. She's wearing a white knitted sweater, delicate over a peach T-shirt and faded denim. Her hair is elegantly twisted into a ponytail, her cheeks a gentle pink, and when I meet her eyes they are suggestive and enticing. I take a deep breath.

"Come with me for a minute." I stand up, pushing my chair out from the table.

"Yeah?"

"I want to show you something."

She rises, smiling. I trail her behind me, our right hands clasped together, and lead her through the drafty living room to the oak-paneled floor of the hallway beyond it. I motion to a set of closed double doors.

"You've never been in this room before," I say. "Nobody from school has."

"What is it?" asks Becs, still frothing with playful energy.

"It's a study, of sorts. Dad used to work in it, but I've taken over most of it. Have a look."

I push the doors open and reach for the light switch. "On the table," I say.

Becs inches across the room, vivacity morphing into curiosity as she approaches the gaming table – like Cortes climbing that peak in Darien to first stare upon the Pacific, I can but hope. She sees the map, the adjacent stacks of grey and blue cardboard in northeastern France, the "Force Pools", the "Faction Aid Cards".

"What am I looking at?" she asks quietly.

"It's a game," I say. "It's called *Totaler Krieg* – German for 'Total War'. It's a detailed simulation of the Second World War, or at least the European half of it."

"A game," echoes Becs.

"Yeah. You know how I'm always talking about how history might have turned out differently? This game allows me to do just that, in a very realistic manner."

"Huh."

"I've basically fought and refought the whole European war 15 or 20 times. Maybe more." I reach over the table and point toward Flanders. "See this here?"

"Yes."

"To answer your question: in 1870, Prussia's army was far superior to France's. In 1914 and 1940, Germany's army was still better, but not by such a large margin. In 1914, Germany's invasion plan was ill-conceived, and its execution flawed, so France survived. In 1940, the invasion plan was daring, its execution was brilliant, and France's defense was bungled, so France was crushed."

"OK."

"But it didn't need to be that way. Take this game, which I played last week as the Axis – it was over pretty quickly, because my invasion of France was driven back with heavy losses. I made a few small mistakes, and I got a few unlucky die rolls, and my opponent punished me severely. As you can see, I've actually lost several armies in the first few months of the battle, and my hopes of a quick victory are now zero. Change a few things around in 1940, and this could have happened for real – the *Wehrmacht* wasn't quite as good as the scoreboard made it look."

"The vehr…what?" Becs is quiet, and her face has gone blank, but her eyes are darting around the room.

"Sorry – the German army. The *Wehrmacht*, as it was called then."

"And you said you were playing the Germans?"

"Yeah. My regular opponent is a guy named Dennis – he was playing the Allies."

"So…" Becs stops. Her head droops downward, and she glances sideways as she haltingly asks, "Are you…some kind of…neo-Nazi, or something?"

"Oh, God no." *Oh boy.* "No! Not at all. Definitely not. That's not…oh. I see what…I think, yeah, this is all…"

"But you said you were the Germans…"

"We take turns. Sometimes I'm the Axis and Dennis is the Allies, and sometimes it's the other way round."

"I don't understand. How can you pretend to be the Nazis?"

"I'm not pretending to…I'm not pretending anything. The Nazis don't come into it."

"But how…"

"I'm sorry – I should have explained all of this better. Or possibly not explained it at all." I slump into the chair on the far side of the table, next to the closed curtains. Dammit. *Godwin's Law is only supposed to apply on the internet!*

"Go ahead," offers Becs. "Try again."

"This game helps us explore untraveled paths through history, and we take turns exploring them from different sides. I don't endorse the Nazis at all, in any way. Thinking about the Holocaust sickens me, as much if not more than anyone else. But sometimes I put myself in Germany's shoes and ponder how it could have prosecuted the war differently. Different strategies, different tactics, those sorts of things. Not that I ever would have wanted the Nazis to win in real life, but I acknowledge that they might have won, and the game lets you explore some of the ways that they could have won."

"OK."

"It's like when a country holds map exercises to ponder what might happen in a future battle or war – someone has to adopt the role of the enemy to make the whole thing work. That's basically what I'm doing when I play the Axis in *Totaler Krieg*. It's no different than when I play the Allies, or when you and I talk about how the war might have ended if we hadn't used nuclear weapons at Hiroshima and Nagasaki. Does that make more sense?"

Becs nods slowly in affirmation, then stares again at the map. After a very long pause, she finally asks, "I take it you're not very good at this?"

"Huh?"

"You lost the war to France. That's not good, is it?"

"Oh. Heh. Yeah…no, actually, if anything the opposite is true."

"Really?"

"I just had an off day. It happens. I'm actually playing an online *Totaler Krieg* tournament against most of the best players around the world, and I've made it to the semifinals."

"Wait, what? You're playing in an online tournament?"

"Yeah. I know, it's a boardgame – but there are ways of playing it via e-mail."

"And you're in the semifinals?"

"I am."

"That's…scary. Can I sit down?"

"Of course. Are you OK?"

Becs sits in Dennis's chair, across the map from me. The color has drained from her cheeks. "How…how do you play the game?"

"Have you ever heard of *Risk*?"

"Yes."

"Well, this is kinda like *Risk* on steroids – there are lots of rules, but the core idea is basically the same. *Totaler Krieg* is particularly complex, so it has a long rulebook, but there are other wargames which are much shorter and easier to teach."

"There are other games like this?"

"Yeah – thousands of them. I have a few in the corner over there, on the shelf. Most of them have nothing to do with World War Two or the Nazis. But mostly I just play this."

Becs cranes her head to look at my small game collection, sorted in chronological order on a shelf half-hidden behind one of the open double-doors – the titles on the shelf read:

Hannibal: Rome vs. Carthage (Valley Games)
Warriors of God (Multi-Man Publishing)
Hammer of the Scots (Columbia Games)
A Few Acres of Snow (Treefrog Games)
Washington's War (GMT Games)
Nations in Arms (Compass Games)
Field Commander: Napoleon (Dan Verssen Games)
Paths of Glory (GMT Games)
Strike of the Eagle (Academy Games)
Axis & Allies (Milton Bradley)
East Front (Columbia Games)
Dai Senso (Decision Games)
Pacific Typhoon (GMT Games)
Hearts and Minds: Vietnam, 1965-1975 (Worthington Games)
Labyrinth: The War on Terror, 1991-? (GMT Games)

"Where did you get all of these?" she eventually asks.

"Some of them were gifts. Others I bought online, from game companies and shops or via eBay."

"How long do they take to play?"

"It varies. *Totaler Krieg* is the longest game – face-to-face, it takes maybe 30 hours for two people who know what they're doing to simulate the full war, although shorter scenarios are also available. By e-mail, games can go on for months."

"Months?"

"But at the other end of the spectrum, *A Few Acres of Snow* features France versus Britain in colonial North America and supposedly lasts about an hour, although I haven't played it yet. Maybe you..." I stop.

"Maybe what?"

"Nothing."

"Sean."

"Yes?"

Becs puts her hands on the sides of her head, blocking her peripheral vision, and says, "You're really, *really* geeking me out right now."

"Even more than usual?"

"*Way* more than usual."

"OK. I just thought, you asked the question about France and Germany, and..."

"Yeah, I know what I asked. By the way, that is absolutely the last time I try to turn on you or anyone else by asking a history question."

"Yeah."

"I need a shower."

"Really?"

"To get the stench of all this Aryan war porn in here off of me..."

"Hey! I just said..."

"I *know* what you said. And I believe you. It's just...urrrrgh!" Becs is now bashing her temples with her knuckles on both hands.

"Look at me for a second, OK?" I ask. "Just look at me."

Becs wipes her face with her hands and sags into her chair. Her chin is in her chest, but she does look up at me. "I just wanted you to know about all of me," I say. "I care about you very, very deeply, and I didn't want to feel like I was hiding anything from you. And I thought maybe, well, who knows? Maybe you might enjoy games like these yourself someday. Not that I'm about to hold my breath."

"That would probably be best." Becs slowly winches her head upwards, then sighs deeply. "I think I should go now."

"OK. Look, I'm really, really sorry."

Becs stands up. "No, it's fine. I just need some space to figure out what the heck you've just shown me."

"Will you be OK for the exam? Anything else you want to study?"

"No, I'll be fine. And so will you."

"Yeah. Let me at least help you tidy your stuff in the kitchen."

"Sure."

Becs beckons me toward her for a platonic hug, which I gladly accept. "You're a sweet guy," she says softly. "But as I get to know you more and more I seem to understand you less and less."

"Thanks."

She stifles a gentle laugh. I walk her back to the kitchen and help collect her books, her notepads, her pens and her markers, and then she's out the side door and tiptoeing to her mother's car. "Have a good night," I call.

"You too."

That went well.

❖ ❖ ❖

The next day is Wednesday, which means it's my turn to bring the cards to the Big Game. Chris brings the cards on Monday, then it's Freddie on Tuesday, me on Wednesday and Melvyn on Thursday; tradition dictates that the biggest winner of the week brings the cards on Friday, but our recordkeeping skills have waned recently, and now several of us tend to bring decks on Friday lest we end up with no cards at all. You'd think that after so many Big Games, this procedure would be less baroque, but as mentioned previously I'm not very good at logistics.

Having won my sledding bet with Chris, I am of course owed a poker-free edition of the Big Game. I have promised to select a card game. However, I have not promised to select a game with a normal deck of 52 playing cards. In fact, I own a simple wargame called *Pacific Typhoon* which has no map and no counters – only two rarely used dice, a deck of 40 "Battle Cards", and another deck of 110 "Force Cards". And today, these are the cards I am bringing to the Muhlendorf cafeteria at lunchtime.

Pacific Typhoon is a multi-player game set in the Pacific theater of World War II. Each player's hand consists of Force Cards representing different Japanese and Allied airplanes and naval vessels or other bonus events relating to command, intelligence or weather. Force Cards are played in a series of historical battles represented by a separate set of Battle Cards, with each battle lasting one round of the table. Either Japan or the Allies will collectively win each battle, and the player who contributes the most powerful card to the winning faction gets to divide the battle's spoils – the Battle Card and the defeated faction's Force Cards – among the winners. As players may freely switch between Japan and the Allies in each new battle (*Pacific Typhoon* is emphatically a game and not a simulation), negotiating the division of spoils after each battle is central to the game's experience.

My reasons for selecting *Pacific Typhoon* for the Big Game are as follows:

1) I'm bored of poker. The Gang of Four ought to broaden its horizons.
2) I'm not sure if Becs will start talking to her friends about *Totaler Krieg*. If she

does, I'd like to inoculate potential critics by demonstrating a less geeky version of my hobby.

3) I want to Becs herself to know games like this exist – games which play fast and work well for veteran gamers and newbies alike.

4) Looking at my game shelf last night made me realize just how many unplayed wargames I own. I should start doing something about that.

5) I consulted BoardGameGeek last night and found not only a clear set of instructions on how to teach *Pacific Typhoon* to non-gamers, but also a cheat sheet which effectively shortens a 24-page rulebook to one page of graphics. I printed five copies of the cheat sheet, and I think I can explain the rules of the game in five minutes.

6) Most importantly, the game is supposed to be lots of fun, and it seems to work best with exactly five players. Perfect.

It's lunchtime at Muhlendorf, and our poorly insulated alcove is radiant with sunlight reflected from the snow-crusted Facilities roof. Several kibitzers are already lurking as I approach the table with my blue backpack slung over one shoulder. The other four players are already present; our fifth today is Nick Simkiss, a brown-haired sophomore none of us know very well. He's next on our list, so it is his turn to join us. He definitely didn't sign up for this, but then, many battles cause collateral damage.

I sit down and let my backpack slide to the floor. Chris is holding court about the evils of Physical Education and the despotic gym teacher known around Muhlendorf as "the Jailer" for his tendency to keep classes locked up in the weight room until nobody has enough time to change clothes before the bell rings. "Little Brian was sitting there," Chris is saying, "hanging onto the rope, too weak to climb but too scared to jump to ground. And the Jailer is looking at him – ah, hi Sean – he's looking at Brian and then he turns to the rest of us and says, 'Which one of you is gonna help him?'"

"Help him climb the rope?" asks Freddie. "How can you help someone else do that?"

"Yeah," says Chris. "So I looked at Brian, and then I looked at the Jailer and said, 'Not my problem,' and walked away."

"Nice," says Melvyn.

"So I got changed on time, for once. Anyway, let's get started."

"Indeed," I say. "So, you remember our little wager the other week?"

"Ah," says Chris. "Collection day, is it?"

"What bet?" asks Melvyn.

"The one we made while you were off with Vicki at the mall," says Chris.

"And I was setting distance records on my sled," says Freddie.

"To summarize, we're not playing poker today," I say.

"Really?" asks Melvyn.

"Um..." says Nick.

"I'll explain everything," I say.

"So, what's it going to be?" asks Chris. "Will this work with five players, or should we allow young Master Simkiss here to be on his merry way?"

"Five players is perfect," I say.

"What is it?" asks Freddie.

"This," I say, reaching into my backpack. Out comes the *Pacific Typhoon* box, which is just over six inches by nine inches in size.

"What the..." says Melvyn.

"Hey – you specifically promised us a card game," says Chris.

"Yes, I did. See here?" I point to the bottom of the box cover – below "Ben Knight's *Pacific Typhoon*", it says "World War Two Card Game".

"What is this?" asks Melvyn.

"It's a sequel to Ben Knight's previous card game, *Atlantic Storm*."

"Is that a joke?" asks Chris.

"Actually, it's not."

"But what *is* this?" repeats Melvyn.

"It's a fun card game with a loose historical theme," I say. "Let me show you..."

"No, I don't think so," says Melvyn.

"Huh?"

"This is the Big Game. The Big Game is No Limit Texas Hold 'Em. Why are you doing this?"

"Because I won a bet with Chris, because Freddie agreed to it, and because you were away with your girlfriend when you could have had a vote yourself."

"Got a point there!" says Freddie.

"But I do have a vote," says Melvyn. "You can't make me play anything I don't want to."

"Got a point there, too!" says Freddie.

"Shut up," hisses Chris.

"You're right – I can't make you do anything," I say. "You don't have to play *Pacific Typhoon*. But I think you're being closed-minded. I think you should give the game a chance. And I think you should give your friends a chance, too."

Melvyn looks at Chris, who shrugs, and at Freddie, who motions encouragingly at the table. I glance at young Master Simkiss, who looks about two feet tall and is yearning to hide under his chair.

"OK," says Melvyn, wearily. "How do you play this damn game?"

"Great," I say, reaching into my backpack. "First, I've printed some copies of a rules cheat-sheet for each of you."

"A cheat-sheet?" asks Chris.

"You can't just teach us the game as we go along?" asks Melvyn.

"I'm trying to make this as easy as possible," I counter. "Just take a look at it."

Melvyn reads from my handout: "'Match Battle'? 'Match Fate'? 'Match Force'? 'Spoils of War'? I think I was right all along." He crushes the paper in his hand.

"Hey," I react.

But Melvyn is already standing up. "Really, you guys have a lovely time," he says. "If there's poker tomorrow, I'll be here. If not, can you let me know in advance?"

"Sure," says Chris.

"Hang on," I protest, but Melvyn has gone.

"Can I go too?" whimpers young Master Simkiss.

"No, you may not," I say. "Look, I'll make this as easy as I can."

"Can we still play with four?" asks Freddie.

"Yes, definitely," I say. "But we can have more than four. Anyone else want to join in? Anyone?" Our kibitzers, who would normally stampede to join an open seat at our table, remain silent and petrified.

"Fine – let me show you the cards." I open the game box – or rather, I try to open it, but the lid is stuck. I shake the box furiously to wrestle it free, but after several seconds I have to extricate a pen cap from my pocket to pry it open. I attempt to carry on seamlessly: "Look at this Battle Card. <u>Midway</u>, it's called – the year is 1942, it's worth six victory points, and the green-and-white icon in the bottom corner means it's also worth half a resource. Everyone starts with six Force Cards, but for each full resource you win, you get to add an extra card, up to a maximum hand size of nine cards. Because the Battle Card has a blue background, it's a Day battle; black cards mean Night battles, while a tan background means it can be either Day or Night. Got that?"

Blank faces.

"I'll continue with the Force Cards. This is the <u>B-29 Superfortress</u>, an American heavy bomber. Every Force Card shows the years in which it can be used, how many victory points it's worth if sunk or shot down, and combat values across the game's three suits – instead of hearts, clubs, spades and diamonds, in *Pacific Typhoon* we have 'Air', 'Surface' and 'Submarine'. The question mark for Air means you get to roll a die and count that as its value, while the half-moon symbol means you add one to its value in a Night battle. At the bottom, '2x Tokyo' means the value is doubled for the Tokyo Battle Card, while the lightning bolt on the side means there's a card in the deck that is fated to kill it if played in the right sequence. Anyway, at the start of each round the 'round leader' takes the top two Battle Cards and chooses one of them. Then he chooses Day or Night as well as the suit – Air, Surface or Submarine, or Combined if he wants to add all three suits together. Then each of us plays one card, or more than one card if you have any Bonus or Event cards – or if you prefer you can discard one card, or discard your entire hand. After everyone is done, you add up the Allied and Japanese totals, and the stronger side wins the battle; the player who has contributed the highest value for the winner then divides the spoils between everyone else on the winning side."

"Sean," interrupts Chris.

"Yeah?"

"I think you've out-dorked yourself."

"It'll all seem much simpler when we play a live hand – let me deal the cards."

"You do that."

I start shuffling the Force Cards – or rather, I try to shuffle them, but wargame cards tend to be thicker than normal playing cards and not as well manufactured, so my dull slide shuffle technique isn't working well, particularly with 110 cards to shuffle. "Chris, could you, you know…" Chris rolls his eyes and starts riffling the Force Cards, while I slide shuffle the smaller Battle Card deck. Finally, Chris hands his deck back to me, and I deal six Force cards to each of Nick, Freddie, Chris and myself in that order. I also turn over the first two Battle Cards: Hollandia, a 1944 Day battle in Western New Guinea worth four victory points, and Kolombangara, a 1943 Night battle in the Solomon Islands worth two victory points.

"I'll be the round leader this time to get things started," I say. "I'll pick Hollandia – it's worth four points, and it's a Day battle. For the suit I'll pick Surface, which is the second number at the top-left corner of each Force Card. And then for my play, I'll select my Kate card – a Japanese torpedo bomber, with a surface value of 3. Nick, over to you."

To his credit, young Master Simkiss can at least hold six cards in a fan shape without showing them to anyone else. However, as his brown eyes dart from one end of his hand to the other, I see a bead of sweat drip down his face. He looks closely at the hieroglyphs on each card in turn, then raises a shirtsleeve to mop his forehead.

"It's just a game, kid," offers Freddie.

"Just pick a card with a Surface value greater than zero," I suggest. "Surface is second from the top, on the top-left corner of the card."

"I don't…I, uh, I don't know what to do," says Nick.

"Shall we play this hand open?" I suggest. "Let's see your cards."

Nick sighs with relief and lowers his hand to the table. I lean forward and immediately understand his difficulty: improbably, young Master Simkiss has only one normal Force Card in his hand, the Japanese Zero (Fighter) card, and it has a surface value of zero. His other cards are all events: two generic cards called Gremlins (Mechanical Failure) and Typhoon (Severe Weather), Japanese cards called Kamikaze (Suicide Pilot) and Tokyo Rose (Radio Propaganda), and an American card called Halsey (Vice Admiral).

"What should I do?" asks Nick.

I stand up, bracing one knee on the seat of my chair, and cock my head to study the text of the six cards on the table. I don't know the cards well at all – this isn't *Totaler Krieg* – but after considering the various options I think Nick's best choice is to attach the Kamikaze event to the Zero card, thereby converting the latter's value from zero to that of a die roll. However, before I suggest anything I look at Freddie and ask, "Do you know what card you want to play?"

"Dude, I haven't understood a word you've said since you sat down," says Freddie.

"Chris?" Chris lowers his cards and silently shakes his head.

"You know what?" I scowl. "Forget it. Forget all of this. Forget I said anything. Give me your cards."

I don't wait for a response. I gather Nick's cards from the table; Chris flings his hand down, and I reach to pry Freddie's cards from his fingers. I whisk my home-printed cheat-sheets from the table. One of our kibitzers, a freshman named Pablo – a freshman! – starts laughing loudly and pointing at me. As fast as I can, with as much dignity as I can muster, I restore the Force Cards and Battle Cards to the plastic trays inside the *Pacific Typhoon* box; I close the box, stuff it and my handouts into my backpack, and silently stand up.

"That was fun," snarks Chris. "I enjoyed that."

"Be nice," cautions Freddie.

I march away from the table, desperate for fresh air and a weapon with which to bludgeon myself. That went *incredibly* well.

4.

Yesterday I came home from school after my *Pacific Typhoon* debacle and buried myself in CyberBoard. It was a cathartic session: CyberBoard doesn't talk back, and it lets me formulate and refine plans and counter-plans for as long as I want without interference or complaint. In light of recent events, I should take this wargaming wonder less for granted.

But now, late on Thursday evening, I'm sitting at the desk in my room when I receive this e-mail from Gregory Spearman via the Automated Card Tracking System die roll server, with the subject, "ACTS: Generic Module: TK Semifinal #2: Allied player action":

> **Die roll request**
> Request: 6-sided die x 1
> 3
> Message from Allied player:
> May-June 1943 – Soviet Blitz Combat:
> 1) 4:1 vs. Taganrog (9:4, HQ/Tank/Air vs. HQ)

I squint at the message in disbelief. Taganrog is a Russian town near the northern tip of the Sea of Azov – one hex west of Rostov on the *Totaler Krieg* map. It shouldn't be possible for Gregory to attack Taganrog during his Blitz Combat phase. What have I done wrong?

My BPA tournament semifinal has reached Summer 1943 – a dangerous time for the Axis in *Totaler Krieg*, but I thought I had taken appropriate precautions. Having captured Leningrad I was able to place the No Retreat marker at Axis Tide 3, but with Gregory due to launch Operational Husky in the West and his Rumyantsev Offensive in the East, I have much defending to do. To that end, I wrote this planning directive:

- **France and NW Europe:** HQ in Le Havre to cover Cherbourg and Calais; strong garrisons in Amsterdam and Brussels shouldn't need HQ support; weaker garrisons in the Bay of Biscay and other French cities; ground units in Copenhagen, Hamburg and the Ruhr to deter raids into Germany or Denmark.
- **Italy and Med:** Evacuate one step from Tripoli. Concede Palermo or Cagliari, but not Messina or northern Sardinia (yet). Guard all Italian ports and cities to forestall Operation Avalanche in the Autumn.
- **Greece and Crete:** Garrison Athens, Salonika, Iraklion and southern Albania (not Khania) – partisans must be restricted to the Peloponnesus.

- **Poland:** Shuffle the usual garrisons through Warsaw, e3904, e3502 and e3402 to prevent partisan outbreaks.
- **Norway:** Garrison the ports – partisan threat safe to ignore.
- **Arctic:** Withdraw Murmansk garrison. Prepare to hold Oulo-Soumussalmi line in Finland by July-August.
- **Russia (north):** Complete phased withdrawal to Minsk-Dvinsk fortresses by July-August; protect Leningrad and Narva river line through 1943.
- **Russia (south):** Start Dnepr fortress line in June-July. Retreat to Bryansk-Kharkov-Rostov in May-June; transfer reinforcement steps and extra HQ south in June-July to hold Dnepr until all fortresses built.

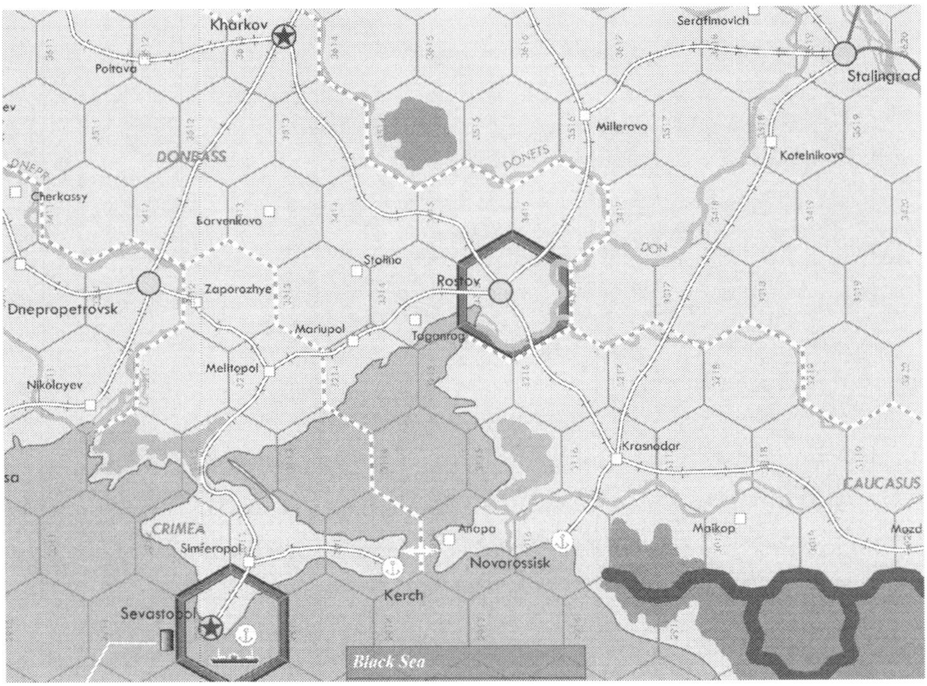

Fig. 10 – Rostov, Taganrog and surrounds

As my next Option Card – <u>Operation Citadel</u> – is a Blitz card, I also analyzed several spoiling attacks in Russia and even one in Tunisia, but none of them promised rewards worthy of the risks they entailed. So I settled on a solid, conservative defense, and after checking and rechecking everything many times, I e-mailed my move to Gregory.

So how did he attack Taganrog? Last night his Western forces crossed from Tunisia into Sardinia and finally encircled Tripoli as expected. But until he sends me his next move file, I won't know how he's managed to attack my HQ in Taganrog with nine factors plus Air support. Maybe his move is illegal? If so, that attack and anything after it will be null and void…but wait, here's another die roll in my inbox:

Die roll request
Request: 6-sided die x 1
4
Message from Allied player:
2) 6:1 vs. e3416 (31:10, HQ/Tank/Air vs. River)

A '4' at 6:1 results in a Dr2, 0/1 – if my HQ has been neutralized, that's probably a big retreat into Taganrog and four or five step losses. What is happening? Here's another roll:

Die roll request
Request: 6-sided die x 1
1
Message from Allied player:
2) 6:1 vs. Rostov (30:10, HQ/Tank/Air/Para vs. City/River)

Goodness. That's a Dr3, 0/1 – and it means his Air unit must be over Rostov itself, because otherwise there would be nobody left in Rostov for Gregory to attack.

I fire off a quick e-mail to Gregory which simply asks, "How did you attack Taganrog in Blitz Combat?" I pace around my bedroom awaiting a response – he can't have used his airborne unit, because it would have to land first and then attack during Regular Combat. Plus, Gregory declared a "Para" combat shift in his attack on Rostov. Gregory doesn't have a Soviet marine unit capable of attacking across the Sea of Azov hexside. And no Soviet ground units already on the map were fast enough to cross the Donets River and move adjacent to Taganrog. Gregory must have made a mistake. He *must* have.

Finally, another e-mail reaches my inbox. This message is from Gregory's own account, rather than the ACTS server: it says "Attack results so far incorporated – HQ decision for you," and attached to it is a CyberBoard move file. I save the file to my computer, and as I watch Gregory's move unfold, I soon discover the awful truth: I've forgotten about the Stavka Logistics marker. At the start of any season, the Soviet player can place the Stavka counter in any Road or Rail hex adjacent to a Russian HQ unit which can trace an overland supply line. So Gregory put the marker in Millerovo, one hex further west than his previous spearhead and empty after my tactical retreat over the Donets, and placed three reinforcement steps there. Those reinforcements were strong enough to cross the Donets and, with Air and HQ support, destroy my HQ in Taganrog.

This is hideous. How could I have been so careless? How can I be so stupid? Gregory will destroy 12 or 13 of my steps this turn near Rostov alone, and there's nothing I can do about it. That doesn't even count the other Blitz attacks he's about to make near Smolensk and Bryansk, or the attritional attacks he's sure to make during Regular Combat across Russia. I've been playing this game since November, and this one mistake could cost me a place in the tournament final. Three-and-a-half months of hard work undone by one tiny, pitiful miscalculation! Arrrrgh!

❖ ❖ ❖

When the smoke has cleared and May-June 1943 is over, Gregory has isolated my two armies in the Crimea and moved adjacent to Dnepropetrovsk at least two turns ahead of schedule. Because my garrison in Dnepropetrovsk is Rumanian, I can't even build a fortress there this turn, so my Operation Citadel reinforcements are urgently needed to hold the Dnepr. If this were a casual game, I'd ask Gregory to let me undo my previous move and fix my blunder, but in a tournament semifinal that option is not available to me.

I remain awake well into the night, staring at my computer and seeking a game-saving alchemy. In the morning, I eat my cereal and drink my orange juice with a side of CyberBoard, and before leaving for school I print several screen captures of the map. I sleepwalk through my classes and duck the Big Game to draw squiggly lines on my printouts between scattered Axis ground units and Kiev, Kanev, Cherkassy and Dnepropetrovsk. When I return home, I expand my planning to France and Italy: from where can I ruthlessly economize to increase my step count along the Dnepr? Or is Gregory already destined to win the game unless he makes his own mistake of similar magnitude?

Around 10 o'clock on Friday night, I take a break and retire to the living room with my copy of *Panzer Leader.* I half-facetiously ask myself WWGD – What Would Guderian Do? – and reread how Guderian recovered from his sacking at the end of 1941. Incidentally, two great facts about Guderian not in *Panzer Leader*:

1) Guderian appeared on the cover of *TIME* magazine in America on 7 August 1944, as part of a feature about his promotion to army chief of staff.

2) In September 1942, Rommel nominated Guderian as the best man to lead *Panzerarmee Afrika* while Rommel himself recuperated in Germany from health problems.

I'm sitting on the living room sofa, reading about Guderian's appointment as Inspector-General of Armored Troops, when I hear a voice from the hallway: "Effing *Panzer Leader*?"

"Yes, Dad – I'm looking up something."

Dad enters the room, doffs his eyeglasses and plunks himself in a chair perpendicular to my sofa. His hair is disheveled, his cheeks are blotched with red, and a second button is unbuttoned at the top of his grey, collared shirt. "Do you have any idea how little truth is contained in that book?" he asks.

"It's a book written by a German general after World War II," I respond. "I have a pretty good idea what to believe and what not to believe."

"In *A World at Arms,* Gerhard Weinberg wrote that in 1942, Guderian 'spent months travelling around occupied Eastern Europe looking for an estate which the government could steal for him.' Hitler massively bribed his generals to ensure their loyalty, you know. But when Guderian was finally offered a suitably huge estate, he didn't think it was adequate. I bet it doesn't say that in *Panzer Leader*."

"Dad, I've had a tough day, OK? This really isn't the time to…"

"It's never the time to obsess about the Nazis. You ought to know better."

"What did I just say? I know who Heinz Guderian really is."

"Have you ever read an independent biography of Guderian?"

"No, I haven't."

"Russell Hart wrote a book you ought to read called *Guderian: Panzer Pioneer or Myth Maker?*"

"Dad…"

"Because that's what historians do. They don't uncritically absorb first-person claptrap from biased sources and form lasting opinions based on it."

"Is that what 'they' do and don't do? Have you ever read *Panzer Leader*?"

"That's not the point."

"Oh, I see – a true historian can know a source is biased without even checking it."

Our voices are rising now. "A true historian doesn't read one book on a subject and think he's an expert about it," says Dad. "He doesn't use Wikipedia for any reason whatsoever. And he certainly won't play a game and attempt to draw historical conclusions from it."

"That's what this is about?"

"Understand this: history is about hard, thankless research in archives and libraries. It's about meticulous footnotes and coordinating thousands of scraps of evidence into a comprehensive whole. You have to put in the hours and the months and the years and study a subject from every angle, not just the angles that interest you, before you can tell someone what they should or shouldn't believe."

"Yeah?"

"History isn't an effing parlor game. You should get that into your head."

"And just what do you know about history?"

"What do I know…"

"You've spent your whole life chasing niches. You've written books with negative market appeal: the average person would pay you to *not* buy one of your books. What do your students tell you to your face?"

"I teach my students about historical process. They respect me for that."

"You don't teach them about the Schleswig-Holstein Question?"

"I do, but that's not what I want them to learn."

"So you could focus on any area of history you want, and you choose obscure social and political topics from countries that don't exist anymore? What kind of history is that? What kind of *life* is that?"

"Given your attitude toward history, you'll never understand."

"I understand the difference between a readable, interesting book and *Radetzky's April* or *Lightening the Yoke*. I also understand the crap I'm being asked to learn in AP European History. People like you…you're co-conspirators in this nonsense."

"That 'nonsense' is history. All of it."

"Yeah. So, what super-important topic are you writing about now? Your doors are always locked – what are you afraid of?"

"None of your business."

"Abstract history, is it? A history of everything and nothing, by J. Alfred Lansbury. 'I have measured out my life with receipts for coffee spoons.' Because in your world, the paupers rule the princes, and a merchant's ledger means more than a declaration of war."

"Yes."

"Well, you're wrong. And you can keep your study doors unlocked. I couldn't possibly care less about what you're working on. I'm sure as hell never going to read it."

"Sometimes I'm tempted to write the complete history of Alfred and Lois Lansbury and figure out what the hell we were thinking when we decided to have you."

"What?"

"You heard me."

"You write that book, and I'll design the game about it. Roll the dice and watch Mom fall down the stairs and break her neck."

Dad whisks his glasses from his pocket and flings them at my head – I duck and they fly into the curtains, which cushion them from shattering as they fall to the carpet. His breaths are short and sharp, his eyes are bulging, and his teeth are clenched.

I stand up. "You started this, so I'm going to finish it," I say. "I'm going to bed. Goodnight."

Dad remains fixed on his chair as I stomp out of the room, up the stairs, down the corridor and into my bedroom. My computer screen still shows the *Totaler Krieg* map, with my grey and purple CyberBoard counters strewn across the Ukraine as my fifth attempt to devise an escape from my mistake against Gregory remains half-finished. My father, my girlfriend, my friends, my defense of Russia…all mistakes, all half-abandoned at just the wrong moment in time. I flop down on the bed and pull the two pillows over my head, straining to block the world from my brain. It isn't working.

PART FIVE

1.

Here's a question: is "mathematics" a singular or plural noun? Because according to my father, in Britain they call it "Maths" instead of "Math". There, you go to "Maths" class. Given that Math, or Maths, is (are?) all about counting numbers and measuring quantities, don't you think the discipline could decide how multitudinous it is?

Needless to say, I hate Math. Math is made for Monday mornings. I'm never going to be a mathematician, an engineer or a physicist, and I don't really care that I tanked my Trigonometry test this morning on – to quote my course syllabus – "Polynomial and rational functions including quadratic functions, higher degree polynomials, real zeros of polynomials, complex numbers, the fundamental theorem of algebra, rational functions and their graphs (including asymptotes)". I rather like numbers, actually – as a wargamer and poker player, I need to understand odds and probabilities, and I like juggling combinations in my head as I search for the 18 attack factors I need to hit Calais with two shifts at 6:1 odds and the other 24 factors I need to blitz Amiens with three shifts at 9:1 odds. I don't always get the numbers right, but I like working to solve the puzzles they pose. But quadratic functions, polynomials and asymptotes? Mr. Prendergast talked about how different subjects can teach you to think in different ways, but I'm never, ever going to think the way my Trigonometry class wants me to, so why bother?

I put this theory to Freddie at lunchtime.

"What about poker?" he asks.

"What about it?" I retort. On the heels of *Typhoon*-gate, the Big Game has been suspended – I'm a poker pariah, at least partly by choice, and Melvyn clearly prefers Vicki to Texas Hold 'Em anyway.

"To play it well, you have to be good at math and probability analysis," says Freddie.

"It may help, but poker still isn't trigonometry."

"What about baseball, then? You're the stat geek, right?"

"Oh, yeah." Without advanced math, sabermetrics wouldn't exist. Perhaps I should pay more attention in class after all.

I think I like baseball for the same basic reason I like history – it's so much fun to discuss and even argue about the past. I'm convinced the Baseball Hall of Fame exists for exactly this purpose. Should 3,000 hits guarantee you an automatic ticket to Cooperstown? Which inductees were the biggest travesties perpetrated by the Veterans Committee? In how many ways was Bert Blyleven a better pitcher than Jack Morris? Through proper statistical analysis, I can definitively answer these questions even if I never watched the players in question – and possibly because I never watched them, as I remain unbiased by misshapen memories and small sample sizes.

Hmmm. Have I just made Dad's argument about *Panzer Leader* for him? I've formed my opinions about Guderian from other sources as well, but historical memoirs can be similar to the nonsense spouted by baseball commentators. I want to vomit when people like Tim McCarver say things like, "I don't care what the stats say – you had to see Jim Rice play in person to understand how feared a hitter he was." Eyewitness reports are valuable historical evidence, but they are also inherently narrow and limiting even when the reporter isn't seeking to distort the truth. Of course in baseball, statistical truth is both finite and nearly exhaustive: with the possible exception of defensive prowess, all of a player's individual contributions to a team's success can now be measured and fully understood in many different contexts. With history, greatness cannot be quantified, because no definitive metrics exist – there are no *Moneyball* formulas, and almost everything is open to interpretation.

Still, on the basis that qualitative subjectivity is better than a quantitative vacuum, let me borrow an idea from sportswriter Bill Simmons and build a World War II "Hall of Fame" with a five-tier pyramid structure. Here's my list of politicians, generals and admirals whose achievements make them worthy of enshrinement, with the best of the best on Level 1 at the top of the pyramid:

- **Level 1:** Roosevelt, Zhukov, von Manstein
- **Level 2:** Churchill, Nimitz, Eisenhower, Slim, Guderian
- **Level 3:** Stalin, Patton, von Rundstedt, LeMay, Rokossovsky, King, Rommel, Marshall
- **Level 4:** Hitler, Spruance, Yamashita, Alexander, Koniev, Halsey, Kesselring, Dowding, Cunningham, Dönitz, Spaatz, Chuikov, Bradley, Montgomery, Vandergrift, Harris
- **Level 5:** De Gaulle, Franco, Alexander, Yamamoto, Doolittle, Kincaid, Ingersoll, Lockwood, Student, Tedder, Chennault, Ozawa, Simonds, Milch, Ridgeway, Model, Patch, Tanaka, O'Connor, Collins, Juin, Smith

- **Honorable Mention:** Gavin, Dietrich, Mikawa, Sprague, Raeder, English, Kurita, Mitscher, Towers, Hausser, de la Borde, Ramsay, Pound, Lütjens, Taylor, Koga, Tovey, Kearney, Halder, Stilwell, Nagumo, Auchinleck, MacArthur

I can also rank the worst of the worst – limiting myself to one per country, I'd go with Voroshilov for Russia, Himmler (in his short-lived capacity as army commander) for Germany, Clark for the US, Gamelin for France, Ritchie for Britain and Homma for Japan. Plus Mussolini for Italy, obviously. Let the arguments begin!

Needless to say, I will not share this list with Becs. We've barely spoken since *Krieg*-gate, and when she comes over later in the week for our next study session, I'm relieved to have something neutral to discuss with her. After a tentative hug and kiss, for my opening gambit I show her a Calvin and Hobbes cartoon in which Calvin is completing a written test at school and is asked when the Pilgrims landed at Plymouth Rock. After answering correctly (1620), he then writes, "As you can see, I've memorized this utterly useless fact long enough to pass a test question. I now intend to forget it forever. You've taught me nothing except how to cynically manipulate the system. Congratulations." Then, in the final panel, Calvin looks at the reader and comments, "They say the satisfaction of teaching makes up for the lousy pay."

Becs laughs as she finishes the strip, and I ask, "That sums us up, right?"

"I wonder what Mr. Prendergast would think about this," says Becs.

"Have you heard of 'Campbell's Law'? Donald Campbell was an American social scientist who once said, 'The more any quantitative social indicator is used for social decision-making, the more subject it will be to corruption pressures and the more apt it will be to distort and corrupt the social processes it is intended to monitor.'"

"Can you repeat that in English for me?"

"Here's a more relevant corollary: 'Achievement tests may well be valuable indicators of general school achievement under conditions of normal teaching aimed at general competence. But when test scores become the goal of the teaching process, they both lose their value as indicators of educational status and distort the educational process in undesirable ways.'"

"In other words, the AP exam is supposed to judge how well we know European history, but because we're being coached to do well specifically on the exam, that judgement is flawed."

"Brilliantly put."

We are now studying World War I. For once I have no complaints – we're covering just the right blend of causes, effects, battles, politics and home fronts. It's only the second-most important war in history, so thank goodness for that. I start by quizzing Becs about the road to war: "What countries were in the Three Emperor's League?"

"Germany, Austria-Hungary and Russia," she answers.

"That's four countries, not three," I joke. Becs looks cross, so I quickly apologize and carry on: "What about the Triple Alliance?"

"Germany, Austria-Hungary and Italy," says Becs.

"When war came, Russia and Italy fought against Germany and Austria-Hungary, not with them. Why?"

"Italy was pragmatic. It waited to see which way the wind was blowing, and then elicited promises of Austrian territory from the Allies before joining the war."

"Very good. What about Russia?"

"The Kaiser thought Bismarck was too pro-Russian – he declined to renew Germany's treaty with Russia and antagonized it into becoming an enemy."

"Which was pretty stupid, of course. What other stupid things did the Kaiser do along the road to war?"

"He tried to drive France and Britain apart in the Moroccan crisis of 1905 but only brought them closer together – the Algeciras Conference left Germany mostly isolated. Also, he instigated a naval rivalry with Britain which served the same purpose."

"I'd say Admiral Tirpitz instigated the rivalry and made the Kaiser buy into his vision of German naval dominance, but yeah, that's about right. Bonus question: how does the Anglo-German naval rivalry compare to the nuclear arms race between the US and the Soviet Union?"

"Sean," says Becs, archly.

"Yes?"

"Can we have fewer of your 'bonus questions' and comments tonight? I want to finish before midnight."

"That's a legitimate question!" I exclaim. "The AP exams often ask questions across different eras like that."

"We haven't studied the Cold War yet."

"But you can answer the question anyway, can't you? This isn't inter-continental ballistic rocket science."

"I would prefer not to."

"Um...OK. Should I continue, or do you want to ask me some questions?"

"You go ahead. Somehow I don't think you need much quizzing."

"We'll see about that. Tell me about Serbia's role in starting the war."

So Becs tells me about the two Balkan Wars and the Ottoman Empire's status as the "Sick Man of Europe". She talks about the Black Hand and the assassination of Archduke Franz Ferdinand, Germany's blank check to Austria, and Austria's long-delayed ultimatum to Serbia. She knows her stuff.

"Let's discuss the war itself," I continue. "When we think about the First World War, we often think about trench warfare, but where was the war more fluid?"

"The Eastern front wasn't as static," says Becs. "Austria-Hungary did well against Serbia, Russia did well against Austria-Hungary, and Germany did well against Russia. Gallipoli aside, Britain eventually conquered most of the Middle East from the Ottomans. And in the West, Germany first had to be stopped at the Battle of the Marne before trench warfare set in."

"Correct again – you're doing great. After the Marne, there was also the 'Race to the Sea' as both sides tried to outflank each other in northern France. In fact, a Bavarian regiment broke through the British lines on 31 October, and Germany easily might have captured the key Channel ports of Dunkirk, Calais and Boulogne. But the men who broke through stopped to wait for further orders and loot a few houses, and a desperate British counterattack plugged the hole and pushed the Germans back. By the by, one of those German soldiers may have been Adolf Hitler himself; if only he had been killed or captured, history might have been very different."

Becs closes her textbook and clears her throat, rubbing her forehead with her hand and then massaging her eyes with thumb and forefinger. "Sean, you really need to stop doing that," she says.

"Sorry," I respond. "I got lost in the moment again."

"I mean you need to stop getting lost in the moment. Do you even realize that you and I are doing two different things right now?"

"I'm asking questions and you're answering them?"

"No, I'm studying for an exam and you're escaping reality."

"We're talking about the facts of the First World War. How is that anything but real?"

"It's not the 'what' that worries me – it's the 'how'."

"I'm multitasking. I'm studying for an exam and I'm indulging a favorite hobby."

"Does your hobby always come back to Hitler?"

"What?"

"We're talking about warfare in World War One, and you bring Hitler into the conversation. Is that a coincidence?"

"Relative to what you're implying, yes, it is. Not that I'm going to apologize for speculating or even fantasizing about how Hitler might have been killed in 1914."

"Sean..."

"This is who I am, OK? If you don't like it..." I don't want to follow that train of thought to a conclusion.

"What happened in the school cafeteria the other day?" asks Becs, quietly.

"What do you mean?"

"You tried to play one of your...'wargames'? Is that what you call them?"

"Ah. I tried teaching a game called *Pacific Typhoon* to my friends."

"So I heard."

"Do you want me to show the game to you?"

"No, I don't."

"Not to teach you how to play it, but to show you why I thought a bunch of normal teenagers might actually like it. It's incredibly harmless – it's a simple card game with a World War Two theme."

"Not that simple, apparently."

"What can I say? I'm a terrible teacher."

"Remember what I said the other night, about you geeking me out?"

"I'm doing it again?"

"Yeah, you kind of are."

I think I've had enough of this, even from Becs. "I don't understand what's going on," I say. "I'm exactly the same person I was a week-and-a-half ago. Have you changed somehow?"

"I don't know."

"Am I behaving differently? I mean, at all?"

"I don't know, Sean. You showed me that game..."

"Doesn't 'that game' fit the pattern of everything else I've ever said or showed to you?"

"Maybe. I don't know."

"At one of our other study sessions you said you were happy that I liked history the way I do, even if you liked it differently. Is that no longer the case?"

"I'm not sure."

"When we move on to the Russian Revolution, I've got this YouTube clip of a song called 'Rasputin' to show you – I know you'll find it as hilariously stupid as I do. But you tell me, is it worth trying to make you laugh anymore?"

"Maybe." A very faint smile creases Becs' lips.

"Shall we carry on?" I ask.

"Yes, I guess so," she replies.

So we talk about the Bolsheviks and the Social Democrats, the roles of women and unions at home, the naval blockade of the Central Powers, the Easter Rebellion and the Treaty of Versailles. I'm very careful not to say anything more than what the course and the AP exam would require. And when we're done, I feel as though I've spent several weeks on the front line at Passchendaele – and not just because we started talking about interwar philosophy, science, art and culture. Who said that love is a battlefield?

❖ ❖ ❖

At the end of a snow-melting school day in early March, I wander around the History classrooms at Muhlendorf and find Mr. Prendergast grading exam papers at a desk. He's wearing an old, brown tweed jacket with black elbow patches, a thin red tie and a white shirt. For Mr. Prendergast, this qualifies as high fashion.

"Ah, Mister Lansbury," he sighs upon glancing up from his work. "The Ned Flanders to my Reverend Lovejoy."

"Huh?" I ask, not getting the reference.

"Doesn't matter. What's up?"

"What are you doing?"

"These?" He motions to the papers sprawled in front of him. "Ninth-grade World History exams. You used to be a freshman, right?"

"Well, yeah."

"How did you live with yourself?"

"I dreamed of one day becoming a sophomore."

"Have you retained any evidence that you were a freshman at Muhlendorf? Do you keep your old essays and test papers at home?"

"Some of them, probably."

"Promise me you'll never go back and read them."

"That bad?"

"Answer me this: the Kellogg-Briand Pact doesn't have anything to do with breakfast cereal, does it?"

"No, it does not."

"I didn't think so." He underlines a handwritten phrase on one of the exam papers with a red pen.

"You'd like to be on the baseball diamond right now, wouldn't you?"

Mr. Prendergast leans back in his chair, removes his glasses and rubs his eyes. Then he says, "If I cared that much about coaching varsity baseball, I'd live in a state where there's no snow on the ground in March."

"Or where it doesn't snow to begin with."

"Indeed. But let's get back to you – there's a question pending. What's on your mind?"

"Yes. I was chatting with Becs – Rebecca – the other night at our weekly study session."

"And how is Miss Fowler?"

"Probably best to ask her that question."

"Really."

"Anyway, I referenced Campbell's Law to her – do you know what that is?"

"Pretend for a moment that I don't."

"Let me ask you this: what would make this year's AP European History class a success in your eyes?"

Mr. Prendergast purses his lips for a moment, then says, "There's no one answer to that question."

"Is your teaching performance judged by how many fours and fives we make on the AP exam?"

"To some extent, yes."

"Is that your focus in teaching the course, then? Trying to get us to do well on the exam, rather than teaching history itself?"

"You make that sound like an either-or question. The best way to do well on the exam is to know a lot of history, don't you think?"

"But you only need to know that history for one three-hour period on a single day in May. If all of our work is geared around cramming for that one day, that doesn't really mean we understand history, does it?"

"To win an Olympic gold medal in the 100-meter freestyle final, you only need to swim well for about 47 seconds. Just because you spend four years preparing for 47 seconds doesn't mean you're not a strong swimmer the rest of the time."

"Well…yeah, I suppose."

After a pause, Mr. Prendergast asks, "What's eating at you, Sean? Why are you here?"

"I'm not sure. I guess…I guess I'm wondering what you get out of our class. Do you enjoy being a teacher?"

Mr. Prendergast grins. "The apple doesn't fall very far from the tree."

"This isn't about my Dad, OK?"

"Sure. No problem."

"How did you come to be a teacher? Did you always want to be one? Or a baseball coach?"

"I always wanted to play baseball for a living."

"Ah. Were you any good?"

"I played Division One ball in college. I thought I was decent, yeah. But there comes a time when you realize very few utility infielders at small liberal arts colleges make a living playing baseball."

I start smirking. "What's so funny?" asks Mr. Prendergast.

"I'm trying to picture you as a utility infielder."

"I didn't always have my current body shape."

"I could see you as a tobacco-chewing first baseman, but a shortstop?"

"Careful – this is the death of my dreams you're talking about."

"Sorry."

Mr. Prendergast cracks a smile. "I majored in History, but to be honest, I only got into teaching when I couldn't think of anything else to do with my life."

"Oh."

"But you know what? However I got here, that's the best decision I ever made, and I wouldn't want to do anything else."

"Really? What about those freshman exams in front of you?"

"I kid because I love. You should have seen the answers they were writing in October."

"Does it ever get boring, teaching the same material over and over again?"

"The topics are the same, but every student is different. There's a type of Japanese bamboo which can grow up to four feet per day – two inches per hour. Observe it long enough, and you can literally see it grow with your own eyes. That's what teaching high school kids is like. I use the same water and the same sunlight every time, but the growth I see can be very different. And I get to watch it happen."

"Huh."

"Are you thinking about becoming a teacher?"

"Me? I've never thought about it before."

"In my experience, most children contemplate doing what their parents do, even if only to reject the possibility."

"I've thought plenty about my father's career, but I've never pondered following in his footsteps – or yours, for that matter."

Mr. Prendergast grins. "What if I give you a test drive?"

"What do you mean?"

"What if I let you lecture our AP class about the Second World War? Your favorite historical subject is World War Two, right?"

"Yeah – how did you guess?"

"I notice things."

"You'd really let me teach the class?"

"I'll give you a few guidelines, but otherwise you can talk about whatever you want. I suspect we might both learn a few things."

"Have you ever done this before? I mean, are you even allowed to let a student teach the class?"

"First answer: no. Second answer: sure, why not? We'll be covering all of the prescribed material. And if you get stage fright or deviate too far from the script, I'll be on standby to step in and take over."

"That sounds…exciting. How long would I have to prepare?"

"About two weeks – I'll confirm the details for you tomorrow. We'll call it an extra credit assignment."

"Thank you, I think."

"Don't mention it. Now, if I may?" Mr. Prendergast points at the papers on his desk.

"Sorry. Enjoy the freshmen."

"Don't remind me."

2.

The best part about being a History teacher, I think, would be bringing wargames into the classroom. If only we had two months in which to study World War II, I could teach everyone *Totaler Krieg*! This is not completely farfetched; I've read on Consimworld about a group of high school kids near Chicago who fell in love with *Here I Stand*, the aforementioned game set in 16th-century Europe, during a game they played in their History class over a 10-week period. What I wouldn't give to be part of that course.

Alas, I'm here again with Dennis, for another Thursday evening session of *Totaler Krieg* at home. He's wearing a tan T-shirt with a black "ATARI" logo on it which looks older than Pong, and his hair seems longer and greasier than usual. *Plus ça change…*

I take the Axis again, hoping to redeem my recent performances against Dennis and also Gregory Spearman, whose lead in our e-mail tournament game continues to widen. My lack of form shows: when placing my airborne unit as a reinforcement step in March-April 1940, I realize Hamburg – my only city within airborne range of Oslo – is already stacked to the max with three infantry steps, and I must kill one of them to ensure Norway falls on schedule.

"At least you didn't lose any panzers in Poland," comments Dennis.

"It's not the step loss that bothers me," I respond. "It's the brain fart that led to the loss which doesn't bode well."

"Give me time – I'm due a few of them myself."

He's right. This time he positions his French HQ in Verdun, where it covers every hex on the French front line but can itself also be attacked directly. It's another experimental defense, but this experiment works less well for Dennis – after blitzing through Belgium as usual, I attack the HQ directly during Regular Combat and manage to occupy both Calais and Lille. In his May-June 1940 turn, Dennis counterattacks Lille with air support and inflicts some damage, but France will definitely fall by the end of the Summer.

Or will it? The Delay rolls at the end of the turn favor me, and I have a two-unit support advantage over the West. I also have a panzer army and an HQ adjacent to the Channel, both at full strength. And London is only occupied by a two-step British infantry army. Hmmm…

"I'll place an Air unit northwest of Antwerp," I announce. "Will you contest?"

"You're not," exclaims Dennis.

"Oh, but I am," I say.

"You're invading Britain before conquering France."

"It's been done before."

"Not by me it hasn't."

"Me neither, but this should be interesting."

"That's one word for it."

In the June-July turn, Dennis contests the placement of my first Air unit, but I successfully deploy two others: one creates a Beachhead in the Channel, while the other interdicts Paris. My panzer army and HQ land at Ipswich, east of London, while in France I kill two British and two French steps, capture Amiens and Le Havre and exploit through Normandy. Then comes the big battle for London – I'm attacking at 4:1 odds, with a 5-in-6 chance of success. And guess what? I roll another '6', for an Exchange result. Unbelievable. But before I can throw my hands up in exasperation or run out of the room screaming, Dennis shocks me by saying, "I'll retreat to Southampton – you lose a panzer step, but you can have London."

Fig. 11 – Britain, Ireland and northern France

"Are you sure?" If Dennis holds London and then regains air-naval parity at the end of the turn, my invaders could be stranded on the beach, out of supply.

"I can't afford any more losses. I've only got three steps in Britain now – how many Brits have died in France already? I might have to evacuate Egypt to keep even a toehold in Scotland."

"But if I'm out of supply…"

"You'll get back in supply soon enough."

"But what if I don't capture Paris next turn?"

"Look at the map. You'll capture Paris."

Dennis is right. The Seine prevents his forward units in Reims and Troyes from redeploying to the west, so I can encircle Paris exactly as Schlieffen envisaged. And when good Delay dice again grant me air superiority for July-August, Dennis's wisdom in pulling back from London into Bristol, Birmingham and Manchester is proven correct. This is all going terribly well.

"Have we played a Sealion game before?" I ask Dennis at the end of the turn.

"I don't think so, no."

"I'm surprised you haven't started whining already. You don't tend to let *Totaler Krieg* get away with this sort of thing."

"No, Sealion is cool. An improvised Sealion while the Germans are still fighting in Flanders, that's weird, but I only have myself to blame – I should have kept another step in London, or saved my Air to protect the Channel, or both."

"How refreshingly reasonable of you."

This is the essence of "Design for Effect" wargame design. In *Totaler Krieg*, the Allies can almost always prevent the *Wehrmacht* from invading Britain. But guaranteeing Britain's safety means hoarding resources and reducing commitments to France and Egypt, so many Allied players – myself included – often gamble as Dennis has. After all, even a successful Sealion will not end the war. The Allies can play Britain Surrenders, giving the Axis a permanent bonus Objective Hex in return for a lengthy truce. Even if Britain doesn't surrender, conquering all of Britain and Ireland only nets the Axis a single Objective Hex (London) and reduces America's impact on the war (in the form of an adverse Delay die roll modifier). Garrisons are required in every city and port to keep Britain subdued. The Soviets can get frisky if the British campaign drags on too long. And if Germany isn't careful, the Allies can ultimately invade France through the Bay of Biscay and bypass Britain altogether on their way to Berlin. Sealion involves significant toil for uncertain rewards, but hopefully also a lot of fun along the way no matter how everything turns out.

In July-August, I capture Paris – triggering France's collapse – as well as Southampton and Birmingham. The next game-year is fascinating:

Autumn 1940: My Treaty card gains Hungary as an ally, but I suffer a Coup d'Etat in Yugoslavia. I ship two more armies to Britain; Dennis holds a firm defensive line at Manchester, but in Egypt he precipitously withdraws behind Alexandria.

Winter 1940: As the *Wehrmacht* bashes into Belgrade and Zagreb to conquer Yugoslavia, another Treaty nets me Rumania. A bloody Exchange in the snow pushes the Brits out of Manchester. In Egypt, Dennis defends behind the Nile with two steps in each of Cairo and Port Said, while an Anglo-Iraqi force captures Damascus to end a short Border War with Syria.

Spring 1941: After I declare war on Ireland, my Operation Marita outflanks Britain's defenses in Cumbria and sweeps through Newcastle to capture Edinburgh.

My increasingly large German-Italian force in Egypt reduces the British garrison in Port Said, leading Dennis to abandon Egypt and Palestine. My Balkan expedition also continues south and conquers Greece. However, the Soviets surprisingly reveal Russia Challenges Germany and successfully declare war (a 1-in-3 chance); Dennis's initial attacks on Königsberg and Warsaw fail, but I must now scramble to form a coherent defense in the East. Dennis also declares war on Persia and moves a New Zealand corps north from Basra toward Tehran.

Summer 1941: I reveal my final Treaty card – meaning the Limited War period will extend into 1942 – while Dennis plays Western Military Aid for Britain and Stalin Orders Attack for Russia. The Soviets lurch forward, capturing Warsaw and Königsberg and crossing the Carpathians into Hungary and Rumania. The Kiwis conquer Persia, but Turkey and Spain join the Axis, and I expel the Allies from Trans-Jordan, Syria and Iraq. Glasgow and Belfast also fall, leaving only five hexes on the map occupied by Western ground forces: Gibraltar (besieged by the Spanish), Basra (besieged by the Germans and Italians), Tehran (cut off from its supply hub at Basra), Malta (in the middle of an Axis lake), and Dublin (threatened by a German army in Belfast). The Turks also creep northwards into the Caucasus, threatening the Objective Hex at Baku.

We end our exhausting but exhilarating session well after midnight, again, at the end of July-August 1941. "Who do you think is winning?" asks Dennis as he packs his duffel bag.

"Honestly? I have no idea," I reply.

"Yeah, me neither."

"I mean, I've reached Axis Tide 2, and my armies cover most of the map. But I am fighting on one, two, three, four…five active fronts, to say nothing of the many garrisons I have to keep. And eventually I'll need to guard Spain – with what, I haven't a clue."

"Feeling overextended?"

"Taking Basra or Gibraltar would help, but who can I spare to do that? The Soviets won't wait for me to march a few armies to the map edges and back."

Dennis nibbles at one of his fingernails, then remarks, "You know it's a great game when both players think they're losing."

"Are you having fun, though?" I ask.

"Absolutely. But you know the board position is completely ridiculous, right?"

"Sure."

Dennis grins. "See you next week," he says, and he's gone.

❖ ❖ ❖

The hypothetical German invasion of Britain in 1940 is a fantasist's paradise. I presume myths about Operation Sealion are popular in the English-speaking world because Britain is an English-speaking country – we can relate to "What if the Germans captured London?" more than "What if the Germans captured Moscow?" (The cover of the second *What If?* book depicts Big Ben and the House of Commons draped in swastikas.) The Battle of Britain's cliffhanger narrative also lends itself to counterfactuals; as the story goes, just when the RAF was starting to crumble under the heat of constant attacks on its airfields, the *Luftwaffe* began terror-bombing London, saving England from invasion just as surely as Trafalgar saved it in 1805. But is that true? And even if it isn't, could Sealion have succeeded under different circumstances?

To answer the first question, current research suggests the cliffhanger premise is demonstrably false, and that the RAF was never in serious danger. Prominent historians like Richard Overy and Steven Bungay now conclude that the main *Luftwaffe* offensive against the RAF between 24 August and 6 September 1940 achieved very little: during this period only two airfields were knocked out of action, neither for more than few hours, and the number of serviceable RAF aircraft and available pilots actually increased. These findings directly contradict earlier works like *The Narrow Margin*, in which Derek Wood and Derek Dempster argued that the RAF was indeed losing the battle of attrition prior to Göring's change in tactics; who you believe depends in part upon how cynical you are about historiography. In the context of Sealion, a prominent game designer once posited on Consimworld that "Military revisionism tends to be based much more on the natural desire of each generation of historians to say something different, rather than any significant change in concepts of strategy" – he firmly believes that the current trend in scholarship favoring the "Axis was doomed to failure" school is generational, and that new historians aiming to establish their own reputations will inevitably swing this trend the other way.

But even if Germany had been winning the Battle of Britain, could an amphibious invasion have succeeded? The RAF could always withdraw northwards and regroup until enemy ships appeared in the Channel – to adequately protect a slow-moving invasion fleet, the *Luftwaffe* required permanent air supremacy, not temporary air superiority. Most of the invading ground forces were to be transported on slow-moving barges designed to navigate the Rhine, not the turbulent waters of the Channel; even getting those barges to the army's staging areas would be difficult, and tugs could tow them across the Channel at a top speed of only three knots. That assumes favorable weather, but the only suitable invasion dates to which Raeder and the *Kriegsmarine* would agree were 22-26 September, during which terrible gales and rough seas would have capsized most of the barges. Even if the *Wehrmacht* had dodged the RAF and the Royal Navy and crossed the Channel as planned, the British Army was rapidly rearming after its escape from Dunkirk and could have wreaked havoc against a first wave scheduled to include exactly six tanks. And even if enough troops had gotten ashore to make a difference, how could they be adequately supplied? The Germans had no Mulberry-like artificial ports to tow across to the Kentish beaches, and the nearest major ports were across the wider part of the Channel, at Brighton, Southampton and Portsmouth. At least Napoleon had a vaguely realistic plan in 1805, whereas Germany's preparations in 1940 were alternately indifferent and delusional; the RAF's triumph probably saved Hitler, Raeder, Göring and von Brauchitsch from a decision they never wanted to make.

Could Sealion have succeeded under different circumstances? Assume no evacuation at Dunkirk, and therefore no BEF in southern England, and assume the *Luftwaffe* wins the Battle of Britain decisively. Suppose Raeder comes up with a plan as imaginative as Operation *Weserübung* (the invasion of Norway) and sorties the *Kriegsmarine* – including Dönitz's U-boat fleet – into the North Atlantic in conjunction with Sealion, leaving the Royal Navy torn between protecting Britain's merchant fleet and running a gauntlet of planes and minefields into the Channel. To Germany, the *Kriegsmarine* was expendable, but to Britain, the Home Fleet was indispensible – in fact, historian John Lukacs believes the Royal Navy was so afraid of losing its prize assets that its battleships would have stayed in Scapa Flow, leaving only smaller craft to oppose any landings. Would Germany have willingly traded a failed amphibious invasion for a chance of knocking out the Home Fleet? Perhaps it should have, insofar as any ground losses could be replaced much more easily.

But even under the most favorable circumstances imaginable, bad weather was still likely, the barge fleet was still inadequate, air supremacy is still different from air superiority, and keeping the troops supplied once ashore would still be problematic. Amphibious doctrine had hardly evolved since Gallipoli – operations like D-Day or the US island-hopping campaign in the Pacific were hardly conceivable in 1940. And how effective would the *Luftwaffe* be against the Home Fleet? In the Battle of Leyte Gulf in 1944, the American carrier force had about as many planes as the *Luftwaffe* in 1940 but was far better trained and equipped to attack enemy ships at sea, and even with uncontested air supremacy it hardly sank every Japanese ship in sight. I think Sealion could have succeeded with a bit of luck, but the odds never could have been overwhelmingly stacked in Germany's favor.

In that context, why would Hitler ever risk a British invasion? Unlike the US and Britain, German military planning was hardly risk-averse, but the worst-case Sealion scenario would have been both highly possible and extremely damaging to the undefeated Nazi war machine. Even after losing the Battle of Britain, Germany was still winning the war by a large margin. Fantasists may syllogize that because a successful Sealion could have won the war, and Germany eventually lost the war, the invasion should have been attempted. But this is hindsight at its least constructive. A disaster in the Channel or a capitulation in southern England could have destabilized every gain Germany had made from 1935 to 1940; besides, Soviet Russia was Hitler's true enemy, and the *Wehrmacht* was designed to win campaigns on land. As such, I think Hitler's decision to turn East was entirely rational. And as a European wargamer once humorously noted on Consimworld, "Assuming that the invasion was repelled and the Axis finally lost World War II, the most serious consequence in my opinion is that 60 years later the Brits would be even more insufferable than they currently are about their history."

Should wargames like *Totaler Krieg* treat Sealion as possible, nearly impossible, or absolutely impossible? Another intelligent Consimworld member once said this: "I do think that games need to reflect contemporary fears, which is why I would support any 1940 game allowing the Germans a chance to conquer Britain, and any 1942 game a chance for the Japanese to conquer Australia. Not because I think that either was likely (I do not) but because games need to reflect contemporary mindsets rather than reality." Again, this is "Design For Effect" wargame philosophy: Britain was worried about a German invasion and took many precautions to guard against one, so British players should be discouraged from frittering away the BEF and RAF in France or sending them away to Egypt. Games following the opposite "Design For Cause" path refuse to give Germany a capability it never had, regardless of what Britain feared. Neither choice is right or wrong, but the existence of such choices demonstrates that wargaming "reality" isn't always absolute.

That said, most strategic-level World War II wargames still make Sealion far too easy. I can picture an invasion in Kent, across the narrowest part of the Channel – but *Totaler Krieg* allows landings anywhere from Devon to East Anglia, and other games can even feature German landings in Scotland or Ireland. An improvised invasion of the sort I executed against Dennis is sheer fantasy. And resupplying my ground forces once ashore in Britain has proven far too easy. However interesting my Sealion campaign against Dennis has been so far, I can't pretend for a moment that we are following a path history might have taken.

But you know what? I don't care. *Totaler Krieg* is a great simulation in many ways, and the ahistorical ease of Sealion doesn't invalidate everything else the game does so well. Anyway, *Totaler Krieg* is a game. Games are meant to be fun. And I can't wait to see what happens next in my game against Dennis. Shouldn't that be enough?

3.

Spring Break started this afternoon. Becs is leaving tomorrow with her parents to look at colleges – colleges! – so we're out on a date tonight. That's the good news; the bad news is that at Becs' suggestion, we're attending a symphonic concert featuring works by Richard Wagner, Béla Bartók and Henryk Górecki. My knowledge of classical music still barely extends beyond placing major composers in their historical context, so although Becs isn't familiar with tonight's program, I'll let her judge whether the visiting Kirov Orchestra is any good.

The campus of my father's College has a large, modern theater – lots of ornate paneling, seats cushioned with sapphire velvet, thick blue curtains to match the seats. Because Becs insists on collecting a program, we arrive slightly late and reach our balcony seats just as the Russian conductor strides to the podium. He is wearing black pants and a black, button-down shirt with long sleeves and no collar. As the initial applause dies down, I mutter to Becs, "He's dressed like a waiter in a pretentious restaurant."

"Behave, OK?" she commands, smirking. She's wearing a green floral dress and black tights beneath her white cardigan.

First on tonight's playlist is the Overture to *Tannhäuser*, by the composer I've heard of. Wonder of wonders, I actually recognize the tune as the love theme from a famous Bugs Bunny cartoon, the one in which Elmer Fudd sings "Kill the Wabbit!" The piece is repetitive, and therefore twice as long as it needs to be, but it's not bad, and I enjoy watching the brass section try to blast the violin section into the audience during the overwrought finale. I give that three-and-a-half stars out of five and can now better appreciate what "Wagnerian" means.

As the second piece begins, I reach to caress Becs' hand on the armrest between our seats, but we are jolted apart by a sudden, swirling rush of violins and then a terrible din of woodwinds. Within 30 seconds, my head is throbbing with loud, scary shrieks from my prepubescent nightmares. This is the suite from Bartók's *The Miraculous Mandarin*, and it sounds like a castrated horse begging for mercy. This is noise, not music, and the conductor seems as confused as I am: his flailing arms don't seem connected to anything I recognize as a beat. And the piece goes on and on and on, for nearly 20 minutes! During a quieter clarinet solo which seems to be causing as much pain to the swaying soloist as my ears, I whisper to Becs, "What *is* this?" She diffidently shrugs her shoulders.

To distract myself I read the program notes and discover that *The Miraculous Mandarin* caused a scandal at its Cologne premier in 1926 and was subsequently banned – a rare success for Weimar Germany, to be sure. The piece is needlessly complex, highly technical, not pleasant at all to the lay listener, blatantly written to demonstrate the composer's own knowledge and self-importance and to appeal only to the smallest audience of pompous specialists. In other words, it's just like one of my father's books. I have begun counting the acoustic panels at the rear of the stage when the piece screeches to a halt, just as suddenly as it started, with four final yelps. I give that negative-two stars and solemnly hope never again to hear anything so foul as long as I live.

The intermission is a welcome balm. "I didn't know that was coming," apologizes Becs.

"Did you like that piece?" I ask. "I mean, at all?"

"I respect the ideas behind it, and the musicianship of the orchestra to play it," she says.

"Musicianship? If someone had played a wrong note, would anyone have noticed?"

"Possibly not."

"If an orchestra plays Bartók in the middle of a forest, and someone makes a mistake, does anyone hear it?"

"That's why the conductor is there."

"Perhaps if they had all made enough mistakes, it would have sounded like Beethoven."

"Or Jimi Hendrix." Becs smiles.

"Or the shop floor of a car factory." I laugh. "So what do you know about Górecki's Third Symphony?"

"Nothing at all. Well, except that Górecki is Polish and was born in 1933," says Becs, glancing at the cover of her program.

"Great," I moan. "More 'modern' 'music'. Do you think *The Miraculous Mandarin* will be topped by *The Vomitous Vomitorium*?"

"If you want to leave now, I'd be OK with that," says Becs. "There's a nice ice cream place near here."

"No, that wouldn't be gallant of me," I respond. "Besides, I'm morbidly fascinated – this is car-crash concert-going."

"The Wagner was good, right?"

"But we're not exactly trending upward."

"I've got an idea," says Becs. "Is your phone set to silent?"

"Yes – why?"

"Why don't you text me a running commentary of the piece? Describe it in your own words as we go along – what you're hearing, what you're thinking, and so on. At worst, you'll have fun during the performance, and I'll have fun after it's over."

"Great idea. Love it."

"Or if needs be, we can quickly escape through the vomitorium. Which is through that archway over there, and not what I think you think it is." Becs smiles and points to the passage leading from the balcony into the bowels of the theater.

"Huh. You are a very clever girl."

"I need to use it myself just now, for a trip to the ladies' room. But once the intermission is over, promise me one thing."

"What's that?"

"Give the piece a chance. We might actually like it."

I shrug. When Becs reappears, the orchestra is nearly ready, and the conductor is accompanied by a large black woman wearing a gold, sequined dress as he marches back onstage. The woman sits in an empty chair which has been placed next to the podium, and as she silently meditates, my one-night-only Twitter feed begins:

8:52 PM: We start – low strings are barely audible
8:53 PM: Testing, testing…Hello? (tap tap tap) Is this thing on?
8:54 PM: If this were on in my car, I'd think I'd hit "Mute" by mistake
8:55 PM: Sinister strings – finally getting louder (and higher-pitched)
8:56 PM: Same sequence of notes, but a bit louder and higher
8:57 PM: Why is the golden woman just sitting there?
8:58 PM: How repetitive is this? How repetitive is this?
8:59 PM: Is the composer tune-deaf?
9:00 PM: A little bit louder now, a little bit louder now…you know you make me want to SHOUT

9:01 PM: The golden woman is STILL just sitting there
9:02 PM: Same notes over and over AGAIN, but now getting softer
9:03 PM: Wagner is sounding really good right now
9:04 PM: Same thing, but quieter – is this it? Really?
9:05 PM: The golden woman stands up! She sings!
9:06 PM: I wish I hadn't asked…SHRIEK
9:07 PM: Great voice, but DULLSVILLE – and not at all tuneful
9:08 PM: Getting powerful now…and now she sits down again!
9:09 PM: And it's the same loud passage we heard before!
9:10 PM: This section brought to you by the Department of Redundancy Department
9:11 PM: Wagner sounding REALLY good right now – Germany beats Hungary and Poland yet again
9:12 PM: A little bit softer now, a little bit softer now, a little…ZZZZZZ
9:13 PM: I've never touched a violin in my life, but I think I could play this
9:14 PM: Is the golden woman about to fall asleep too (like me)?
9:16 PM: I hope the golden woman isn't getting paid by the word
9:18 PM: FINALLY finished – but that's just the first movement (oops)
9:20 PM: Brighter start to Part 2 – the golden woman is standing up again
9:21 PM: She sings…not exactly a sing-along
9:23 PM: If I were a witch, I'd be digging this
9:26 PM: Not the Happy Fun Bunch in here – I think the bassoonist wants to slit his wrists
9:28 PM: Rehearsals for this must have been HILARIOUS! Laugh-a-minute stuff
9:29 PM: Second movement finishes – film at 11
9:31 PM: Third movement is the bastard child of the first two
9:32 PM: At least Bartok had a pulse
9:35 PM: Operation Shutdown takes effect – I've had enough

I nudge Becs, draw a finger across my neck and ostentatiously switch off my phone. She glares back at me, then faces forward and softly sniffles once.

As the music meanders, rises, falls and meanders again to its conclusion, I contemplate life as a Pole born in 1933. I can think of few worse eras and places in which to grow up: as a youngster Górecki would have lost his national identity and experienced constant violence, depravity and austerity under the Nazis before settling into a rut of dull despair after the Soviets moved in and the Cold War began. If I were creative and had grown up in that environment, I'm sure my poetry or music would have sounded similar to Górecki's. That doesn't mean I have to enjoy it, though.

Eventually, the music fades into gentle oblivion. Our audience erupts with applause – Becs jumps from her seat and claps furiously, and as I rise more slowly I notice a tear running down her cheek. I clap as well, more for the performance than the music, and accept that I'm a cultural philistine on unfavorable ground. As the curtain calls finally cease and the patrons around and beneath us head for the vomitoria, Becs slumps again into her chair, so I sit down as well.

"That was…incredible," she stutters. "So…deep, and powerful. Sad, and moving, but tender."

"Yeah…"

"Wasn't that amazing?"

"Um…"

"Oh, sorry – it's on my phone, isn't it?"

As Becs reads my verdict, I scan the emptying stage. Several violinists remain, chuckling to one another as they slowly inch toward the wings, while the petite harpist is struggling to corral her instrument and drag it off stage right. Honestly, why would a small woman ever choose to play a harp or a double bass? Carriage and transport alone would put me off even if I could reach the strings with my arms.

When I look again at Becs, her phone has been sheathed and she is staring down at the floor. Clearly, I have misjudged my audience. I tap her on the shoulder, and she peers up at me. "You have a lot to learn about minimalism," she murmurs. "In every sense."

"Probably," I respond.

"Let's go," she says.

"OK."

Without speaking, we don our coats and file slowly down the balcony stairs, through the marble-dappled foyer, out the double-doors into the chilly gloom, and along the sidewalk to the parking lot and the white Ford owned by Becs' mother. The drive to my house takes less than ten minutes; for at least five of those minutes, Becs stays silent, and I wait anxiously for her to make the first move.

Finally, while waiting for a traffic light at deserted intersection, Becs clears her throat. Then she says, "I can't believe you ruined that piece of music for me."

"Ruined it?"

"Did you read the program notes?" she asks.

"I was kinda busy writing my own."

"The piece is all about separation through war, as seen by parents who have lost children and by a child separated from her parents."

"Oh."

Becs continues through clenched teeth: "In the second movement, the soprano was singing a prayer written by a high school girl on the wall of her Gestapo jail cell."

"Are you OK?" I ask.

"Yes," she grunts. She falls silent. The light turns green, and we drive on. A left, a right and two lefts later, we are parked in my driveway.

Becs sighs and closes her eyes. I ask, "I take it you don't want to come inside?"

"Correct."

"Are you going to be OK to drive home?"

"Yes," she whispers. Then she asks, "You liked the Wagner, then?"

"Yeah, I did," I respond.

"Why am I not surprised?" she mutters.

"I know, I liked the piece with a melody – I'm a heathen."

"Do you know who Hitler's favorite composer was?"

"Yes. Wait…what does that have to do with anything?"

"You tell me."

I'm flabbergasted. "*You* brought Hitler into the conversation this time, not me."

"You're the one who wrote, 'Germany defeated Poland again'."

"I included Hungary in that, and for the record I liked the Bartók even less than the Górecki. But really, are you implying that I shouldn't criticize any artistic work referencing the Holocaust? If I say that *Schindler's List* is…"

"Shhhh," commands Becs. "Shut up for a minute."

I exhale loudly through my nose. Becs hangs her chin in her chest, closes her eyes and paws at the vinyl on the steering wheel in front of her. "What is it?" I ask.

"I…I'm sorry, but I can't get past this," she says, slapping the wheel before turning to me. "I just can't. I need to take a break."

"What do you mean?"

"I think we should stop seeing each other for a while."

"What? Why?" This can't be happening.

"It's that game."

"It's *a game*."

"Do you know what I heard in the Górecki tonight? Women and children. Groans of pain and agony. The separation and loss caused by war. As long as you think war is a game, you'll never hear that yourself."

"That's not true."

"Sean..."

"Becs. *Rebecca.* I love you – I really do. Please take some time to think this through."

"Goodnight, Sean." She turns away from me.

"This is all a terrible mistake..."

"Good*night*, Sean."

She stares resolutely forward, not engaging me, not allowing me space for rebuttal. I feel light-headed and hot; I open the car door and feel as though I'm floating right through it onto the driveway. "Becs, please," I whimper.

"I'm sorry," she says, but I don't think she means it. She turns the key in the ignition, the motor starts, and she drives away. Separation and loss, I mutter to myself – separation and loss. Then, as the car drives off and she's much too far away to hear, I cry out: "Here's what *I know* about bloody *separation and loss*!"

❖ ❖ ❖

Rage. Emptiness. Despair. Numbness. How can you describe the indescribable?

From my driveway, I enter my house and collapse onto the living room sofa, curling into a defensive ball. I lay motionless for many minutes. Is this what Becs felt during Górecki's symphony? It must be worse, right?

I can hardly think. Three weeks ago, we were perfect together. Was Becs not who I thought she was? Am I so different from the man she said she loved? Can a game really ruin a relationship?

That game...

Eventually, I push myself up and resolve to visit the crime scene. Along the coffee table, around the sofa, through the archway, to the double doors of the study, a flick of a switch: the ceiling lights shine on the room where *Totaler Krieg* poisoned Becs. And this...this...

What?

No.

No!

Aaaaaargh!

The plexiglass pane atop the *Totaler Krieg* map has been twisted and juddered out of position. One corner dangles out from the table, over the leather chair nearest the curtained window. Stacks of counters have been toppled over and whisked together. Twenty, maybe thirty pieces have fallen into the chair by the window. The plastic tray for the unused Soviet and Western counters, which had been on Dennis's side of the table by the southeastern corner of the map, has been flipped over, and most of the units which were in it now mingle prematurely on the wooden floor. None of the game's components seem to be damaged, but my Sealion adventure with Dennis is clearly over: our latest war cannot be salvaged.

I grind my teeth together, and a monstrous groan rises in my throat. Becs didn't do this, did she? She hasn't been inside since…no, she wouldn't have anyway. An army of cats, perhaps? Or maybe…

DAD!

Anger swells within me. I grunt, then splutter a cough, then run from the room toward the front staircase. I ascend the stairs two at a time – if he wants to play rough, I can follow suit. Enraged, I'm ready to bust down the locked door of his study, to kick his little stacks of books and notes into a messy pile…I'm at the door, I bash into it with a shoulder, I grab at the handle, and, and…

The door opens. I stumble inside – I wasn't prepared for that – but quickly regain my balance. On the floor, there are no documents for me to kick; the thick, asparagus green carpeting I've rarely seen before is unexpectedly bare. However, my father is himself on the floor, twisted and lying on the carpet next to the dark pine desk across the room from me. He's snoring quite loudly, and his greying hair creeps out in messy swirls from the black headphones encasing his ears. Attached to the headphones is an iPod which has escaped his clutches and rests near his left hand. He's wearing a white dress shirt with thin blue pinstripes, a untucked corner of which flaps out from his blue jeans. Black socks cover his smelly feet, but his breath is far worse and reeks of booze; a mostly empty bottle labeled "MACALLAN 18" rests sideways on the floor, perpendicular to my father, with a thin layer of amber liquor inside the bottle and a small patch of liquid staining the carpet near the uncorked top.

Dad's desk is tidy: a stack of blank note cards and several Post-It pads flank an old desktop computer and its chunky monitor. A pair of glasses, a stapler and a cup full of pencils and pens also rest nearby. And then there are the bottles: a half-full bottle of gin, an unopened bottle of vodka, three unopened bottles of scotch. And on the wall of bookcases behind his desk, the empties: one, two, three, four, five see-through bottles, neatly aligned with the labels facing away from the room and toward his yellowing stores of *And I Have Forgotten It* and *The Salons of Vienna.*

This is my father: a slumbering, drunken wreck, sleeping on the floor without a pillow. I don't know which of us is doing worse, but surely he deserves his fate much more than I do. I pull a pen from the cup on Dad's desk and scribble two Post-It notes – the first reads:

THANKS FOR RUINING MY GAME – I APPRECIATE IT!

And the second:

YOUR NEXT PROJECT SEEMS TO BE GOING REALLY WELL.
—SEAN

I peel each note from the pad in turn, then bend down without inhaling and stick them to my father's shirt. And then I walk away. Dad deserves a good kicking, but that's not the kind of violence I'd ever dish out.

I go to my room. I sit down at my desk. I've received an e-mail from Gregory Spearman – he's just captured Naples, Minsk and Bucharest. I search for and find a complete recording of Górecki's Third Symphony on YouTube. I open CyberBoard. And I listen, and play, listen, and play, listen, and play, until my soul is empty and the sun comes up.

PART SIX

1.

I don't wake up until Saturday afternoon. When I come downstairs, Dad has left this note on the dining room table:

I'M REALLY SORRY, SEAN.
I'LL BE GONE FOR A WHILE – WE'LL TALK WHEN I GET BACK.

Huh. Dad often departs for a week or more when researching a book, but I didn't think the College's spring break coincided with Muhlendorf's. I'll worry about him later, though. I'm angry he messed up my game with Dennis – potentially one of the great counterfactual wars of my generation – and I wish I had taken detailed photos of the map and Force Pools to help us recreate it. But I would happily let Dad wreck several other games to get another chance with Becs.

❖ ❖ ❖

Sure – I didn't need to show *Totaler Krieg* to Becs. That's ground zero, my assassination-of-Franz Ferdinand moment. But if we had stayed together, she was bound to find out anyway. If the Archduke had survived, something somewhere else would have triggered the Great War, right?

That said, I could have introduced *Totaler Krieg* to Becs in a more circumspect manner. What if I had shown her a simpler game first, or explained what she was about to see before the game was thrust upon her? What if the Archduke had gone straight back to Vienna after attending Austria-Hungary's military exercises in Bosnia, instead of touring Sarajevo on 28 June?

I'm sure the *Pacific Typhoon* episode didn't help – I misread my audience badly and made a public spectacle of myself. What if the Archduke's driver hadn't taken a wrong turn, separating his car from the protective motorcade heading away from the city center, or if the car hadn't stalled just as Gavrilo Princip emerged from an adjacent delicatessen?

❖ ❖ ❖

Even then, there were other proximate causes. What if I hadn't mentioned Hitler or invoked the nuclear arms race during our World War I study session? This was the framework which made subsequent events at the concert possible. What if Bethmann Hollweg had been shunted aside and Germany hadn't offered its "blank check" to Austria-Hungary on 6 July?

What if I had accepted Becs' offer to leave the concert during the intermission, and we'd enjoyed a nice ice cream together? Gallantry is for suckers. What if Russia had explicitly and publicly withdrawn its support for Serbia, leaving Serbia no choice but to fully accept Austria-Hungary's ultimatum of 23 July?

What if I had rejected Becs' suggestion to do a running commentary, and hadn't committed myself to an irreversible course of action? None of the texts I sent could be edited or recalled after the fact. What if Russia hadn't mobilized, partially or otherwise, following Austria-Hungary's declaration of war against Serbia?

What if I had looked across at Becs and gauged her reactions to Górecki's symphony? Surely I would have toned down my comments accordingly. For that matter, how did I fail to spot the obvious warning signs in the concert program? I must have read the same information Becs did about Górecki's piece while trying to ignore the Bartók, but I must have forgotten it during the interval. What if Britain had waited several days or weeks before committing itself, instead of declaring war on Germany on 4 August?

❖ ❖ ❖

What about systemic causation? Did I have to constantly spew historical anecdotes and musings at Becs? The debate about Hiroshima, the Top Ten Moments in History list, watching *Bridge Too Far* together…this is who I am, but did I always need to be so brazen? Was the Kaiser bound to antagonize Britain and France in his quest for German naval and colonial supremacy?

I told Becs I was worried about the future; she assumed I was trying to avoid the present by living in the past. Should I really be so worried about the future? Did the Great Powers really need to entangle themselves in a web of permanent alliances which would prove so inflexible when a major crisis began to escalate?

For that matter, what if I had never chatted with Becs at the Homecoming Dance, and we'd never started our study group or fallen in love? Would the German people have been better off without Bismarck, and to have gained independence years later within a less powerful, less aggressive and less militaristic country?

❖ ❖ ❖

One final question: was Becs correct to assume that World War II wargaming might be a haven for Nazi sympathizers?

I have now discovered a firestorm of posts on Consimworld regarding a magazine article called "Sleeping with the Enemy: Pro-German Bias in WW2 Wargaming". Even discounting the tiny minority of shaven-headed, swastika-tattooed wargamers who wish *Iron Sky* were a documentary, the author – a gamer named David Hughes – believes many wargamers subconsciously embrace a Cold War mentality in which the Soviets are bad and the German army fought bravely only to be corrupted by the meddling of Hitler, the Nazi Party, the SS and the Gestapo. Left to its own devices, so this story goes, the *Wehrmacht* would have conquered all before it, and conquered it in a professional manner – as proven by the chivalrous Rommel and the behavior of normal German soldiers fighting against British and American forces in particular.

Meanwhile, Hughes argues, wargame companies pander to their audience and cater demand for German-centric products by amply supplying them. Games with "Hitler" in the title far outnumber those with "Stalin", "Roosevelt" and "Churchill" combined. Why is Operation Bagration, the huge Soviet offensive in 1944, so under-represented in gaming terms relative to German offensives like Operation Barbarossa and the Battle of the Bulge – and why should Decision Games' simulation of the Bagration offensive be called *The Destruction of Army Group Center*? GMT Games' two simulations of the French campaign in 1940 are called *Victory in the West* and *Case Yellow*, not *Disaster in the West* or *The Fall of France*. There are more than 100 English-language games in BoardGameGeek's database with "Panzer" in the title, roughly double the number of games with "Tank" in the title even counting *Thomas the Tank Engine*. And so on, and so on.

Speaking of which, why do so many wargamers think the word "panzer" sounds cooler than "tank"? Is my regular use of terms like *Wehrmacht* and *Luftwaffe* instead of "German army" and "German air force" merely precise shorthand, or does it indicate a more general fascination with foreign-language terminology… or am I subconsciously fascinated with terms rooted in the ethos of Nazism? Why do so many games (including *Totaler Krieg*) depict normal German units in one color and SS units in an eye-popping white-on-black, even when (unlike *Totaler Krieg*) there is no functional difference between them, and when elite units of other nationalities aren't similarly recolored? Why does so much wargame box art feature so many German soldiers – and so few Soviet soldiers – in heroic poses? Is it coincidental that wargamers on BoardGameGeek once voted the German army in World War II to be their favorite army in military history?

Honestly? I think there's more smoke than fire here. From what I've seen with Dennis and read on Consimworld, geeky wargamers obsess about the subjects of every game they play. World War II, Napoleonics, American Civil War, nuclear armageddon, Dungeons & Dragons, Star Wars, zombie invasions...gamers are willing to play anything and immerse themselves in any faction, historical or fantastical. Because World War II in Europe is so interesting, and because the vast majority of its campaigns, battles and skirmishes involved German soldiers, the *Wehrmacht* is the most gameable army in military history – if you've played any board wargame, at some point you've probably played as the Germans in World War II. There's nothing wrong with that. However, the *Wehrmacht* and Nazism cannot be separated. Atrocities were frequently perpetrated by "ordinary" German soldiers and commanders and not just the SS *Einsatzgruppen* trailing in their wake. If an outsider like Becs can understand that, wargamers like me should understand it even more and respond accordingly.

For my part, I henceforth resolve not to say "panzer" when "tank" works perfectly well, carefully consider my use of terms like *Wehrmacht*, and above all recognize that Dad might be right about Heinz Guderian. Becs is wrong about me and my hobby. But why should I make it so easy for someone as smart as she is to draw the wrong conclusions?

2.

The difference between Becs breaking up with me and the start of World War I – well, one of the differences, although proportionally I think both caused equivalent damage – is that none of the major actors in 1914 really wanted to avoid a war. Germany, Russia, Austria-Hungary, France and Britain all knew war was coming, but they didn't know what war would look like or how long it would last, so they fell into it willingly. But I certainly didn't want to break up with Becs, and every one of my counterfactual scenarios involving her was within my power to change. Why, why, why?

So I mope through Spring Break. I cancel my Thursday session with Dennis and apologize for the paternal meteor that detonated our game. I resign my BPA tournament semifinal against Gregory Spearman – he hasn't made a mistake and isn't going to, and I feel inadequate enough as it is. After reading hundreds of posts arguing for or against the existence of a pro-Nazi bias in wargaming, Consimworld seems a very lonely refuge. I try to read the rules to *Field Commander: Napoleon*, which is designed as a solitaire game – a very popular genre within the wargaming universe, for obvious reasons – but my heart isn't in it and my brain won't engage. Mostly, I slump around the house eating microwaved meals and watching television in my underpants.

When school finally resumes on Monday morning, I'm walking from English class to Math class when I see Becs standing at her locker, talking to Chris. They're both laughing, and Chris is rakishly bracing his elbow above his head against an adjacent locker; the *Casablanca* magnet I'd given Becs is nowhere to be seen. This sends me into another downward spiral, and when AP European History comes along I make sure to arrive early, sit in a back corner of the room and keep my head down until the class is over. This must be the bottom of the crevasse. I just know Becs and Chris are going to form their own study group, start dating, get married and do non-history things with their kids.

After school I talk to Freddie, the last piece of duct tape holding the Gang of Four together. "If Becs and Chris are an item, that's the first I've heard of it," he assures me.

We sit outside on a park bench, facing a soggy practice field now bereft of snow. I tell him how I miss Becs and don't know how to approach her now, and how cool it was to share the geek inside me with someone who seemed delighted to listen. Then I tell him about Dad, the ruined game, the floor of his study, the bottles.

"Have you seen him since it happened?" asks Freddie.

"Nope."

"Have you heard from him at all?"

"He texted me yesterday to say he'd be home soon. It's not unusual for him to be away for days without contacting me."

"That doesn't sound normal," says Freddie. "What do you think he's been up to?"

"What do you mean?"

"The last time you saw him, he'd drunk himself to sleep on the floor. Then he left and didn't tell you where he was going. He's been gone a week-and-a-half. Where do you think he is?"

"I don't know."

"Maybe he's embarrassed about what he did and is staying in a hotel near your house."

"There isn't a hotel near my house."

"OK, any hotel within 200 miles of here. For all you know, he could have been kidnapped."

"Kidnapped?"

"I know, there's no ransom note, but it's still early – you never know with these things. Or he could be dead."

"What?"

"Maybe someone murdered him and texted you to throw the police off the scent."

"What are you talking about?"

"Maybe he's run off to Wyoming with his mistress to start a new life without you."

"Freddie…"

"And he'll keep stringing you along with occasional messages until it's time to fork over your college tuition."

"Shut up."

"C'mon, it's your turn. We're up to number five in the Top Ten Silly Places Sean's Dad Could Be."

"Maybe he's hiding in the woods over there, holding a sniper rifle and aiming it at your head."

"Oooh, I like that. I hope for your sake he's a good shot."

"This is ridiculous."

"I'm just trying to distract you from thinking about Becs."

"Oh. Thanks, I guess."

"Is it working?"

"It was until just then."

"Ah." Freddie switches gears. "Anyway, let me ask you something else."

"What?"

"The game you showed to Becs…what's it like?"

"*Totaler Krieg*?"

"Gesundheit."

"*Totaler Krieg* is German for 'Total War'. It's like *Risk* on steroids."

"Yeah?"

"No, not really," I sigh. "It's way different from *Risk*."

"Is it like that card game, the one you tried to teach us?"

"*Pacific Typhoon*? No, it's much more complicated than that."

"Is that even possible?"

I roll my eyes. "*Totaler Krieg* tries to realistically simulate World War Two in Europe. You're either the Axis or the Allies, and you plan your strategies and tactics and fight your battles in great detail. To get all the details right, the rules have to be very complex. But when you're done, you have a real insight into the decisions the real commanders made during the war, and you can get a sense of how the war might have turned out differently."

"Huh." Freddie seems legitimately impressed. "Could you teach me how to play it?"

I laugh. "*Totaler Krieg*? Really?"

"Sure, why not?"

"That's not the first game I'd pick to teach you," I say. "Against an experienced opponent, it takes about 25 or 30 hours for me to finish a full game."

"Oh."

"Also, if you couldn't handle *Pacific Typhoon*, you're not going to manage *Totaler Krieg*."

"What about *Pacific Typhoon*, then? Can you teach me how to play that?"

"I don't think so. I tried that once already, didn't I?"

"You'll do better next time."

I grimace. "There won't be a next time. Wargames and Muhlendorf don't mix."

"I bet there are guys in the Chess Club who would play them with you," suggests Freddie.

"Chess is so two-dimensional. Besides, do I look or sound like a member of the Chess Club?"

"You just admitted you're a geek. Be true to yourself. Embrace the geek within."

"Yeah, I don't think that's going to happen. I tried with Becs, and it didn't work."

"I'll help you. Can I borrow your copy of *Pacific Typhoon*? Maybe I can figure it out myself."

"You're a good guy, Freddie. Thanks for being my friend. But simply making that offer is kind enough – there's no need to follow through on it."

"I'm not trying to be kind – I want to learn the damn game."

"You're not pulling my leg?"

Freddie frowns. "Can I borrow it or not?"

"Sure, if you insist. But you know, it's not a two-player game – you need at least three players, and preferably at least five."

"I'll cross that bridge when I get to it."

"OK, fine. I'll bring the game into school tomorrow."

"Great. We'll start with *Pacific Typhoon* and see what happens next."

Freddie must be winding me up or plotting something devious; there's no way a friend of mine from school would want play a World War II-themed game with me. But then I ask myself, what's the worst that can happen? It's not like a second encounter with *Pacific Typhoon* could be any worse than the first.

❖ ❖ ❖

On Tuesday, I again hide from Becs and Chris in the back of the AP European History classroom. Wednesday is different, though. I can't hide from anyone on Wednesday.

"Yesterday we discussed several '-isms' pertaining to European government in the 1930s," begins Mr. Prendergast, who today is wearing mustard-colored cords and a dark green sports coat which could have come from army surplus. "We had authoritarianism, totalitarianism, socialism, fascism and communism, with a side of Stalinism. Today we're going to cover two other '-isms' which came together in the 1930s in the worst possible way: that old villain, anti-semitism, and a new upstart, Nazism. Together they created World War Two and the Holocaust, and to lead us through a discussion of those two topics, I'm pleased to announce that we have a guest lecturer with us today. Ladies and gentlemen, please give a very warm welcome to your friend and mine, Mister Sean Lansbury."

A collective "Huh?" ripples through the classroom as I rise from my desk and walk forward with my speaking notes. I begin by joking, "Mister Prendergast doesn't actually know anything about World War Two, so he's asked me to help." Several heads turn toward Mr. Prendergast, who shrugs jovially.

"Here's an interesting statistic," I continue. "Of the Top 100 movies as rated on the Internet Movie Database, no fewer than 11 feature World War Two and/or the Nazis. Has anyone here not seen at least one movie which involves Nazis or the war in some way?" Nobody in the room raises a hand. "For what it's worth, my favorite is *Casablanca* – if you haven't seen *Casablanca*, you should."

I glance at Becs, who seems to be squirming in her seat. I had previously hoped this might be a pleasant surprise for her.

"The Second World War remains very prominent in popular culture," I say, "but popular culture doesn't always teach the right lessons. For example, did you know that the Soviet Union probably could have defeated Germany on its own, but that the US and Britain probably couldn't have? I know Miss Fowler does, as we once discussed this at great length" – yep, Becs' face is reddening – "but that's not a lesson you'd infer from *Saving Private Ryan*. Did you know that Hitler and the Nazi Party came to power entirely legally and democratically? Did you know that Britain and France could and should have stopped Hitler long before the war started, if only they'd believed the plans he'd published in the 1920s? Did you know that the war directly led to the invention or perfection of radar, sonar, jet airplanes, rockets, the jeep, penicillin and many other medical innovations, the computer, synthetic rubber and fuel technology, and nuclear weapons? And did you know that until 1942, the Nazis planned to exile all of the Jews to Madagascar, rather than killing them?"

"Sorry...did you say 'Madagascar'?" interrupts Jenny Pedersen.

"Yes," I answer. "I know, it sounds crazy and impractical, but much of Nazi Germany was crazy and impractical. Hitler governed Germany by letting his ministers and generals squabble with each other – this meant nobody could ever consolidate power and threaten his leadership, but it also meant Nazi government was terribly inefficient, and wild schemes like the Madagascar Plan could be taken seriously. On which note, let's go back to the beginning and look at the rise to power of the National Socialist German Workers' Party."

So I talk about Hitler's ascension to *Führer* and his personal popularity, the Nazi state and German society, appeasement and the road to war, the course of the war itself – stopping briefly to watch a History Channel clip about the battle of Stalingrad – and the rise of industry and technology. Nothing in voluminous detail, nothing earnest students of the war wouldn't know by heart, but enough to keep my classmates scribbling furiously in their notebooks. Then I carefully and compassionately portray the Holocaust as a culmination of the long history of European anti-semitism without glossing over the gruesome specifics – the Wannsee Conference, the *Einsatzgruppen*, Auschwitz and the gas chambers, the six million dead.

"I've always wondered something," interjects Tim Rogers, facing Mr. Prendergast. "If the Jews knew the Nazis wanted to kill them, why didn't they resist, and maybe at least take a few Germans down with them?"

"Sean can answer that, I'm sure," says Mr. Prendergast, as all eyes turn back to me.

"There are several reasons," I say. "The Nazis were very careful to make it seem as though the Jews were being deported for resettlement, not mass execution. Virtually nobody in occupied Europe knew what was going on, and even when rumors about the death camps started filtering back to the ghettos, few people believed them – the whole idea of mass genocide was simply too new and difficult to comprehend. Also, centuries of bitter experience had taught the Jews to cope with persecution through compromise and negotiation, rather than resistance. The Jewish ghetto in Warsaw did rise up against the Germans in 1943, but they were obviously poorly armed and very ineffective – around 13,000 Jews were killed against an official total of only 17 Germans, and the survivors were shipped to the death camp at Treblinka shortly thereafter."

I pause for a moment, then ask, "Any other questions?" I'm not going to lie: it feels great, sharing my knowledge outside of the Consimworld debating chamber.

"Realistically, could the Nazis have won the war?" asks Hugh Johnson.

"Yes, I think so," I say. "After conquering France, Hitler could have ignored Russia and instead attacked through Egypt towards Turkey and the Middle Eastern oilfields – that might have been a winning strategy. As it was, Germany came very close to capturing Moscow in 1941, which could have triggered a Soviet collapse along the lines of what happened in 1918. As the war dragged on and the United States got involved, an Allied victory became increasingly assured, but yes, Nazi Germany conceivably could have won the war and dominated Europe."

"What about Japan?" asks Felix Randolph. "Could they have won in the Pacific?"

"Almost certainly not. America's military leadership, its government and its industry were all far superior – Japan's only hope was to grind America down and make the US unwilling to suffer the casualties it would take to win the war. But the surprise attack at Pearl Harbor guaranteed that wouldn't happen."

"So did we have to use the atomic bomb against Hiroshima and Nagasaki?" asks Belinda Macintosh.

"Yes, I absolutely think we did. Miss Fowler, would you like to elaborate?"

The classroom heads turn to face Miss Fowler. "Why are you doing this?" asks Becs, quietly and resignedly.

"I don't need to hog the limelight, and I happen to know you know the answer to Belinda's question," I answer.

"I mean, why are you teaching us at all?" continues Becs.

"How do you know all this stuff?" asks Felix Randolph.

"Yeah, why *are* you such a geek?" asks Chris. A few voices titter within the classroom.

I thunder back at Chris, "Are you suggesting that knowledge is a bad thing? That it's somehow wrong to know more about what we're studying than what Mister Prendergast might teach us? That learning more that what's absolutely necessary about our past is somehow 'uncool'? This is an 'Advanced' class – many of our friends will never study such complex material so intensely, and eventually some of us might even study History in college. You should get used to that idea, and embrace the geek within yourself." Several of my classmates start laughing, and Chris is now blushing.

"But to answer Miss Fowler's question," I conclude more gently, "Mister Prendergast asked me to teach today's class a few weeks ago, and I was happy to say yes. I hope it's been worthwhile for most of you."

"I couldn't have done any better myself," says Mr. Prendergast. "Literally, I couldn't have, because Mister Lansbury knows way more about World War Two than I do. And next time" – the bell to end the class begins to drone – "next time our scene will shift from this hot war to a Cold one, so stay tuned for some exciting Communist-on-Capitalist action!"

I stand motionless at the lectern as the class files out. Becs and Chris skulk away, embarrassed and reticent, but Tim Rogers supportively pats me on the back, and several others say "Well done" or "Good job". When everyone has left and the hall outside is bubbling with commotion, I thump my forehead and mutter, "I forgot to answer Belinda's question about atomic weapons, didn't I?"

Mr. Prendergast smiles and asks, "You like baseball – have you seen *The Natural*?"

"Of course."

"At the end, when Roy Hobbs hits the home run and circles the bases as the lights explode and sparks rain down on the field? That's what your smackdown of Chris felt like – the exclamation point at the end of a masterpiece."

"Thanks, I think."

"You're going to have to come back and deliver that talk for me again next year. Did you enjoy that?"

"More than I thought I would, yeah."

"You were a natural. I'll see you later."

Mr. Prendergast's eyes soften, and he smiles warmly at me. I won't be hiding in the back of the AP European History classroom tomorrow.

❖ ❖ ❖

On Friday evening, I'm on the sofa in my living room reading Russell A. Hart's *Guderian: Panzer Pioneer or Myth Maker?* – it arrived in the mail yesterday – when the doorbell rings. So I mark my page, slip past the coffee table between the comfy chairs, stroll through the hallway to the foyer, and open the front door.

"Hello, Sean."

It's Dad. He looks pale and gaunt, and despite the warm spring evening and the grey overcoat he's wearing, he seems to be shivering. At his side is the leather garment bag he takes with him on business trips – often he carries another hold-all, for books and other documents, but I don't see that anywhere.

"Can I come in?" he asks, unsteadily.

"This is still your house, right?" I respond. "Why did you ring the doorbell?"

"I don't know."

"Why are you at the front door instead of the side door? Did you park your car out front?"

"It seemed like the right thing to do."

"Where have you been? What's going on?"

"I'll get to that in a moment." Dad steps inside and pulls the door shut. "Are you OK if I get myself a drink first?"

"Sure. I'll be in the living room."

"I'll meet you there."

Dad's face twitches – I can't tell if he's grimacing, trying to smile, or trembling with exhaustion. But I let him trudge into the kitchen as I wander back to the sofa.

I'm halfway through Hart's short book – I should finish it tonight – but its thesis was clear from its introduction:

> Heinz Guderian has been lionized by many as the legendary father of the German armored force and brilliant practitioner of *Blitzkrieg* maneuver warfare. Guderian created this legend with his own highly influential, yet self-serving and distorted memoir, which remains one of the most widely read accounts of the Second World War. Unfortunately, too many of Guderian's biographers have accepted Guderian's view of his accomplishments without sufficient critical scrutiny. The result has been an undeserved hagiography of Guderian. While undoubtedly a great military figure, Guderian was a man of appreciable ego and ambition – a volatile, impetuous, and difficult personality determined to achieve his vision of a war-winning armored force, irrespective of the consequences. He proved naive enough to fall under the sway of Hitler and National Socialism, yet arrogant enough to believe, late in the war, that he could save Germany from inevitable defeat despite Hitler. In spite of his later disapproval of Hitler, he proved unwilling either to participate in attempts to remove him or to denounce as traitors the conspirators that did. In the end, he proved to be a man prepared to distort the truth in order to establish his place in history. In doing so, he denigrated the myriad important contributions of other Germans as he took personal credit for what were, in reality, collective accomplishments. He succeeded in creating a legend that has endured long after his death. This brief biography begins to put the record straight by endeavoring to place Guderian's career and accomplishments into sharper and more accurate relief. It seeks the real Heinz Guderian, not the man of legend.

What is a boy to believe? If Hart is correct, my mental image of Guderian – shaped not just by *Panzer Leader*, but by hundreds of lateral references in broader historical works – has been a sham, and several generations of historians have much to answer for. Some revisionists seem motivated by the desire for notoriety in a crowded academic landscape, but I don't sense that Hart is one of them. In a bibliographic note, Hart cites several historians (Citino, Corum, Senff, Weinberg, Goda) who previously uncovered telltale imperfections in Guderian's account, but he also references others – notably the distinguished John Keegan and Kenneth Mackesy – who bought the *Panzer Leader* myth and failed to correct it in their broader biographies of Guderian. I always suspected that *Panzer Leader* contained exaggerations and half-truths; most memoirs do. But Hart's book, published in 2006, is the first holistic attempt to debunk *Panzer Leader* as a self-serving façade. How could 60 years of postwar history fail to correct such an appreciable wrong? This isn't a classified, ULTRA-scale secret withheld from the public; this is an important and, presumably, easily verifiable element of the generally accepted story of World War II. I think my father's profession requires more professors.

But my exploration of Guderian's career can wait. Dad, now wearing a light grey suit and pale blue shirt but no tie, enters the living room carrying a tall glass of clear liquid and ice. "Is that water, or something stronger?" I ask.

"Funny you should ask that." Dad puts the glass on a coaster and collapses into the chair to my right.

"By the way, see this?" I show Dad the book I'm reading. "On your recommendation, I hasten to add. You seem to be right about General Guderian."

Dad smiles. He looks tired. "Sean, for the past two weeks I've been in rehab."

I'm startled. "Rehab? Where? For what?"

"I'm an alcoholic, Sean."

Dad removes his glasses and rubs his moistening eyes. His jaw is still gently quivering. "What does that mean?" I ask, still not comprehending.

"It means I drink too much. It means whenever I have one drink, I have another, and another, and another. It means I can't stop drinking, regardless of the consequences."

"Oh."

"At the clinic where I was staying, they say their patients are not bad people trying to be good, but sick people trying to get well. So that's what I'm trying to do now. Alcoholism is a disease, and I'm a sick person."

I've never heard my father talk like this. "How…how are you feeling?" I ask.

"Not great. Detox isn't pleasant. But the important thing is that I'm sober now."

"What happened two weeks ago, the night before you left?" I'm struggling to look Dad in the eye.

"Yeah, about that." Dad sniffles, sips his drink, and continues even more haltingly. "Sean, I'm really, really sorry for messing up your game. I don't know why I did that. I probably wouldn't even remember doing it if you hadn't written your note. And thank you – really, thank you for that. It was the final push I needed to get help. I'm glad I forgot to lock my study door."

The penny finally drops. "You haven't been working on another book at all, have you? You've been going upstairs and drinking."

Dad smiles grimly. "For such a bright boy, you can be terribly thick sometimes." He sniffles again and pulls a handkerchief from a pocket inside his suit jacket. He's right – I wouldn't make a good detective. "No, I haven't been working on another book. I haven't been teaching my students very well. And I certainly haven't been a good father to you for quite a long…time."

And now he's really fighting back tears. Trying to be stoic, sticking fingers in the dyke and hoping to stem the flow. For now, at least, he succeeds. I study the thread patterns in my jeans, unwilling or unable to respond.

Dad takes another deep, jagged breath. "I'm not sure what you think of me right now, but that's OK," he says. "I don't deserve anything from you. But I hope you'll give me another chance. Here, there's something I want to show you."

Dad reaches into his rear pants pocket and fishes out a folded piece of worn yellow paper. He hands it to me and leans back in his chair; I unfold the paper and am astonished to see the following words in large, black letters:

THE WARGAMERS ALLIANCE
EVERY THURSDAY – DAMSON HALL
7 p.m. until the last battle is won
LOOK LIVELY!

"Where did you get this?" I gasp.

"It's posted on several bulletin boards at the College," Dad answers. "I saw this several months ago."

"There's a wargame club at your College? A bunch of gamers close to my age, living on my doorstep?"

"I don't know. I haven't investigated further."

"Why didn't you tell me about this before?"

Dad sighs. "I wasn't sure I wanted you to know," he says. "Like I said, I haven't been a good father."

"Dad…"

"I've never appreciated your hobby. I never realized how incredible it was to have a son more deeply fascinated with history than I ever was. I thought you were perverting history, instead of embracing it in your own way. So when I left for rehab, I took a copy of the *Totaler Krieg* rulebook with me."

"You did what?"

"Of course, when I started reading it late one night in my room at the clinic, I immediately discovered that there's a section in the scenario book called 'Playing *TK* for the First Time', and I didn't have the scenario book with me. So I haven't gotten very far yet."

I'm dumbfounded. My gast is well and truly flabbered. I finally stutter, "You're willing to learn…how to play *Totaler Krieg*…with me?"

"Yes, Sean. I am."

This is probably the nicest thing Dad has ever thought to do for me. I don't know what to say, so after several seconds I say this: "The first training scenario covers the German invasion of Poland. It's very short and will be a good learning exercise for you – I'll install CyberBoard on your computer and show you how to move the pieces around. You can practice over and over again until you get the hang of it."

"That sounds great, Sean. Thank you. And really, I'm sorry about all this."

Dad stands up, leans over to me and gently tousles my hair. Then he picks up his glass, squeezes between the coffee table and the two comfy chairs, and disappears again into the kitchen. I start to cry.

3.

"Did you know there was a wargaming club at the College?" I ask Dennis, shortly after he arrives for our next gaming session. He is wearing a black T-shirt captioned "SPOT THE NINJA" and showing a neat rectangular grid of white stick figures in which one space on the second row appears to be blank.

"Yes," he answers, not skipping a beat.

"And you didn't tell me this…why, exactly?"

"You never asked."

"Seriously?"

"Seriously. Besides, the club meets on Thursdays, and we play on Thursdays."

I'm incredulous. "We don't play *every* Thursday. And we don't *have* to play on Thursdays, do we?"

"You wouldn't want to hang out there. College kids are weird."

"So are you," I respond.

"So are you," retorts Dennis. Touché.

As usual, for the first session of a new game I have set up the maps, force pools and counters with pinpoint precision, waiting for the invasion of Poland to provide a first shock of entropy. However, Dennis is playing the Axis faction this time, and he claims to have spotted a mistake even before we begin. "See the Polish reserve corps?" he asks. "It's in the wrong place."

"I know Poland is going to fall in one turn," I respond, "but just in case you do something stupid, the Polish reserve corps should start in the Force Pool, just as the Polish cavalry starts in the Delay Box."

"No, I mean the Reserve corps is in the wrong Force Pool."

"It's in the Western Force Pool."

"Can you move it to the Soviet Force Pool, please?" Dennis grins – he's choosing to make Poland a Soviet ally.

"You're going East First?"

"Do you have a problem with that?"

"You could have warned me in advance!"

"Where's the fun in that?"

"I haven't played an East First game in so long, it'll take me forever to figure out what to do. Like trying to unclasp a girl's bra behind her back – you might have fun along the way, but you're never going to feel like an expert."

"I haven't studied this either – I just thought it'd be fun to try something different. We don't have to rush. We can take things nice and sloooow…" Dennis suggestively raises an eyebrow.

"Ewww. Are you implying Röhm purged Hitler and is leading Germany? I'm pretty sure there's a book about homosexuality in Nazi Germany called *The Pink Swastika*."

"I'll pretend my army counters are brown and not grey." Then, in a camp German accent, Dennis says, "Now is ze time on Sprockets ven ve march!"

When Germany goes East First in *Totaler Krieg*, Britain and France are paralyzed by their "Appeasement" policy and remain inactive while the Axis player drives east as hard and fast as possible before (usually) imposing the <u>Ostland Accord</u>. Patterned on the 1918 Treaty of Brest-Litovsk, this Option Card reduces the Red Army to 10 steps and converts certain Soviet regions into German vassal states if German ground units control Minsk, Kiev, Sevastopol, Rostov and/or Baku. After a lengthy truce, Russia can rise again; meanwhile, with Britain and France now fully prepared for war and the Maginot Line likely extended to the Channel, Germany must engage in an attritional bloodbath and forcibly evict the Allies from the Continent to vanquish France. By 1942 the map of Europe will normally revert to something resembling history, but the road taken to get there is less travelled by far.

On the continuum of ahistorical situations in *Totaler Krieg*, East First isn't as wacky as the "World War One Revisited" scenario, while a campaign game starting in 1937 – which we have thus far avoided – can see a belligerent or neutral Britain stand alone after a Franco-Russian Entente. In truth, the Ostland Accord model seems perfectly plausible, but it also remains purely hypothetical, and I've never gone East First as the Axis myself. But if my aborted Sealion game against Dennis taught me anything, it's that a fun game is a good game: historical plausibility can be overrated.

After Dennis rolls through Poland, we grapple near the Russian border through the Winter. In March-April 1940, Dennis declares war on the Baltic States and zooms into Riga, while three Soviet armies are surrounded and destroyed in the western Ukraine. I should have constructed my defenses one hex further back, but no matter: at least I'm holding firm so far in the north, and because Dennis gets no more than one Blitz marker per turn during Limited War, he can never attack forcefully in both the north and south. As predicted, though, I'm struggling to choose a Soviet strategy; I prioritized infantry production (Wartime Mobilization) in Winter 1939-40, but I also desperately need a second HQ and my Interceptor support unit.

"I probably should have demanded the Baltic States in the Winter," I say to Dennis at the end of March-April 1940. "I'd be getting my second HQ about now, plus you'd have had to fight for Lithuania, and declare war on someone else with Weserübung."

"Remember, the Ostland Accord will zap most of your army," says Dennis. "So it doesn't really matter what you play now."

"But I don't want to let you get beyond Minsk and Kiev. See, this is why you should have warned me you were thinking East First."

"I think you're trying to say you suck at *Totaler Krieg*," jokes Dennis.

"You're laughing, but I don't think I've a won a game of *TK* this year," I remind him. "Before our Sealion game, I lost the BPA tournament semifinal, and you diced me in France, and before that we abandoned the World War One game as well. What was before that? La Coruña and the 'Sideways Shift'?"

"You won an Axis ATV somewhere in there as well, but I take your point."

Fig. 12 – Position at the end of March-April 1940, after Dennis goes "East First"

"And that doesn't even count showing *Totaler Krieg* to Becs, which was the biggest loss of them all."

"Becs is your girlfriend, right?" Dennis asks.

"Ex-girlfriend," I correct.

"Oh. I'm sorry to hear that."

"I hadn't told you, had I? She couldn't get over…well, this. She couldn't get over *Totaler Krieg*. I thought I knew what I was doing when I showed her the game – maybe I should have shown her *Axis & Allies* instead."

"Maybe I should have dated Becs, and you should have dated Carolyn Johnson."

"Yeah, that's exactly what should have happened."

Because April-May 1940 is a Mud turn, Dennis has few decisions to make. He moves adjacent to the Dnepr, capturing the towns of Cherkassy and Kirovograd; in turn, I disengage from Army Group North, leaving blocking armies in Dvinsk, Minsk, Kiev and Dnepropetrovsk but withdrawing key units to Luga, Orsha and Kharkov. Few of those place names should mean anything to a junior at Muhlendorf High School, but they all do to me.

As I finish my turn, I ask Dennis, "How old were you when you got your first wargame?"

"I think I was nine when I bought Avalon Hill's *Panzer Leader*," answers Dennis, leaning back in his chair. "When I was your age, wargames were sold in toy stores. Buying games was the easy part. The hard part was figuring out how to play them, and finding friends who could understand them with you."

"Did you have any luck?"

"Not with *Panzer Leader*. I played *Midway* a few times with a kid in my class named Daniel, and I may have played *D-Day* once or twice, but mostly I just collected games and waited for e-mail and the internet to be invented."

"Did you ever play games with your father?"

"God, no. He was an insurance salesman – he didn't have the time, interest or brainpower for wargames."

"Oh." After a pause, I continue, "For what it's worth, my Dad is actually learning how to play *Totaler Krieg* himself. It was his own idea and everything."

"Really? Good luck with that."

"So I may need to pick up this game at some point – I'll take pictures of the map and record where all of the pieces are so we can resume it later."

"Sure."

"By the way, Dad apologized again for wrecking our Sealion game. He's still really, really sorry about that."

"Apology accepted."

We again drift into silence, and Dennis leans forward to contemplate his May-June 1940 move. He scrapes a fingernail across his front teeth, then scratches that same fingernail across his beard. Then he holds his chin in thumb and forefinger and purses his lips, glaring quizzically at the map while drumming his suction tweezers on the table. Reaching for the map, with the tweezers he then levers his Second Panzer Army – currently on its reduced 5-4-4 side – into the air from its starting position in southeastern Lithuania, pulls it above and along the map to the east, and gently drops it into the empty hex containing the town of Mogilev, halfway between Minsk and Smolensk and adjacent to my three armies in Orsha. A warm, tingly sensation flows through my body, and I smile gently to myself. Repeated a thousand-fold every game night, this is the wargamer's sacred ritual: the intense burst of thought, followed by the perfunctory levitation of the cardboard square. It is not a ritual of elegant physical performance; the calculations which define it are often exquisitely crafted, but the bodies performing it rarely are, and the awkward silences and stilted conversations either side of it reflect this. But that's perfectly OK. I'm not sure Dennis is what I want my future to look like, but I can think of worse ways and worse people with whom to spend a Thursday evening.

❖ ❖ ❖

"Time's up! Please put your pencils down."

The shrill call of my female proctor echoes around Robinette Gymnasium, the smaller of Muhlendorf's two gyms but a cavernous exam venue for 18 people. I'm surprised her call has any effect – my pencils have been resting on my foldable table for almost half an hour already. Fifty-five minutes is an absurdly long time in which to answer 80 multiple-choice questions, no matter how long or difficult they might be. I mean, no question on the AP European History exam can be more convoluted than this:

27. *"The power of population is infinitely greater than the power in the earth to produce subsistence for man. Population, when unchecked, increases in a geometric ratio. Subsistence only increases in an arithmetic ratio. A slight acquaintance with the numbers will show the immensity of the first power in comparison with the second." This argument is fundamental to:*
    a) Adam Smith's belief in the natural laws of production and exchange
    b) Hegel's theory of the process of change

c) Malthus' belief in the inevitability of working-class poverty
d) Charles Darwin's theory of biological evolution
e) Marx's theory of class conflict

Even then, how long does it take to read and process these words on the page? Twenty seconds? Maybe less? Then, either you know the answer, and fill in the correct circle on the answer sheet with your No. 2 pencil, or you don't, in which case you guess and move on anyway. At most, 30 seconds per question times 80 questions equals 40 minutes, leaving plenty of time for double-checking your answers – or double-shading them, if you brought No. 3 pencils to the exam by mistake. And yet, several of my peers were clearly flustered by the proctor's call to stop. Faith Evans, seated in front of me, is edging toward hyperventilation.

Our proctor, who is not from Muhlendorf, is wearing an olive blouse, a baggy grey skirt and thin-rimmed glasses. "Please remain seated and face forward while I collect your answer sheets," she says. She's actually quite pretty, although I may have convinced myself of this while staring at her for half an hour. Can the polar opposite of beer goggles have similar effects? As she approaches my table, my gaze instinctively follows her to my side, and as she collects my answers she mutters "Eyes forward, please" in a tone as neutral as Switzerland.

When she's done, we have 15 minutes to stretch, use the restrooms and water fountain, and worry about the Free Response section. Best case? I could get a question like this one from the 2006 AP exam:

Considering the period 1933 to 1945, analyze the economic, diplomatic, and military reasons for Germany's defeat in the Second World War.

On the other hand, all six FRQs could be like this one from the 2010 exam:

Compare and contrast the goals and achievements of the feminist movement in the period circa 1850-1920 with those of the feminist movement in the period 1945 to the present.

Our individual exam tables are spread well apart from one another across the gym. Mine straddles one of the three-point arcs on the main basketball court, so as I stand up to stretch I step behind the table and shoot an imaginary jumper toward where the rim would be if the backboard weren't retracted to the ceiling.

"Airball!" chants Chris, who has snuck up behind me.

"Swish, more like," I respond.

"Your technique is all wrong. Half the girls' JV team could have blocked that."

"Gee, thanks for the tip."

Chris smiles. "You know nothing is happening between me and Becs, right? She's way too dorky for me."

"Remember what I said when I taught the class? Embrace the geek within yourself."

"Today, yes," he says. "Tomorrow, probably not."

"Do what you want," I respond. "She's a good study partner, at least."

"I know. Anyway, I thought I'd ask how you did on the multiple-choice section," he says. "But I can piss off if you'd prefer."

"I'm doing well so far. You?"

"Not too bad. The hard part is yet to come, of course."

"Indeed. Good luck with that."

"Same to you."

Chris slinks away. I shoot another imaginary jump shot, this time pronating my wrist above my forehead, then sit down again. I stare off into space. Chris was my best friend once, wasn't he?

A hand comes to rest on my back. "How are you doing?" asks a female voice.

I turn around – it's Becs. She's wearing black jeans and the grey sweater she likes because it's comfortable but which I think makes her look fat.

"Ask me in three hours," I respond. "Or in thirty years."

"I never properly thanked you for helping me prepare for today," says Becs. "Thank you."

"You would have done fine without me," I say.

Becs looks at me, and I at her. She wants to be polite, and I have so much to say. But now is not the time; indeed, that time may never come. "Good luck on the rest of the exam," I whimper.

"You too."

I bury my head in my arms on the table. I've spent countless hours preparing for this exam both at home, in class and at several after-school study sessions organized by Mr. Prendergast – never mind the lifetime of reading and study which made me want to take AP European History in the first place. But it's always the thing you're unprepared for which hits you the most.

By the time the cellophane-wrapped Free Response section arrives at my desk, I am numb with nihilism. If I get the right questions, I'll get a better score, even though my level of knowledge won't be any different. So by definition, the AP exam cannot accurately evaluate my understanding of history. Why, then, should the exam exist? Perhaps this is a grand experiment to teach the capriciousness of academia, and of life itself. But then, I didn't need a year's tuition to tell me that; the dice in *Totaler Krieg* teach that life isn't purely meritocratic. Before promoting any officer, Napoleon's first question was, "Is he lucky?" If the FRQs are all terrible, maybe I'll shoehorn that into one of my answers.

My peers have drifted back to their tables, and our pretty proctor stands up. "You will have 130 minutes to complete the Free Response section," she announces. "First, there will be a mandatory 15-minute reading period in which no writing will be permitted – you may read through the document-based question and the two sets of three thematic essay questions. After the reading period is finished, you can begin writing your answers: you are advised to spend 45 minutes answering the document-based question, and 70 minutes answering the two essay questions you have chosen. Does everyone understand those instructions? Are you ready to begin?"

No, but let's get this over with.

"Good – you may open your packets and begin reading. Good luck."

A sharp crackle of plastic ripples through the gym, then all is quiet save the muted rustling of pages. I quickly scan the DBQ:

How did the life and achievements of Sir Christopher Wren (1632-1723) reflect the age in which he lived?

Yawn – an Age of Enlightenment question. I skip to the back of the booklet… and read the first of the six thematic essay questions:

1. *The Prussian military theorist Carl von Clausewitz wrote that "War is the continuation of policy by other means." Analyze the truth of this saying, citing wars involving European powers in three different centuries since 1500.*

❖ ❖ ❖

"You'd think that would be a dream question for me," I say.

Mr. Prendergast nods. The AP exam finished an hour ago, and I've tracked him down in a vacant classroom – he's wearing jeans and a blue T-shirt bearing the white image of a man holding a mallet and riding a chicken above the word "POLLO". He must have stolen the shirt from Dennis's closet.

"Was it not?" he asks.

"It was – and yet, that was all I could think about. What should I say? Which wars should I write about? How can you pick just three? In the end I chose the Thirty Years War, Napoleon's campaigns from 1805 to 1815, the Franco-Prussian War, and of course World War Two."

"That's at least four wars," says Mr. Prendergast.

"I know, but the question referred to wars in three different centuries, not three different wars. Anyway, before I knew it I'd spent nearly an hour answering that question alone, so I'm afraid I rushed through the DBQ and the other FRQ."

"Which other FRQ did you choose?"

"The one about ethnic minorities in the Austro-Hungarian Empire."

"What was the actual question?"

"I can't remember – don't you know the one I mean?"

"I won't see the essay questions until they're posted online tomorrow." Mr. Prendergast smirks. "And you may find this hard to believe, but you're the first student I've talked to since the exam was over."

"Oh. What did you do while we were taking the exam?"

"For me, AP exam day is like sending your son out in your car by himself for the first time – you pace around a lot, fretting and hoping that you and his driving instructor have prepared him well enough to get home without breaking anything."

I chuckle. "I think I got home without breaking anything. But I guess I'll have to wait until July to find out."

Mr. Prendergast smiles warmly at me. "You remember me telling you about my nephew who plays the clarinet?" he asks.

"Yes."

"Last year, Justin auditioned for the All-State Symphonic Band in Louisiana. My sister told me how despondent Justin was when he came home – he'd botched one of his audition pieces completely, his tone was messed up, he wasn't going to make the band at all, he was a failure, and so on. Next week he found out that he'd made first chair, same as the year before, and would again get to play an important solo. As Einstein once said, everything is relative."

"I see."

"If you don't get a '5' on the AP exam, I will eat the chicken on my shirt. But here's a dirty little secret: your score on the exam doesn't matter. I mean, it would matter if you were to major in physics at college and the '5' lets you skip the History class you'd otherwise have to take. Otherwise, the hour you put into that one essay question is much more significant. Ultimately you will have to figure out what gives your life meaning, but let me tell you something: only film and music critics measure success and satisfaction on a scale of one to five."

Goosebumps envelop me. "Thanks for that, and for all you've done for me this year," I gush.

"What a change nine months can make, eh? Now, get out of here before I beat you with a baseball bat," says Mr. Prendergast, grinning. "Can't a teacher live in peace for a few minutes?"

❖ ❖ ❖

The AP exam does not end my school year at Muhlendorf. I may be walking the halls in a permanent daze, but with several weeks until the end of our third trimester, most of my classes are getting more intense, not less. Even Mr. Prendergast still has a final exam to administer, as AP test scores aren't calculated quickly enough to contribute to our grade point averages.

Three days after the AP exam, I wander to the school cafeteria after third-period Chemistry with my usual brown-bagged sandwich, grapes, pretzel packet and cookie. The day is warm and sunny, and as I queue to buy a soft drink, I ponder eating outside, lounging on the grassy slope by the lower playing fields and perhaps napping until either someone wakes me or fourth-period Trigonometry is finished. But as I'm paying my dollar to the elderly cashier, Freddie intercepts me.

"Come over here," he says. "I want to show you something."

I shrug my shoulders and assent. He leads me through a forest of tables and chairs toward our familiar alcove at the rear of the room. "You haven't raised the Big Game from the dead, have you?" I ask.

"Even better," says Freddie. "Look."

Seated at the round table in the alcove are Jeremy Bressler, president of the Muhlendorf Chess Club; Helena Thompson, another junior I vaguely know from several classes; and Nick Simkiss, the brown-haired sophomore last seen wetting himself during our final Big Game. Also on the table are two dice and the Force Card and Battle Card decks from *Pacific Typhoon*.

"Everyone is all set," says Freddie. "Will you join us for a game?"

"Wow. I mean, um, yeah." I look quizzically at Freddie, who smiles toothily in response. After an exchange of hellos, I sit with Freddie to my left and Helena to my right and ask, "Shall I explain the rules to everyone?"

"We've played the game twice already," says Jeremy.

"Really?"

"It's actually a lot of fun," says young Master Simkiss. "Freddie is a good teacher."

I'm astonished. I mutter, "Can you explain the rules to me?"

Freddie grins and deals each of us six Force Cards. "Don't worry, we shuffled and cut the decks before you got here," says Jeremy.

"How did you..." I stutter. "I mean, how is this happening?"

"I told everyone today was your birthday," says Freddie.

"He didn't, actually," corrects Jeremy.

The first two Battle Cards are Vella Lavella, a 1943 Night Battle worth two victory points, and Java Sea, a 1942 Day or Night Battle (round leader's choice) worth four victory points plus a Resource. My opening hand is weak but diverse: I have the Japanese Hiryu (Aircraft Carrier) and Haguro (Heavy Cruiser), and the Allied Santa Fe (Light Cruiser), Mitchell (Medium Bomber), PT 109 (Patrol Torpedo Boat) and Coast Watchers (Field Intelligence).

Freddie announces, "Let's up the stakes and start with Java Sea. I'll make it a Night Battle, the Suit is Surface, and I'll play this to start." Freddie lays down the Japanese Kirishima (Battlecruiser) card, which has a Surface value of four.

"Very strong," says Jeremy. Jeremy has clipped black hair, wears black-rimmed glasses and possesses the overbearing, know-it-all demeanor one would expect from a math whiz and the president of the Chess Club.

Nick goes next. He studies his cards, then plays Canberra (Heavy Cruiser) – "That's worth two Surface for the Allies, but I'll play a bonus event as well," he says. He then lays down Holy Moses (Aircraft Rockets), which has a "+1" Surface value.

"You can't play that," says Jeremy. "It has to be attached to a parent *aircraft*, and Canberra is a *ship*."

"Oh, OK..." stammers Nick. "I'll just take the bonus card back into my hand."

I ask Jeremy, "Did Freddie teach this game to you, or did you teach it to Freddie?"

"I'm a fast learner," he says, laying down Indianapolis (Heavy Cruiser) and the bonus card Fire Control Radar (Gunnery Direction), which together are worth four Surface. The Allies are now winning the battle six to four.

Helena squints at her hand – her somewhat spotty face is improved by striking brown eyes and wavy black hair which curls gently over her shoulders. She turns to Freddie and says, "I can put Japan into the lead if you promise to give me the Java Sea card as my spoil. Or I can guarantee an Allied victory, and you'll get nothing. Your choice."

"Sold," says Freddie. "You're a wench, you know."

"I can make the same offer," interrupts Jeremy.

"Too late," says Helena. "Not that I trust you anyway." Helena plays I-168 (Submarine) and the bonus Long Lance (Superior Torpedoes) card for a combined four Surface; Japan is now winning eight to six, with just me to play.

This is good. "OK, folks – let's make a deal," I announce. "I can win the battle for either side, so my terms are the same as Helena's. Freddie: cancel your deal with Helena and give me Java Sea. Or Jeremy, promise me Java Sea and the battle is yours."

"Deal," blurts Jeremy. Freddie and Helena are still looking blankly at each other.

I smile. "Actually, it's too early for broken promises – I won't do that to the two of you. So, here." I play Henley, worth one Surface, and the two bonus cards PT-109 and Coast Watchers, each worth +1 Surface, and the Allies win nine to eight.

"Yes!" says Jeremy. Freddie shrugs.

"Henley is nearly an anagram of my name," muses Helena.

"Did you know there was actually a *USS Helena* in World War Two?" I say. "She was a light cruiser."

"Cool!" says Helena. I like that.

"She was sunk in 1943, though."

"Ah. Still, though!" Helena is beaming.

"Ahem – to the spoils," continues Jeremy. "The rules say I don't have to honor my promise, of course, so…"

"But of course you don't want to have everyone hate you this early in the game, either," I remind him.

"…so of course I'll give Java Sea to Sean." Jeremy frowns. "Four points for him, and I'll take Kirishima for three points, and Nick can have I-168 for one point."

"That's a good boy," I say.

Freddie grins again and starts dealing new Force Cards to everyone. "See?" he says. "This is great fun. One for me, one for young Master Simkiss, two for Jeremy, two for Helena, and three for Sean."

"I get four cards, actually," I correct. "I played three, plus I get an extra card for the Resource."

"Four cards for the man with the target now on his back," clarifies Freddie. He turns to me as we collect our cards and says, "By the way, did you hear Vicki broke up with Melvyn?"

"No!" I exclaim. "Really?"

"Yeah, he's in a state of shock."

"What happened?"

"I don't know. Maybe it's just that Vicki's a senior, and she's graduating soon? Anyway, everyone in the Gang of Four is single again, at least for now."

"For now?"

Freddie glances furtively at Helena, who instantly blushes and looks away. "The two of you?" I ask.

"No, you dummy," says Freddie. "I think you…never mind."

"Me? Is that why…"

"We'll talk about this later."

"Hello?" interrupts Jeremy again. "Can we fight the next battle now?"

One of our old Big Game kibitzers, Michael the sophomore, passes by our table. "Are you guys playing *Magic* or something?" he asks me.

"Or something," I respond. "Something better."

"Cool – can I watch?"

"Sure."

Michael hovers behind young Master Simkiss, our new round leader, as he chooses between Day Battles: Pearl Harbor (1941) is worth seven victory points and a Resource, while Bismarck Sea (1943) is worth only three victory points and half a Resource. Nick bites his lip as he studies his hand, presumably deciding if he has a good enough 1941 card to play. Jeremy huffs, silently urging Nick to get on with it. Helena's brown eyes peer out from behind her cards. I look at Freddie, and he looks back at me – he smiles encouragingly, and I shake my head in wonderment. Maybe Michael was actually right: Freddie is full of magic just now.

4.

Gliwice is a city in southern Poland, roughly 50 miles west of Krakow and 40 miles northeast of Ostrava in the Czech Republic. Gliwice's radio transmission tower, rising to a height of 387 feet, is the tallest wooden structure in Europe and probably the world now that most timber transmitters have been dismantled. Near the base of this tower, Franciszek Honiok – a German Silesian known to have strong Polish sympathies – became the first of the 60 million people killed in World War II.

From 1526 until 1945, Gliwice was known as Gleiwitz, having passed from Hussite Bohemia first to the Austrian Habsburg crown after the Battle of Mohács and then to Prussia after the Silesian Wars of the 1740s. After World War I, a plebiscite and further arbitration by the League of Nations determined that Gleiwitz should remain just within Germany, even as most of the rest of Upper Silesia was awarded to the newly reconstituted country of Poland. So Gleiwitz became a border town, rife with simmering Polish-German tension.

According to the sworn affidavit of SS Major Alfred Naujocks at the Nuremberg Trials, an incident was staged at Gleiwitz on 31 August 1939 on the orders of Reinhard Heydrich, head of the SS, and Heinrich Müller, chief of the Gestapo. A group of seven German operatives led by Naujocks briefly seized the radio station in Gleiwitz and broadcast a short anti-German message in Polish. To make their "raid" seem more convincing, Honiok – who had been arrested by the Gestapo the previous day – was dressed to look like a Polish saboteur, drugged into unconsciousness, shot in the head and left for dead at the scene, so that he appeared to have been killed while attacking the station. Reports of the raid were quickly broadcast across Germany and echoed around Europe; the next day, Germany invaded Poland, and Hitler cited Honiok's corpse and other previous border incidents in justifying the "defensive" nature of Germany's attack to the Reichstag, the press and the world.

The Gleiwitz Incident is utter lunacy, right? After years of rearmament, posturing, scheming, annexation and betrayal, nobody could really believe that the carefully planned invasion of Poland was an act of self-defense. But this is how lowly individuals like Honiok are sucked into history's vortex and become answers to trivia questions. Hitler, wanting to cover Germany's impending attack with a fig leaf of legitimacy, gives Heydrich and Müller their orders. Heydrich has Naujocks prepare a plan. Müller calls his local bureau chief in Silesia and finds a suitable patsy. One of Naujocks's subordinates drugs Honiok, and another shoots him. Two days earlier, Honiok had been an anonymous, 43-year-old Catholic farmer living in the small village of Polomia, north of Gleiwitz. Now, he was the "cause" of World War II.

Some people believe the tiny act of a butterfly flapping its wings can trigger a chain of events leading to a tornado or hurricane on the other side of the world. If anything, I believe exactly the opposite: big actions with hurricane-like impact ripple around the world and can cause momentous effects upon incidental actors. World War II alone spawned millions of variants of the chain leading from Hitler to Heydrich to Naujocks to Honiok; I wonder if the poor paratrooper about to land on a burning building in Ste. Mère-Église on D-Day might have blamed the Tehran Conference or Eisenhower's invasion plan for his imminent death. And yet, I hardly believe in historical determinism either. Hitler might not have craved a *casus belli*; Naujocks could have devised a different plan; Honiok himself took part in the interwar Silesian Uprisings and was a known Polish nationalist, yet remained in Germany; the paratrooper volunteered for airborne school instead of waiting for his draft number to come up; I didn't have to show *Totaler Krieg* to Becs. Outcomes can seem chaotic, but pure luck only exists in dice and other games of chance; most of what we call "luck" is the confluence of many freely made and independent decisions, all subject to change until they are actually made.

Dad doesn't see things this way. The other day, he shared his views on socio-economic determinism with me, quoting Hegel and of course Marx: "Men make their own history, but they do not know that they are making it." And: "In the social production of their life, human beings enter into definite and necessary relations which are independent of their will." I asked where he drew the line between free will and determinism – surely the very existence of the former must exclude the latter? He patiently explained that if a man is hungry, he will need food: he might visit the supermarket and buy ingredients with which to cook his own meals, or he might visit McDonald's three times a day until his arteries clog and his heart explodes, but the basic need remains the same, and if his access to food is restricted, what Marx called "class struggle" must commence. And then he surprised me by saying this: "When I was running through the 'Case White' training scenario in *Totaler Krieg*, I could have moved all of my pieces to the west, away from Warsaw, and lost the game – that was a choice freely available to me. But the scenario is engineered to make you attack and occupy Posen, Krakow and Warsaw; if you don't do that, you can't win, and by not trying to win, you're not actually playing the game."

"Wargames are all about counterfactuals!" I exclaimed. "You can't cite *Totaler Krieg* in support of determinism!"

"I think I just did," said Dad, smiling.

I suppose when Hitler, Heydrich, Müller and Naujocks conceived the Gleiwitz Incident, they knew the game they were playing: for Germany to "win", it needed to gain sufficient *Lebensraum* in Poland and the Soviet Union and confirm its mastery over Europe. Franciszek Honiok was the first pawn sacrificed to that end, just as Gleiwitz itself was sacrificed and became Gliwice again when Stalin's own pursuit of "victory" – security and hegemony for himself and the Soviet Union – moved Poland's borders to the west. But here's the thing: in life, unlike *Totaler Krieg*, we all get to set our own victory conditions, and we can change them as often as we like. When Hitler was my age, he dreamed of studying at the Academy of Fine Arts in Vienna. And when Honiok was my age, he probably dreamed that his

Silesian village would one day be part of a reconstituted Poland. Honiok may have been a pawn in someone else's high-stakes game, but six years after he died, one of his own most important victory conditions – a cherished ambition he voted for and even fought for – was finally fulfilled. Who scored higher in the game of life?

❖ ❖ ❖

Dad and I have been getting along much better lately. Between his professorial assignments and continued rehab meetings, he's not home much, and last week he had several men with big muscles and beards and tattoos – bodily attributes never seen in my house – over to talk about whatever it is people in rehab talk about with each other. That was weird. But he's making time for me as well, as demonstrated by our determinism discussion. Before he went to rehab, we'd never discussed history as equals; now he's even asking me for advice in conceptualizing his next book. That's very exciting, even if he is still wrong about nearly everything.

I certainly never imagined Dad and I might one day sit on opposite sides of the *Totaler Krieg* map, as we are now. It feels…not like a dream, but rather the first moments of consciousness after a night's sleep. I'm disoriented: groping for the end-table, hoping not to shove my alarm clock to the floor. I know hours have passed, but not how many, and my memory of them is dim and distant. Do I feel better for having rested? I'll know soon, but I can't tell yet. Can I remember my dreams? What might they mean? I'm tempted to retreat beneath the covers and postpone these reckonings. But the day is new, pregnant with possibility, and history doesn't write itself.

It is a Saturday in May. Normal people are outside, enjoying the bright sunshine and liberating warmth of late spring, and even we have opened the curtains in the gaming study. Wargaming and natural light make strange bedfellows; but then, so do wargaming and alcoholic Marxist History professors. My chair faces the window, and in looking at Dad or the map I am peering toward the brightness – you could say Dad holds the weather gage.

We are playing the second training scenario: "Barbarossa". Axis versus Soviets, five turns only, and then:

> **Victory Conditions:** At the end of the September-October 1941 Game Turn, count the number of Soviet Strategic Hexes that are under Axis control. If the number is three or greater, the Axis faction has won. If the number is two or less, the Soviet faction has won.

Minsk and Kiev? For sure. Leningrad, Moscow, Rostov or Sevastopol? Perhaps. Forget the West and the Med; this is the heart of the war, and the distilled essence of *Totaler Krieg*.

Dad is the Axis, because it's easier to pinpoint holes in a defense than construct a defense without holes. He has rolled up the sleeves on his white dress shirt with the thin red pinstripes. He bites his cheek as his eyes dart around the map – "Everything looks different than it does on the computer," he says.

"Do you need help getting started?"

"No, I'm fine." He reaches for a stack of infantry steps in his Force Pool.

"There are easier wargames to learn, you know. I could have started you on..."

"Shhhh," says Dad. "I'm placing my Seasonal Reinforcements."

He remembers to use his HQ in East Prussia as a reinforcement hub. He knows how to combine individual steps into armies, and he places his Air support units for maximum effect. He twice reduces infantry armies and stacks them with pairs of armored units, combining striking power and exploitation capability within an advanced tactic even Dennis could barely fathom. Wow. Is my father some crazy combination of Gregory Spearman and Anakin Skywalker?

"All of your defenses are in units of three and six, so I've constructed my attacks in multiples of three and six," says Dad. "It's not that difficult."

"But still! This game isn't that easy to figure out."

"Whatever you may think of me, Sean, I'm not a dolt." Dad smirks. "I've practiced this move several times in CyberBoard – a good historian must always be meticulous. You didn't expect me to come to this table unprepared, did you?"

Dad smashes my defenses in Lithuania and Eastern Poland and kills my HQ in Latvia. I blame the scenario setup – I never defend with my HQs that far forward at the start of Barbarossa. But for a '6' at Lvov, my HQ in the Ukraine would be dead as well. Dad calls my dice tower "a silly contraption".

The German spearhead in Byelorussia is Second Panzer Army – which, I've decided, may or may not be commanded in this cardboard reality by Colonel General Heinz Guderian. Does it matter? Narrative considerations do not influence my decision not to counter-attack hex e4106; instead I abandon Minsk and combine a weak screen of Second Panzer with a mix of sacrificial speedbumps and defensive strongpoints.

"Unorthodox," comments Dad.

"I know it looks weird, but *Totaler Krieg* is what they call design for effect..."

Dad holds up his hand, stopping my apology. "I like what you've done," he says. "A brilliant defense with limited resources, actually. Clever boy."

I roll the Delay dice. Cardboard airplanes stream out of invisible factories. Cardboard armies are forged with imagined tanks and guns. My destroyed HQ unit will return before the end of August.

"Now the hard part begins," says Dad. "What to do next?"

Dad scrunches up his face and pulls his eyeglasses to the tip of his nose. He scratches his head and pores over the map, scanning it from south to north and back again. Perhaps he sees a puzzle of rising complexity, one which started with 47 pieces on the map but now has 68. Perhaps he sees the story of a war without garlands, a clash of cultures and societies full of atrocities and brutality and sacrifice and patriotism and military genius and unbelievable stupidity. Perhaps he finally sees all of the roads not taken, the forked paths of history which forever intersect and between which all men must freely choose. I hope he sees all of these things, and that we get to talk about them later. I just hope he doesn't see the gap I've left in my defenses – I've just realized that if Dad is very clever, he could bypass Dnepropetrovsk and advance two of his steps currently in Odessa beyond the Dnepr and all the way to Rostov. That would be a true disaster.

References

Several passages from old discussion threads on Consimworld have been quoted more or less verbatim – specifically:

- "Was Denmark to blame for World War II?" *(Part Three, section 3)*: Quotes by Lawrence Duffield, Andrew Taubman, Robin Griller, Éric Grenier, Louis Capdeboscq, William Terdoslavich, Charles Vasey, Scott de Brestian and Lars Rasmussen
- "Could Sealion have happened?" *(Part Five, section 2)*: Quotes by Ted Raicer, Louis Capdeboscq and Nicholas Barker

The article referenced in Part Six, section 1 by David Hughes – "Sleeping with the Enemy: Pro-German Bias in WW2 Wargaming" – appeared in the #5 (November 2010) issue of *Battles* magazine.

Other sources referenced through the book include the following:

- John Birmingham, *Weapons of Choice: World War 2.1* (Penguin, 2006)
- Ed. Robert Cowley, *What If?: Military Historians Imagine What Might Have Been* (Pan, 2001)
- Ed. Robert Cowley, *More What If?: Eminent Historians Imagine What Might Have Been* (Pan, 2003)
- Richard B. Frank, *Downfall: The End of the Imperial Japanese Empire* (Random House, 1999)
- Heinz Guderian, *Panzer Leader* (Classic Penguin, 2000)
- Russell A. Hart, *Guderian: Panzer Pioneer or Myth Maker?* (Potomac, 2006)
- Julian Jackson, *The Fall of France: The Nazi Invasion of 1940* (Oxford, 2004)
- John P. McKay, Bennett D. Hill and John, Buckler, *A History of Western Society Since 1400* (Houghton Mifflin, 1991)
- C. L. Sulzberger and David G. McCullough, *The American Heritage Picture History of World War II* (Outlet, 1987)
- Adam Tooze, *The Wages of Destruction: The Making and Breaking of the Nazi Economy* (Penguin, 2007)
- Gerhard L. Weinberg, *A World at Arms: A Global History of World War II* (Cambridge, 2005)

31652831R00171

Made in the USA
Charleston, SC
24 July 2014